FIVE

The Hell Trials

JEREMY S. PRATTE

VERTICAL HOLD PRESS

PUBLISHED BY VERTICAL HOLD PRESS

verticalholdpress.com

Book and cover design by the Author.

ISBN: 979-8-218-45248-3

ACKNOWLEDGMENTS

First and foremost, I must thank my good friend of twenty-eight years, Julie Sondra Decker, a fellow author, fellow creator, and fellow troublemaker. She has supported me, inspired me, and pushed me to be a better writer for decades. I would not be here without her. And that statement has more than one meaning.

I also need to thank Priscilla Wagner, fellow author, and beta reader for an early draft of the manuscript. Without her insight, suggestions, and commentary, the book wouldn't be where it is today.

Big thanks go out to Jennifer Burke for all of her love and support during the development of the final manuscript for this book, and her encouragement as I continue my journey as a published author.

Many thanks also goes to my good friend and o.g. beta reader SPC Jamie Meeks. Her discussions with me about the story beats and her in-depth analysis helped me shape the story into what it is today.

Fellow author Carla Edwards deserves many thanks, for offering so much support, and for beta reading the book. Her commentary and suggestions helped the book become what it is today.

Thanks to Maryssa Gordon for doing a great job of being my developmental editor, which vastly improved the manuscript.

Finally I thank my mom for raising me to be a kind person, for kindness is one of the themes of this book, and for encouraging my creative pursuits.

CHAPTER ONE: Interrogations

"**A**RE YOU sure there isn't a camera or something? That we're not being watched?" Chloe looked around the room once, then again, to make sure nobody else was there. She swallowed nervously as she was fairly certain that she was in way over her head. Her heart skipped a beat when she heard a single drop of water drip from a pipe.

"It's fine," said the Deelooveren scientist. "No surveillance is in this room. Our supplier wouldn't like being watched. She hates being caught."

"How much?"

"People who catch her tend to end up dead."

"Then why deal with her if she's that dangerous?"

The room was dimly lit. It was somewhere in the bowels of the *Arkenstar* Station near the waste recycling facilities, so it wasn't a very popular spot. It was cool in there, a bit too cool for comfort. The unpleasant room had a mild odor of mildew in its humid air. Chloe shivered. Less energy for environmental systems was dedicated to this section of the station.

"She's very resourceful," the Deelooveren said. "She's one of the few people who can get you doses of the serum." They looked around the barely lit room nervously.

Chloe shrugged her hands up. "I'd have thought an actual Deelooveren would be more likely since, well, it comes from your planet."

"She's a criminal. I'm not. Well…not usually. Do you think I want to get caught smuggling this stuff from the labs or the medical bay?"

"Good point," Chloe said. "So, let's go over this deal again…"

She pointed up a finger for each point she made next. "You give her the gold she wants, she gives me the doses, and then when you're on Earth, I provide you with ten thousand pounds of spending money. I just want to get this straight."

"Twenty thousand," the scientist said.

"Oh, sod off! You can't double it now!"

"Do you know how much trouble I could get into for doing this?" They shot their arm up in the general direction of the station headquarters many floors above. "I mean, I had to temporarily deactivate certain security measures put in place ever since Slank's attacks just so this woman could get access to the station. With all the rules I've broken in the last few hours, I could be extra fired. Or even worse."

"Fifteen!" Chloe exclaimed.

The Deelooveren sighed. "All right. Fine. So what do you want this stuff for, anyway? The Contest is over. You won. And you've probably got a little of the serum still in your system."

"I have nightmares every night because of what Slank did to me. Plus, I have a disease. It kills a lot of my kind. It is dormant…at the moment. But I'm terrified of what would happen if it came back."

"It doesn't cure diseases," the scientist said.

"But it heals, and that might be all I need. It could heal my immune system, right?"

"Possibly. Maybe. And maybe not. It usually just heals bones, tissues, blood vessels, those sorts of things. A super dose can regrow lost limbs."

"I hope I never need *that*!"

The Deelooveren's communicator beeped. "She's here."

A shower of sparkles entered the room. A woman appeared through the sparkles. Her transporter certainly differed from the Deelooveren's. The woman wore a dark green cloak and a hood. Chloe couldn't see her face very well. It was mostly hidden in the shadow of the hood. She had a small metal case in her hands. Chloe also couldn't help but notice that the woman had visible weapons. There was a knife holstered on each side of her belt.

The woman cocked her head a little to the side as she looked at Chloe. "What's your species? I've never seen anybody like you before."

"That's not your bloody business," Chloe replied. "Do you have them? Are they in that case?"

"Yes," the woman said. She held out the metal case. Chloe reached out for it. The woman snapped it away. "Ah-ah-ah! Where's the gold?"

The Deelooveren scientist grabbed a large metal case that had been hidden in the shadow of a waste tank. "Here it is." They handed it to the woman.

She grabbed it with her other hand. The woman fumbled with the case and opened it while still holding the serum case. She inspected the gold. "Good. It's all here." She closed the case and put it down on the floor but between her legs. She held out the small metal case again.

Chloe reached out for it. This time, she was allowed to take it. She opened it up. All the vials that were promised were there.

"Don't use it all up at once. These are difficult to get. I had to kill more than one person to get this."

Chloe's eyes almost popped out of their sockets. "You what?!"

"You can't buy these at a corner market, girl!" the woman exclaimed. "These are very hard to come by! I kept a few doses for myself in case I ever needed them."

Chloe swallowed hard. She breathed deeply. "I didn't want anybody to die," she whispered.

"Boo hoo," the woman said. "Are we done here?"

"Yes," said the scientist. "I need to get the security systems back up as soon as possible."

"Fine," the woman said. She clicked a button on her communicator. She beamed away.

Chloe unzipped her tote bag and put the case in it. "I've got to go. I'm late getting to the airlock. They're going to wonder what's taking me so long."

The scientist clicked some commands into their handlink. "Whew. Everything is back to normal. Okay, fine, get gone. Get up to your friends." They pointed toward the nearby stairs.

#

"Who was the scientist who helped you, Miss Thompson?" The Deelooveren investigator clicked information into their thin, clear, plastic tablet. They were in a small room in a containment facility in Loovian City. Chloe knew that "containment facility" was a nice way of saying "jail."

"I didn't get their name," Chloe answered. Her eyes were sore from all the crying she'd been doing. She was tired and hungry. She was weary of wearing the same plain gray uniform every day.

"This will go easier for you if you say who it was."

"Trust me, I want all this to go easier on me!" Chloe yelled. "I don't bloody know the wanker's name! I mean, how many Deelooveren scientists went down to Earth?! Four? Five? It isn't an epic mystery! It had to be one of them!"

"We're very thorough, Miss Thompson," the investigator said. "And I would appreciate it if you kept your cool. I don't enjoy being yelled at." They leaned forward onto the table, separating them. "It makes me grumpy." They leaned back. "So, tell me, if you didn't know their name, how were you going to get the cash to them?"

"Secret drop-off meeting in London," Chloe said. "I never had to get their name." She buried her face in her hands. "Can I please have more water?" her muffled voice asked. "I'm thirsty."

"Yes," the investigator said. They got up, headed to a nearby wall, clicked some commands into a replicator panel. A glass of water appeared. They grabbed it and handed it to Chloe.

When she heard the glass land on the table, she grabbed it and gulped down the entire glass. She swallowed and sighed in relief. "I'm also hungry."

"We'll feed you soon," the investigator said. "Trust me, it won't be those luxury catered meals you got on the Arkenstar. But don't worry, it will be adequate. We're not cruel. We're civilized, unlike humans."

Chloe buried her face in her hands and started sobbing again. "I'm sorry! I'm so sorry! You have no idea what I go through, most nights, the nightmares! I'm terrified of my leukemia returning! I didn't mean to—"

"Ambassador Karak informed you why we have to restrict the enhancement serum! Which is why we have to have severe restrictions on it and why there are stiff penalties for misuse or illegal distribution of it." The investigator moderately slammed the tablet on the table. "This makes us very angry. This is serious. Look, I have sympathy for you. I do. I like you. And your friends. Your Contest win was great. And you all risked your lives over and over to get the Loovestones. You helped the station when the Jistari attacked. So yeah, I like the five of you. Normally. But now I'm not a big fan of yours anymore. But if you can give me any more information than you have, I might like you a bit more again."

"Where's my attorney?" Chloe said. "You said you'd get me a Deelooveren lawyer, possibly a human one, too!"

"We've contacted Earth. Let me tell you, you'll get one soon enough. A lot of very distinguished attorneys are keen to take your case. And not just from your region or nation but all over your planet. I mean, going to another world, representing somebody in an alien court, on an alien planet, trust me, you won't have to pay them a single pound…or whatever your money is. They really want your case."

"Great, but I don't want to say anything else without an attorney of some species present," Chloe replied as she wiped her eyes. "I know my rights, Investigator Charlock."

The investigator tapped something into their tablet. "Do you? Do you know what rights you have? Because, to be honest with you, I don't even know. This is unprecedented. We've arrested aliens for doing this before, but never a Terran. This is big news here, too. I mean, you were famous already, here and on your planet. But you were caught committing one of the highest crimes we have a law for. All Deelooveren are hooked to their news feeds about this. A lot of humans are, too, I heard."

"So my friends know?"

"They know. Well, except for Mr. Chase."

"Why doesn't he know?"

"Quite simply, we don't know where he is."

Chloe looked at Charlock, her eyes wide in surprise. "He's missing?"

"I wouldn't be worried. I think Miss Mackenzie knows where he is. Farine, Deelan, Woo'cha, and Barchell are also missing. That's a bit conspicuous. They're probably all headed off to the same place. Probably to steal something."

"Fine, but the other three, are they coming?"

"They're all on their way, along with your human attorney," Investigator Charlock answered. "They all love you, especially Mr. Henderson. It's sweet that as soon as they heard, they all three dropped everything and begged to be brought here."

Chloe looked down. She felt like crying again. "I love them, too. They're all the loveliest friends I've ever had."

"Then why did you risk this? Why did you risk all this trouble?"

"I already told you!"

"But I still don't understand." Charlock slowly shook their head. "This is one of my people's worst crimes. I know I've said that a lot in the past three hours, but it's just one of those things that cannot be emphasized enough. You remember what Slank looks like, yes?"

Chloe buried her face in her hands again. "That's not fair! Don't bring him up!" A few memories of him torturing her flashed in her mind.

"The point is, that's what it does to people. That's what it would do to you, given enough doses and time. Your friends, that you love so much, you could have dragged them down into this, too. Because they all knew."

Chloe looked up, alarmed. "Oh my god! Are they in trouble,

too?!"

"Luckily, no. Given, well, everything and the fact that they did help save the *Arkenstar*, we decided to let them slide. But you got Ambassador Karak into hot water. They and Commander Vot had an agreement to let this slide. Now that Vot is dead, that left them your only Deelooveren advocate. They're facing disciplinary action over this. They might not have the title of 'Ambassador' much longer."

Chloe, once again, buried her face into her palms.

"Now, if you have any more information about this scientist, then, well, it might help your case."

"All I can do is describe them!"

"Well, you can do better than that," Charlock said. They put the tablet down in front of her. "These are images of all the Deelooveren climate scientists. Pick out the one."

Chloe looked at the tablet. "Fine. It's...this one." She was hesitant. She really did not want to get anybody else into trouble.

"Ahhhh, Analyst Feerjon! Wow. They just had another child. Such a shame."

"What?! Oh my god!" She shook her head, and tears streaked from her eyes again.

"They're going to lose their job, their freedom, and their new family!"

"Stop it! I feel bad enough!"

Charlock quickly stood up. "No, you don't!" Charlock leaned on the table to bring their head closer to Chloe's. "Do you see, do you see now, the trouble that breaking this law causes?! Do you?!"

"Yes," sobbed Chloe, her face buried in her arms. She snuffled.

#

Alice was in her bed on her phone, mindlessly scrolling through Facebook. Her dorm room was mostly dark, only lit by the soft glow of her touch-controlled nightstand lamp. It was late, and she felt sad. She was worried about Jacob. He was gone yet again with no guarantee of returning. Her heart hurt. So many of her friends had posts where they were doing things with their boyfriends, girlfriends, husbands, wives...Alice couldn't figure out why she did it to herself, scrolling through all of that, just causing herself more pain. When she saw a post with her sister and her boyfriend near the rocky Oregon coast, she'd had enough. Maybe her friends were right: she was silly to be on the social media website that only the "old people" used. She clicked her phone off and set it aside.

But then it vibrated. Who the hell was calling at 2:00 AM?

She looked at her phone. It was Wyatt. Why was he calling? It was 4:00 AM where he lived. She clicked the button on her earbuds to answer the call.

"Hello?"

"I'm sorry I'm calling so late! Or…so early! I needed to talk to you!"

He sounded distressed. Alice immediately grew worried, furrowing her eyebrows and staring at his name on the screen as if that would help her see him.

Alice shifted her position in her soft bed to sit up straighter. "What, Wyatt? What's wrong?"

"They took her! They…they…they beamed down, and they took her!"

Alice put her hands up defensively as if he could see her. "Wait, wait a minute, Wyatt, back up, slow down. Who took who?"

Wyatt breathed heavily. She could hear him swallow. "Chloe. Deelooveren guards beamed down and took her! They arrested her!"

"Oh my god! Because of those serum doses she had?"

"Yes, yes, umm, her friend said she heard her say something about the enhancement serum! That must have been it! Oh, Alice, I had just talked to her on the phone! Oh my god, what are they going to do to her?!"

"Do the others know yet?"

"No! You're the first one I called!"

Alice tried her best to keep her own cool. Wyatt needed her, and he needed her to be supportive and calm. There was a reason he called her first. She tried hard to keep her own mind from going into a frenzy of emotions.

"Wyatt, listen to me, just…I know that you're rattled, okay? Just hold on a sec, please. Listen, Chloe is tough and strong. You know she is! If anybody can get through this, she can!"

"She's gonna be in an alien jail, Alice!"

Alice needed to get him to calm down somehow, or he was going to spiral. She'd never heard him so upset and emotional. "Wyatt, stop! This is not the Wyatt Henderson I know! Listen to me! We need a plan! You do the plans, right?! You're the man with the plan! And a strategy!"

"But, but, but…"

"No buts about it, Mister! Pull it together! Chloe needs you! She needs you to pull it together and come up with a strategy. You can't help her like this. But you can do this! I believe you can!"

"But I don't how their legal system—"

Alice actually held up her right index finger. "Wyatt, what's step one?!"

"But—"

"Wyatt! What is step one? What is the very first thing we need to do for her? Think! Use that awesome brain of yours and think!"

Wyatt grew quiet, but he audibly sighed.

"Wyatt, I know you're overwhelmed. So just think of the very first step. Just the first one. I know you always think three or four steps ahead, but this time, just step one. Let's start with the first step. Can you do that for me? For her?"

"I can't…I can't think right now. All I can think about is Chloe, how helpless she must be…"

Alice grimaced and shook her head. She shook her finger at her phone as if Wyatt would see her angry gesture. "Okay, look, first of all, she is not helpless! You know she's not. You know how strong that woman is. Second, you need to get some sleep. It's four AM in St. Louis. I don't know if you were up all night or got up super early, but either way, it sounds like you need sleep. Step one: get that sleep! That's the first step of your master plan. Right? Doesn't that sound like a good first step?"

"Um…yes, Alice."

"Good! Then after you get that sleep, we can work on the second step of what I'm sure will be your best master plan yet. Okay?"

"Yes," said Wyatt, who finally sounded calmer. "Thank you, Alice. I knew calling you was a good idea. Maybe that was the first step of my master plan."

"You're right. It was. Now, promise me you're going to get some sleep. We'll talk again tomorrow…or…later today. Okay? And we'll also get in touch with Jamar and…well, Jamar. Okay?"

"Okay. I promise. Thank you. Goodbye."

"Goodbye, Wyatt."

Alice sighed. Jamar and…Chase. That's what she'd wanted to say. But he was gone, and there wasn't a way to contact him. She had tried to call his communicator with her handlink but it wouldn't connect. Either he didn't have it, or he was too far away. Maybe he was still in the Far Lands; he hadn't stuck to his original plan of just going to Slithertown, which infuriated her. So the gang wouldn't be all back together to help Chloe. But maybe the three of them would be enough.

CHAPTER TWO: Breaking News

T HE NEXT morning, Alice was tired. She was up too late, and when she went to sleep, she only slept a little. Alice needed a large coffee. She bought one in the little coffee shop on the bottom floor of her dormitory. With her coffee in hand and her backpack on her shoulder, she headed for the door.

Alice opened the main door to her dormitory building to head out into the cool, overcast spring morning. Chirping birds and the floral scents from a nearby flower garden greeted her.

She was not expecting nor prepared for what else was out there to greet her.

There were dozens of reporters with cell phones and microphones, and cameras pointed at her. They had been waiting for her to emerge.

"Alice, what are your comments on Chloe's arrest?!"

"Did you know she had the super serum?!"

"Have you talked to the aliens?!"

"How will this affect their help in the climate crisis?!"

"Are you going to her trial?! We heard there'd be a trial!"

"I'm gonna need a bigger coffee," Alice mumbled to herself. She had a worried and overwhelmed expression in her eyes as she looked upon the sea of reporters.

Her phone rang. Alice ducked back into the building. She retrieved her phone from her pocket. It was Jamar. She answered it.

"Hey, Alice! There are like a hundred reporters outside my damn house!" Jamar exclaimed. "They're all yelling something about Chloe. The hell is goin' on?!"

Alice noticed a television monitor on the wall of the coffee shop. It was on CNN. It was on mute, but a male reporter was saying something and a picture of Chloe was in the top right corner.

"Alice? Are you there?"

"Yes, sorry, Jamar. I'm here. But Chloe isn't. She was arrested for having illegal doses of the serum. She's on Loovian, I think."

"So *that's* what this is all about! Holy shit, girl! She's in big trouble, isn't she?"

"Yes, she is."

"Damn, Jam," said Darnell as he looked out the window. "They all want your autograph or something?"

Jamar was still on the phone with Alice, using his air pods. He looked out the window again. "Something big is going down, bro. No, not you, Alice. You, you're a sis."

"What is it?" Darnell asked.

"You know Chloe? My British friend?"

"Yeah?"

"She got arrested by the aliens for having vials of that super drug."

"They took her to the alien jail or whatever?"

"Yep!" Jamar pointed out the window at the reporters and TV station vans. "And they have questions about it!"

"Damn, dude," Darnell said. "They're getting all *Law & Order* up in space."

Jamar held his finger to his right air pod to hear Alice better. "Mmm mm…oh, she's getting a lawyer?" He turned to Darnell. "CNN report on this says she's getting a lawyer."

"Like a space Perry Mason or some shit?" He counted all the vans and reporters. "Man, they are all up in our shit, ain't they?"

"What is all this?" Phyllis said as she bounded down the stairs. "I thought all of this died down after your last TED talk."

"Hey, Mom," Jamar said. Then he pointed to his air pods. "I'm on the phone with Alice."

"Tell her I said 'hi!'"

"Yeah, Mama says…oh, *right now*?" Jamar snapped his fingers and pointed at the TV. "Turn it on CNN!"

Phyllis turned on the TV and found CNN.

"…First time a human being will ever have had a trial on an alien planet," said the brunette female reporter. "Analysts are already calling it 'The Trial of the Century.' Twenty-year-old British college student Chloe Thompson is facing up to several decades in an alien prison for illegally obtaining and possessing unauthorized vials of the enhancement serum or the superpower serum that she and her friends used during the alien contest…"

"Like, twenty years?" Jamar said.

"Yes, or longer!" Alice replied as she looked out the window. Her reporters weren't going away, either. Several of them took pictures of her through the window. "That's what a Deelooveren they'd interviewed earlier said. Yes? Oh, tell her I said 'hi,' too! And your brother. Where's your other brother? Oh well, tell him I said 'hi' to him, too, when he gets back. Well, I don't know! Push 'em out of the way. I know, right?! I gotta get to class, too!"

"Can you two get rid of those reporters?" Phyllis said. "I gotta get to work."

"Ditto!" Darnell said.

Jamar slowly shook his head. "Fine, I'll do it! Listen, Alice, we'll talk later. I'm gonna try to get rid of these jerks. Yeah. All right, bye." Jamar hung up, strode over to their front door, and opened it. The reporters immediately flooded him with questions. He tried to answer as many as he could while also trying to tell them all to go away.

As Alice put her phone away, there was new breaking news about the story being announced on the television. The coffee shop employees had unmuted the monitor a while ago so everybody could listen.

"…Famous UK lawyer Vincent Franklin won the bid to go to the Deelooveren home planet Loovian and be Miss Thompson's human attorney. You might remember a few years ago, he successfully defended a UK football star on trial for sexual assault. Oh, wait, here he is right now…let's go live to his press conference in London."

The scene switched to a middle-aged man with a dark suit, blue tie, and dark, slicked-back hair. Alice noticed that this man had a *very* square jaw. He stood behind a podium, taking reporters' questions.

"Yes, you from the Sun," Vincent said.

"I heard that the aliens actually have video evidence showing Miss Thompson having the vials of the drug. Isn't that pretty damning?"

Vince cleared his throat and smiled. "Well, that evidence was illegally obtained, according to our laws at least. The surveillance they conducted on my client was not authorized or legal. I plan to have that evidence suppressed. They may have this trial in an alien court with a different legal system, but she is a UK and Earth citizen, and I will make bloody sure that our own laws are respected!"

He pointed to another reporter. "Yes, you?"

"Surveillance?!" Alice said. "They had cameras in her *bedroom*?! What the *hell*?!" She ran back up the two flights of stairs to her floor. She entered her dorm room and looked around everywhere for a hidden camera. She almost tore her dorm room apart, looking for anything that looked like a camera. Alice got out her phone and called her mother.

"Hello, Mom, yes…yes, I know. I heard. It's all over the…no, Mom, look, let's…I have something important here. Listen! Check the entire house for cameras! I think the aliens have been surveilling us. Yes, secret hidden cameras! Maybe! Look, I'm looking through my dorm room. I gotta go. Look, Mom, no…yes, tell him hello… look, I gotta go! Love you, bye!"

After moving more items around the next five minutes, Alice finally noticed a tiny black dot in one of the ceiling corners. She got up on her bed so she could reach it, but she was still too short. She tried hopping up and down on her bed to reach it. "Dammit! I hate being short sometimes!"

She got out her little broom that she used to clean up her room. She could knock the tiny black device down using the broom handle. It fell on her bed. She threw the broom aside, plopped down, and grabbed the thing she was pretty sure was a very tiny camera. She examined it by bringing it as close to her eye as she could. It indeed looked like a tiny lens.

"Ambassador Karak! Are you on the other side of this? Jeelork maybe? Farrstead? Whoever you are, go to hell, all right! You had no right to do this! You hear me?! Giving us yet another reason not to trust you people anymore!" She flipped the camera off, ran to her bathroom, tossed the camera in the toilet, and flushed it. Then she texted both Jamar and Wyatt and told them to look for the cameras in their house and dorm room.

"This is the last straw!" Alice yelled to the ceiling. "Because we won't be—" But then the last several words of the sentence she was trying to yell were silent. Her eyes opened wider. She mouthed, "NO!" Her voice box had stopped working.

"Did you do this?!" she silently mouthed to the walls and ceiling. She jumped up and down. How petty! She was furious. Did they actually remotely shut off her voice box?! She got so angry that she grabbed a small, pink piggy bank she'd had on her dresser and threw it against the brick wall of her room. It smashed into it, sending bits of pink, ceramic piggy and coins everywhere.

Then she realized how sweaty she was from frantically tearing apart her dorm room. She calmed down and realized her neck was very sweaty, as her head and chest were. She took a tissue and wiped the sweat off the voice box and the skin under it. Then, she carefully placed it back in its spot. "Testing…testing…oh, thank god!" It was just the sweat. She looked at the smashed piggy bank and change all over her bed. She sighed heavily. "Good once, Alice. Good one."

She headed for her bathroom to have her second shower of the young day.

#

"Hello. I'm Counselor Vache," a Deelooveren attorney said as they approached Chloe's detainment cell. "I'll be representing you, along with your human lawyer. I know the Deelooveren side of the law."

Chloe turned her head and looked at them with her tired, bloodshot eyes. The attorney wore a dark suit of Deelooveren design, which meant it had some dressy frills.

"The trial starts in just two days. What took you so long?" She got up from the bench she was sitting on and approached the force field.

A guard standing by the attorney used their handlink to turn the force field off. "We'll go to the conference room. Behave yourself, Miss Thompson." They trained a phaser set to stun on her.

"Whatever," Chloe said.

In the conference room, Chloe sat across the table from Counselor Vache. Chloe grabbed the cool glass of water the guard had given her. She drank some. There was also a plate of little hard pretzels in front of her for a snack. She nibbled on one.

"So," Chloe said, "what's the plan?"

Vache swiped and scrolled through some information on their tablet. "Well. I'll be honest with you: this isn't good. I mean, it's pretty obvious that you illegally obtained some doses. You're on camera with them…"

"That's rubbish, I say! They had no right to get any of that evidence. No search warrants or anything, and they were spying on me!"

"You make good points," Counselor Vache said. "But, please don't forget, we have different laws on Loovian."

"We have different laws on Earth."

"There isn't a law against the type of surveillance we did. It was for your protection. It saved your lives from the vehicle bomb. We saw the people put the bomb under the car."

"Don't even try to tell me it would be legal for you to secretly put a camera in the house or bedroom of somebody you know if you say it's just to protect them."

"Your circumstances were special. Look, I am on *your* side. Stop getting antagonistic, please."

"Well, then, if you're my attorney, then please look into this for me!" Chloe said. "Can you at least *try* to suppress this evidence?"

Counselor Vache frowned for a moment. They looked at something else on their tablet. "Well, there might be something. The cameras could have caught other people who were *not* under our protection…that could be a problem. But it's a legal stretch. Look, Miss Thompson. I recommend pleading guilty, and you will get a reduced sentence. I hear the same thing can work on your planet."

Chloe looked at the Counselor angrily. She slowly reached for the translating communicator in her ear, took it out, and slapped it onto the table.

"Feeker firrjirr v'lah vooginarr shzinser, farrjinzz et?" Vache said, which, translated to English, would have been: *That's one way to reject my advice, isn't it?*

Vache sighed. They clicked something on their tablet. He used it much like Alice had used hers. "You have made your point," a Deelooveren voice came from the device. Chloe still gnashed her teeth and narrowed her eyes at them. But she grabbed her communicator and put it back into her ear.

"Well," Vache tried again, "another option is pleading not guilty via fleeting insanity or extreme situation anxiety."

"On my world, pleading insanity can help you avoid prison but then get you committed to a mental facility."

"Not in this instance. It was just temporary. You experienced trauma, and you are terrified of your disease returning. It *might* work. But with the seriousness of the charges against you, I would not bet on that working."

"Well, I would bet a little on that working!" A human had walked into the room. He was the Earth attorney Chloe had been promised.

Chloe smiled for the first time in weeks. But only a little. "Oh my god, you're Vincent Franklin! *You* are my human attorney?!"

He held out his hand to Chloe. She shook it. "Nice to meet you, Miss Thompson! I will represent you via the human side of this legal trouble, and I'm just going to be straight with you, we have quite a challenge ahead. Oh my god, I still can't believe that I just traveled through space, and I'm on an alien planet." He looked around the room. Then he put his own tablet on the table, which was his iPad.

"Well, wow, thank you for coming!" Chloe exclaimed. "You just traveled hundreds of light years to get here!"

"Our planet is only about *nineteen* light years from yours, Miss Thompson."

"Whatever, Vache!"

"Well, anyway," Vincent said, "on the way here, I read up on all of their laws relevant to this case. I was surprised to find many of them similar to Earth laws." He suddenly looked irritated and fiddled with his air collar. He looked right at Chloe. "Question: do these things *always* chafe you?"

"Sometimes, if you sweat a lot," Chloe said. "Try loosening it a tad."

Vincent pulled it away from his neck a little. "Ah, that loosened it…a little bit." Then he saw the pretzels. "Oh, are these pretzels?"

"Yeah," Chloe said as she slid the plate toward him. He grabbed one. He tried to put it in his mouth too quickly. It almost bounced back.

"Oh," he said. Then he tried again more slowly and got it through the air collar field. Then, he could put it in his mouth. He happily crunched on it. "That was weird."

"You get used to it," Chloe said. "Then eating and drinking with the air collar becomes second nature."

"Mmm," he said. He nodded to Vache. "These are good. You're good at human food."

"I didn't make them, but sure, thanks," Vache replied.

Vincent took a drink of his own glass of water. "Ahhh, okay. Now your trial is in two days." He looked at his iPad, scrolling through some items. "We are going to file motions to suppress almost all the evidence gathered against you. And your supposed confession. Because confessions are only supposed to be made in the presence of counsel and preceded by the words 'I confess.'"

"This is going to be interesting, working with you," Vache said. "If this were strictly Deelooveren law we were concerned with, the judges would summarily deny the motions. You're right about the confession, though. I don't know what the investigator was thinking."

"Judges, plural," Vincent mumbled. "Right, right. You have a three-judge panel. And a six-person jury." Vincent realized he just thought of something. "Wait a minute. It can't be a jury of her peers. I should have come with more people than just my two paralegals. How can she get a fair trial with a six-person *Deelooveren* jury?"

"Fair question," Vache said. "I mean, we are very fair people, I wasn't concerned about it."

"Well, you should have been," Vincent said. "And if we can't resolve this somehow, I will push for a mistrial." He grabbed a few more pretzels.

"Mr. Franklin," Vache said, "I'm sorry, this may sound rude, but we are a more advanced people. We have a greater ability to be fair and impartial, to remove biases, than you Terrans."

"Terrans?" Vincent said with his mouth full of pretzels. He finished them and swallowed. "Oh, I see. Well, I prefer 'humans.' But anyway. Doesn't matter. She is both a client of mine and yours, which means human law, more specifically, British law, is relevant, and being tried by a jury of your peers is the cornerstone of our justice system."

"Same here," Vache said. "So what's the problem?"

Vincent looked at Vache. "You said something very interesting a moment ago, Counselor Vache. You talked about how more advanced your people are. Which means you admitted that a six-person Deelooveren jury couldn't *possibly* be a jury of her *peers*."

Chloe listened to both of them, resting her chin in her hand. She was getting bored…until the thing that Vincent just said. That perked her up a little.

"Very good point, Mr. Franklin," Vache replied. They frowned. "Let's go to the High Judge about this."

"Wow," Chloe said, "if you can turn an insult into an advantage like that, you *must* be an excellent lawyer."

Vincent chuckled a little and tried to appear humble. "Oh. I'm only the second-or-*third*-most famous lawyer in the UK." He shrugged. "But, rest assured, you *are* in good hands, Miss Thompson."

"I bloody hope so," Chloe mumbled.

CHAPTER THREE: Pressers and Pressures

ALICE, WYATT and Jamar all three flew to the United Nations headquarters in New York City to give a press conference about their friend Chloe, as well as meet with human and Deelooveren diplomats. Chloe's trial became somewhat of a diplomatic crisis between the planets. Human trust in the alien species was never very high, to begin with, but the fact that they just beamed down and arrested an Earth citizen without checking with an Earth government or law enforcement agency first put relations between the two species at an all-time low.

The Deelooveren diplomats that had been invited to sit in on United Nations meetings had expected the four other humans to take their side. Or, at the very least, try to be diplomatic between the two sides. What they did not expect was for one of them to be missing and the other three to turn against them.

Wyatt and Jamar both showed up wearing dark suits. Alice had a pantsuit on. They hadn't dressed up like this since they did the TED talk and press conferences after they had arrived home from the Contest.

Wyatt still felt uneasy and sporadically emotional from Chloe's plight. He was also nervous about the press conference. But he didn't have an issue with previous ones. Alice and Jamar both agreed that he was not himself.

"I think he's just still reeling from what happened to Chloe," Alice whispered to Jamar when Wyatt was elsewhere out of earshot. They were all three backstage, waiting for their turn at the podium. They observed him take his glasses off and rub his eyes with his thumb and forefinger.

"Whatever it is, I haven't ever seen him struggle like this.

Dude is, like, thrown. He must really, *really* care about her."

"Oh, he does. He's terribly worried about her. So am I, but, it's like, he's so unusually cynical about it. He's usually so much more optimistic. Or at least realistic."

"He needs to regain some of that confidence and optimism before he goes out there in…" Jamar looked at his smartwatch. "… Five minutes."

Alice cringed. "Maybe we should do most of the talking?"

"Maybe."

"Wait. I will try a last-minute pep talk."

Alice strode up to Wyatt. She tapped him on the shoulder. Wyatt turned around.

"Oh, hey, Alice."

"Hey, listen, we go on soon."

"Yeah." He hung his head down briefly.

"Look at me."

Wyatt brought his head back up and looked at Alice. She reached up and put her hands on his shoulders. "You can do this. I know you can. I believe in you. You're struggling. And I understand. But we, and, most importantly, Chloe, need you to be the Wyatt that we know you can be, the confident Wyatt who had all the brilliant strategies and ideas during the Contest and the Quest. We need him back."

Wyatt sighed. He nervously straightened his shirt collar. "I don't think he's here."

"Yes, he *is*. I'm looking at him. He's right here." Alice pointed right at his heart. Then she cupped his face with her soft hands. "And I think he needs a hug. Come here." She gently embraced him. He hugged her as well.

Alice was much shorter than Wyatt, but he could still smell, in her hair, the floral scent of whatever shampoo she'd used that day. He bent down and kissed the top of her head. "Thank you, Alice. This is what I needed."

When the hug ended, she kept her hands on his arms. "Good."

"You often seem to know just what people need. It's why we've told you that you're the heart of the team."

Alice only half-smiled and sighed. She looked back at Jamar. "Some team. Just three of us now."

"We'll be back together soon, all of us," Wyatt replied. "You'll see." He put his arm around Alice and nudged her to walk over to Jamar with him. "Come on. Let's do this! Let's defend Chloe! Here at this press conference, and then go back to Loovian and help defend her there, too!"

An official came to them and told them it was time. All three of them came out to stand at the podium for their press conference. They answered numerous questions and took turns doing so. Yes, they would go back to the alien planet. Yes, they fully supported their dear friend Chloe. Yes, they were going to help her defense during her trial in whatever capacity they could. But after all those softballs, a hard question came.

"Did you know she had those doses of the super serum?"

All three of them waited a second, seeing if one of the other two would answer. Finally, Wyatt cleared his throat and responded, "I knew." That caused a bit of a stir in the press corps. "But, I convinced her that it was wrong to have them and that we needed to get rid of them, and that she needed to stop using them. She did."

"Where are the doses now?"

That was actually something that Alice and Jamar did not know. They looked to Wyatt to answer that question, too.

"I disposed of them."

This caused an even bigger stir.

"Where?!"

"How?!"

"I disposed of them, and that's all I'm saying."

After the press conference was over, Alice practically yanked Wyatt to get backstage faster.

"What did you do with them?!" she asked in a loud whisper. "How did you dispose of them?"

"Yeah, man," Jamar added. "Dude, please tell me you didn't just pour that shit down the drain."

"What? I just…disposed of them."

"Wyatt," Alice said, getting more upset, "if you did anything other than shoot them out into space or give them back to the Deelooveren, you probably made a *big* mistake."

"What would happen if that shit gets out into the environment?" Jamar asked.

"I…well…I didn't know what else to do, I flushed the serum, destroyed the vials."

"Dude!" Jamar's eyes almost popped out of his head. "You *flushed* them?! That shit's out into the ecosystem now, man! What's *that* gonna do?! Are there like supercharged snakes now or something, in some swamp somewhere?! The sewage treatment plants don't get everything!"

Alice slowly shook her head at him. "Bad move, man. Bad

move. The EPA will probably call you soon to *insist* you tell them how you disposed of it."

"I didn't know how else to dispose of them! I'm sorry! I needed to get them away from Chloe. I couldn't hide them, or else I would have gotten in trouble for possessing them as well. We might *both* be in alien jail now if I'd done that!"

Jamar sighed and pursed his lips tight. "Well, I understand, but I really hope there aren't bad consequences from that."

"They were microdoses, they don't last long, they deteriorate quickly," Wyatt said. "They probably just dissipated."

"I sure hope so," Alice said.

#

The trial date came. Deelooveren and Earth media were all over the trial. It wasn't as big of a deal on Deelooveren as it was on Earth, but it was still significant on Loovian because Chloe was a Contest winner. But the Deelooveren allowed a crew of Earth media to their planet and they were all over the event. They could broadcast their signal using the wormhole network. That made their broadcast nearly live. There was only a slight delay.

All over the planet, humans glued themselves to their televisions, computers, tablets, and smartphones, watching the nearly live feed of the trial.

Alice, Jamar, and Wyatt arrived on Loovian several hours before the trial was to begin. They were allowed to visit with Chloe after she had one last pretrial meeting with her lawyers.

"Oh my god, they're here!" Chloe yelled when she heard them knock. She was in a dormitory-type room very similar to the ones they had used on the *Arkenstar* Station. She ran to the door and opened it. Chloe opened her arms wide, grabbed all three, and hugged them. Her eyes immediately became wet. She hugged them tightly. "You guys, I'm so glad you're here!" Chloe said between muffled sobs. Then she parted and looked at Wyatt specifically. "Oh, darling!" She then hugged only him, so warmly and firmly it was like she'd never get to hug him again.

"I'm so glad to see you again!" Wyatt said. He noticed she felt thinner and lighter than she did the last time he hugged her. He could feel her ribs, vertebrae, and collarbone.

Wyatt ended the hug and looked Chloe up and down. "Hon, are they feeding you?"

Chloe sniffed. She wiped her eyes. "Yes. But…I have not been very hungry."

They hugged again. "Oh, Wyatt, what if they find me guilty?"

"They won't," Wyatt said. "You've got one of Earth's best lawyers on the case. And…you've got us."

"Not Chase, though?"

"He's still in the Far Lands or Slithertown," Alice said. "At least, I think he is."

"It's okay," Chloe said. "I'm sure he'd make his way back here if he knew."

"If he isn't…" Alice didn't finish the sentence. "Never mind."

Chloe put her arms around Alice. "He's okay, love. I believe he is. We saw how capable he was out there during the quest. Have faith."

Alice smiled. "Thank you," she whispered, then she hugged Chloe warmly. Then she also whispered, "I love you." She then separated from the hug and looked at Wyatt and Jamar. "I love all of you."

"We love you, too, Alice," Jamar said.

A subtle smile came onto Alice's face. "Umm…this is going to sound *super* cheesy…"

"If you're about to say that the power of our love will help save Chloe," Jamar said. Alice, Wyatt, and Chloe raised their eyebrows at him. "…Then get me some crackers. 'Cause I am ready for that cheese."

They all smiled. Alice and Chloe chuckled a little. "You know what?! I don't care how cheesy it sounds! Jamar is right! Guys, I've never had better friends than you all. And, yes, the power of our love and friendship will help Chloe. It has to! Look at what all we've been through, all the dangers and near-deaths. Are we going to let something like *this* break us up?"

"Hell to the no, girl," Jamar said. He held out his fist. Alice fist-bumped him. Then the others did.

"No!" Wyatt exclaimed. "We are not!"

Chloe felt warmth and love for the first time in over a week. They also helped her feel optimistic. She smiled as she looked at each of them. "Wow," she whispered, "I am almost speechless."

Alice pulled her voice box away. "Me, too," she mouthed. Chloe chuckled. "Oh, come here, love! I need another Alice hug!" She grabbed Alice and hugged her.

As much as the hug felt good, Chloe's stomach tightened. She was still terrified of the upcoming trial.

CHAPTER FOUR: The Trial of Chloe Thompson

T HE TRIAL started the next day. None of the humans had ever seen a courtroom so large. Its design was also fairly alien, but yet some things looked familiar. The judges sat at a table in the front. They all either had special wigs or they had their hair done the same way, poofed in the front and braided in the back. They all wore white robes. To the right was the jury box, three Deelooveren, three humans. Chloe's lawyer halfway got what he'd wanted.

There was a gallery of Deelooveren sitting in floating chairs behind the judges. Their purpose was mysterious. There were large monitors directly behind the judges. The desks near the front for the prosecution and the defense looked familiar, except for the fact that they were both large computer panels that were all black until the apps were activated. Seats for spectators filled the rest of the room. The three most important spectators, seated directly behind Chloe, were Wyatt, Jamar, and Alice.

Deelooveren guards stood near the judges, who probably served the same purpose as court bailiffs.

Counselors Vashe and Franklin sat by Chloe at the defense desk, along with Franklin's paralegals: a young man and a young woman. At the other desk was the prosecutor, also flanked by two assistants. The Prosecutor was one of the Deelooveren who seemed to favor a gender, as they looked more feminine than masculine. They had shoulder-length curly brown hair and wore a violet Deelooveren formal outfit.

Counselor Franklin could see that Chloe was uncomfortable. She had just consumed her second glass of water, and the trial had not even begun.

"Miss Thompson," he whispered to her, "I believe you will

win this case. I got them to allow three human jurors. There's no way they will vote to convict you."

"Don't get cocky," Chloe warned. "I may know nothing about lawyering, but you don't know as much as I do about how things work out here on alien worlds or in space. You never quite know what to expect. There are surprises at almost every corner."

"Even if you are convicted, Miss Thompson," Counselor Vashe said, "our prisons are much more civilized and safe than what I have read about Earth prisons. You live in a nice dwelling, and all your food…*and medical care*…is provided. You just have to do some chores in exchange."

"Just can't leave, right?" Chloe said before taking another drink of water.

"Actually, there are occasional field trips."

"Lovely."

"I'm just trying to help you feel better," Counselor Vashe said. "If you're convicted or not, your life won't be horrible, either way."

"I'm going with 'not,' Miss Thompson," Counselor Franklin added. He gently patted her shoulder.

A pleasant *booping* sound rang across the room. All the chatter hushed. The judge in the middle made an announcement, "This court is now in session! I am High Judge Kellnan. I am joined by Judge Jenker to my left, and Judge Dakarr on my right. Before us is the case of the Deelooveren People versus the human Chloe Marie Thompson. The charge is illegal obtainment and possession of improper enhance-ment serum. At the arraignment yesterday, the defendant pleaded *not guilty*. Opening arguments may commence, beginning with the pros-ecution."

"Before opening arguments," Counselor Franklin said, "I in-voke a…" He looked at his notes on his tablet, "…discovery of mo-tions, which I believe is proper at this time. I filed three motions, one to suppress surveillance evidence against my client, one to suppress her confession, and, since there is no other compelling physical evi-dence against my client, a motion to dismiss this case."

High Judge Kellnan swiped through something on the com-puter panel in front of them. "Yes, I see the motions, Counselor. Sup-pression of the confession is granted since the lead investigator used improper procedure." A look of extreme annoyance came over the

Judge's face. "But, both the other motions are denied."

"Your Honors," Franklin said, "I know that I am new to Dee-looveren law and court proceedings, but on Earth…"

"You are not on Earth, Counselor. The other two motions are denied. Do you want to be found in contempt of this court?"

"Uh oh, will this be like *My Cousin Vinny*?" Wyatt mumbled to Jamar.

Jamar frowned and nodded to Wyatt. "I sure hope so. Vinny won."

Wyatt raised his eyebrows. "Actually, that's a good point."

"May I please inquire as to the nature of the denial?" Franklin asked. "I believe I can request this."

The High Judge raised their eyebrows at Vincent. "As for the motion to suppress the evidence, the surveillance was indeed proper as we considered the humans under our protection. Now denying the case dismissal is obvious. If nobody has anything else, we will proceed with the trial, starting with opening statements."

The prosecutor stood from their seat. "This is a fairly straightforward case. In Deelooveren society, it is highly illegal to possess unauthorized enhancement serum, as we believe it would lead to massive misuse and a public health crisis. It could also lead to the total extinction of the flora on our planet that the key ingredient is derived from. The defendant, Chloe Thompson, obtained microdose vials of the serum from the known intergalactic criminal Leeka Shaffle. Miss Thompson is in visual evidence proving possession of the substance at her Earth dwelling. We expect justice to be done here, judges, jurors, please find her guilty."

Counselors Franklin and Vashe stood. Vashe gestured to Franklin to go first. "I plan to show this case against my client, Chloe Thompson, is *not* that straightforward. The evidence against my client is *not* that compelling, plus there isn't a confession to this crime. She is a human from my planet, who your people, I need to point out, *abducted* against her will, brought her to your space station where she was not kept safe enough from a violent criminal, which caused her trauma. And for that Contest, she was freely given a rather large dose of that enhancement serum, which may have led to her being addicted. But in spite of all that, she showed bravery and fortitude in a quest that she believed was to save your planet. And then she also helped defend your space station against an enemy attack. She risked her life doing these things many times over, and I want to point out that maybe this should grant her some leniency. Thank you."

Vashe then spoke, "My co-counselor is correct. This case, indeed, is not so straightforward. We will show that the evidence against Miss Thompson is weak, even by human standards. Thank you."

Counselor Franklin gave Vashe a bit of side-eye over their last comment.

From there, the case proceeded. The prosecution's first witness was the Deelooveren scientist who had facilitated the deal between Chloe and Leeka. They testified against Chloe. What the humans did not know was that it was in exchange for a reduced sentence. The prosecution's second witness was an audio/visual expert who showed the video of Chloe with the doses in her bedroom, even injecting a dose once.

On the cross-examination of that witness, Franklin struck a blow. "So, tell me, Expert Grake, how do we know, just from watching the video, that there is enhancement serum in those vials?"

"Well, I know you don't read Deelooveren, but the vials were labeled as such."

"Is it possible that they were mislabeled? Does the video conclusively prove that enhancement serum was in the vials?"

"No, it does not. Although her reaction to the injection sure does strongly suggest it."

"There are many drugs on Earth that cause a similar reaction to the one seen on the video."

The Prosecutor stood up. "Prosecution objects. Counselor did not ask a question. He offered testimony."

"Okay, okay, I'll rephrase," Franklin said. "Have you ever seen a person on video having the same reaction to some other drug?"

Expert Grake hesitated but then answered, "Yes, I have."

"Nothing further," Franklin said.

Vashe's cross-examination was brief. "So, Expert Grake, have you ever been wrong about thinking somebody on video was taking the serum and they were not?"

"Yes, once or twice."

"Nothing further."

The defense's witnesses were character witnesses. He called

Alice, Wyatt, and Jamar to the stand. They each spoke about how wonderful Chloe was, what all she'd been through, and they each emphasized the difficulties and life risks the quest presented. They also pointed out how they saved the *Arkenstar* Station. At one point during Alice's testimony, Counselor Franklin pointed out the disability that the quest caused her.

"And what did she do to you?"

"She…destroyed my—"

"Wait," Franklin said, holding up his hand. "Please remove that necklace you're wearing, then try to answer my question."

Alice nodded. She removed it. Then she tried to answer the question. But she could only mouth her answer. "Destroyed my voice."

The prosecution stood. "Prosecution objects. This witness's answer to the question was not audible."

"That's the point, Your Honors," Franklin argued. Then he looked at Alice again. "Please put it back on and answer the question."

"Leeka destroyed my voice out of pure malice after she captured me during the quest."

Franklin gestured toward her. "Do you think that this is one sign of how dangerous that quest was?"

Alice sat up in her seat a little. "Absolutely! Just one of the many!"

But when the prosecution asked Alice about that, they asked her a slightly uncomfortable question.

"When Ambassador Karak asked you if you wanted to participate in the quest, what was your answer?" They looked at Alice sternly as they awaited her answer.

Alice hesitated. She cleared her throat. "I…I said, 'I'm in.'"

"So you and your friends totally voluntarily signed up for that quest?"

"Yes."

"Why?"

"Because…" Alice sighed. "Because of how much the Deelooveren were helping my planet. Because I trust—I *used to* trust Ambassador Karak."

"But you were not coerced in any way?"

"No."

Then Alice was done. She did all she could for Chloe. She

hoped it was enough.

Now it was time for the prosecution's other star witness. Several armed guards brought Leeka in, who was heavily restrained. She looked weird to the humans, just wearing that same gray uniform. She grinned at them as she passed by them.

"Please state your full name for the record," Prosecutor Veeloren requested.

"My name is Leeka Shaffle."

"What is your occupation?"

"I'm a professional baker."

This caused quite a murmur in the court audience.

"Leeka, you are *not* a professional baker!"

Leeka grinned.

"We remind the witness of the penalty for perjury in this court!" Judge Jenker said.

"I am fully aware of it," Leeka said. She fluttered her eyelashes playfully and grinned again. Then she looked at Chloe and grinned even more.

"If you do not answer the prosecution's questions honestly, you will be found in contempt of this court."

"Honey, contempt is *all* I have for this court."

Jamar turned to Wyatt and whispered, "Hey…do we like Leeka now?"

"Geez. I dunno."

The Prosecutor continued. "Did you or did you not sell the defendant illegal vials of the enhancement serum?"

Leeka smiled at Chloe. Then she answered, "No."

This time, the murmur in the court was louder. Judge Dakarr clicked a button on their computer panel. This caused loud, dinging noise. "Order in the court, please."

Prosecutor Veeloren looked at Leeka, then down at the tablet they were holding, then back up at Leeka.

"You said in your deposition that you did."

"Oh, I lied in that deposition. I merely sold Miss Thompson some bread."

Veeloren suddenly shriveled their face into a look of intense anger. "You are under oath, Miss Shaffle!"

"Oh, oh, thanks for reminding me, I also sold her some donuts."

"Judges, we are now treating this witness as hostile."

Leeka leaned forward. "Get these restraints off of me, and I will show you *hostile*!"

"I again ask you, did you sell vials of the enhancement serum to Miss Thompson?"

"No. And let me make one thing abundantly clear." Leeka leaned forward again. "I will not help your government do *anything*. Even if it's to prosecute somebody I don't like." She smiled at Chloe again. Chloe couldn't help it; she smiled back at Leeka.

"Well, her testimony sure is entertaining, eh?" said a familiar voice.

Alice whipped her head to her right to see Chase suddenly sitting right next to her. Wyatt and Jamar also looked over at him. He had a full beard, as opposed to the short stubble he usually had, but it was him.

"Jacob!" Alice said in her loudest whisper. "You…you're here! *With a beard*! But…how are you here?"

Chase gestured behind him. "The front door?" He smiled. She smiled back. She hugged him tightly.

"Now the gang's all back together," Jamar whispered, "what're you doin' here, man?"

"Oh, I couldn't miss all of this," Chase whispered, still hugging Alice.

"Oh no," said Alice. She noticed a scar on his face. It ran from his right cheekbone down to his chin. She traced the scar down with her finger. "What happened?"

"I was just in a battle where I'd really wished I'd had the super juice," Chase replied. Alice gently brought his face to her lips, and she kissed it. He smiled. "Too bad I didn't have it. But maybe the scar is a good thing. Makes me look all rugged, doesn't it?"

"Maybe his new nickname can be 'Scarface,'" suggested Wyatt.

Alice pointed ahead. They all looked. Judge Jenker looked directly at them. Alice put her finger to her lip and shushed them.

"Spare the Deelooveren People, Leeka," the Prosecutor said. "You are not friends with Miss Thompson. You two were in a fight to the death once, right?"

"Um, we're both still living."

"You know what I mean!"

"Okay," Leeka said, sighing, "the humans have a saying that I recently learned that I really like. 'The enemy of my enemy is my friend.' So, she's kind of my friend now."

"We are *not* her enemy."

Counselor Franklin stood up. "Objection, Your Honors. Does Prosecutor Veeloren have a question? Or are they just going to waste the court's time with this banter with the witness?"

High Judge Kellnan surprised Chloe's defense team. "Objection sustained. Let's move along, Veeloren. Do you have any more questions for your witness?"

Veeloren looked at the judge with a slightly puzzled and annoyed look on their face. "Fine." They turned back to Leeka. "Do you regularly steal and/or sell doses of enhancement serum?"

"Objection, relevance," Counselor Vashe said as they stood up.

Veeloren turned to the judges. "I am trying an alternative means of establishing a chain of evidence since my witness is lying about her direct involvement."

"Objection overruled. But get to the point, Veeloren. Witness will answer the question."

Leeka grinned. "No, of course not. Not ever. Because that would be illegal." She tried to look as coy as she could.

A look of barely suppressed rage came upon Veeloren's face. "Miss Shaffle, if you do not stop lying, you will find these perjury charges adding significantly to your sentence for your own crime in this matter."

"Oh, will you add a few more years to *forever*?"

Chloe couldn't help it. She smiled again. She enjoyed this.

Veeloren looked even more angry. But they decided to cut their losses. "We have nothing further for this witness."

Counselor Franklin stood up and approached Leeka. "So… would you say that you are *friends* with the defendant now?"

"Oh, yes. Absolutely."

"But would you engage in criminal activity with her?"

"Objection!" Veeloren stood up. "Defense knows she's going to lie!"

Vincent looked at the judges and put his hand on his heart. "You Honors, surely you know that we humans are not a telepathic species. I don't know what she's going to say."

Judge Jenker sighed. "Objection…" They hesitated. Everybody

in the courtroom hung on that word. "...*Overruled*. Answer the question, Miss Shaffle."

"No," Leeka answered. "I would *never* do such a thing."

"Did you ever previously engage in criminal activity with my client?"

"No, *of course not.*"

Counselor Franklin turned back to look at Chloe, then turned back to Leeka. "The Defendant is a lovely woman, isn't she?"

"Objection!"

"Yes, of course she is."

"Sustained!"

Leeka winked at Chloe. Chloe blushed a little. She winked back.

Vincent held up his hands. "Withdrawn! I have nothing further."

Counselor Vashe stood and approached Leeka. "So, *how* lovely would you say she is?"

"OBJECTION!"

High Judge Kellnan looked angrily at Vashe. "Sustained! Is Defense done with this witness?!"

Vashe smiled. "Yes."

"Guards, take Leeka back to her holding cell," ordered Judge Dakarr. Four guards came and collected Leeka. She smiled and winked at Chloe as she passed by on her way out.

"Well," Chloe whispered to her legal team, "that was inappropriate, but...I liked it?"

Vincent chuckled. "Oh, just a bit of courtroom theater. The jury loved it. It'll help them love *you*. I know it's inappropriate, but sometimes it helps me get acquittals."

"I agree," Vashe said, "and I am seeing why he is such a popular lawyer on your planet."

"I have an objection," Wyatt mumbled to Jamar.

"You don't think she's lovely?"

"Well, I...well, I object to *him* saying it!"

"Does anybody have popcorn?" Chase said. He pantomimed eating popcorn. Alice giggled. He half-smiled and winked at Alice, then pretended to eat another piece. "Mmm. Extra butter."

"Give me some!" Alice grabbed some of the imaginary popcorn. She pretended to eat the pieces she'd pretended to grab.

Jamar looked over at them. "Y'all got some pop—" But he noticed they were pretending. "Dammit."

Soon, it was time for closing arguments.

"Wow. I guess people have a right to a speedy trial here, too," Wyatt said. "I mean, closing arguments already?" He looked at his smartwatch. "It's only been six hours since the trial began."

"Takes longer to make chili in the crock pot," Jamar said.

As was Deelooveren custom, the prosecution delivered their closing argument first. They stood and paced back and forth in the area before the jury box.

"Judges, members of the jury, ever since we discovered the enhancement serum, including the plant we get the main ingredient from and the correct recipe to make it, we knew that it would be very helpful to our world. But we also quickly discovered how dangerously it can be abused.

"Centuries ago, abuse and illegal obtainment of the serum and its ingredients almost led to the plant going extinct, as it was massively over-harvested. We successfully cracked down on misuse and maldistribution of the serum, and now we *mostly* have that under control. The serum is very useful. It can save lives. We put it to good use in the Contests as an incentive to participate because they can be dangerous. We have helped so many worlds, saved trillions of lives because of the Contest, and part of the reason we have the Contest is the enhancement serum.

"The accused human, Chloe Thompson, illegally obtained vials of the serum, doing her part to unravel the fabric of our system of control over the helpful but dangerous treatment. She was on video with the vials. We had one witness testify to the facts of the deal. True, another witness recanted, but she is a known criminal and liar, and we know she lied on the stand! The defense says that we can't prove that serum was in those vials. But use your sense of logic! Everybody in this room knows what's true. You have a duty to convict Miss Thompson of this crime for our people and for our continued use of the serum! Thank you."

Counselor Franklin stood up and approached an area near both the jury box and the judges' desk. "Your Honors, ladies and gentlemen, and neutrals of the jury, we believe we have showed that you cannot convict my client, Chloe Thompson, of the crime of which she was accused. Now, this is not a principle that's explicitly defined in the Deelooveren justice system, although I believe it is implicit, but a cornerstone of most modern justice systems on Earth is that to convict, you must not have *any* reasonable doubt of guilt, no matter how small.

"'Beyond a reasonable doubt.' That's what we say you have to have to convict, in the United Kingdom, the part of Earth I am from, but also in the United States and Canada, the nations that her friends are from. The prosecution's star witness said that deal that they are trying to convict my client of didn't happen. The supposed video evidence of my client having vials of the serum does not prove, *beyond a reasonable doubt*, that the serum was actually in any of them.

"And what of the vials? They're gone. The prosecution didn't have those as evidence, nor did they have my client's fingerprints or DNA on that evidence. Because, again, it's gone. You cannot, in good conscience, convict my client of this crime. You can't. I know this is a very serious offense on your world, and I understand why. But it's not fair to make an example of my client for it if you are not absolutely one hundred percent sure she's guilty. My client needs to go home, back to her family, back to her life, a life that, I remind you, almost ended several times over as *she tried to help your planet*." He said that last bit while specifically looking at the Deelooveren members of the jury. "You must acquit my client, Chloe Thompson. Thank you."

Counselor Vashe stood up to give their closing argument. "My co-counselor is right. There is not one bit of totally credible evidence of my client's guilt. The human Chloe Thompson should not be found guilty of this crime. As Counselor Franklin pointed out, we don't explicitly have the phrase 'beyond a reasonable doubt' in our justice system, but being certain of the guilt of the accused before conviction, that *is*. 'Absolute certainty of guilt' is what we say on *this* planet. And the prosecution here did not provide that. It is essential to adhere to that principle.

"Thousands of years ago, when we Deelooveren were more primitive, all the regional justice systems were awful. There were show trials, people convicted of crimes with very little or no evidence, and many barbaric executions were carried out. When we started this age we are in now, the Civilized Age, we wrote our World Constitution to enshrine new fair and just laws, and included in that was a new fair way to enforce our laws.

"'Absolute certainty of guilt' is a fundamental principle in our justice system. You have a duty to not only acquit my client but also to show our human guests that our justice system is just as fair, if not more fair, and cherished as theirs is. If you unjustly convict my client, you will sow much distrust between our peoples, between our worlds, and it will sour the budding relationship we have with them for a long time.

"In closing, as was already pointed out, no good evidence exists, their best witness recanted, and there is no confession to the crime. They have almost nothing. You must acquit the human, Chloe Thompson. Thank you."

Vashe returned to the defense desk, and the jury was ushered away to their chamber to decide the innocence or guilt of Chloe. Butterflies zipped and zoomed around Chloe's stomach as if they had injected some of the serum. She grabbed her glass of water and took a large drink of it to moisten her dry throat.

"I think we're going to win," Vincent said as he turned and smiled at Chloe.

"How can you be so sure?" Chloe asked.

"Well, I'm not sure, but yeah, I think there's a very good likelihood of acquittal."

"I agree," Vashe said. "I have to admit, during the investigation, I thought they had you. I had my doubts, I'm ashamed to admit it. But the prosecution failed to provide that absolute certainty of guilt."

"So," Chase said, "do we still hate Leeka? I mean…after what she did to Alice, I probably still do, but…that was pretty cool, what she did there, for Chloe, wasn't it?"

"I admit, I'm conflicted," Wyatt said.

"I don't hate her, despite everything," Alice said. "I really don't. And Jacob, you don't have to hate her." She grabbed her voice box and pulled it away from her neck a little. She mouthed, "I have this." Alice let it snap back into place. "But…this isn't what I want most of all."

Jacob smiled at her.

"Do *you* know what *you* want most of all?" she asked him.

Jacob's smile faded. "I…don't. I…never have."

Alice frowned, and she looked down.

"Correction," Jacob said, "I did. One time. In my life. Recently. I…actually…there's two things I want most of all. And I wish I could have them both."

"Life has hard choices sometimes, doesn't it?" Alice said.

"Yes, it does."

"What does your heart tell you, Jacob? It always tells the truth. It tells me the truth, at least."

"It tells me I love you. More than anybody or anything ever in my life. That I am certain of." He reached out and moved a stray lock of her blonde hair out of her eyes and back into her hair. She smiled.

He leaned in and kissed her.

"Are we in court or a soap opera?" Jamar asked.

After a few seconds, she giggled. "I've never kissed you with a full beard before! It tickled a little!"

"Sorry, babe, not a lot of time for shaving running all around the galaxy."

"Did you save those kids?"

"Yes, we did. We freed all the kids at Slithertown. And some we found in the Far Lands. But there's lots more kids to save."

"I know, but I'm so glad you rescued them," Alice gently stroked Chase's beard.

Suddenly there was some activity going on at the front of the court. Everybody in the courtroom began low-key chatting. All four of them looked toward the front to see what was going on. They saw the six jurors coming out and filing back into the jury box.

"They're done deliberating already?" Wyatt said.

Jamar raised his eyebrows. "Now that is either a really good sign or a really bad one."

The three judges stood. The six jurors did as well.

"Members of the jury," High Judge Kellnan said, "have you reached a verdict?"

"Yes, we have, Your Honors," said one of the Deelooveren jurors, who held a clear, thin Deelooveren tablet.

"What say you, Juror?"

"We find the defendant, Chloe Marie Thompson…without guilt! We declare she is innocent of all charges."

Chloe gasped! She shot up out of her chair, her mouth open wide in happy shock. "Oh my god!" Tears came to her eyes. She hugged Counselor Franklin and then Counselor Vashe. She whipped around to look at her human friends. Alice, Chase, Wyatt, and Jamar flew out of their seats to pile a hug on her.

"I was acquitted!" Chloe yelled from inside the hug pile.

The High Judge repeatedly clicked a button on their desk computer panel to make a loud beeping noise. "Order in this court!"

Chloe and her friends quieted down and turned to look at the judge. They looked angry. They pointed at Chloe.

"You, human, were found without guilt, and you are free to go. But we know what the truth is. I would suggest that once you leave this planet, you do not return." Then the High Judge addressed every-body, "Court is adjourned for the day!"

Chloe, her eyes still wet, turned back to her attorneys. "Thank you both so much!"

"You're welcome!" Counselor Franklin said. "But the plea-sure is mine! I am very pleased that you get to go free. Plus…bragging about being the first attorney to help get a human acquitted in an alien court for the first time in human history? I will enjoy having *that* flex added to my website!"

Chloe chuckled. "I'm sure you will!"

"I don't think this will make me as popular on this planet as it will for him," Counselor Vashe said, "but I am still very glad about this outcome!"

Wyatt extended his hand to both attorneys. "Thank you so much for helping Chloe go free. I appreciate what both of you have done." He shook both their hands.

When the five humans exited the courtroom reporters from Earth and Deelooveren media met them. They tried to answer as many questions as they could.

"I am very glad to be free and go home!" Chloe said to one reporter. "And I'm so glad to be going home with my friends!"

#

A few hours later, a Deelooveren ship was ready to take all the humans home who had traveled to the planet. Chase agreed to go home with them and celebrate at a party at Chloe's house.

"I can't believe that I just had a court case on an alien planet," Vincent said to the Five as he was about to board the ship. "I am still processing all this!"

"Don't worry, Mr. Franklin, you get used to it," Alice said as she smiled at him.

Vincent and Chloe and her friends were the final six to board the ship. He went through the door and then looked backward to see the others enter. But…they were gone.

The pilot looked toward the door. "Five more were getting on, right? The Five Contestants?"

Vincent looked all around. "I don't know where the hell they went. They were right behind me." He stepped back off the ship. He looked all around outside, too.

"They're…gone."

CHAPTER FIVE: Taken...Again

A S WYATT awoke, as his mind returned to the waking world, he found himself quite confused. He lay on a grated floor that was made of either metal or hard plastic. He couldn't decide which at first. But either way, it was not comfortable. He opened his eyes and looked straight up. He was in an enclosure of some kind. It was mostly open to the sky above like it was some kind of cage. And it was nighttime wherever he was—the light from the moon reflected off the edges of the cage above. He blinked several times. His vision wasn't clear. His glasses were gone. The moon provided just enough light so that Wyatt could discern his surroundings. The air was cold but smelled fresh. There was a subtle floral fragrance to the air, along with a mossy odor. Was he in a forest?

He sat up. He noticed he was wearing the Deelooveren human team uniform again. It was red and black and somewhat form-fitting, precisely as it was before. But why was he wearing it? Where was he? He again noticed it was cold. He hugged himself and shivered. The uniform was thick, though, and he wondered how much colder he'd feel if he had regular clothing on.

"What the hell is going on?" he said. He looked around. It was like a big, domed cage. Chloe, Alice, Jamar, and Chase also lay on the floor of this…thing he was in. They stirred. Wyatt fumbled around for his glasses. He found them lying next to him. But the left lens had a crack in it. He put them on anyway. When he looked at his surroundings more closely, he noticed this enclosure, which was indeed a cage, was high in the air. Right beyond this enclosure to his left was a thick tree trunk.

Were they in a giant tree?

Wyatt crawled to the edge of the enclosure. He could see that the greater landscape was that of a vast jungle or rainforest. And they were indeed on a huge branch of an enormous tree. The enclosure looked to be about the size of a high school gym. The sounds of nocturnal creatures, insect and animal, filled the air. Wyatt looked around some more and noticed more enclosures like that one atop unusually large branches of other trees nearby.

"What?"

Wyatt looked to see that Alice was waking up. "What's going on?" she asked. She looked around and saw Wyatt. "Wyatt...where are we? What the hell is going on? Why is it so cold?"

"I am just as confused as you are," Wyatt said. "We appear to be in some sort of enclosure, a domed cage of sorts, in...a giant tree... above a jungle."

"What the hell am I wearing *this* again for?!" She looked at Wyatt. He wore it, too. She looked around at the others, who were still unconscious. They all wore that damned uniform. Her brain suddenly became fully awake. "Wyatt, what the hell is going on?!" She stood up. "What's the last thing you remember?"

"Ummm...let's see...it's coming back to me...Chloe's trial... found not guilty...ummm..." He scratched his head.

"Yes, the trial! On Loovian! Are we on Loovian?!"

"No," Wyatt said. He looked up. "Loovian has two moons. I have no idea what planet this is. Which...is...very worrisome." He checked his neck. He still had on an air collar. So did Alice.

"We need to wake the others," Alice said, but suddenly, her voice had lost volume. It sounded more tinny. She thumped it. "Testing...there, now it sounds normal."

"I hope it's not running out of charge."

"Ambassador Karak said it'd last years. Wait. Do I have the batteries with me? Do we have *anything* with us?" That's when they noticed five small black cases placed around the tree trunk. She walked over to them. Each one had a small square painting of each of their faces. Each painting depicted their faces as if they were gray and dead.

"That's...ominous." She opened the case that had her dead face on it. Inside was a small, shiny battle knife, an ear communicator, a small metallic case, a canteen that appeared to have water in it, a bowl of red berries, and a small, white card about the size of a business card. She picked it up. Something was written on it. It was in

English. It read, "He's in love with Farine."

"The hell?" She flicked the card back into the bottom of the case. "What kind of bullshit is *that*?"

Wyatt, nearby, was also going through his case. He was also reading his small, white card.

"What's yours say?"

Wyatt flipped it around. "It says 'she doesn't love you.'"

"Somebody is playing some sort of sick game with us! What is this?!"

Wyatt shook his head. He did not know what it was. "What did yours say, Alice?"

Alice's hand trembled slightly as she read it. "It said, 'He is in love with Farine.'"

"Farine? But…he's in love with *you*."

"He has been around her a lot lately, and I've seen how he'd look at her…"

"Don't, Alice, don't. You're right. This is a game or something. Somebody's messing with us. Don't let them. Clearly, it's a subtle thing to get into your head."

Alice opened the small metal case. Inside was a small vial with a needle with a plastic lid on it. "Is this a super serum microdose?"

Wyatt looked inside Alice's case. "You've got all the same stuff I do."

"Is this…food?" Alice picked up one of the berries. She examined it.

"*I* wouldn't eat it."

"I don't plan to." She put it back in the bowl. But she picked up the canteen. She unscrewed the lid and smelled the liquid inside the canteen. It was odorless. "I guess this is just water." She dipped her finger inside and was about to lick her finger.

"Wait," Wyatt said. "Are you sure you want to do that?"

"I think it's just water." She put her tongue on her finger and scooped up just a tiny drop of it. She brought her tongue back into her mouth and tasted it. "Yeah. It's water."

Wyatt got his new communicator out. He put it in his ear. As soon as he did, it started beeping. He pressed the button. "Hello?"

"Mr. Henderson! Finally! What is going on?"

The voice was familiar. *Oh!* Wyatt thought. "Coordinator Jeelork! Look, I don't know what happened or where we are. How long have we been missing?"

"How should *I* know? Do *you* know where we are?"

"Do *I* know where *you* are?" Wyatt said. "I'm…so confused. Why would I—?"

Suddenly, Wyatt heard a far-off tinking noise that sounded like somebody banging metal against metal. It echoed into the night forest air. Wyatt looked out to their left. He saw something, or somebody, moving in one of the other dome cages.

"Did you hear that?" Jeelork asked.

"Yes. Was that *you*? Are you in that other…*tree cage*?"

"Yes!"

Alice approached Wyatt as she took a drink of the water. She wiped her mouth and said, "Who are you talking to?"

"Put your communicator in your ear. *Now*." Alice went back to her case, plucked her communicator out, and put it in. It immediately beeped.

"Hello, Alice?" Ambassador Karak's voice asked.

"Ambassador Karak?" Alice said.

She and Wyatt heard Jamar groaning.

"I'm afraid it's just Karak now," they replied. "I no longer have a title for anything. But that's not important right now. Do you five know what's going on?"

"No, when you called, I hoped *you* did!"

Wyatt turned to Alice. "Jeelork and Karak are over there in that cage." He pointed to it. "They were abducted, too."

Karak continued to talk into Alice's ear, "Coordinator Jeelork, myself, Farrstead, Captain Flarr, and Assistant Meel, we are all in a cage like yours. And we are just as confused as you are."

"The hell?!"

"Jamar's awake," Wyatt said.

Alice noticed Chase moving around. She went to him.

Jamar rolled over and looked around. He looked down as he noticed he wore that uniform again. "What the hell is happening?" He rubbed his arms. "It's chilly."

"We are all in some sort of tree cage. Five Deelooveren are over in that cage, including Jeelork and Karak, and we are not on Loovian, and that's all we know," Wyatt said to Jamar. "I guess we were abducted…by *somebody*…as we were about to board the ship."

Jamar slowly stood up. "I'm getting real tired of this space shit." He looked around. "What are these?"

"Cases, we each have one," Wyatt replied. "One of them is yours."

"This is a pic of me *dead*!" Jamar exclaimed when he studied his case. "Oh, I do not like *this*. No, sir." He noticed the small card. He read it out loud. "Her family will take her away from you." He flashed the card at Wyatt. "The hell is *this*?!"

"It's something to mess with us," Wyatt said. "Alice and I got similar cards. Don't let it get into your head."

"Alice?" Jacob mumbled as he fluttered his eyes open. "What…? Where are we?"

"On another alien planet, in a big tree cage," Alice answered.

"Huh? What?"

Chase quickly sat up. He looked around and up at the moon.

"We don't know what planet this is," Alice said, "but it's cold here." She shivered.

"I wish I knew," Chase said. He noticed that his breath condensed into small white clouds. "And yeah, it's a bit chilly. But I'm kind of used to cold like this." He moved to get up. Alice grabbed one of his arms and helped him up. He patted her arm and smiled at her. "Thanks, hon." He kissed her.

"No problem," Alice said

"Chloe's awake!" announced Jamar. He knelt by her side as she rapidly blinked her eyes.

"Where the bloody hell are we?" she asked. She sat up. The others came over to her until they were surrounding her. Wyatt explained the situation to her.

"No!" Chloe yelled. She scrambled to stand up. She whipped her head all around. "I was free! I was going to go home!" Her screams echoed off into the night.

"Chloe, shhhh, shhh," Wyatt said as he grabbed her shoulders. He looked into her eyes. "Whatever this is, we will get out of it. We will win, like we always do, okay? But maybe we shouldn't yell."

"Wyatt—"

"Chloe, please, we don't know who's listening…or *what* is listening."

Chloe looked around at their surroundings suspiciously. "This is a bunch of rubbish!" she muttered.

Soon, they had all gotten into their cases and had their communicators on.

"Your father doesn't love you," said Chloe's card. She tore it to shreds and tossed the pieces back into the case. "Wyatt said the card was just to mess with us!" she said to herself. She slammed the case shut. But she had a drink of the water.

"What did your card say?" Alice asked Chase.

He shook his head. "I didn't get a card," he lied.

"But why did we all get one, and you didn't?"

"What does it matter? They're just messing with us with them. It's not like I'm missing out on something."

"But it's a small mystery as to why you didn't get one."

"Let's solve the big mysteries first, okay?" Chase actually seemed annoyed with Alice. He examined his vial of the serum. "Like…is this really super serum in these vials? Or some poison?"

"Hmm. Who wants to be the guinea pig?" Alice said.

Chase briefly considered the advantage of having the serum again, but decided there was no way he would be a test subject. "Not me, that's for sure."

"Well, not me, either," Alice said, but it sounded like the volume of her voice box was malfunctioning again.

"Is something wrong with your voice box?" Chase asked. He looked at it.

Alice sighed. "Dammit. I hope not. It did that a few minutes ago, too, when I was talking to Wyatt."

Jacob put his hand to her soft face. "Have I told you yet today how beautiful you are?"

Alice smiled. "No. You just woke up. But you can keep telling me." She giggled.

Wyatt approached them. "I hate to interrupt, but I have a suggestion.

"What's that?" Chase asked.

"If your voice box is running out of charge, Alice, I mean, if that indeed is what the problem is, then I recommend being light on the talking. Y'know, make the charge last longer. Just a suggestion. I don't know what this thing is that we're caught up in, but I have a sinking feeling that it's not supposed to be a pleasant vacation."

"Polite way of telling me to shut up, Wyatt?" Alice smiled at him and lightly chuckled.

Wyatt also snickered. He grinned at her. "Oh, I'd never tell *you* to shut up."

"You tell me to shut up," Chloe grumbled. She was suddenly standing behind Wyatt.

Wyatt looked at Chloe, slightly annoyed. "*When*?"

"Remember that time that your mom was being rude about British people, and I complained?"

"Well, you complained a little overzealously. You talked bad about my mom."

Chloe snickered. "Mama's boy."

Wyatt squared his jaw and looked straight into Chloe's eyes. "Honey, I say this with all the love in my heart…*shut up*."

Chloe brought her face closer to his. She narrowed her eyes at him. "Why don't you *make me?*"

Wyatt smiled. "Oh, *I will*."

"Seriously, you two, get a room!" Jamar yelled. He shook his head.

Alice giggled.

Chase looked around. "Looks like separate rooms is something we don't have the luxury of right now." Then he looked at Alice and smiled. "Dang it." Alice giggled again.

"Aw, hell," Jamar said, rolling his eyes. "Here we go again. You four, I swear, I have had it up to *here* with this PDA…especially since I can't have any!" He held his hand up over his head.

"Awww, Jamar, we're sorry," Alice said. She came over and hugged him.

Chloe did, too. "Yes, love, my apologies, too." They both snuggled him.

Jamar looked at them, then looked up and smiled. "Okay. I'll take it."

Wyatt looked at Chase. "Are we going to have to kick his ass?"

Chase chuckled. "Looks like."

"Or maybe we should snuggle him, too?" Wyatt said.

Jamar looked at both of them with a slightly amused look on his face. "No thanks!"

Chloe and Alice laughed. They stopped the snuggling.

"Humans," Karak's voice said in their communicators. "We need to communicate more, figure this out. We see the tree cage...or whatever we're supposed to call them...next to us has Fargles, and I recognize Barchell. They're big, orange, hard not to notice. That's another winning team...which just so happens to be the year that the first human team participated. I don't think we have to recap what went wrong there."

"So," said Wyatt, "we have two Contest-winning teams up here and five Deelooveren. Could this have something to do with the Contest?"

"Maybe," Karak replied.

"Hopefully, others will also get their communicators in," Jeel-ork said. "So we can all talk and get a better idea of what's going on."

"Hi everybody!" Farrstead said. "We have not talked in a while."

"Hi Farrstead!" Alice said.

"Hey there, Former Number Three," Chase said, "how's it hanging?"

"How is *what* hanging?"

"Never mind," Chase said, "I mean, how are you?"

"I am very confused at the moment. Like I don't know where we are, what's going on, and if I got that title."

"Title?" Alice said.

"Well, the last thing I remember was my titling ceremony. I was about to become Engineer Farrstead. But I don't remember if it concluded before...*this* happened."

"Well, I'll call you Engineer Farrstead if you want," Alice said.

"Yeah, me, too," Wyatt said, "let's all do it."

"Awww, you humans are so kind," Engineer Farrstead replied. "I mean, of course you are. You won the Contest."

"Hello?" a new voice said over the communicator. "Who all is receiving this?"

"Hello, Barchell," Karak said, "we Deelooverens and the five humans can hear you."

"Chase?" Barchell said. "You're there?"

"Yeah, I'm here. Did you get the kids to that home on Tarf?"

"Yeah, right before I ended up here...wherever the hell here is!"

"You all don't know where here is, either?" Farine asked.

"Farine is here!" Chase announced. "Are you with your former team?"

"Yes, I am with my Norfan team."

"That's three teams of winners," Karak said. "I think our idea of this having something to do with the Contest is becoming more likely. If this is so, then Woo'cha's team could be here."

"What about any others?" Wyatt asked.

"Most of the teams of winners are gone," Karak replied. "There aren't winners very often. Most of them are too old and probably dead. The last team to win before Woo'cha's and Farine's teams that could possibly still be alive were the Wistwills, from seventy-five years ago. The last winning team before that was well over a century ago."

"Yes, we're here," Woo'cha said in his usual grumpy voice. "All five of us."

"Trust me," said another Doo'chen voice, "we're not exactly pleased to be hanging around this grumpy shit again."

"Well, you smell, Tak'mer," Woo'cha said, "they don't wanna be around you, either. Even Tork'chee thinks you do."

"I do not! I never said that!" Tork'chee sighed. "Sorry, this is the first time our entire team has been together in over a decade. We don't exactly get along."

"We are here, too," said a strained, cracking but feminine voice.

"Are you from the Wistwill team?" Karak asked.

"Yes, we are," said that same voice again, "all five of us." The person audibly swallowed. "Funny…I didn't even know we were all still alive."

"You don't sound well," Karak said.

"I am ninety-one years old, Deelooveren. How well am I supposed to sound?"

"We haven't even all seen each other for…what…twenty years?" said another raspy voice, this time masculine.

"Wow, that's old!" Woo'cha said.

"That's not appropriate!" Tak'mer exclaimed.

"It's not groovy!" Farine added.

"Not cooly-cool," said another Norfan voice.

"Who are *you*?" asked a Fargle who hadn't spoken yet.

Then, several aliens spoke at once. Wyatt couldn't distinguish between them. "This is getting crazy."

Chloe counted. "Five, ten, fifteen…there are twenty-five people on the channel at once."

As all the voices became a cacophony, Karak had enough.

"Everybody, silence!" Karak exclaimed. "We need to come up with a better system of communication here. Can each of you designate a team leader to speak for your entire team, *please*? And turn off your communicators while you argue about it. But when you decide, speak your name and what your role was on the team."

The humans didn't need to. Alice pointed at Wyatt. So did Chloe. Chase frowned. Then he shrugged and pointed at Wyatt. They all looked at Jamar. "Well, it ain't me. Wyatt's fine."

"I, Wyatt, speak for Team Earth," Wyatt said, "I was the strategist."

"I will speak for the Deelooveren," Karak replied, "and until recently, I was an Ambassador."

"I am Streen," said a feminine voice. "I was the strategist for Team L'Norfa."

"I am Tork'chee," said another feminine voice. "I am the strategist for the Doo'chen."

"You always have to be in charge, don't you?!" Woo'cha said.

"Shut up, Woo'cha! Seriously!"

"I am Barchell, I'll be the leader of Team Fargle, I was the thief."

Chase smiled. "Oh, the thief is the leader of the Fargles," he quietly mumbled. He turned to Alice. "Maybe I gave up too easily." She smiled at him and kissed his cheek. Then she shushed him.

"I am Johanne, of the Wistwills," said the same feminine voice that had first spoken for them. "I was…" They could hear Johanne audibly sigh. "…I was the strategist. Sorry, it was seventy-five years ago. My memories of our Contest aren't very clear in my head. Not much is. I don't know what this…this malevolent alien species has in store for us, but this will be hardest on us, I fear. One of us is confined to a hover chair and can't get around very well."

Alice sighed. Her face drooped into a look of sadness.

"Well, looks like for most teams, the strategist is the leader," Karak said, "so let's come up with a plan."

Suddenly, a large globe ascended from the ground so that it floated in the air in the middle of all the tree cages. It glowed brightly and lit up the area. "*We* will tell you what the plan is!" a feminine voice echoed from it. The globe pulsated with every syllable of the words that spoke.

"Well," Wyatt said, "they're finally showing themselves."

"Silence, human!" the voice blared. "Or do you want to lose *your* voice, too?!"

"I hope Woo'cha speaks out of turn next," Chase whispered as silently as he could to Alice. She tried hard to keep herself from laughing.

"I suppose you all wonder why you were brought here! Well, here is the answer. See, we have decided to put on a little…*contest*… of our own! You will go through a series of trials, but I promise you they will be far less fun this time. And the prize you win at the end? *You get to live.*"

"Aw, shit," Jamar said under his breath.

"Now," the orb spoke again, "here is the first trial. It's rather simple and straightforward. It's just a decision. Some of you are very good decision-makers, right? Decide which member of your team to sacrifice before this contest proceeds, which will be with only four-person teams. If you cannot decide, then your whole team will be eliminated. And we mean 'eliminated' literally. Which is a great and quick way to be the first losing team."

The humans all looked at each other, horrified looks on their faces.

"You have ten minutes to decide!" the orb yelled. Then it descended.

"Oh my god," Chloe whispered. Her heart pounded. The blood in her veins felt like ice water. She looked upon the others with pure fear in her eyes.

"This…this must be a test," Wyatt said. "It…it can't be serious! It's…it's a moral test, and, and…"

"What if it's *not*?!" Chase yelled. He looked at Alice. He embraced her. "It's not her! You hear me! No way, it's her! I will kill any of you who—"

"Stop!" Jamar yelled. "Jesus, Chase, *nobody* would choose Alice! Pull yourself together, man!"

They could hear echoes of yelling and arguing from the other cages.

"Holy shit," Wyatt whispered. "Listen to them. This is bad. This is so bad. These aliens are evil."

Chloe turned to face the other four. "Well, it's not *me*! I just won a trial and was supposed to bloody go home!" Tears trickled from her eyes. She was utterly terrified.

"Well, *I* don't wanna die, guys!" Jamar said. His eyes teared up.

"Better you than Alice, Jamar!" Chase said.

"Well, why don't you just die protecting your woman, then, Canada?!" Jamar replied. "Sacrifice *yourself*!"

"That's it, as I always suspected, Jamar," Chase said. "I *knew* you didn't like me!"

"STOP!" Alice yelled as loud as her voice box would allow her voice to go. "Stop, please…stop." She let a sob escape her throat. "I'll go. Because I could not bear to see *any* of you die and me live! It would tear me apart! I wouldn't want to live!"

"Everybody, listen!" Wyatt said, holding his hands out. "Stop arguing about this. We're *not* arguing about this." He pointed out to the other cages. "We can't be like *them*. We're not going to fall apart. Listen to them. Some of them are threatening each other now. No. *Not us*! I…I am just gonna declare it. This is a test. This is the greatest test of our friendship that we have yet faced. And we will pass it, damn it. *We will pass it*. We choose *nobody*, got it? *Nobody*."

A moment of silence followed. They all stood there, looking at each other. All of them were crying now, some a little, some a lot. "Come here," Alice whispered. She opened her arms wide. "*Please*." Everybody converged on her. They all hugged each other. She whispered again, "Nobody dies. Or we all do. Wyatt's right. This is how we pass this first trial. *Or it's how we fail it*."

All of them murmured words of agreement.

"Ride or die," whispered Jamar.

"Ride or die," everybody else, at once, echoed him.

They all separated, but not completely. The five of them stood in a straight line, holding each other's hands in a defiant show of solidarity. They strengthened their grips until their knuckles were almost white and the skin on their hands creaked.

But all of their hearts pounded in their chests. They were all afraid.

Moments later, the globe returned.

"Have you all decided?" the voice boomed.

Chloe trembled. She sobbed. She looked like she was about to vomit.

"Chloe, Chloe, please," whispered Wyatt, "please, please hold it together. *Please.*" He tightened his grip on her hand.

"Anxiety…attack…" Chloe mumbled. She gasped. Jamar, who held her other hand, looked at her with fear in his eyes.

"Chloe, Chloe, you can do this, girl, you can do this. Just hold on another minute."

The glowing orb shined a slightly brighter beam of light on them. "The humans have made an interesting choice." Then, it shone a brighter spotlight right on Chloe.

With the spotlight on them, the pupils in her blue eyes shrunk to tiny dots. "*Noooooooooo!*" she screamed.

"She is having an anxiety attack!" Wyatt screamed. "We don't choose her! We don't choose *any* of us! We will not choose, damn you!"

"Hmmmm," the globe voice said. The brighter spotlight on Chloe disappeared.

Chloe was hyperventilating. "Wyatt…can't…breathe… can't…breathe…"

Finally, the light on the group faded. They could let go. Chloe collapsed. Wyatt held her and collapsed with her. She desperately gasped for breath. "Breathe, baby, breathe…please breathe for me… you're okay, baby, you're okay…" Wyatt said.

The globe slowly showed spotlights on each cage, one, then the other, then the other, until it had shone a light on each of them. "Well, well, well. Interesting. All of you refused to choose. How touching! Maybe this whole thing ends right now." Weirdly, the globe voice…sighed. "We had all these fun plans, though! Damn all of you. Fine! You all pass the first trial! Nobody dies…*yet.*"

"Babe, you hear that?" Wyatt said. Chloe was still having trouble breathing. "We're all fine. Nobody is dying. We're good, baby, we're good."

"Okay, okay, good," Chloe said, heavily sobbing. Wyatt hugged her tightly.

"Time for the second trial!" the orb said. "I have an important question for you! How many of you know what a sniggle is?"

"Oh shit!" Jamar exclaimed. "Aw nah nah…NO!"

The globe giggled. "At least one of you does!"

CHAPTER SIX: The Sniggle Trial

WYATT HAD never seen Chloe so terrified. She gripped his arms so tightly her hands were completely white. She again trembled with pure fear. "Wyatt…Wyatt…I can't do this! I can't do this!"

"Chloe, listen, none of us look forward to this, okay? But I will do whatever I can to protect you. I won't let you—"

"I'm afraid for *you*!" Chloe yelled. Then she looked around. "And *all* of us!"

"We've each got one vial of the super serum," Jamar said. "We can use it with the sniggles."

"What if they only give us one vial for this whole thing?" Chase asked. "What if there's something *worse* after that?"

"I am having a real tough time imagining something *worse*," Jamar said.

"Let's wait until we get more details," Wyatt said. "We still don't know exactly what they're going to do with the sniggles. Or how we're gonna fight them. Or…whatever."

"Wyatt's right," Alice said, "let's…" But the word "wait" didn't come out of her box. She blinked several times. She tried to talk again, but nothing came out. Alice gently tapped her voice box. They could hear her finger thump as if she had been thumping a microphone attached to a speaker. "Testing…testing…oh thank god."

Jamar sighed and furrowed his eyebrows together. "Aw, no. I hope it doesn't give out."

"I hope so, too," Alice said.

"The sniggles will kill us!" Chloe yelled. Alice, her boots clanging on the metal cage floor, walked over to Chloe and Wyatt.

She firmly put her hand on Wyatt's shoulder. "Excuse me."

Wyatt let Alice push him away from Chloe. Alice put her hands up on Chloe's shoulders. She had a very firm look on her face, which was highlighted and shadowed from the moonlight above. She almost looked angry. White clouds of condensed breath not only came out of her mouth, but her flared nostrils as well.

"Alice, what—"

"Do you remember the first night in that room, Chloe?"

Chloe hesitated, shivering in the cold. "Um, yeah."

Alice put her hands on her hips. "Do you remember how I was that first night?"

"Well, sure…"

Alice angrily pointed at herself. "I was a pathetic, anxious mess! Wasn't I? It annoyed you! No. It pissed you off! Didn't it?!"

Chloe stammered. "Uh um uh, I…*yes*."

"You wanted to beat me unconscious."

Chloe looked into her eyes. She blinked. "I…I…I wanted to…I wanted to…*strangle* you. And…yeah…beat you, too." She heavily exhaled, sending little white clouds up into the cold air.

Alice raised her eyebrows. "Well, okay—"

"But, but darling, I—"

"Let me *finish,* Thompson!" Alice stopped to point at Chloe. "What the hell happened to you?! Where'd you go?"

"I'm right here."

"No, you're not! Let me tell you something. About another woman who isn't standing in this stupid cage right now. That pathetic little girl that pissed you off that day. The girl who…" Alice stopped. She swallowed. "…The girl was such an anxious mess that she tried to kill herself by slitting her wrists two years ago." She pulled her sleeves down and revealed the scars on her goosebumped wrists. "There's a reason I always hide my wrists with long sleeves or a watch or brace-let or something. I told Ambassador Karak and Commander Vot to never make my uniform sleeves short…except at that disc game."

Jamar and Wyatt gasped. Chase sighed. He was the only one, until now, that she'd told.

"And that girl thought about doing it again later that night in the space station dorm. But something happened since then. We, like, did a body swap! Like we're in a goddamn sitcom! What happened, Chloe? I really want to know something. That tough bitch who wanted to strangle me that first night, I wanna know where the hell she went! 'Cause I'm not lookin' at her! I'm lookin' at *me*!"

Wyatt tried to step toward Alice. Jamar put out his arm and stopped him. "Wait, Wyatt, wait," he whispered.

Chloe's expression changed. Her nostrils flared. Her mouth became tight. "I was beaten half to death! Did you forget that?!"

"Maybe these evil aliens should finish the job then, Chlo—!"

Chloe slapped Alice in the face; the sharp, loud noise of it clapped out into the cold air. But all Alice did was put her hand to her face and look Chloe directly in her eyes again.

Alice smiled. "There's that tough bitch you need to be again. You need to be her to survive whatever shit these aliens have in store for us! *Be her again*!"

Wyatt had had enough. "You are out of line, Alice! She's experienced major trauma!"

Alice whipped around to face him. "No, Wyatt, I am *not*!" She walked toward him. "If we are back on Earth, on the street, or at one of our homes, I agree, I'd be a monster right now! But if we don't snap her out of this, she will *die*! Whatever these demented aliens have in store for us will kill her! And she'll let them!" Then Alice, in a lower voice, added, "And she almost did moments ago."

Chloe became enraged. "I was having an anxiety—!"

Alice whipped around and attacked Chloe. She tried to punch her, but Chloe's martial arts and fighting instincts kicked in, and she blocked it. Alice tried to punch her again, again Chloe blocked it. They began full-on sparring. But each one blocked every punch. Their heavy breathing shrouded both of them in tendrils of white.

"Hit me, Chloe!" Alice yelled. "Come on, hit me!" Chloe tried, but Alice blocked it. "What's wrong, Chloe?! You've been doing this longer. Hit me!" Chloe then tried several more times, each time blocked, and she blocked several punches from Alice. But finally, Alice missed a block, and Chloe punched her in the face. Alice collapsed to her knees. Both women breathed even more heavily. Chloe looked at her fist, then at Alice.

Warm blood trickled from Alice's nose onto the cold skin of her lip and chin. She could feel the burning pain in her nostrils. Alice wiped them with her wrist and loudly sniffed. She looked at the blood on her wrist, then, through a few sweaty locks of her blonde hair, back up at Chloe. "There. *Now you're back.*"

Chloe looked at Alice in silence for a moment. Then, a slow smile spread across her face. "Thank you."

Chase knelt down to Alice. "Al, lemme see your nose."

"I'm fine!" Alice said. She used her sleeve to wipe more of the blood away.

Chase pointed at Chloe. "Bloody her nose again and—"

"Chase, *enough!*" Alice stood up and faced him. She pointed at him and then actually pushed him backward with her finger into his chest. "You're not my personal bodyguard. I'm not a baby. I don't need that! That's not what I need from you! *Stop it!*"

Alice made a disgusted face and walked away.

Wyatt looked around. "Okay, so, are we all good here?"

"We're about to see some sniggles again," said Jamar, "so *no*, we are *not* good."

"What are 'sniggles?'" came a voice to their communicators. It was Streen.

"A highly feared rodent animal that originated on Clokia-4," answered Karak. "But because of its vicious nature and swarming capabilities has been bred across the galaxy, and they have many nefarious uses."

"You do *not* wanna mess with them!" Jamar exclaimed. "Those things almost killed me and several of my teammates! Even when we had the super juice!"

"*Even with the serum?*" Tork'chee asked. "Oh my god."

The glowing orb ascended again. "Now it's time for some *real* fun. But before we begin, we highly recommend you use that one dose of the enhancement serum we gave you. As much as we would enjoy seeing you all die horrible deaths, we think we should give you a sporting chance. There's not a chance that you'd survive a sniggle attack without it. And we have much more fun planned for you in the next week or so. So, start injecting, folks! You have five minutes to prepare!"

The orb descended.

"She doesn't have to tell *me* twice!" Jamar was already taking the plastic lid off of the needle on his dose. "Inject this stuff into your thighs, folks. Best place."

"Wait!" Wyatt said, throwing out his arms. His eyes were wide with worry. "Everybody else here might be fine, but we've had our lifetime limits, haven't we?"

"Farrstead said we could possibly have three big doses and not suffer the addiction and withdrawals," Alice said, despite feeling worried about it, too.

"We don't have a choice!" Chloe exclaimed. "We're facing another horde of bloody sniggles! Fighting them again without the serum is riskier!"

"It's a small dose anyway!" Jamar said. "It will probably only last during this trial. We need to stop arguing about this and inject… *now*!" Jamar injected his into his own left thigh.

"Ugh. Needles, though," Chloe grumbled as she examined her vial.

"You're tough again, Chloe, remember," Alice said to her. Then she injected herself. She grimaced as she did so.

"Well, actually, I'm concerned, folks," Jamar said. "I'm not feelin' the usual euphoria. You know what that means. Maybe Wyatt was right."

"We *have* had too much already," Wyatt said. He had just injected himself. "I'm not feeling it, either. Yeah, I think we've reached that limit."

"You humans might not feel the usual euphoria," Karak warned, "since you've had more than one super dose. After this… whatever this is…you should never have anymore the rest of your lives."

Chloe got her knife out of her case. "These are our only weapons. They've got to be bloody kidding. Last time, we had phasers."

"These are malevolent beings," Wyatt said. "They don't seem to be concerned with fairness."

"We're going to have super speed and strength and healing," Alice said. "We've got to use all of those things to their full advantage. If we do, we can survive. We might not even need the knife."

Jamar furrowed his eyebrows and turned up his hands in confusion. "But last time—"

"Last time, we didn't use the serum to its full potential!" Alice said. "I remember we didn't use our super speed or strength enough. People, we can do this! Sniggles be damned!" Alice put her hand up. "All in favor of winning this next trial, raise your hand!"

Everybody else raised their hands.

"You are just full of useful speeches tonight," Wyatt said. He smiled at her.

Alice smiled, too, and tried to say something else. But nothing came out. She tried again. Still nothing. She tapped her voice box several times. "Hello?" She sighed. "I may not be able to deliver many more speeches." She closed her eyes and buried her face in her hands.

Chloe approached her and put her hand on Alice's shoulder. "Alice," she whispered, "you're a tough bitch, too. Don't forget. With or without your voice."

Alice looked up at Chloe. She smiled. "Thank you."

A few moments later, the orb returned. "Are you all ready for some fun?"

"No!" said somebody on one of the other teams.

They all heard a noise that sounded like a metal latch opening. And then, suddenly, there was no longer a floor below their feet.

Everybody yelled as they fell to the forest floor. For a few terrifying seconds, they all cut through a chilly breeze until the fall came to a violent end.

Alice landed flat on her back. She heard and felt her spine crack. Her head hurt like hell. She gasped for breath as the wind was violently knocked out of her. Alice desperately tried to breathe. She tried to move but couldn't. The ground was hard and cold and only partially covered in grass and vines.

Wyatt landed on his feet. It broke both his legs and both of his feet. The most intense pain he'd ever felt shot like lightning up through his legs and hips. He yelled in pain. It echoed up through the night air.

Chloe, like Alice, landed on her back. But, unlike Alice, it knocked her unconscious.

Jamar landed on his side. It knocked the wind out of him and broke his right arm and hip. He gasped for breath as the intense pain from his broken bones throbbed.

The fall was the worst for Chase. He fell on a rock. It broke his neck. Along with the horrific pain of the rock banging his head and the ground slamming into his back, he could feel that something was terribly wrong with his neck and the way his head was bent. "Oh my god!" he said with a crooked mouth.

Numerous other screams, cries, and yells echoed across the forest.

Alice felt the weird sensation of her vertebrae un-breaking. She heard the pieces of them crackle back into place. She also felt the fracture at the back of her skull fuse back together. As soon as she could, she scrambled to stand back up. "Is everybody okay?!"

"NO!" Wyatt yelled. He yelled in pain again.

She noticed Chloe lying there still with her eyes closed. Alice almost ran to her, but it horrified her to see Jacob's condition.

"Jacob!" Alice ran over to him. "Oh my god, oh my god, oh my god…"

Chase tried to smile at her. "This trial…is a real…pain…in the neck…"

"Your neck is not supposed to bend like that!"

"No…shit…" But then his neck crunched and popped as it popped back into place and started healing. He grunted as it did so. "Oh…oh my, that is a really…really…weird…feeling."

"Chloe!" Wyatt yelled. He crawled over to her as his legs were still healing.

"Lie still, Wyatt, or your legs won't heal properly!" Jamar exclaimed.

"Wyatt, I'll check Chloe," said Alice, "please, you've got to stop moving." She ran over to Chloe. One of her legs was bent awkwardly. She took her leg and carefully placed it back into the proper position.

Chloe murmured and groaned. Her eyes fluttered open. She smiled when she saw Alice's face. "Hey, love." Then she shut her eyes tight. "Argh, everything hurts!"

Alice heard a female voice across from them wailing.

"He's dead! He died! Tak'mer is dead!"

"How, Flee'cheer?!" Woo'cha exclaimed.

"He was too afraid of needles. He didn't inject himself!"

"Morla, wake up!" Farine yelled. "Morla, come on, my cutie, wake up!"

"Danfer!" yelled Johanne's voice. The Wistwills were further off from the humans than the others were. But her voice was still loud and clear. "Wait, I think he's alive!"

Alice looked around at all the carnage and misery. But she

noticed a bright spot. All the Fargles were perfectly fine, standing and talking to each other. Chase noticed it, too. "Oh yeah, it takes a lot more than that fall to hurt a Fargle. Trust me."

"Morlaaaaa!" Farine cried. "Morla's dead!"

The orb descended, so that it was closer to the ground. "At first, we thought you all didn't like us, but we are pleased to see that you all have now fallen for us!"

All the Norfa and all the Doo'chen were screaming and crying.

"Oh, look, we've had our very first casualties!" the orb continued. "Congratulations!"

Chloe quickly stood up and looked around. She grabbed a rock off of the ground, zeroed in on the orb using her super vision, and hurled the rock at it. The orb quickly moved upward, and the rock barely missed. A phaser blast shot from the orb and hit Chloe, knocking her to the ground.

"Now, now, humans, we will have no more of *that*!"

Wyatt ran to Chloe. "You okay?!"

Chloe grunted and sat up. "It was just a mild stun, I'm fine!"

"Holy shit, these aliens ain't screwin' around!" Jamar said. "Two dead already!"

"Now," said the orb, "are you ready to pet some sniggles?"

Chloe thought of something. "I have an idea. Where's my case?" Everybody realized the cases had to have fallen with them. After rooting around a moment, she found her case. Inside it was a violin. It wasn't her Stradivarius violin. It was a rather plain-looking one. But it still might work for her idea. She pulled her violin out.

"What's your idea, English?" Jamar asked.

"I wonder what effect music will have on the sniggles?" Chloe said.

"Like a pied piper, maybe?" Chase said as a smile spread across his face.

"Why did you get something special like that?" Alice asked.

"I got an instrument during the actual Contest," Chloe said, "so maybe they gave us musicians an instrument in our cases for the same reason. I mean, this is a very twisted version of the Contest?"

Then they heard it: that terrifying sound: sniggles chittering. It sounded like hundreds of them. Maybe more. It was hard to tell exactly how many there were with all the echoing.

"Sweet Jesus," Jamar mumbled. He looked all around so he could locate them. The others did the same.

Chloe found a nearby tree stump. She scrambled on top of it. "Musicians on the other teams! Did you get an instrument in your case?! If you did, I have an idea! See if your music affects the sniggles!"

A single sniggle dropped out of a tree. It landed in front of the tree stump. At first, it looked at Chloe with its big, adorable eyes. It tilted its head in a very cute way as if pleading for a good petting. Chloe held her violin bow with one hand and slowly slid her knife out with the other.

They heard more thuds of things hitting the ground. Sniggles dropped out of the trees all over the area.

Chloe looked at her sniggle with intense anger in her eyes. She gritted her teeth. "Come on, then, you little hellspawn. Have a go at me! I'm ready!" The sniggle hissed at her. "There it is!"

She heard sniggles hissing all over the landscape.

"Keep them away from your neck and head, everybody!" Wyatt yelled as loudly as he could so he could be heard over all the hissing.

And then…the sniggles attacked.

It was not the enormous wave of them like the humans had fought back at the riddle maze, but it was bad enough. The sniggles painfully bit and clawed as they attacked. Screams and cries of pain echoed all over the area, as well as continual sniggle hissing.

Chloe, with her knife, made quick work of the first one that attacked her, but another five or six followed that one…all at once. She used her super vision and speed to kill all of them before they could even make a single bite on her. One of them clawed her leg badly, but the slice to her thigh quickly healed.

Alice used mostly her super speed and fighting skills to fight them off. With quick punches and twirling kicks, she kicked most of the ones attacking her far away.

Wyatt used his super speed to quickly dig up dirt and bury himself into the ground except for his face and hands. He grabbed and stabbed sniggles as they ran over him to attack others.

Chase and Jamar just basically brawled with the sniggles, stabbing, punching, kicking, and tearing them apart.

"What were we so…scared about…Jamar?!" said Chase as he fended several off and smashed two together with his bare hands.

"There's more coming, man!" They saw another wave of sniggles drop out of the trees.

An intense scream from one of the female aliens ripped through the air.

That distracted Jamar. He didn't notice a sniggle jump onto his shoulder and bite at his neck until it was too late.

"Aw, shit!" he yelled as it sank its sharp, venous teeth into his neck. He tore it apart, but the venom took immediate effect. He felt dizzy and fell to his knees.

"Jamar!" Chase yelled. He helped fight sniggles off of Jamar to protect him.

Farine and her remaining Norfan teammates danced around the sniggles frenetically, kicking, punching, and stabbing them with sublimely violent dance moves. But after a few moments of that, their musician, Murr, readied his instrument as the human Chloe had suggested.

The Fargles destroyed most of the sniggles attacking them, sometimes obliterating them into gnarly clouds of blood, tissues, and fur. When Chase saw that, he felt a little jealous of how little effort they needed.

The Wistwills fared the worst. Even with the super serum, they couldn't move quite fast enough to effectively fight the sniggles off. They screamed and cried as the sniggles piled onto them. Alice gasped, horrified, as she glimpsed that scene while fighting off her own sniggles.

Chloe finally freed herself enough to have time to ready her violin. She played a sweet melody. She jumped back on the stump. Many of the sniggles stopped attacking. They all slowly turned toward Chloe.

Across the clearing, she heard a flute, also playing a sweet, calming tune. Chloe mused that it sounded similar to the flute theme music in the old nineties *Titanic* movie. She looked to see that the Norfan musician was playing it. He looked at Chloe and smiled as he played.

"Chloe and Murr are playing their instruments!" Karak yelled. "It's working! Come on! All musicians play your instruments!"

Flee'cheer, the Doo'chen musician, played smooth, pretty music from what looked like a tiny harp.

Chloe got a good look at the Wistwills for the first time. They were completely pale, as in not a single pigment in their skin, and each had a head full of blue hair. They indeed looked very old, as many wrinkles folded across their faces. Some of them now had blue, bloody wounds, as blue must have also been the color of their blood. One of the males, even with several bites on his arms and hands, struggled to play a small guitar.

Hancharree, the Fargle musician, also played her instrument. It was like a violin, but it was longer, and she played it with two bows.

Soon, not a single sniggle was attacking anymore. They slowly gathered around the five musicians.

Jamar observed this happening from his vantage point on the ground. The venom coursed through his veins, almost paralyzing him. He gasped for breath. But despite all that, he found himself impressed with what the musicians were doing, and he was also impressed with the fact that it was Chloe's idea.

Wyatt got up, wiped all the dirt off of himself, and used his knife to stab the nearest sniggle in the head. Then he used his super speed to kill a dozen more in just a few seconds. Chase stood next to Wyatt with his knife. Soon Alice stood there, too, with her knife. "Let's kill them all," Chase said. They nodded at each other. The sniggle slaughter began.

The other aliens in the other teams copied what they were doing. Soon, with super speed stabbing of all the sniggles, the trial was won. The musicians stopped playing.

Everybody took a silent moment to take an inventory of the situation. The injured were tended to. Fortunately, nobody else died. The woman with the loud scream was Alannis, the thief of the Wiswills. She nearly died, but eventually, the serum brought her out of a brief coma. Their teammates buried the two that had tragically died.

The Norfans held a brief ceremony where they all, led by Farine, gracefully danced around the grave of Morla, their fallen scientist.

"Okay, let's clean this place up," Wyatt suggested. Using their super speed, they threw most of the bodies of the sniggles deeper into the forest. They kept a small group of them.

"If that glowy orb thing leaves us alone long enough, let's build a fire," Alice suggested as she rubbed her own arms up and down to warm them up.

"It's campfire time!" Chase said. "Did anybody bring any chocolate or graham crackers or marshmallows?"

"Fresh out, dude," Jamar said. He went to work finding dry sticks for the fire.

"Is anybody hungry?" Wyatt asked as he examined one of the sniggle bodies. "Because I sure am."

"Are you suggesting that we have a sniggle dinner?" Chloe said.

"Well, why not? We don't have any food except for those berries in our cases, which I still say we shouldn't touch."

Karak gathered some sticks, too. "Building a warm fire sounds like a great idea, Miss Mackenzie. This planet is a bit too cold for humans, Deelooveren, and, judging by how much everybody else is shivering, most of the other species here as well."

Wyatt took the large pieces of wood that they'd gathered so far and started building a small log-cabin-like structure in the middle of the forest clearing.

"Interesting," Chloe said when she saw what he was doing.

"One of the best ways to build a fire," Jamar told her. "I learned that in the Scouts."

"Oh, I see you were in the Scouts, too," Wyatt said as he added another layer.

A tall and orange Fargle approached. He frowned and nodded. "Yeah, I approve of this. This will work excellently." Then he extended his hand. "I am Barchell. The only one of you humans I've met so far is Chase."

Wyatt shook his hand. "I'm Wyatt. This is Chloe."

"Pleasure to meet you both," Barchell said. "How about I light this thing when you're done?"

"Go right on ahead," Wyatt said.

"What is this?" Woo'cha said as he approached. "We need to build a fire, not a tiny log cabin!"

Barchell sighed. "Woo'cha, you really test my patience."

Chase chuckled. "And Fargles are known for their high levels of patience!"

Barchell took his knife and a flat rock he'd found and used his super speed to quickly shower the potential campfire with sparks. It didn't take long before this produced a huge, roaring fire. Everybody eagerly gathered around it, most sitting in the grassy patches, some finding suitable pieces of wood to sit on. The humans loved the smell of the campfire, as it was pleasant and interesting like the alien wood that was burning was a cross between pine and cedar, mostly patchou-li, but with a prickly, cooling, camphoraceous aroma. That paired well with the satisfying sizzling, fizzling, popping, and whooshing sounds of the fire.

Jamar was curious about something. He turned his air collar off and tried to breathe the planet's air. He found it difficult, but not impossible, to breathe. Jamar felt light-headed, as if he was at a high altitude on Earth.

When he started wheezing, Chloe turned to him. "What the hell are you doing?"

Jamar turned his air collar back on. He took in a deep breath. "Oh, I was just curious about how the fire was burning, wondering if there's at least some percentage of oxygen in the air. And I guess there is—enough for a fire. But not quite enough for our lungs. Keep your collars on, fellow humans."

"Other gasses burn, right?" Alice asked.

Jamar shook his head. "For combustion, like a fire, with a few limited exceptions, oxygen is the only game in town."

"Well, if the science lesson is over, I say it's time to make din-ner," Wyatt said as he held his knife in one hand and a sniggle carcass in the other.

"You know, it's weird, but I'm looking forward to trying snig-gle meat," said Chloe.

"Well, I'll try almost anything," Chase said. Alice looked skeptically at the sniggle. But then she shrugged.

CHAPTER SEVEN: From Terrifying to Tender

LATER, EVERYBODY sat around the large fire. Jamar, while holding a cooked sniggle leg, slowly chewed on a bite.

"You know what? Sniggle isn't bad!" He raised his eyebrows and bit another piece off. "It's kinda got a sweetness to it, like pork! Hey, I don't hate these things as much anymore!"

"I agree," Wyatt said as he chewed on a bite. "It's surprisingly delicious and tender."

"I would even use the word 'succulent,'" Chase said. He tore a piece off his sniggle thigh and chewed it.

Alice looked longingly at it. Chase looked at her. "Hungry?"

Alice nodded. She was starving. Alice was about to try one of the berries, but the meat looked so much more appetizing, especially since she was still worried that the berries were poisonous. She unconsciously licked her lips while staring at Chase's sniggle thigh.

"I thought you were a vegetarian," Chase said. "I mean, you don't want to eat the flesh of those innocent animals—"

"Screw the sniggles," Alice said, "gimme a bite." She grabbed a piece and put it in her mouth. She closed her eyes as she chewed. Alice was in food ecstasy. "Oh my god. Sniggles are *delicious*!" She grabbed at Chase's piece. "Want more!"

"Well, I'm glad there's still more cooking," Jamar said.

Farine stood up and danced in front of the fire. Her dance moves looked even more elegant, silhouetted against the bright orange flames of the campfire. "I call this dance 'Deliciousness of the Sniggle Meat,'" she said.

Jamar chuckled. "Meat so good there's a dance about it now!"

Farine's dance movements transfixed Chase. He studied every detail of every movement of her body.

"Jacob?" Alice said. He didn't hear her. "Jacob!" When she said it louder that got his attention.

"Oh, hey Al, what is it?"

"Umm…nothing."

Wyatt turned to Chloe. "Maybe we need a song about the sniggle meat, too. You've performed plenty of songs. Ever written one before?"

Chloe sighed. "No. I'm not very good with the *words* part of songs." She took a bite of her sniggle leg. It was the last bite. She tossed the bone into the fire. "Are there any legs left?" she asked with her mouth still full of sniggle meat.

"It's very odd," Karak said, "I don't think I've ever read or heard an account of anybody actually using sniggles for food. Surely *somebody* before now tried it."

"I say we write a song about it and translate it into as many languages as possible," said Furk, the Norfan linguist. He savored another bite of his sniggle thigh.

Alice smiled at him and gave him a thumbs-up.

"What does…oh, is that an Earth signal of approval?" Furk asked. Alice nodded.

"Are you finally trying that talking-less thing?" Chase asked.

"Yes," Alice replied, "I'm worried it's almost out of juice." She tapped her voice box.

"Wait," Karak said as they swallowed a bite, "the battery in the voice box is almost dead? That shouldn't be possible. The initial battery should have lasted at least two years. Something else must be wrong with it. I wonder what sort of transporters these people use. They might have damaged it. Some transporters can damage electronics."

"What's wrong with her natural voice?" Johanne asked.

"It was destroyed," Chase answered. "There's this device that does that. An enemy of ours used it on her."

"I dunno if she's my enemy anymore, though!" Chloe said. "She helped me get off on a possession charge!"

"Okay," Johanne said, "I think I want to hear this whole story."

#

For the next several hours, everybody traded stories around the campfire and ate sniggle meat. It was actually a pleasant experience, and after what they'd been through so far in that ordeal, everybody welcomed it. Most of the stories revolved around cultural differences and their accounts of the Contest that they'd taken part in. The most interesting story for most of them was how they figured out the end of the Contest, how they gave the Zerrdon the food.

"We'd planned on giving them the food before we even entered the simulation," Johanne said, "not to brag, though. But we thought it was disgusting how they were going to use the food for bait. We figured there had to be something else to it."

"They were one of only three winning teams in the history of the Contest to figure it out that early," Karak added.

Then the stories returned to the Loovestone quest, and when the humans talked about the Jistari, the people who hadn't heard of them yet were very intrigued.

"These are people I'd never want to encounter!" Jonnifer, the Wistwill, said.

"Oh, nobody would, trust me," Coordinator Jeelork said. "And their weapons, they don't use phasers or lasers very much. They prefer more traditional weapons. They have the sharpest swords and daggers in the galaxy, they blow poison darts that cause you to live out your most desired fantasies in your head before you die, they have bomb ships that pursue an enemy ship forever, wire weapons to slice heads and limbs off as if their swords and knives weren't good enough...I could go on..."

"The Jistari are people you do *not* want to tangle with," Chase said.

"They are *not* groovy!" Farine added.

After another few hours of stories, some of the aliens were falling asleep. Some made little beds with bush branches and slices of sod. The campfire died down. Some wondered where the orb went and why it hadn't bothered them for so long.

"I'm tired," Chloe said. She yawned. She lay down and snuggled into Wyatt's lap. He massaged her shoulder.

Wyatt noticed something.

"Hey, has anybody else wondered why the sky hasn't changed at all?" he asked.

"What do you mean?" Chase said. He looked up at the sky.

Wyatt looked up. "The only thing that's moved is the moon.

And shouldn't the sun be rising by now? How long are the nights here?"

"Well," Chase said, "I've been to a lot of planets on my galactic travels. The timelines of days and nights vary."

Jamar yawned. "Right, it just depends on the planetary rotations. Some are slower than others. One day on Venus is about two hundred forty-three Earth days. Some planets are tidally locked with their star. There's a night side and a day side, and it never changes."

"So," Chloe said as she yawned, her eyes barely open, "you're saying that maybe…the entire time we're here…we might never see…sunlight?"

"That wouldn't be groovy," Farine said. She was sleepy, too. "I think it's time…for sleep dances." She snuggled with Furk, her team's linguist. They both looked sleepy. Chase looked at them. Alice looked at him, looking at them. It might have been her imagination, but she thought she detected a mild annoyance vibe from him. She touched his arm.

"Are you okay?" Alice asked him.

Chase looked at her. He narrowed his eyes at her. "I'm fine. Why?"

"It just…I dunno…it seemed like something was bothering you."

"Well, other than the fact that we're trapped on some planet and some aliens have nefarious, potentially lethal plans for us, I'm doing alright."

She stroked his beard. "So, when we get back, you gonna keep this?"

He smiled. "I might. Does it suit me?"

Alice frowned, thinking about it. "Hmmm. I still haven't decided. I might lean toward 'yes.'"

Wyatt looked down at his lap. Chloe was still except for her breathing. She was fast asleep. He smiled down at her. But then he frowned. "Well, how am *I* supposed to sleep now?"

"Somebody's gotta keep watch," Jamar said. "Hey, with as much D&D you play, you gotta know all about that. One character always keeps watch when they're camping."

"So you're saying that should be me?" Wyatt said as a loud pop sprang from the campfire. He yawned. "I'm so tired, though. I

still never got over that space lag from that trip from Earth to Loovian."

"Hey, who all is still awake?" Jamar asked.

"I am," Barchell said, "barely."

"We are," Chase said. But then he looked down in his lap. Alice had fallen asleep, too. "Scratch that. *I* am." He rolled his eyes. "Oh
great, I'm in the same situation, Wyatt."

Wyatt leaned over. "Maybe we can just…lean…slowly…
down to the ground…and they won't wake up."

Seconds later, they saw a bright light flicker. Wyatt, Chase,
Jamar, and Barchell looked up. A bright light several yards away and
about ten feet off the ground flashed.

"The hell is *that*?" Jamar said. The light flickered, flashed, and
crackled. Then, it shot a beam of intense light down to the ground.
Somebody fell down from the crackling light, down the beam, and to
the ground. That somebody looked very large.

The person grunted after hitting the ground. Then, the orb reappeared. "Sorry," it said, "I'm sure you all missed me. I was off looking for somebody. And look! I found him! A sixth human for our fun
games! Besides the five who are already here, he is the only surviving
member of the only other human team!"

"Oh no!" Chase said.

"Oh god!" Wyatt said.

"Aw, hell no!" Jamar exclaimed.

Chloe woke up. "What…? The orb is back? Who—?"

The man who came out of the light sat up. He looked through
the campfire at the humans…at Chase in particular.

Chloe gasped.

Slank glared at Chase. "*You!*" he yelled.

CHAPTER EIGHT: The Phobia Rooms

S LANK SLOWLY stood up. He looked around. "Where the hell am I? What planet is this?!" He looked at Chase again. "Are you and your pathetic bleeding heart brigade behind all this?!"

Then he noticed Chloe. He grinned at her. "Hello, gorgeous."

"Go to Hell!" Chloe yelled.

"You first," Slank said.

Slank jogged toward the humans.

"No, no, none of that!" the orb yelled. It shot a stunning phaser blast at him. He yelled in pain as he flew backward onto the ground. After a few seconds, he sat back up. He growled.

That woke Alice and a few of the other aliens. She looked at Slank. "Oh my god, what's he doing here?"

"Behave, Jeffrey!" the orb voice said. "You won't be killing your fellow humans—or anybody else here—that's *our job*! You won't take away *our* fun!"

"And who in the actual hell *are* you?!" Slank yelled up to the orb.

"Oh, you'll find out in due time!"

"I'll be *killing you* in due time, whoever you are!"

Chloe yelled up at the orb, "Hey! Will you let *me* kill *him*?!"

The orb laughed. "Oh, I like *her*! But, no, sweetie. We can't allow that, either."

Slank scoffed. "Like she even *could*!"

"Why did you bring him here?" Karak asked, looking at the orb.

"To make this event a little more fun," the orb replied. "Each team is going to have to work together to survive this and we thought, what if we add the serial killer to the human team? We thought they all loved each other just a little bit too much. So we thought it'd be very interesting to add a member to the human team that they all hate and who hates them. Fun, huh?"

"What kind of event *is* this?" Slank asked as he stood up again. "Why are all these aliens here…" He looked around the campsite, then with disdain, he added, "…*camping*?"

"We decided to host our own contest," the orb said. "Why should the Deelooveren have all the fun?"

Slank looked around. "Humans…Fargles…Norfan…those are all winning teams. Are these all Contest winners?"

"Correct," the orb answered. "Well, except for you, you loser. And the Deelooveren team. We just wanted them to have a taste of their own medicine."

Slank lumbered over to the campfire to be closer to the humans. "I'm not working with these idiots." He looked back at the orb. "You can kiss my ass."

"Yeah, we're not excited about this idea, either, you piece of shit," Wyatt said.

"Yeah, how about I almost kill ya again?" Chase said. "Or, better yet, *actually* kill you."

"Yeah, that was pretty clever, huh?" Slank said. He laughed. "You know what? As much as I hate you, I have to give you props. Not many people have bested me like that. You are in small company, Chase."

"Gee, thanks, let's do it again sometime," Chase replied.

"Oh, and keep the beard. I like it. Keep it the rest of your short life. Because, you know…"

"Yeah, yeah, yeah, you'll kill me soon, blah blah blah…you have a one-track mind, don't you?"

"Well, this time," Slank said while glancing at the orb, "I think these people will kill you. Either way, I'll enjoy watching you die."

The orb talked again, "As much as this banter is entertaining, I'm going to leave you alone again for a while. I suggest getting more sleep because you will certainly need it." The orb then ascended into the sky until it disappeared.

"Oh, like we'll *really* get sleep now," said Alice.

"Well, you're all pretty lucky, in that I would actually like to get some sleep," Slank said, "see you in the morning." He walked off out of the clearing and into the thicker brush. He found some soft bushes to lie in.

"Let's take turns doing watch," Chase said to Wyatt. "I'll go first."

"All right," Wyatt said. He and Chloe cuddled together on the bed of leaves they'd made and soon fell asleep.

#

Hours later, everybody awoke to an obnoxious, blaring, beeping sound. The orb was there, flashing a blindingly bright light with every obnoxious beep. "Time to wake up! Wake up, everybody! We're going to have lots of fun today!"

The first thing Alice noticed was that the night sky was still overhead. Perhaps it was indeed a world of permanent night. And she felt cold again, as the fire had died down to just some smoldering embers.

There were lots of mumblings and grumblings as everybody woke up.

Jamar smacked his lips and rubbed his eyes. "Now, that's just rude."

"More or less rude than dropping the floor from beneath us and letting us fall for about thirty feet?" Wyatt asked.

"Okay, less," Jamar admitted.

Alice noticed Karak awakening. "Ambassador Karak…"

"It's just Karak now," they said, their voice subtly quivering in sadness.

Alice sighed and frowned at them. "Well, um, so who are these people? Haven't you figured it out by now? It has to be one of the losers who are bitter about the loss. I mean, that's the prevailing theory. Don't you remember a loser planet that's like this?"

"My colleagues and I have conferred about this, and we can't recall any Contest losers who have a planet like this," they replied. "We don't yet know who they are."

In small swarms of sparkles, six small buildings appeared at the campsite. Wyatt and Alice noticed they were about the size of a typical backyard shed. Each one had a different color. One was red, one was orange, one was brown, one was emerald green, one was purple, and one was just gray. Wyatt assumed the colors matched the teams. Red was theirs. Green was for the Norfans. Brown was for the

Doo'chen. The orange was for the Fargles. The purple was for the Wistwills. And that left the plain gray one for the Deelooveren.

"You all might have noticed something new," the orb said. "These are what we call the 'Phobia Rooms.'"

"This doesn't sound pleasant," Chase said.

The orb continued. "Each and every one of you is required to enter the Phobia Room at least once—but as you'll soon see, nobody wants to enter it more than once—and inside, you will face your greatest phobia. And if you don't each go in, I will randomly select one member of your team for execution. Your goal is to last at least five minutes in the room. The team that logs the most minutes, collectively, in the room wins the challenge. Understood?"

"Bloody hell," mumbled Chloe.

Slank was just coming out of the nearby bushes. He looked at the orb. Then at the buildings. He laughed at the orb. "Good thing I don't have any phobias!"

"*Everybody* has a phobia, Jeffrey!" the orb replied.

"That's not my name anymore!" Slank yelled.

"Oh, oh, we're so sorry, Jeffrey. We'll get it right next time, Jeffrey."

A furious look tightened on his face. "Oh. You think you're funny! Fine. Call me whatever the hell you like! It doesn't matter!"

The orb giggled. "Okay, people. Now it's time to decide. Who goes first? When you decide that, head for your team's Phobia Room. We will observe all the fun. Ta ta!" The orb ascended and vanished.

"Well, *I'm* not going in there!" Woo'cha yelled.

"One of us is already dead, Woo'cha!" Flee'cheer replied. "What's wrong with you? You were not like this during our Contest win!"

They continued arguing as the humans all got together in a huddle.

"So, who wants to go first?" Wyatt whispered.

"Not me," Chloe mumbled.

"Does it matter?" Chase said. "We all get a turn, don't we?"

"Rock, paper, scissors?" Jamar suggested.

"I'll go first," Alice said.

"Wow, Alice," Wyatt said, "you're brave."

Alice shrugged. "What does it matter? Like Jacob said, we all get a turn. Let's just do this and get it over with."

"But wait," Wyatt said, "realize that's some sort of holo-simulation room…probably. Whatever's in there might not be real. Keep that in mind. Maybe we can beat it if we convince ourselves it isn't real. I mean, how can it be real if there's going to be a different phobia in there every time one of us enters?"

"Good point," Jamar said, "like, meditate or something. Get it in your mind that it's not really there…whatever nightmare awaits us."

Heavy footsteps on the ground approached them. "So, what's the plan?" They all looked to see Slank standing right there by them. They all reacted by scrambling a few feet away.

"Oh, come on!" Slank said. "Do you think I want to be stunned again? I'm not gonna kill any of you. Look, like it or not, I'm a member of your team, so I should be in the team huddles. Don't you think?"

"No," Wyatt said. "Serial killers aren't welcome in our huddles!"

"Go to hell, Slank," Chase said.

"Eat shit and die, you sodding cunt," Chloe added.

Slank opened his eyes wider. "Wow. Do you kiss your mother with that filthy mouth, Chloe?"

"He has a point," Alice said. They all looked at her. "Why do you think he's here? I mean, besides as another means of torturing us? We're meant to work together with him, and he with us, despite how much we will all mutually hate it. I have a feeling that not working together with him will end up being worse, somehow, than doing it."

Wyatt sighed. "As much as I hate to admit it…I think Alice is right."

"She is," Slank said, "and it doesn't take a genius IQ, which I have, by the way, to figure that out."

"Besides, look at him," Alice continued. "He's still 'roided out with the super serum. It's almost always coursing through his veins. That could be advantageous. We each only got one microdose, and we already used it."

"Another good point, Blondie," Slank said. He turned to Wyatt. "And here I thought you were supposed to be the smartest one here, Missouri."

"I never claimed to be the smartest, alright, but I know what I'm good at, and that's winning," Wyatt replied. "And we're going to win this. And if we have to work with the likes of you to do it, then so be it. This means we have a sixth person, so potentially more minutes."

"Fine," Slank said. "Now, I think I heard the blonde say she was going first?"

"My name is Alice," she said. "And if we're going to work together, call us by our names."

"Okay, fine, *Alice*," Slank replied, saying her name with a level of disdain in his voice.

Alice stood up. She brushed some dirt off of her rear and legs. "Time to do this."

"Good luck," Jamar said.

Alice approached the door of their Phobia Room. She noticed that the room next to theirs was the Norfan. Farine was about to enter.

"I see you're going first, too, my cutie," Farine said. Her hips swayed back and forth slightly.

"I just wanted to get it over with," Alice said as shrugged her left shoulder toward her door.

"Good luck in there," said Farrstead, who was about to enter the Deelooveren's room.

"Just remember that whatever is in there, it might not be real," Alice said. Then she gestured for the two of them to come closer to her. "Come on, a hug first. It'll help."

They came in for a three-person hug. It was warm, and it helped.

After that, they all turned to their doors. The butterflies in her stomach went crazy. She trembled a little. "Whatever it is, Alice, it's not real," she whispered to herself. She approached the door, and it slid open. It was dark inside. She couldn't see what was in there. She nervously swallowed and hurried inside. The door shut behind her.

At first, it was pitch black. She couldn't see anything. "Hello?" Her voice didn't echo. She turned around and around. It was still totally dark.

Suddenly, she thought she felt something scurry over her left boot. She heard it, too.

Oh god, oh god, oh god, oh god, oh god…

She trembled again. She was well aware of what her worst phobia was. But how did these aliens know unless they could read her mind? She didn't recall ever writing it down anywhere. Only her family knew.

Then, a disturbing thought occurred to her.

What if they messed with my fam—

A single, dim light on the ceiling flickered on. Her heart stopped. Her lungs almost collapsed. Every muscle fiber in her body tightened.

Spiders were everywhere. They crawled. They hung in webs. They scrambled around. They were of various sizes and species.

"Not real," she grunted. "Not…real…not…real…"

She looked down. A line of them just crawled over her feet. She whimpered.

"It's not real," she squeaked. A fleeting thought occurred to her: it was impressive that her voice box could even do that in a squeal.

One of them, a large tarantula, dropped on her shoulder. Her heart stopped again. She gasped for breath. Her whole body convulsed. She couldn't breathe. Tears sprung from her eyes. She brushed the spider off her body. Another dropped on her other shoulder. She quickly brushed that off. She wheezed air into her lungs as she tried to breathe.

She shut her eyes tight, as tightly as she could shut them. "It's…not…real…" she said between wheezes. But she could hear them scurrying about. She could feel them. Alice could even smell them. She'd never even thought about spiders having any particular odor. The big ones smelled like vinegar, others like fresh shrimp. Alice stutter-sobbed. More crawled over her feet. She felt another one land on her left shoulder.

Then she felt one plop onto her hair. Alice couldn't take it anymore. She screamed as she smacked it off her head, testing the limits of her voice box's volume. She turned around and headed back for where the door should be. It was beyond the scope of the light. But she ran into it. She pounded on it with both fists. "You've made your point! Let me out! I don't care about the time! Please! You want to hear me beg! I'll beg! You can have that satisfaction! Please, please, please let me out! PLEASE! I beg you, PLEASE! PLEASE! Oh god! Just kill me instead!" She felt spiders crawl down her back. She screamed and screamed and pounded on the door some more. Then she finally had the presence of mind to actually feel for a door handle. She found one. With all her might, she yanked on it. It actually opened the door!

Alice stumbled out of the room into that cool night air. She collapsed to the cold, hard ground. Her stomach heaved and heaved, and she couldn't hold it in any longer. She violently vomited.

"Holy Christ," Jamar mumbled when he witnessed Alice come out of the room. "The hell did she see in there?!"

"Oh my god," Jacob whispered. He ran to her, terrified that she was seriously hurt, mentally or physically, or worse.

Wyatt gulped. "So…it doesn't look very fun, then."

A few tears sprung from Chloe's eyes. She wondered what was in store for herself. Fear gripped her entire body as she tensed up.

Jacob almost slid to the ground to get to Alice quicker, like a baseball player sliding into a base. "Alice, Alice! Are you okay?"

She wheezed and wheezed as she tried to breathe normally again. "Water…need…water…"

"Water!" Jacob yelled to the other humans.

Slank detached a little container of water that was attached to his belt. He tossed it to Chase. He caught it. He was shocked. Chase sat there for a second, holding the water, utterly dumbfounded that Slank had actually helped.

"Well, what are you waiting for?!" Slank said. "Give it to her!"

Alice tried to reach for the water. "Gimme…gimme…water!"

Chase handed her the container. She quickly unscrewed the lid, put it to her lips, lifted her head back, and gulped it all down.

Chase looked back at Slank. "Why did you do that?"

"New stupid rules, remember? Gotta work together. Right?" He shrugged. "Look, don't overthink it! Alright? I figure maybe if I help you all enough, you'll reciprocate. If I like…I need help."

Chloe looked up at Slank with pure hatred in her eyes. "Not a chance in Hell of that."

Slank pointed toward Alice. "Looks like Hell is already here."

"So…who's next?" Wyatt said. Nobody answered. "Come on now…don't everybody volunteer at once!"

Farrstead suddenly burst out of their room. They rolled to the ground. "Oh, thank Molltock!" they yelled. They wheezed. "Oh, that was horrible!" Karak and Jeelork ran over to Farrstead to help.

Jacob then gently put his hands on Alice's shoulders. "What did you see, babe? Do you want to talk about it? What can I do for you?"

"Don't…wanna…talk about it…" Alice's breathing finally returned to normal.

"Okay," Jacob said. He hugged her. She wrapped her arms tightly around him.

Farine collapsed out of her room. She was screaming and crying. She just fell flat on the ground and writhed around, continuing to cry. Farine frantically swatted invisible things off of her limbs.

"Farine!" Chase said. "Are you—" But two of her teammates scrambled over to her to help her. Chase wanted to hug her, too.

Jamar stood up. "I'll go next." He slowly walked past Chase and Alice and stood in front of its door. He sighed. "Let's get this over with."

"You sure, man?" Chase said.

"Yes. I just wanna get it over with." He inched closer to the door. It slid open. He took in a deep breath. Then he went in. The door closed.

It was pitch black inside. Jamar couldn't see anything. "Well, I was scared of the dark when I was a kid," he mumbled to himself. But then, a dim light flickered on. What he saw chilled his very soul. The room was filled with holes. Hole clusters covered the floor, walls, and ceiling. They weren't holes like something had poked holes in the structure. They were patterns of holes, like those that might be useful to insects for nests or holes that resembled zoomed-in images on insect eyes.

"Oh no, oh hell no," Jamar whispered as he looked around. "These aliens know I have trypophobia. How the hell did they know that?" Then, the holes started moving like they were alive. They made little moist, squishy noises as they did so. He could feel the holes he stood on, shifting and slurping around.

"Ah!" He jumped around. His heart thundered in his chest. His breathing became labored. "Oh…you…you assholes!" He tried shutting his eyes. But then he could still hear them moving. He could hear slurping and sucking noises. "Oh god, no!" he yelled. He shivered. Breathing became more difficult. But then he remembered what Wyatt and Alice had said. *It's not real*! He bent over, still trying to keep his eyes shut. "Not real, not real, not real…"

The ceiling lowered down to where it touched the top of Jamar's head. He could feel the holes on his short-haired scalp! He yelped and squirmed and fell to his knees. But then he could feel the holes all over his feet, shins, and knees. And he could smell them. They smelled like old, moldy dirt, and, at times, they also smelled like bug spray.

He looked upward and yelled, "Awww, I hate you guys!" He wheezed for breath. He shut his eyes tighter. He clenched his fists tightly. Jamar sweat profusely. "No! It's not real! I know it's not real! You hear me?! I can do this all day. You just watch me."

He thought of Min. He thought of her pretty face and how lovingly she'd look at him. Nobody had ever looked at him like that before. The noises got louder, like they did not like being ignored. Soon, it became a cacophony. He held his hands over his ears. He screamed.

"Fight it, Jammy," Min said in his head. "You can do it! You're stronger than you think!"

"I am!" Jamar yelled out loud.

But then he heard Min's real voice outside his head. "Jamar, help!"

He opened his eyes. "Min!" But she wasn't there. Instead, his eyes were mistreated to a more intense, more horrifying look at the holes. They were right up in his face. He could see tiny insects and larvae in them.

Jamar screamed. He slammed his eyes shut again. He couldn't take it anymore. He wasn't sure if he'd been in there long enough. But he no longer cared. "Let me out! Let me out!" Jamar got up and ran for the door. But all he saw were the holes. He turned around. Only holes. Which way was the door?! "Where the hell is the door?!" He looked up. "Please show me the door! Please!"

Some holes in the wall in front of him vanished, revealing a flat door handle. He grabbed at it. He slammed the door open and scrambled to get out. Once out, he fell to his knees onto the cold ground. He gasped and wheezed for air. He closed his eyes. But when he did so, all he could see in his mind's eye were those holes. "Oh god, oh god," he said between gasps for breath.

"Jamar!"

"Jamar!"

He heard both Chase and Alice call his name. They ran to him. They both embraced him. He cried as he hugged them back. He was so glad to smell Alice's hair versus the horrible scent inside the room.

"Oh, you guys, it was horrible, horrible."

"You're out now, man, it's okay now, you're out," Chase said.

"We got you, we got you," Alice said. She grabbed his hand. "You're with us now, not what was in there. We got you." He gripped her hand tightly in return.

Slowly, Jamar's breathing returned to normal. Wyatt and Chloe also entered the embrace. "We all got you, man."

Large, deep footsteps approached. "You alright?" It was Slank.

Jamar looked up at Slank. "*Wh…wh…what*? What do *you* care?!"

Slank frowned. He shrugged. "Just…curious. I *don't* care!" He walked away.

Chloe stood up. She clenched her fists tightly. "I'm ready. I am terrified. But I am ready."

"Are you sure?" Wyatt said. He grabbed her hand.

"Ready as I ever will be," Chloe mumbled. She let go of his hand. She walked up to the door. It slid open for her. She went inside.

It was pure dark inside. She couldn't see anything. But then a tiny window appeared. It was slightly rounded as if built into a curved structure. A light shined through the window. Then she heard sobbing. Suddenly, it felt like something was pressing against her back. No. Actually, it seemed like she was lying down on something and no longer standing.

"What?" The window was too close to her face. She tried to back away from it. No. She couldn't.

"No…*no, no-no-no-no-no!*" she whispered when she realized she was lying in something…a box…a *coffin*?! Was she in a *coffin*?!

What was the sobbing she heard? Then she saw part of her mother's face through the window. It was her. "Bloody leukemia took my baby. It wasted her away!" Her mother sobbed. "I begged her to hold on!" She cried and cried.

"Mum!" Chloe yelled. Her heart pounded. "I'm here! I'm alive! Mum!" Chloe banged on the lid of the coffin. She desperately banged some more. "Mummy!"

But she tried to calm down. "It's not real, like Wyatt and Alice said. It's not real. It's not real. This is like a holosuite. It's a simulation." She swallowed. She shook her hands a little, trying to loosen herself up. "I can do this. Just lie here for five minutes. Easy peasy. Just lie in the fake coffin. You can do this, Chloe."

But she had much difficulty calming down. Enclosed spaces terrified her more than anything else. The tighter the space, the more terrified she became. When she first got sick, she had an MRI done. She had a full-blown panic attack while in there. They couldn't finish the scan.

Then, the coffin banged around. She was moving. "Goodbye, love," her mother sobbed. It felt like she was being lowered. She could see through the tiny window that walls of brown and black dirt rose around her.

"Oh bloody hell no…bloody hell no…" Chloe's heart pounded again. All her muscles tightened. "No, please, no." She swallowed hard. It got darker. And darker. And then she heard clumps of dirt hitting the coffin. "No, no, no, no, no," she whimpered.

THUMP!

A big clump of dirt hit the window. Then, she was in total darkness. She kept hearing and feeling clumps of dirt thump onto the coffin. Her whole body shook.

"It's not real…it's not real…" But she couldn't convince herself that it wasn't. Chloe could feel it getting warmer. She could smell the musty dirt. She could smell the sharp, varnished wood of the coffin. It became harder to breathe.

"Enough! Enough!" Chloe screamed. She banged on the coffin. "Oh god please stop…please stop…no please no…"

The thumping of the dirt got quieter and quieter, indicating she was buried under more and more dirt.

Chloe couldn't suppress it anymore. She trembled, and then

she screamed. She screamed louder than she'd ever screamed before. Then she screamed again. She kicked and punched the lid of the coffin. "Noooo! Nooo! Let me out! LET ME OUT! PLEASE, PLEASE, PLEASE LET ME OUT! I CAN'T TAKE IT ANYMORE! I can't BREATHE!" She gasped for breath. She was out of air. She was starting to suffocate. "I…can't…breathe…please…please…PLEASE!" Chloe sobbed as rivers of tears flowed from her eyes. She gritted her teeth. She gave that coffin lid the most powerful kick she could muster.

The door to the room opened. Chloe flew out of it. She tripped over her own feet, trying to get as far away from that box as possible. She rolled onto the ground, screaming and crying. Wyatt sprinted over to her.

A few seconds after that, another member of Farine's team stumbled out of their room and onto the ground, screaming, too. Then, Karak tripped and fell out of the Deelooveren's room. They trembled and sobbed while in the fetal position. Nobody who knew Karak before that day had ever seen them like that. They were used to seeing them stand up so straight, so strident in how Karak usually held themself.

"Chloe, my god!" Wyatt exclaimed. He tried to hug her.

"No, NO, NO!" She actually punched his arms away with her own, then punched him away from her, right into his eye. He flew backward and fell to the ground.

"Jesus, Mary, and Joseph!" Jamar yelled.

"Leave me alone, LEAVE ME ALONE!" Chloe screamed. She continued to lie on her back, her entire chest heaving up and down with sobs and deep gasps for breath.

"Ow, ow," Wyatt said as he stood back up, holding his eye, "that's gonna leave a mark."

Chase grabbed him, pulling him by the collar. Wyatt opened his eye, the one that wasn't swelling up. Sheer terror was in Chase's wide eyes.

"Dude, what's in that thing?! What's in it?! What do you think's in it?!" He pointed at Chloe. "That was the worst one yet! I'm terrified of what's in it! What's in it, man?!"

"How the hell should I know?!"

"Did you see Karak?! Look at Karak!" Chase pointed at them. "LOOK!"

Wyatt grabbed both sides of Chase's face with his hands. "Calm down, man! Calm down! You're acting like you've already been in there! Pull yourself together, Chase!"

Chase grabbed Wyatt's wrists. "I don't wanna go in there, man. I really, really don't."

"Chase, I've never seen you like this!" Wyatt noticed that Chase's skin was totally pale. It had lost all color. "Breathe, man, just breathe. *Breathe.*"

Alice wrapped her arms around Chase from behind. She hugged him tightly. "Wyatt's, right, baby, breathe. Just take a moment and breathe. I saw spiders. It was awful, but I got through it."

Suddenly, they heard the loudest scream any of them had heard yet, even louder than Chloe's. One of the Fargles burst out of their room, screaming bloody murder. He actually ran right out of the campsite. His teammates pursued him.

When Chase saw that, it made him panic even more. "Oh my god," he whispered.

"Jacob, turn around!" Alice ordered. "Turn around! Look into my eyes!" Jacob hesitated. "JACOB!"

She actually forced him to turn around and face her. "Look into my eyes! LOOK AT THEM!" Jacob did as he was told. She put her hands to his face. "Look at me. Just at me. Nothing else. Just my eyes. And breathe. Just look at me and breathe." She briefly glanced at Wyatt. "You go next!" She looked back at Jacob. "Just breathe for me, baby. Come on."

Jacob calmed down. It was working. "Alice, I'm scared," he said.

"Listen to me, Jacob, this is what they want," Alice said as calmly as she could. "They want to terrify the ones not in there yet from having to look at what it's doing to the others. They want to torture and kill us, Jacob. They want one of us to refuse to go in there, at least one of us. Do you understand?"

"I, uh…"

"Tell me you understand! Do you understand what I'm saying?"

Jacob swallowed. He breathed. He swallowed again. "Yes. I understand." A tear sprung from one of his eyes. "I, I get it. You're right. You're right." He gently put his hands on hers. He wrapped his hands around Alice's soft, delicate hands. Chase actually smiled as his breathing returned to normal. "You…are my rock," he whispered.

"And you…*rock*!" She smiled at him. He smiled back. She pulled his face to hers, and she passionately kissed him.

Slank approached them. "How touching," he said. They stopped kissing. She looked at him with hatred in her eyes. "Go to Hell, Slank."

"Are you a little bitch, Chase?" Slank asked.

Chase clenched his jaw. He looked furious. "No."

"Then stop acting like one!" Slank said. "There. That's the best I can do for a pep talk! Take it or leave it! Just…tryin' to be useful!" With a wave of his hand, he walked off.

Wyatt entered the room. The door shut behind him. There was a very dim light on the ceiling. He could barely see where the walls were.

"Okay, do your worst, Phobia Room," Wyatt said. He looked around in fearful wonder. Then, it started filling with water.

Wyatt sighed as it got ankle-deep. "Great. Just great. My greatest phobia is drowning. So, of course, it's water. Well-played, assholes, well-played."

The water reached his shins. He looked up. "I can hold my breath, you know. I once did a breath-holding contest. I lasted over a minute." The water reached his knees. He shook his head. His heart rate increased slightly. "Hey, this is actually great. I was feeling sweaty. I was dirty after what I did to avoid the sniggles. I had wanted a bath. So, thanks for this. I'm going to enjoy getting clean! You hear me?"

The water reached his hips. "I won't scream," Wyatt said. "Nope. Not gonna scream." He held his hands on his hips as he watched the water get higher. "I guess you don't know me. I almost always win. I've been counting. It's been about three minutes. I estimate that…the water will reach higher than I can breathe in…hmm… yeah, about another two minutes. Give or take. Give, I hope." Then he had an idea. "Oh, hey, I'm thirsty. I'd wanted some water." He cupped some in his hand and drank it. He had to immediately spit it out. It tasted dirty and horribly salty. "Oh, okay. Clever. So drinking a bunch of it to give me a little more time is out of the question, I see."

Soon, the water was halfway up his chest. "Let's see," he mumbled, "how long has it been? Four minutes?" His heart rate increased more. The water reached his neck. His heart now pounded. "Gee… phobias…are interesting…I know…intellectually…I'm not really gonna drown, but…" Wyatt gulped. His breathing speed increased. He lifted his chin up. Wyatt started to float. He put his head up to the ceiling. "Don't panic, Wyatt…don't panic…" His voice echoed off the ceiling and the surface of the water. Despite putting almost all of his mental energy into suppressing panicking, he panicked. Soon, the room was almost filled. Only his nose was above the water, and it was right against the ceiling. He entered full-on panic mode when water entered his nostrils.

That's when he began banging on the ceiling. He swam over and banged on the wall. He tilted his chin up as much as possible to get his mouth out of the water. "Okay, you win, let me out! I'm done! Let me—" But just then, the water reached the top. Wyatt was completely submerged. He couldn't breathe. He swam toward the door. He banged on it. It wouldn't open! He pounded and kicked and pounded on it, each bang muted by the water. He tried yelling, "Let me out, please!"

Wyatt meditated a few seconds, then kicked that door harder than he'd ever kicked anything before. It opened. Then he and hundreds of gallons of water flooded out of the room and onto the ground. He gasped for breath. He hyperventilated. Chloe splashed through the water to get to her boyfriend.

"Darling, are you okay?!" Chloe knelt to him.

Wyatt coughed and spurted some water out of his mouth. He gasped for more breath. "No…not really. Are *you*?"

"Ohhhh," Chloe said as she noticed his swollen eye. "I'm sorry for punching you, love! I was not in a good mental state! But I'm okay *now*!"

"No, Chloe, it's okay! I…understand!" Wyatt's breathing was still somewhat labored.

"Good job, Missouri," Slank said, who was nearby, "no screaming." Just then, perfectly timed, somebody, somewhere, screamed. A female somebody.

"Go to Hell," Wyatt mumbled. He struggled to get up.

"Lemme help you, darling," Chloe said. She helped him stand up. They slipped a little in the mud, but they got it done.

Slank scoffed. "Can you people be a little more original? Hey, talk to your girlfriend Chloe here. She's got some foul-mouthed British zingers. Get a few pointers from her." Slank lumbered off.

Alice massaged Chase's shoulders. "It's your turn. You can do this, hon."

"You're right. I can."

"You can," Jamar said. "I just saw some holes. Chloe said she was even buried alive. But we got through it, man. You'll be alright."

Alice patted Chase's back as he walked toward the door. "Yeah, babe, listen to Jamar." Chase took in a deep breath, let it out through his mouth, and hopped up and down a little to loosen himself up. Then he walked close enough to trigger the door to open. He stepped inside.

Like with everybody else, it was pitch black. He couldn't see anything. But unlike the others, that didn't change.

"Hello?" Chase said. There was no echo at all to his voice. It barely created any sound wave at all. "Hello?" he said again. It felt eerie and disturbing how his words just absorbed into the nothingness ahead of him. He'd never felt or heard anything like it before. Chase felt around. He couldn't feel anything. He couldn't see anything, hear anything, or smell anything. He tried to think of what phobias he might have, trying to imagine what sort of hellish jump scare was ahead. Did he even have a phobia? He was afraid of stinging insects. Would that be it? He soon realized that they wouldn't be it, that it was something much worse.

"I am in…nothingness," Chase whispered. He realized he couldn't even feel the floor anymore. He was just floating out in pure nothingness. Chase thought of sensory deprivation chambers, and maybe this was like that. But it didn't feel good. The pure nothing ahead, above, behind, and below started to terrify him. A voice in the back of his head wondered if he'd be stuck in this void forever.

Alice saw spiders. Chloe was buried alive. Jamar saw the holes. Chase actually longed to see those things…or see *anything*, no matter how disturbing they were. Those were actually preferable to what was going on now. As the minutes of nothingness went on, it gnawed at his mind and spirit. He felt deep sadness, despair, and loneliness. It actually felt like he was the only soul or the only *thing* in the universe.

Outside the room, Alice stared at the door in nervous anticipation. She chewed on her fingernails.

"He's dead!" somebody yelled. Alice, Wyatt, Jamar, and Chloe looked around. They located where the yell had come from. It was the Wistwill's room. Johanne was tending to one of her teammates, who lay flat on the ground. "He had a heart attack!"

Jamar sprang into action. He ran over to them. "I know CPR!"

Jamar knelt down to the male Wistwill. He put his hand over the man's mouth and nose. He didn't detect any breathing. But not knowing this alien species' anatomy, he didn't know where to feel for a pulse. "Where do you feel for a pulse for your species?"

"Here," Johanne pointed to a point in the middle of his neck, "but we already checked this!"

Jamar felt the man's chest. "Where is the heart? Do you breathe through your mouths?"

"Yes, we do, and our hearts are here!" Johanne pointed to his chest, but on the other side, where a human's heart would be.

Jamar started CPR on the man the best he could, but with the unfamiliar anatomy, he doubted he could help. But he tried.

Sadly, Jamar failed in reviving Danfer. "I'm sorry…he's gone…I tried," Jamar whispered after he gave up. He could not even get the slightest response. Danfer, their musician, was dead. Jamar wiped tears from his eyes.

Johanna grabbed Jamar's hand with her thin, bony, wrinkled hand. "Thank you! Thank you for trying! We appreciate it!"

"I wonder what he saw," Jamar whispered.

Johanne looked down. "The spiked roots of the latava tree, one of the most terrifying things on our planet. He was yelling about it when he burst out of the door. Then he collapsed. If you venture too near a latava tree, its spiked roots slither out of the ground and grab you. It injects you with a neurotoxin, and then, when you can no longer move, more roots come out to envelop you, and then it releases acids that slowly consume you while you're still alive."

"Oh my god," whispered Jamar.

"The only reason we haven't eradicated that damn tree from our planet is that people like to eat those roots," Markonis, their scientist, said as he moved closer to Jamar in his hover chair. "It's a delicacy. You have to wear a special suit to collect them." He slowly shook his head. He sighed. "Misguided greed and gluttony."

Jamar stood back up. "I'm so sorry for your loss. And for your evil tree."

"Jacob!" Alice yelled.

Jamar left the Wistwills and ran over to his team. He saw Chase slowly stumbling out of the room. He was almost as pale as the Wistwills. Alice tended to him. When Jamar got closer, he noticed Chase had a completely blank expression on his face. He just looked straight ahead at nothing.

"Jacob! What did you see?" Alice asked. She tried to get his attention, tried to get him to look at her, but he wouldn't stop staring straight ahead.

"Nothing," he whispered.

"Nothing?" Chloe asked. "Well, that doesn't sound…" But then a realization hit her. She studied Chase's expression again.

"What do you mean?" Alice said. She grabbed his face and forced him to look at her. "What do you mean 'nothing?' Please, please talk to me. I've never seen you like this. I'm worried."

"Total…nothingness," Chase replied. Alice had forced him to look at her, and even though his eyes pointed toward her face, it still didn't seem like he was actually looking at her. His eyes were cold and almost dead-looking.

"Aw man," Jamar said, "sounds like he literally stared into the cold abyss of complete nothingness. I mean, you hear it in poetry and such, but to *literally* do that, that's gotta mess you up."

All the humans—except for Slank—converged on Chase to offer him comfort. Alice hugged him tightly. He didn't hug back. He continued to stare ahead, almost unblinking.

Slank was nearby, though. He knelt down so he could look into Chase's eyes. He waved his hand a little in Chase's field of view. His expression stayed the same. "Are you in there, man?"

"This is gonna take time," Wyatt whispered. They all started a group hug around him and Alice.

"Chase, we're here for ya, man," Jamar said.

"We love you, Chase," Chloe added.

Slank stepped back a little. This was frightening. Chloe looked up from the hug at Slank. At first, it was a hateful look that would have shot daggers at him if it was possible, but then she saw something in Slank's expression, in his eyes, that she had never seen in him before.

Fear.

Slank was next and last. Chloe had never in a million years expected to see somebody like Slank terrified. But he sure seemed like he was.

"Your turn, Slank," Chloe said, her statement dripping with hate.

"Yeah," Slank said, "give me a minute."

"You're afraid, aren't you?" A slight smile brought one corner of her mouth up.

"I'm not afraid of *anything*."

"Then go. See what's in there. *Do it*."

Then they all turned to look at Slank. They all saw what Chloe had observed: Slank being fearful.

"Get your ass in there, Slank," Jamar said. "What's the hold-up?"

Slank suddenly and forcefully changed his demeanor. He stood up straighter. He jutted his jaw out and tightened his fists. "I'm goin' in." He stomped past them and to the door of the room. It slid open, he entered, and the door slid closed.

Like with the others, at first, it was pitch black in there. Slank put his hands on his hips and scoffed. "Come on! Let's get this over with!"

A moment later, a light from above flickered on. The very last thing Slank ever wanted or expected to see appeared: a middle-aged woman with short, curly brown but graying hair. Her wide, lipsticked mouth curled up into a sinister smile.

"No," Slank whispered. Chills danced up his spine.

"Hello, Jeffrey," the woman said.

Slank looked upward. "You sons-a-bitches!"

The woman groaned. "Is that any way to greet your mom-my?!"

"You're not my mommy!" Slank yelled at her.

"Well, with your filthy mouth and disrespect, sounds like you need a punishment!" The woman wagged her finger at him. "You were always such a naughty boy!"

"Shut up!"

"Okay, it sounds like you need another week under our bed to think about how bad you've been!"

"GET AWAY FROM ME!" Slank exclaimed as he backed

away from her.

Meanwhile, back outside in the cold, dark campsite, Chase finally started to snap out of it. He slowly raised his arms up and wrapped them around Alice. Chase closed his eyes. He sobbed. Everybody around him hugged him tighter. They heard somebody screaming in the background. But it didn't phase them.

"Alice, I thought I'd never see you again, or any of you," Chase sobbed. "Or…anybody. I can't…I can't find the words to describe the despair and loneliness that it smothered me with…you can't imagine it…"

Alice kissed the top of his head and hugged him tighter. "Oh, Jacob," she whispered, "it sounds so awful. I'm here for you. Just let it all out, okay?"

"I fear what's next," Wyatt mumbled to Jamar. "I mean, that was a nightmare. How they gonna top it? People are actually dying."

"Are we gonna all survive this?" Jamar looked at Wyatt with sad and worried eyes.

Wyatt sighed. He let out a deep breath. "I want to say that we will. But this…what they're putting us through…we are powerless to stop it."

"What about the first trial? We are not powerless. Not as long as these aliens want something from us."

"Good point. But unfortunately what they want from us is entertainment. And a means to revenge."

"It's still something," Jamar said.

"We've got to somehow find out more on these aliens. We may not have any more super juice. But if we can't get it, our power can be information. Like who these aliens are and what their motivations are. This is gonna sound cliche, but I think it's literally true here, knowledge is power."

"They're bitter about losing the contest."

"I don't think that's it. Or…I don't think it's that simple. But the Contest is definitely something to do with it."

"Oh god, no! Eeler is dead!" they heard one of the Fargles scream.

They looked in their direction. A female Fargle—Eeler, presumably—hung from a tree branch. She'd hung herself with a vine. The body slowly swung to and fro, the tree branch creaking as it did so.

"Jesus," Jamar whispered.

"My god," Wyatt mumbled.

"That leaves us and the Deelooveren as the only two completely intact teams left," Jamar said.

"Yeah, all five of us are still left," Wyatt replied. "Or…all *six* of us." Then, they both looked at the room.

"How long has he been in there?" Jamar asked.

"Ummm…I dunno. Three, four minutes?" A slight breeze moved through the campsite. Wyatt shivered and rubbed his arms. "I hate this planet."

"Oh no!" Chase said. "Barchell. I need to go to Barchell!" He ambled away from Alice. He was still very pale and, despite the chill, sweaty.

"I'll go with you," Alice said. They walked over to the Fargles. They passed Karak, who was just then finally trying to stand up from their ordeal.

"You okay?" Alice asked them.

"No, Miss Mackenzie, I'm not," Karak replied. They rubbed their eyes with their fingers. Chloe appeared, She held her hand out. Karak took it, and Chloe helped them up. Alice hugged Karak and then continued on with Chase.

"What did you see?" Chloe asked.

Karak looked down. They let out a tortured sigh. "On my planet…there's a…a kind of stinging insect. They…they swarm…sometimes." Karak put up their hands and shook their head. "No, no, I don't want to talk about it any further." Karak looked at Chloe. "What did you see, Miss Thompson?"

"Buried alive," Chloe said. She shivered.

"Did you die of the leukemia in the sim?"

"What?" Chloe looked confused and suspicious at Karak. "How did you know about that?"

"Why are you surprised? We vetted the five of you before the Contest, remember? We knew almost everything about you. Your bravery and survivability that we chose in you had to do with more than your martial arts and fighting ability."

"Well, if you know so much about us, then what the bloody hell do you know about these people?!" Chloe pointed at the spot the orb usually hung out in. "You must have some idea as to who they are by now."

"Like I already said, we can't think of any Contest losers who are on a planet like this!"

Wyatt and Jamar appeared. Wyatt said, "Hmmm. What about Contest *winners*?"

"Winners?" Jamar said. "What?"

"Well, it has something to do with the Contest. So, if they aren't *losers*, then is it possible that they're bitter…*winners*?"

"Why would a *winner* be bitter?" Jamar asked.

"What if the solution didn't work?" Wyatt asked. "Or…made things worse? Has that ever happened, Karak, with any winning teams?"

Karak blinked a few times. A look of surprised realization came upon their face. "It's rare. But…it unfortunately has happened. We've had solutions not work. And, yes, only twice, you could say that the solution made things worse. But it's been over a century since the last time that happened. It was before my time running the Contest. I learned about it in a history class like a lot of other Deelooveren students."

"Karak," said Wyatt, "there's a saying on my planet, 'revenge is a dish best-served cold.' Do you recall what sort of planet those winners had?"

"I remember," Coordinator Jeelork said. They were suddenly standing nearby. "It bothered me so much when I learned about it. It was unlikely that I would ever forget it. It was the Hellkorians. From the planet Hellkor. A, uh, planet tidally locked to their star. Does this sound familiar?"

"Hellkorians!" Karak exclaimed. "Yes, I remember now! They had a fertility problem. Their annual birth rate had plummeted to only a few hundred per year. And…I just remember learning that our solution made things worse."

"I remember," said Jeelork. "The solution we gave them was two-pronged, but both went very, very wrong. A disease pandemic had spread across their globe; the virus spread to every person, and even though the females would survive the infection, almost none of their fetuses would. Our solution was to release a kind of radiation to kill the virus. It's something that we'd done before with perfect results. And it did reduce the virus somewhat. But the problem was, it made most of the males infertile, too. Our other solution was for them to find the females that were still fertile and treat them like royalty, give them their every need, keep them in perfect health. And that… that went horribly wrong, too."

"Let me guess," Wyatt said, "those females became prisoners, didn't they?"

Jeelork sighed. "They twisted our advice. They imprisoned all the fertile women they could find and put them in breeding camps. We abhorred what they did. We condemned it. And then, well, the story goes, Deelooveren troops went down to the planet to put a stop to the breeding camps. Things got…out of hand. It all ended *very* badly. Things got violent, and most of those women ended up dead."

"My god," Jamar said.

"But here's the thing, though," said Jeelork, "the Hellkorians should have been extinct by now. Their population was only about one-and-a-half-billion to begin with, as most of their population was limited to the narrow band around the planet between the permanent night and permanent day. The permanent day side is way too hot, several hundred degrees. And the cold side is too cold. But the point is, the Hellkorians, I mean…they shouldn't exist."

"But is this planet Hellkor?" Wyatt asked.

Jeelork looked around, their eyes slightly narrowed, their lips pursed together. They shivered as a breeze went by. "Well…it sure seems to fit. Yeah. I think so."

"Wait a minute," Jamar said, "if we are on the permanent night side, it should be a *lot* colder than *this*."

"The book on the Hellkorians I read said that the night side got enough heat to make it bearable via jet streams in the upper atmosphere, bringing warm air from the day side to the night side. Ocean currents from the day to the night side had the same effect. Some Hellkorians actually lived on the permanent night side."

"Apparently, they're highly technological people, with all this tech they have," Wyatt said, "like those awful rooms."

"They were," Jeelork said. "They were dabbling in artificial intelligence at the time of their Contest."

"Maybe they found a way to extend the lives of the ones that were left," Jamar suggested.

"It's possible," Karak said, "but that would involve pretty radical DNA tinkering."

"Some of our human scientists are already looking into that," Jamar replied.

Farine danced up to them. "Did I hear that you figured out who these people are?"

Suddenly, they heard a loud banging noise. They all looked toward the humans' Phobia Room. It was rattling. Something slammed into the door. With another loud bang, the door flew off and landed near the campfire. Slank ran out of the room and collapsed to his knees.

"Well, looks like he's done," Wyatt said. "I wonder what he saw."

The orb descended. "Well, we have the results! The team who racked up the most minutes was the human team! Congratulations, Terrans!"

"Okay," Wyatt said, "so...what do we win?"

"You get to avoid ten whole seconds of excruciating pain!"

The orb shot a narrow beam of light at everybody else at the camp but the humans. They all fell to the ground, doubled over in pain, screaming in agony. They writhed on the ground and continued screaming.

"NO!" Alice screamed. "Stop it, please!" She wished they hadn't won. She felt terrible guilt that others were going through that torture, and she was not.

"My god!" Wyatt exclaimed. "What is it doing to them?!"

In a few more seconds, that nightmare was over. The beams of light vanished. Then the orb did. In its wake, everybody not from Earth lay on the ground, groaning and crying.

Alice knelt down to Jeelork and Karak and put a hand on each of their trembling shoulders.

Chase knelt down to Farine. "What was it like? What did it do?"

Farine, between sobs, said, "It...felt like...knives were...cutting up my insides!"

"That was a game I did not like winning," Jamar mumbled.

"I don't think any of us did," Chase said.

Over the next ten minutes all the crying and painful groans

slowly subsided. Even the Fargles looked miserable in their recovery time. Chase had never seen Barchell in such anguish. The Wistwills took the longest to stand up again. Markonis remained hunched over in his hover chair for a while, breathing heavily and wheezing.

It was quite some time before the campsite mostly calmed down. But unbeknownst to everybody there, soon the campsite would be anything but calm.

CHAPTER NINE: Imposter Syndrome

A FTER THE Phobia Rooms, and the punishment for the non-winners, the mood around the camp was dour. Misery and grief were everywhere. Everybody was upset. Some people were catatonic after their experience in the Phobia Room. Others were crying. Morale was low. They rebuilt the fire, but there would be no more sniggle meat to eat. All the sniggle corpses had turned. But they had the berries that were in each of their cases. They turned out to not be poisoned. But…

Alice made a sour face as she ate one of the berries. "God, these taste bad," she said, "they're so bitter and sour."

"It's our only food, though," Jamar said, "but yeah, they're disgusting."

"Another way to torture us," Wyatt said as he angrily ate one.

"Better than starving," Chloe said ruefully. She put one in her mouth. She almost spit it out. She had to force it down. Chloe quickly drank some of her water to make the taste go away.

Everybody tried to get as much enjoyment out of the campfire as they could. They tried telling stories again. At some point, everybody fell asleep.

\#

Five hours after the last person drifted off to sleep, the orb returned. It awakened everybody with the obnoxious beeping again and flashing of its intense light.

"Wake up! Wake up!" the orb's voice cheerily yelled. "Time for another day of fun! And we have something *really* fun in store today!"

"I just wanna go home," Jamar whined. He still lay there flat on his back. He wiped his eyes.

"Dammit," Wyatt mumbled as he stirred awake.

Everybody else groaned and cussed in their own languages as they awoke.

Karak stood up quickly. "Please stop this! This isn't anybody else's fault but our own, the Deelooveren. Please let everybody else go. We figured it out. You're the Hellkorians, aren't you?"

"Oh, you figured it out?" the orb said. "I suppose one of you at some point would. Well, I guess that takes some of the mystery out of all of this. But…no matter. Because we just happen to have a mystery in store for you today! You all like figuring out mysteries, don't you?"

"Please, what Karak said, let them go!" Coordinator Jeelork yelled. "You wanted revenge on *us*, didn't you?"

"Yes, it's just us you'd wanted revenge on!" Assistant Meel said. "Let the others go!"

"Watching your precious Contest winners die, one by one, that seems like a satisfying revenge for us," the orb replied. Then it laughed. "So stop that pathetic begging! Anyway, onto today's agenda. While you were all asleep last night…well, it's still night, but… while you were asleep, we replaced one member of your team with an imposter! You will spend the rest of the day…about six hours or so… trying to figure out who the imposter is!"

Alice, who had been snuggling Chase, looked at him. She crept away from him.

The orb continued, "What makes this mystery even more fun is the fact that when you think you've figured out who the imposter is, one of you must kill the imposter!" The orb giggled. "So, of course, you'd better be sure that you're right! Oh, and if you don't do this, the imposter, if you haven't figured it out before time's up, he, or she, or they will kill one of your real team members. So…good luck, teams!"

The orb ascended.

All the humans looked at each other. They all looked at Slank. He looked at them.

"Oh, this is diabolical," whispered Wyatt.

Alice looked at Chase again. "It could be any of us."

"It's not me," Chase whispered. He reached out to touch Alice.

She slid away. "What if it *is* you?!"

"Oh lord," Jamar said, "no, no, no…this is horrible."

Chloe looked upward with pure anger on her face and in her eyes. "Wankers!"

"Don't give them the satisfaction, Chloe," Wyatt said.

"You know what I'd like to give them?" Chloe replied. "I'd like to shove a sniggle up their arses!"

"I second that!" Jamar said as he held a finger up.

Alice looked at Wyatt, then Jamar, then Chloe, then back at Chase. "I don't like this. I don't like it at all."

"It could be just a test," Wyatt said, "like maybe none of us is an imposter."

"Which is exactly what the imposter would say!" Jamar said as he pointed to Wyatt. "What if it's *you*?!"

"Well, it's not me!"

They looked around. They could hear and see arguments from the other groups springing up all around them.

"Jesus, it's not taking long to get to chaos," Chase whispered.

Wyatt looked down, like he was in some deep thought. "Let's really think about this, okay? Let's ask each other questions only the real person would know."

"That's no good, Wyatt," said Alice. "The Hellkorians know almost everything about us somehow. They knew our phobias!"

"Well, let's try it anyway! They can't know, like, *everything*! Unless they're telepathic."

"But *we* don't know everything about us!" Jamar argued. "As good of friends as we are, I still don't know any of y'all's favorite colors."

"Blue," said Chase.

"Red," Wyatt said.

"Purple," Chloe said.

Alice sighed. "Mine's yellow."

"And mine's red also," Jamar said. "So that was useless, though."

"Mine is black," Slank said. They all looked at him. They hadn't even known he was standing there yet.

Wyatt held up his finger. "Technically, black isn't a—"

"Shut up!" Slank rolled his eyes.

"It's Slank!" Chase said, pointing at him.

Slank chuckled. "Really? Oh, yes, of course it's me! The evil one!" He sighed. "Come on, nimrods, do you really think they'd make it that obvious? Or easy?"

"Well, that's what the imposter would say!" Chase said. "Maybe that's exactly why they'd make it you!"

"Hey, moron, listen, would any of you really be bothered if you killed me, accidentally identifying me as the imposter? I'm surprised one of you hasn't tried to kill me already. Oh, and don't try it unless you want my dagger sticking out of your brain."

Chase sighed. "Well…he has a good point."

Some of the arguing around the camp escalated. They got louder. The humans looked at the Deelooverens. They were still keeping their cool. But they were having an animated discussion, though.

"We'd least expect it to be Alice!" Wyatt said. "I mean, she's the sweetie of the group."

"Stop it!" Alice yelled. "I'm getting really scared!"

"Gee, I thought you were beyond that now," Chloe said. "You were over all that anxiety stuff. Hmm?" She got her knife out.

"No, please, no, it's not me!" Alice said. She drew her knees up to her face, just like she had done that first night in the room.

"It's Chloe!" Chase exclaimed. "Look, she has her weapon drawn already."

"But the imposter wasn't supposed to attack till the end of the day!" Jamar said.

Chloe still held a tight grip on her knife. Alice breathed deeply. She sat normally again and got out her own knife. "It's…not…me," she said in a shaky voice.

"Well, let's make sure," Chase said. "Take your voice box off. If you can talk, then it's you!"

"Do you really think they'd be that dumb, Chase?" Wyatt asked.

"Maybe whatever process they used to make the clone, they got it right, down to the finest details," Jamar suggested. "I mean, the Alice imposter would be made not to talk without the box."

"Or it's not a clone at all," Wyatt said. "I mean, it could be a solid, touchable hologram with advanced artificial intelligence. I mean, why would the Hellkorians disguise one of their own with the risk of him or her being murdered?"

"You guys are a bunch of idiots!" Slank said. "I think the worst thing about all this is being stuck with you imbeciles for...I don't know how many days!"

Chloe pointed her knife at Slank. "Why don't we just kill this pratt for the funsies, whether he's the imposter or not?!"

Slank pointed his knife back at her. "Brain...dagger!" he reminded her. He raised his eyebrows at her.

"I have an idea," Wyatt said.

"What if you are the imposter?" Jamar said to him. "Then we can't trust any of your ideas!"

"Well, why don't you at least *listen* to my idea first before deciding that?"

They heard Woo'cha screaming. "I'll kill anybody who comes near me! Anybody who comes near me is dead! It'll be self-defense!"

"Calm down, Woo'cha!"

Jamar sighed. "Some of these teams might not last six hours."

"But *we will*," Wyatt said, "and here's how we're gonna do it. Let's just have a long conversation. *Talk.* And try to pick up on things. The imposter will slip up at some point. Especially if it's an advanced A.I."

"Turing test!" Jamar exclaimed. He excitedly pointed at Wyatt. "If it's an A.I., it might fail the Turing test."

"Exactly, Jamar!" Wyatt replied. "If...you are indeed Jamar."

"Turing test?" Chloe said. "What's *that?*"

Wyatt explained, "It's basically if you can have a conversation with an A.I. that seems totally natural and organic, then that means it passes the test, which could mean it's sentient or self-aware."

Farine appeared. She danced, as usual, but only a little. "This is very *not* groovy, my cuties. A couple of my friends think that *I* am not *me*."

"I think we are all suspicious of us all," Wyatt said with a sigh. "And I thought your species was telepathic...or at least some of you were. Can't you read each other and figure it out?"

"The Hellkorian is using some sort of telepathy-dampening field today," Farine answered. "We can't use our telepathy right now."

Barchell, in his dark orange and brown uniform, also approached the humans. "So what do you all think? Any ideas? Chase? How about you?"

"I think this all sucks beyond the definition of it," Chase replied.

"I've been talking to a few of the other thieves," Barchell said. "We need to try to steal the orb."

Chase frowned. "And then do what with it?"

"Get information out of it?"

"Oh yes, let's torture it for info. Sure, that should work."

"Well, we could interrogate it."

"It can fire phaser blasts!" Chase replied. "Unless you like getting your hands blown off, it might just be a bad idea."

Barchell scoffed. "Well, at least it's a start! Y'know, *trying* to think of an idea!"

"Sorry, Barch," Chase said. "I'm just…feeling really cynical after all this. Especially after…what I saw in that room."

"What I saw messed me up, too," Barchell replied. "But, I still say we thieves gotta get together and hatch some sort of plan. Hmm. I wish Deelan were here, too."

"Don't you think we should figure all this shit out first? Before we do that? Make sure we're talking to the real…*us*?"

Farine danced into the conversation. "The sooner we do something, the better. People are dying. More die with each of these trials."

Barchell gently put one of his huge orange hands on Farine's shoulder. "I'm very sorry about Morla."

A tear came to Farine's eye. She looked down. "It was so senseless how she died! Just from a cruel fall! These Hellkorians have no heart at all!" Farine's voice shook.

Barchell sighed. "Seeing Eeler hanging like that…I don't think I'll ever get over seeing that. We all loved her."

"Team Earth is very sorry for your losses," Wyatt said.

"That's kind of easy for you to say," Barchell replied. "You haven't had a loss yet."

"You have our sympathies, regardless."

"There's no need to be mean to them just because they're all still here, Barchell," Farine said.

"I know, I know. These damned aliens. This is what they're doing. They're eating away at us. Changing us for the worse."

"This might be the worst way yet that they do it," Chloe said.

"You know what we need before we begin the conversations," Wyatt said. "We need a good fire again. Last night's is almost gone."

"Yeah, let's get some more wood and do that," Jamar said as he got up. "I'll help."

"Me, too," Alice said. She got up as well. On her way to the tree line, she passed Team Doo'chen. They were almost literally at each other's throats. Their arguing was intense.

Soon, the fire roared again. Everybody sat as close to it as possible. It seemed colder now than it had been. But the coldness of the awful situation could have caused it.

"So, Alice, tell me about your early home life," Wyatt requested.

"I'm supposed to talk less, remember? In case my voice box is almost out of power."

Wyatt looked irritated. "Fine, then pick another topic of conversation! One that won't need as many words."

"Okay. Favorite movies. My favorite movie ever is *Arrival*. Because of the language-translation aspect of the plot."

"And the main character was talking to aliens," Wyatt said, "how 'bout that?"

"Life's weird lately," Alice said.

"Understatement of the year," Jamar mumbled.

Wyatt looked at Chase. "Okay, what's *your* favorite movie?"

Chase was playing with a stick when Wyatt asked, sticking it in the fire, trying to get the tip to light up. "Favorite movie? Hmmm. *The Matrix,* I guess. Unoriginal, I know. Me and about five hundred million others."

"Nothing wrong with that, great movie. How about you, Jamar?"

Jamar sighed. "Movies. We're talkin' 'bout movies. Here. Now."

"We need to talk about *something*."

"Fine. *Avengers: Endgame*. About as epic as you can get. When they all assemble…that was a hell of an assemblin'."

"Here, here!" Wyatt held up his water canteen. "Jamar, actually, I've never heard it said better. 'A hell of an assemblin'!' So, Chloe, what's yours?"

"*Pride & Prejudice*. Sometimes, you just can't beat Jane Austen."

"*Avengers* beat the hell outta her," Jamar said.

"Whatever," Chloe shot back. "Sometimes you blokes are so basic." She eyed a berry in her hand with hunger and disappointment. "I'm so bloody hungry. And these are rubbish!" She ate it anyway. She almost gagged, but she got it down. "Why are they doing this to us? We don't deserve this!"

"We're gonna have to hunt for better food." Jamar slipped out his knife. He looked at the firelight reflecting off the metal blade.

"I was never much of a woodsman or a hunter type," Wyatt said. "Like that Bear guy on TV. I am not sure I could hunt and kill an animal if I tried. But with just a knife?" He shook his head.

"What is *your* favorite film, Wyatt?" Chase asked.

"*Lord of the Rings: Return of the King*," he answered. "Put a still from that film next to the word 'epic' in the dictionary." He turned to Slank. "Okay, just out of…morbid curiosity…what's your favorite movie?"

"*A Clockwork Orange*," Slank replied. He smiled. "Certain parts of that film, well, I just like to replay over and over."

"Why am I not surprised?" Wyatt asked.

"What's… 'clockwork orange?'" Alice asked.

"I'm not sure you *wanna* know," Wyatt replied.

"Oh, I heard about that movie," Jamar said. "Yeah, Alice, steer clear of that one. Take my word for it."

"Okay, so what have we learned?" Wyatt asked. "That if one of us really is an imposter, these aliens, hundreds of light years away from the Terran system, know about Earth movies."

"They're telepathic or something," Jamar said. "They must be."

"Or this imposter thing is a sham," Wyatt replied.

"That's what the imposter would try to get us to believe!"

Chase said. He eyed Wyatt suspiciously. "I think it's *you*! You're mining for information from us to use in your ruse. Aren't you?"

"I'm trying to find out who the imposter *is*, Chase!" Wyatt then looked at him suspiciously. "You seem to be awfully accusatory. I think that makes *you* suspicious."

"I'd like to circle back to Alice being the one we'd least suspect," Chloe said. "Sorry if I'm wrong, love, but if I were these aliens, I'd make *you* the imposter."

Alice stood up. "Okay, Chloe. Why don't you and I both prove we're not? Let's spar. Come on. Let's fight. These aliens can do research about Earth media, maybe read our minds, but can they suddenly know human fighting or martial arts moves?"

"We no longer have super healing!" Chloe exclaimed. "I *don't* want to fight you! Not now!"

Alice gestured to Chloe. "Well, I think we might know who it is now."

"I don't wanna break your bloody leg again! Not when you can't heal it! Not with another fresh hell awaiting us tomorrow!"

"Prove you're not the imposter!" Alice approached Chloe threateningly. Chloe stood up quickly.

"I'm not bloody fighting you!" Chloe yelled.

"Come on! You've never backed down from a fight before!" Alice tightened into a fighting stance.

"Stop it, Alice! I'm not fighting you!"

"Hey, cut it out, you two!" Wyatt exclaimed. "Alice, lay off her!"

"I need to know who it is!" Alice yelled. "I can't...I can't take it anymore! I need to know! Fight me, Chloe!"

"No!"

"FIGHT ME!" Alice took a swing at Chloe. She blocked it. Alice swung at her again and successfully punched her in the jaw.

Wyatt scrambled up to them, grabbed Alice's shoulders, and pulled her away.

"Let go of her!" Chase yelled.

Alice squirmed around and punched Wyatt in the chest. He stumbled backward but stumbled forward again and swung at Alice, but she dodged it. Chase punched Wyatt in the face.

"STOP THIS INSANITY *NOW*!" Jamar screamed. He jumped

between Chase and Wyatt as he was about to hit Chase back. "STOP! STOP!" He held out his arms. "We can't do this! We can't let these aliens do this to us!"

Slank sat nearby. He laughed. "I wish I had some popcorn right now!"

"Stop fighting, my cuties!" Farine yelled.

Chloe recovered from Alice's punch. She gritted her teeth. Her face filled with rage. "You wanna see my bloody fighting moves?!" She yelled like an animal would, and she ran toward Slank.

"Chloe, no!" Wyatt screamed.

Slank stood up, but he wasn't quick enough. Chloe kicked him as hard as she could in the face. He fell backward off his log and onto the cold ground.

"That's it, bitch!" He spit blood out of his twisted mouth. He stumbled up to a standing position. Chloe punched him twice in the face, with one fist and then the other. He stumbled backward.

"This is what you did to me!" Chloe screamed. She tried to punch him again, but he blocked it. She tried to punch several more times, but Slank blocked them all. Then he grabbed her by the sides and restrained her arms. She kicked him several times in his mid-section, but it didn't injure him. He smiled, then head-butted her. It immediately knocked her out. He threw her to the ground.

Wyatt sprinted over and hit Slank in the chest with a flying kick. It only knocked him backward. Suddenly, a bright phaser blast hit the ground between them. It knocked Slank and Wyatt away from each other. The orb had reappeared.

"Boys, boys, boys!" the orb yelled. "As much as I'd love to see you all kill each other, Slank was probably about to massacre all of you. It wouldn't have been fair."

Wyatt crawled over to Chloe to examine her. Slank just sat up and looked at the other humans with intense hatred.

Jamar glared at Alice. "Look at what you did. You started all that. I don't know if you're the imposter or not, but either way, I can't look at you right now." He turned and sat back down on his log.

Alice looked down at her feet.

Slank looked down at Wyatt and Chloe. "Man, your girlfriend really needs to get over it!" Then he walked back to where he had been sitting.

Wyatt ignored Slank. He cleaned up Chloe's bloody nose. He gently tapped her cheek. "Chloe…Chloe…are you there?" His eyes glistened as they narrowed in sad concern. He picked Chloe up off the ground and headed back to the campfire. He gently placed her on the ground in front of his sitting spot.

#

For the next hour, none of the humans talked to each other. They just watched the flames of the fire slowly die down. Chloe groaned. She was awake. She sat up while holding her head.

"What happened?"

"You were knocked out," Wyatt said. "How do you feel?"

"Like…a small freight train hit my head," she weakly replied.

"This is all my fault," Alice said. "I'm sorry, Chloe. I apologize to all of you." She looked at Jamar. "I'm sorry."

Jamar reached out and touched her hand. "Hey. Look, this is what those aliens want. To, like, do this to us."

While they were quiet, there were sporadic arguments going on around the campsite with the other teams. But the human team was the only one so far that had erupted into physical violence.

"What's happening to us?" Chase said.

Alice tried to reply, but no voice came out. A look of distress came over her face. She thumped her voice box a few times. "Testing…oh, thank god it's still working."

"I wonder how much longer it's gonna last," Jamar said.

"What's happening to us is exactly what the Hellkorians want to happen," Wyatt said.

"We need to make a promise to each other," Alice said, "right here, right now. That we will always be friends. No matter what. *Ride or die*. Like what we said when we got here."

"I'm all for it," Wyatt said. "What about everybody else?"

"I'm in for that promise," Chase said.

"Same here," Jamar said.

"I'm in…but…my head hurts so badly," Chloe said, "and my ears are ringing badly. It's hard to…think…clearly."

"You might have a concussion," Wyatt said. "Just lie down,

honey, get some rest. I guess there's no Tylenol or aspirin in any-body's case?"

"Nope," Jamar said.

The argument that the Norfans had been having heated up. They suddenly got louder.

Streen, their strategist, seemed particularly agitated. "I am telling you, her dancing is different!"

"My dancing is different because this place is different!" Farine yelled.

"She's right," Furk said, "it's affecting all of us! It doesn't mean she's the imposter!"

He and Streen, wearing angry grimaces on both of their faces, stared at each other as they slowly circled each other, swaying their hips back and forth in a rather disturbing sort of threatening dance.

"Look more carefully at her dancing, Furk!" Streen exclaimed as she pointed her knife at Farine.

"I agree!" Murr exclaimed. He also pointed his knife at Farine.

"Wow," Alice whispered, "it's bad over there."

"Yeah," Chase said.

"It was bad over here a while ago," Jamar replied.

Slank, who had been using his knife to whittle a sharp point on a stick, stopped. He appeared to notice something that the others hadn't. He stared at the other humans for a moment. But then, he shrugged and continued whittling.

"Jonnifer is the imposter!" The argument was getting loud amongst the Wistwills, too. Alannis, their thief, had accused their lin-guist of being the imposter. "She doesn't remember that we lost the Grid Disc game!"

"That was over seventy-five years ago!" Johanne exclaimed.

The Fargles got loud as well.

"Turakell keeps accusing everybody else of being the im-poster, so it must be him!" Seeka, their scientist, yelled.

"Well, I think he was right when he accused *you*!" Hancharree, their musician, yelled at Seeka. "You've been looking dodgy at me all day so far!"

"Oh my god," Alice whispered. She pointed over at the

Doo'chen group. One of them had the other at knifepoint.

"Should we break it up?" Jamar suggested.

"And one of *us* get stabbed?" Wyatt said as he threw out his arms to gesture to their entire group.

"I want to help!" Alice said.

"What if we make it *worse*, not better?" Chase asked.

"What if the one they're about to kill is actually their imposter?" Slank asked. "We should just mind our own business."

"But I can't stand to see that!" Alice said as she pointed at the Doo'chen. Tears were in her eyes. She buried her face in her hands. "I can't stand to see *any* of this! This all is a waking nightmare!"

"That's the point, isn't it?" Jamar mumbled. His eyes were also growing wet.

"I just wanna wake up!" Alice said, her face still in her hands. She sobbed. "I just want all this to be a nightmare and wake up!"

Chase wrapped his arms around her and hugged her. "I don't care if you might be the one. I can't stand to see you so distressed, my love." He kissed the top of her head.

#

Over the next few hours, as the deadline approached, the bickering and violence around the campsite continued. The Doo'chen were all ready to kill each other. They had completely broken down into a fever of paranoia. The Fargles were screaming at each other, looking like they were about to break out into violence at any moment. And the Norfans were in complete disarray, they were actually all hiding from each other. Even the Deelooveren's arguing finally turned heated. They had remained the most civilized team, but cracks in their cool demeanor were showing.

Team Earth, while faring better than all the other alien-winning teams, was dangerously close to imploding, too.

"My family has lots of money," Chloe said as she stood in the middle of the group near the fire. "We, we, we're very wealthy, just reveal yourself, we won't kill you, you don't kill us, come, come live on Earth, you can live in luxury the rest of your life!"

"They don't want money, Chloe!" Chase exclaimed. "They want vengeance!"

"Come clean!" Wyatt exclaimed as he pointed his knife at the others. "Chloe has a point. Maybe we don't kill you, you don't kill us, we work out a deal! Come on! You can be reasoned with, can't you?!" He pointed the knife at Alice, Jamar, Chase, even Chloe. "Please, we can be reasonable! There doesn't have to be murder and death!"

"Please," Chloe pleaded with whoever was the imposter. "I can't do it! I can't kill another human person! Please don't make me! I can't do it! I can't!"

"Pull yourself together, Chloe!" Alice stood up. "Come on! Don't come apart on us now!"

"Don't *you* start again!" Jamar yelled. He stood up and stood between Alice and Chloe. "We ain't having a repeat of this morning!"

"Leave her alone!" Chase exclaimed. He pointed his knife at Jamar.

"Put it away, Chase! I am not about to attack Alice! I'm trying to *prevent* more violence! Chill the hell out!"

"How much time is left?" Alice said. "Does anybody know?"

Chase came closer to Jamar with his knife.

"Put it away, Chase! I'm warnin' you!" Jamar pulled out his own knife. But he backed away from Chase.

"I told you yesterday, Chase, you're not my personal bodyguard!" Alice yelled. She grabbed his knife-holding arm. "Stop being a prick, will you?!"

Screaming rattled the campsite. It was Farine. She came bolting by the fire pit. Furk was chasing her, murder in his eyes, wielding a knife in each hand.

"It's you! I know it's you, Farine! Streen was right!" Furk screamed. They ran right by Alice and Chase.

"Oh my god!" Alice said. She looked at Chase. He didn't seem to react to it at all.

"That's it," Slank said. He sighed, rolled his eyes, and got off his log.

"I said put the knife away!" Jamar exclaimed. "Come on, man, please!"

"Put yours away first!" Chase said.

But then, suddenly, a knife flew through the air and impaled Chase right in the face between his eyes. He stumbled backward, then fell to the ground.

Alice screamed as loud as her voice box would go. "JACOB! NOOOO!"

"Alice! Alice, shut up!" Slank said.

"JACOB!" she screamed again.

"ALICE!" Slank boomed so she could hear him over her own screaming. "It was Chase! He was the imposter! I figured it out! Settle down!"

Alice looked from Chase's body, back to Slank, to Chase's body, then back to Slank. Everybody was stunned. They just froze in place for a moment.

"It was...him?" Alice whimpered. "But...but..." Chase's body started melting into a fleshy goo. "Oh my god!" But she looked at Slank. "How...how did you figure it out?"

"Well," Slank said, "I'm gonna let you in on a little secret, sweetheart. Chase? He's really into that green Norfan chick. He's got it *bad* for her. I've noticed that over the last couple of days. Apparently, none of you other idiots did. He barely flinched when she ran by, running for her life. The imposter was also an idiot and also didn't see that, either. But *I* did. So the good news is, the crisis is over for our group, but bad news is, your boyfriend is in love with somebody else." Slank smiled and laughed. He retrieved his knife from the melting goo that used to be the Chase imposter. Then he went back to his log.

Then he thought of something. He turned to the other humans. "Oh, and...*you're welcome.*"

Alice slowly looked up from the goo and at everybody else. Tears dripped down her face. She blinked several times. She was utterly speechless. For a quiet moment, they all were.

"But...where is he?" Alice finally said. She looked around.

The orb appeared. A beam of light appeared from it, aimed at the ground near the humans. When it vanished, Chase was on the ground where it had shone. He lay there still and quiet.

Alice ran to him. She knelt down. "Jacob, are you okay?" He wasn't awake. She checked his pulse and breathing. "He's alive!" she announced. She tried to drag him to the bed of leaves they'd been sleeping on. But she had to use all her strength. She wished she had the super serum again. Jamar came over to help her, but she waved him off. She wanted to do it herself. After another try, she succeeded.

She looked up at Wyatt. "Now, we have to help Farine."

Chloe looked confused. "But, Farine, Slank said Chase—"

"I don't care!" Alice said. "She is still our friend! She fought by our side! And we're gonna save her!"

"What if she's their imposter and Furk and Streen are right?" Jamar asked.

"Everybody, we have lost our way," Wyatt said. "This torture has messed us up. We need to be the team that won the Contest again, that gave the Zerrdon the food, that…that didn't let the Deelooveren rebuild their weapon! We are going to help Farine! She could be their imposter, but we're gonna play the odds! There's only a one-in-four chance she is! Come on! Let's be a guiding light, damn it, like we were before!"

"Yes!" Alice said. "Yes, Wyatt, yes! Enough of this bullshit!"

Farine, screaming, ran by again. Furk still chased her. Alice quickly stood up and stuck her leg out. Furk tripped over her leg and tumbled to the ground. Alice got her knife out. She jumped on top of Furk and held her knife to his neck.

"You're gonna stand down, Furk!" Alice yelled in his face. "YOU HEAR ME?! You are not gonna kill my friend Farine!"

"Let me go!" Furk grunted. "Farine is the—"

"I have faith that she's *not*! Now, why do I have more faith in her than *you* do? Her loyal teammate?"

"Get off me," Furk said in a strained voice.

"Promise me you will stop trying to kill Farine."

"Fine! I promise! You have my word."

Alice withdrew her knife and got up. Furk stood up, too. "You'd better be right," he said as he did so.

The orb descended. "You all now have two minutes left! Looks like the humans are the only ones so far that figured out their imposter! They won the challenge, but, sorry, that doesn't mean it's over!"

The orb stayed in the air. Alice mused maybe it wanted to watch the carnage that was about to unfold.

She caught a glimpse of the Deelooveren team. They all calmly stood up. They all got their knives out. Four of them pointed their knives at Assistant Meel. Meel pointed their knife at Karak.

Farine approached Alice. "Oh, my cutie! Thank you for saving me!" She held her arms out. Alice smiled at her and embraced her.

"No problem, Farine! I'd never let anybody hurt you!"

Chloe watched their embrace. It warmed her heart. She whispered to Jamar, "I've said before, I'll say it again. She's such a better person than I am. I love her."

"Same, Chloe, same," Jamar said.

Alice, who was facing them, smiled at them. She looked happy and loved.

Then, her eyes bulged out. She suddenly looked very surprised. She and Farine stopped hugging. That's when they saw it: Farine's knife, covered in red blood. Alice, a shocked look on her face, took several steps backward.

"No," whispered Chloe.

Farine turned around and smiled at the humans. Furk appeared, and he looked at Alice. He looked at Farine. He ran at Farine wielding his knife, but she spun around, and before he could change course, she stabbed him deep into his gut. He looked shocked like Alice did. Farine pulled her knife out, and he fell to the ground.

Alice fell to her knees, reached around, and felt her back with her left hand. She brought it back in front of her. Her shaking hand was covered in her blood. The orb beamed up the fake Farine.

Wyatt, Chloe, and Jamar sprinted over to Alice. She was still on her knees. Her entire body trembled. At the same time, Murr and Streen ran to Furk, screaming and crying.

"Alice!" Wyatt yelled as they got to her.

They heard the entire Fargle team yell and scream, but they had a higher priority.

Alice, her eyes still almost bulging out of her sockets, fell into Wyatt.

"Wh…wh…Wyatt," she whispered, "d-d-don't…don't let me…die."

"Oh my god!" Chloe said as her eyes filled with tears. She saw all the blood on Alice's back. Jamar, panicked, looked, too.

"Shhhh, shhh," Wyatt said, "I'm not gonna let you die, okay, Alice? Not on my watch. You hear me? You're gonna be okay."

Wyatt picked her up and took her back to their area by the fire. Jamar quickly jumped ahead of them and rolled Chase off of the leaf bed. He decided Alice needed it more. Wyatt lay Alice on it, face down. "We need something! We need to apply pressure! Is there anything like a towel around?!"

Oh no, no, no, not Alice! Wyatt thought. As his hands trembled, he grabbed at the tear in Alice's uniform where the fake Farine had stabbed her. He tore it open more. The wound gushed more blood. His mind and body hummed in anxiety. He then tore a strip off the uniform. He was glad it wasn't a Deelooveren-issue uniform, as those were almost impossible to tear. For once, he was glad for a cheap knock-off.

"We don't have towels!" Jamar said.

Chase stirred and grumbled.

"I got it!" Wyatt said as he applied pressure to her wound with the torn strip of cloth. "We can tear these cheap knock-off uniforms! We need more strips!" Wyatt looked at the location of the stab wound. It was on the upper part of her back, so he hoped it hadn't stabbed into her liver or intestines. And it wasn't over her spine.

Chloe used her knife to cut a strip of her uniform off of her midsection. She gave it to Wyatt. Jamar copied Chloe.

"Wyatt!" Alice said. "It hurts!"

"I know, shhhh, we're gonna take care of you," Wyatt said.

"We're here for you, love," Chloe said. She knelt and brought her face down to be eye level with Alice. "We're gonna take good care of you! You're gonna be okay, we promise!"

Jamar knelt down to her other side. "We got ya, girl, we got ya!"

Meanwhile, the real Farine beamed down to the campsite, just as Chase had. The other two remaining Norfan team members ran to her. The Deelooveren had guessed correctly when they killed the fake Meel. Soon, the real one beamed down to them.

The Doo'chen also guessed correctly.

The Fargles did not.

The orb flashed. "Oh no! The Fargles killed the wrong one! Oh, what a failure they were! Now there's only two Fargles left! But congratulations to the Doo'chen and the Deelooveren for guessing correctly!" Then, the orb ascended.

Alice's skin grew pale. Very pale. Wyatt became more scared.

"I'm not feelin' so good," Alice gasped.

"We need…something!" Wyatt said. He had a powerful urge

to panic. "Uhh. Uhhh." Out of all the times in his life that he absolutely could not fail at something, it was *now*!

"Medicine!" Jamar said.

"Yeah, sure! Let's go down to the nearby Walgreens!" Wyatt exclaimed.

"The forest! We've got to, uhhhh, see if there're any herbs or leaves with medicinal properties or something!"

"This is an alien planet, Jamar!" Chloe said. "We don't know—"

"Well, let's get to knowing!" Jamar said. He grabbed his knife. "Let's all put a small cut on ourselves and then try various leaves, plants, that are out in the forest and see what helps our cuts heal!"

"If this wasn't a dire emergency, that would be a very, very bad idea!" Wyatt said. "But…ride or die, ride or die, we might all die, but let's do it! For Alice!"

"I'm…scared…" Alice said, her voice box barely audible.

"We're taking care of you, Alice," Wyatt said. "Please have faith. You're gonna pull through. Just hold on! Okay?! Hold on! Stay with us!"

Jamar and Chloe frantically ran through the edge of the forest, grabbing as many different kinds of leaves, grasses, and roots as they could. They ran back to the campsite. They each cut a finger with their knives and tried various items out.

"Ah, shit!" Chloe yelled when she tried one leaf she'd gathered. It burned her cut badly. She tried another one. It did nothing.

Jamar also found something that burned. He tried something else.

Wyatt continued to apply pressure. For a brief second, he lifted the bandages to see if the bleeding was still as profuse. It was. But then he noticed something else. The skin around the cut was rapidly turning red, and it wasn't from the blood that had gushed out.

"Oh no," he whispered to himself. *Infection.*

Slank walked over to them. "That's getting infected."

"No shit!" Wyatt said. "Go away!"

"Listen, ummm, Wyatt," Slank said, "I, uh, I wanna help."

Wyatt scowled at Slank. "Now is not a good time for jokes!"

"I don't know…what's…coming over me," Slank slowly said, "but…I…I don't like seeing her like this." The way he squinted his eyes showed that he indeed looked troubled.

"Did your cold, dead heart start beating again?!"

"I, umm…"

"If you wanna help, then do what Chloe and Jamar are doing!"

Slank stomped off to do just that.

"Wyatt…" Alice's barely audible voice said.

Please don't die, Alice! Please! Wyatt internally pleaded. If she died, he wasn't sure he could keep them together without the heart of the team. They'd all fall apart without her!

Wyatt lightly petted her soft hair. "Stay with us, Alice! You can do it! I believe in you! Umm. Hey, hey, did your umm family ever have a pet?"

"Yes…"

"Cat? Dog?"

"Cat…Whiskers…"

"What color was Whiskers?" Wyatt waited for a response. "Alice! What color was Whiskers?!"

"Or…orange…"

"Stay with me! Tell me all about Whiskers!"

"She was…cute…she…she…slept in…" Alice trailed off. She became still.

"Alice! Alice, stay with me! Alice!"

Jamar tried the last sample he had. He rubbed it on his cut. It started fizzing. At first, that frightened him. But then, something amazing happened. It was a miracle. The cut started healing almost as quickly as if he had injected himself with the super serum.

"I found something!" Jamar said. He showed the leaf to Chloe and Slank. "Get me more of these! *Now*! I got it from that plant over there!"

He ran over to Alice and Wyatt. "Here!" Jamar said. "I don't know if there's a god up there watching us or not, but it's some kinda damned miracle, man. This stuff is like the super serum."

"No shit?!" Wyatt said. He crushed the leaf up and rubbed it on Alice's stab wound. The fizzing alarmed him, too. But then he saw it working. First, the redness went away. But then, the cut slowly began to heal.

Wyatt looked at Jamar, dumbfounded. Then he whispered, "Dude, get as much of this shit as you can."

"Chloe and Slank are already on it."

"Get on it, too," Wyatt whispered, "and without the orb hearing or seeing."

After Jamar ran off, Wyatt had a thought. *What if it's not a miracle? What if this is the plant the super serum's key ingredient came from, and they tried to grow it here?*

"What the hell is going on?!"

Wyatt looked up. It was Chase. He was awake.

"*A lot,*" Wyatt replied.

"Oh my god, what happened to Alice?" He knelt down on the cold, hard ground.

"She was stabbed in the back by the fake Farine," Wyatt said, "and now I'm healing her with a super plant."

Chase looked very confused. "*What?*"

"There's a lot to unpack, man."

Jamar, Chloe, and Slank came back with more of those leaves. Slank had secretly shoved many of them in his own pocket.

Alice groaned and moved.

"Oh, thank god!" Jacob said. "Alice…are you awake? Can you hear me?"

"Jacob?" She turned over on her back. She looked up at everybody.

"Oh, Al, you're okay!" Jacob smiled real big. He was so happy.

"You are, too!" Alice said. She smiled at him. She sat up and hugged him.

"I love you!" Jacob said.

"I love you, too!" Alice said. But then something occurred to her. She quickly separated from Chase and looked at Wyatt. "Hey, how am I still alive?"

Wyatt gestured for everybody to come in for a quiet huddle.

"Alice, we may have found the super serum plant on this planet," Wyatt whispered.

"Really?!" Alice exclaimed.

"Shhhh!" Wyatt said. "We need to keep this discovery quiet. *Very* quiet. The orb can't know that we know. This will give us an advantage.

"We need to make the leaves into the serum, though, some-how." Wyatt looked at Jamar. "Can you figure that out, Science Guy?"

"I'll see what I can do."

CHAPTER TEN: Alternative Medicine

FORTUNATELY, THEY still had the empty, injectable vials in their cases from the microdoses of the super serum. This gave Jamar something to put the homemade serum into…*if* he could make it. As he gathered them up, Wyatt and Alice explained the whole imposter trial to Chase. It deeply disturbed him.

But they had more important things to discuss.

"So, how did that plant get here?" Chase whispered to Wyatt as they had a hushed conversation by the fire.

"No idea, but I have a theory," Wyatt replied. "If the Hellkorians really were on the brink of extinction and couldn't have any more children, what's the second best thing to do? Immortality for the Hellkorians that already existed."

"So they get a hold of as much super serum as possible," Chase said. "To heal the body from almost anything. And they live longer. Maybe centuries."

"And if they can't find the serum, make it themselves," Chloe suggested. "Maybe grow the plant here. Maybe that first dose they gave us wasn't Deelooveren. Maybe it was Hellkorian."

"How do the plants grow here, anyway?" Chase asked. "I mean, *any* plant? Without any sunlight?"

"Alien world, adapted to different conditions," Wyatt said as he shrugged. "Maybe it's something other than photosynthesis for energy. I assume this super plant also adapted somehow."

Alice shook her head. "Why would it be growing wild? Out in the open? That doesn't make sense."

"We know almost nothing about this world," Wyatt said. "It's a weird planet with weird people. Who knows?"

"So Jamar is trying to make a serum from it?" Chloe asked.

"Secretly, in the woods," Wyatt whispered.

"I think we're moving too fast," Chase said. "We know almost nothing about what this other serum will do."

"It saved my life."

"Sure, but there are these complicated rules about the Deelooveren serum. About how it's addictive, how many lifetime doses you can have, all that. What if a side effect from this one kills you later?"

"Well, I sure hope not."

They heard sobs through the crackling fire. Barchell and his only remaining teammate, Seeka, held each other's hands and wept. The Fargles had mistakenly thought that Turakell, their strategist, was the imposter and killed him. The fake Seeka was the imposter, though, and killed Hancharee, their musician, before they figured out their terrible mistake.

"Seeka's their scientist, right?" Alice asked. "Maybe she could help Jamar."

"She doesn't look like she's in the mood for that right now," Wyatt said.

Chloe looked at the Deelooveren team, who sat across the fire next to the two remaining Fargles. They were talking to them, maybe offering them comfort. "We should keep this a secret from *them*, too," she whispered to Wyatt.

"Good idea," Wyatt said. "We can't exactly trust them anymore. And if they find out there's another source for the serum, they would likely try to control it. You're right. We can't tell Karak or any of them."

"It's really sad," Alice said. "Before that sham quest, the Deelooveren would have been the first people I'd want to confide in. It really sucks that we have this distrust of them now."

Wyatt wanted to take a sip of water from his canteen. It was almost empty. "We have another problem. We need more food and water. If I have to eat another one of those berries, I'm gonna find other imposters to kill."

"We need to become hunter/gatherers again," Chloe suggested.

"Should I put on some leopard skin clothes and drag you around by your hair?"

Chloe took a deep breath in and slowly let it out. "Why in the bloody hell did that make me a tiny bit horny?"

Wyatt chuckled. "Let's not kinkshame ourselves."

Alice cleared her throat. "It uhhh…also…made me just a tad bit horny."

Chase looked at her and snickered. "Oh really?"

Wyatt sighed. "I can't decide if I'm more hungry or horny. I think it's actually hungry. All we've had to eat the past few days are those damned berries. Chloe, let's go see what we can find. Chase, Alice, why don't you two stay here for when Jamar comes back?"

"Sure, no problem," Alice replied.

Chloe pointed at the other teams nearby. "Why don't we get others from other teams to help…hunt and gather?"

"Good idea."

#

Meanwhile, Jamar was in a spot in the woods near a small stream of water. He was experimenting with crushing and liquefying the plant in varying concentrations and ratios of leaf matter to water. He used a makeshift mortar and pestle—an empty berry bowl and a smooth, roundish rock he'd found by the stream.

When he arrived at a consistency he liked, one he thought would be easily injected, he got out his knife. He sighed. He hated cutting himself. He gritted his teeth and made a small slice on the palm of his hand. When he felt the sharp, burning pain, he cursed under his breath. Then he applied some of the serum he'd made into the wound. It quickly healed.

"Now, *that's* the stuff," he mumbled to himself. He got out an empty vial. He sighed again. "This ain't sanitary." He wished he'd had some sort of alcohol. Then he thought of something. He remembered the berries were extremely acidic, one reason that they tasted so awful. He got an idea.

"Citric acid can be a disinfectant," he said to himself. If the berries had some sort of citric acid in them or some alien equivalent, he could use the juice to disinfect the vials and the used needles. So he squeezed some of the berries onto another stone he'd collected and did just that.

"Where are all the animals?" Wyatt mumbled to himself as he traipsed through the woods. He gripped his knife tightly and listened for animal sounds. He heard them. There were various animal calls. But he didn't see any. Maybe he only heard birds and then were high in the trees.

Then he saw something he hadn't expected. He came upon a nest. It had quiet baby sniggles in it. "Well," he mumbled, "I guess we killed your mommy and daddy." They were so adorable. They looked like baby ferrets, only cuter. But his stomach rumbled.

He did not want to kill cute little baby animals. But the babies looked at him…then hissed at him. When they crawled out of the nest toward him, he no longer felt guilty about it. He readied his knife.

Chloe, along with Farine, Seeka, Woo-cha, and Barchell, found various wild nuts, legumes, and berries out in the woods but didn't have any idea how poisonous they could be.

#

An hour later, when they all met back at the campfire, they had the makings of a feast.

Jamar examined the berries, nuts, and legumes that were gathered. "Hmm. The nuts are probably fine. Legumes, too. But I wouldn't trust the berries."

Chloe whispered in his ear, "The super serum could be an antidote."

"We don't want them to know about it," he whispered into her ear. "The D-bags are right over there. We'll do the berry experiment when everybody else is asleep."

"All right," Chloe whispered back.

"Jamar, we talked about this earlier when you were in the woods, but how do any plants even grow here if they never get sunlight?" Wyatt asked.

"Chemosynthesis, probably," Jamar replied. "It's how plants at the bottom of the ocean grow where it's way too deep for any sunlight to reach. Instead of photosynthesis with sunlight, they must convert carbon-containing molecules and other nutrients into organic matter as a source of energy. Bacteria also do it."

"Hmm, adapted to different conditions," Chloe said, "like you said earlier, Wyatt."

Wyatt took a bite of baby sniggle meat. "Yep. Just like my diet is adapting right now. Mmmm. Even more tender than the adults!" He'd found dozens more nests after the first one.

Alice grabbed a kabob that had been sitting in the fire cooking some baby sniggle. She was about to take a bite, but then she looked at Chase, then Wyatt. "Nobody back on Earth finds out that I ate meat here, got it?"

"Your secret is safe with us!" Chase said. He got his own kebab. "Let's dig in!"

Chloe and a few of the Doo'chen grabbed kabobs, too. Chloe moaned in food ecstasy as she tore into her first bites. "Oh my god, finally, some real food again!"

"Mmm," said Wyatt as he chewed, "we bring some sniggles back to Earth, have sniggles farms, we'd become filthy rich."

"I sure hope you're joking," Jamar said. "I mean, talk about *invasive species*!"

"Yeah, I was kidding…sort of. I mean…this sniggle meat will be the only thing I miss about this hellhole."

Farine danced in front of the fire again.

"Hey, Farine," Alice said to her. "I'm really sorry about what happened with Furk. He was right about your imposter. I feel like it's my fault that he's dead."

"I'm really sad about him, but I don't blame you, my cutie," Farine said. "Plus, you got stabbed in the back. And I'm really glad you survived. And even though I didn't do it…I feel terrible. Because it was almost like it was me."

The horrible memory of the event quickly ran through Alice's mind: how the loving embrace suddenly ended in one of Farine's hands violently punching her in the back. For the first few seconds she didn't even realize Farine had stabbed her, but she was still extremely shocked and confused, nonetheless. The evil grin on Farine's face, which was still only inches from her own, was one of the most disturbing things Alice had ever seen.

But Alice shook her head to get the memory out of the front of her mind. That was not the woman she was talking to *now*. For a few seconds she looked into the real Farine's face and conjured up some happy memories with her.

"But it wasn't you, though," Alice said. She stood up and opened up her arms. "Come here, my friend."

She hugged her warmly.

Chase watched them hug. At first, he didn't realize that Jamar, Chloe, and Wyatt were watching him watching them. But then he looked around and saw it.

"What?" he said.

"Nothing," Wyatt said.

When they were done with the hug, Farine danced away to continue her dance tour around the fire. Streen also danced by, followed by Murr, their fighter/musician.

Jamar looked up at the night sky. He was sick of looking at a dark sky filled with only stars and a moon. "I sure hope the sniggle meat, or those awful berries, have vitamin D because I am really missing sunlight."

"It's gonna start affecting our health, our mood, just another reason this place sucks!" Chase exclaimed.

Chloe sighed as she threw a tiny sniggle bone into the fire. "At least in those two weeks we spent on that space station, we got some bright lights and some simulated sunshine!"

"We've got to do whatever we can to keep our spirits up," Wyatt said. "We will not survive this if we don't. These aliens want to wear us down, destroy our spirits and morale. They do not want us to survive these…these *Hell Trials*."

"We need to get the hell out of here," Chase said. "I mean, I haven't seen a fence or walls. Let's just leave."

"But go where?" Alice asked. "We have no idea exactly where we are on this planet. We don't know how far we'd have to travel… *on foot*!"

"Maybe we'll, um, find a way to travel faster soon," Chase said. He winked at her.

Alice shot him a sly, angry "Shut up" look on her face.

"Oh," Alice said. "Jacob…when were you going to tell me that you have feelings for Farine?"

"Umm…what?"

Alice put her hand on his leg and looked him straight in the eyes. "Be straight with me. Please. You owe it to me."

"Okay, okay, I like her," Chase said, "she's lovely, I admit it. Yeah, I crush on her a little."

"This is how Slank knew you were the imposter. You didn't react to her life being in danger. He said you had it bad for her."

Chase slowly shook his head. "Al, look, that's not true, I

wouldn't describe it like that."

"Then how *would* you describe it? Tell me the truth."

"I did."

"Are you in love with her?"

"No!" Chase sighed. He looked down. "Look, I'm trying to tell you the truth the best I can. I admit it. I think I have feelings for her, yes, and this is extremely hard to tell you. I don't want to hurt your feelings." He looked back up into her eyes. "Because I am totally in love with *you*."

"Thank you for telling me the truth," Alice said as she patted his leg. "I appreciate it. It doesn't hurt my feelings. I know that these things can happen. And I am in love with you, just in case that wasn't clear."

Jacob reached out and ran his hand through her hair. He looked deep into her eyes. "I've never loved anybody like I love you."

Chloe looked at her sniggle kabob. "I'm losing my appetite now. Thanks." But she laughed.

Alice looked playfully at Chloe. "Oh, just shut up!"

The orb descended into the campsite. "Okay, who is ready for some more fun?"

"No!" Chloe yelled. "You didn't even let us sleep this time!"

"So, here's the thing, so listen carefully!"

It hesitated. Everybody awaited its next words.

"*We don't care*!" Then the orb giggled. "So, the next trial starts soon. This one is going to be interesting. Maybe even more interesting than the imposter thing."

Jamar's face heated up into a look of anger. "I am gettin' real tired of this shit."

Barchell stood up and pointed at the orb. "Go to Kanthos!"

"You might not want to do that, Mr. Lorken," Karak warned him.

"I do not like being interrupted, Fargle!" the orb boomed. "Now, as I was saying, for this trial, you're going to go through an obstacle course with the goal of saving the life of one of your team members. And if your strategist is still alive, that's the one you have to save. Your team is going to have to come up with plans for getting

through the course without them!"
    Wyatt sighed. "Well…shit."

CHAPTER ELEVEN: The Missing

EVER SINCE they had vanished from the Loovian capital, media coverage of the disappearances of the human team had been almost non-stop, both on Earth and Loovian. Of course included in the Loovian coverage was the missing Deelooveren staff. Security camera footage caught them being beamed away, both on Loovian and the *Arkenstar* Station.

"WHERE IS TEAM EARTH?" was the top headline on CNN's website for days. The "CHLOE THOMPSON ACQUITTED" headline barely had time to shine before being usurped by a sudden, bigger story. The abduction of the five humans was international news on Earth. Theories ran wild as to what had happened to them, who may have snatched them, and for what purpose.

On the fourth day of their disappearance, tensions were high.

"Do you have any clues yet at all?!" Hank yelled at his laptop. He was having a video conference with Ambassador Harklon and Co-ordinator Philk, who were on the *Arkenstar* Station.

"Mr. Mackenzie, we only have a few long-shot theories," Ambassador Harklon replied. "We are working around the clock trying to figure out where the humans went. We assume they are in the same place as my predecessor, Karak. We have four other staff members missing. Trust me, we are doing everything we can. We have Level Five scans going to detect radiation trails from ships, and transporter signatures. Whoever abducted them has very advanced cloaking technologies."

"Tell me what the long-shot theories are!" Emma exclaimed. "I need to know where my little girl is!" Her eyes were bloodshot. That and the dark circles under her eyes illustrated a worn-out, cried out mother sick with worry about where her daughter was. Hank did not look much better.

"Ambassador, I just got her back after all those years," Hank pleaded. "You must tell me anything you know!"

"All right, Mr. Mackenzie. Until yesterday, our prevailing theory was that it was the Jistari—"

"Those, like, space ninjas, right?" Hank said.

"Yes, but this morning, we got word that other teams of former Contest winners also vanished from their planets. They never had any contact with the Jistari."

"So, now you're thinking, what, it has something to do with that Contest they were in?"

"Yes, that's what we are now thinking."

"Bitter former Contest losers?" Hank asked.

"Well, yes, most likely, but we're talking about *hundreds* of teams it could have been. Although we have narrowed that list down to about fifty-three teams, or planets, that were really bitter about losing, planets that suffered the catastrophes we could have helped them with."

"There was also that one winning team," Coordinator Philk said.

"A winning team?" Hank looked confused. "Why would a winning team do this?"

"There was a team that won the Contest," Harklon said, "and our solution made things worse, and they hated us after that. But it was over a century ago."

"Ambassador, there's an expression on our planet, 'revenge is a dish best-served cold.'"

"We are aware of the expression, Mr. Mackenzie, but the Hellkorians are extinct by now. Or, they *should* be. They could no longer conceive new children, and all the Hellkorians who were alive at the time should be dead by now. Their normal lifespan was about seventy years. Trust us. It's not them. It has to be one of the Contest losers. There's one particular planet that's at the top of the list, Fenzzera, a highly technological species that specialized in cloaking tech, but they lost two years ago. An asteroid hit their planet and did catastrophic damage. If they'd won, we would have helped them avoid the collision."

"Well, I can see why they'd be pissed!" Emma exclaimed.

"Honestly, why do you people do that? Why don't you help them all?!"

"We help those that are worthy," Coordinator Philk answered. "They lost the Contest, they weren't worthy. Until recently, they traded in wars and genocide."

Hank sighed and shook his head. "So do *we*," he said under his breath.

"Yes, but be very proud of your daughter and her teammates. They showed that you humans have great potential for compassion and reason. She is the primary reason that your planet's team won."

Hank suddenly got choked up. "That's my girl!" He sniffed. Emma grabbed him and hugged him.

"We're proud of her, too!" Emma said.

Hank looked at the computer again. He wiped his eyes. "So you're gonna check out the…the…Fender…"

"Fenzzera, and yes, we are investigating them, as well as about a dozen other planets simultaneously. Now, if you will please excuse us, we have a meeting scheduled with Mrs. Thompson in a few minutes. We are doing everything we can to find your daughter. I believe that we will prevail in doing that. Harklon out."

Hank closed the laptop lid. "I dunno. My money is on those Contest winners. Those, um, Hell people."

"But they said that it couldn't be them."

"Well, just imagine how pissed off we would be at them if that carbon capture machine they gave us suddenly made the climate *worse*."

Emma breathed deeply. She slowly let it out. "Whoever it is, what could they be doing with them? I mean…why haven't they contacted anybody? Demanded a ransom? I don't understand these *aliens*…any of them!"

Hank hugged his wife close. "Have faith, honey. Have faith that they'll find her. I do."

"I do, too," Emma said. "Oh god…just think. If they hadn't time-traveled the first two times, how worried we would have been while she was gone, especially the *first* time!"

"You were," Hank said, "I mean like…in another timeline, like before she came back." He shook his head. "Thinking about time travel stuff makes my head hurt."

"Maybe…maybe all this will be erased? They'll time travel

again?"

"No, not this time," Hank said. "They said no time travel this time because they weren't in control of the event in which they left. Or some crap like that."

"Oh honey…this is so much worse than her being kidnapped by some human! Aliens, they're, well, so alien to us! And she could be so far away! Like…a thousand light years or something!" She broke down, weeping into her husband's shoulder.

Hank let her cry for a moment. But then he nuzzled her slightly away so he could look into her eyes. "Hey, listen to me. Our daughter is tough. She learned how to fight, martial arts, how to use weapons before that quest they had. They tell me that she is a *badass* now. Remember that. Alice is a badass now. She's gonna make it! Believe me!"

Emma nodded. "Right…she…" She actually stopped crying to chuckle a little. "She told me that she shocked the British girl by beating her once. And that girl had trained almost all her life." She chuckled again. "That's our Alice. Always full of surprises!"

"Yes, she never fails to surprise us," Hank said as he stroked her back. "That's why we'll see her again."

They heard their front door open and close. "Am I too late?" It was Cassie.

"Sorry, Cass, you just missed it!" Hank said.

"Dammit!" Cassie came into the kitchen and threw her purse down. "I couldn't get out of class in time. What did they say?"

"They have some theories as to who took them," Emma answered, "but nothing solid. They have some suspects. Well…suspect planets."

"Do you think they'll find her?"

"Yes!"

"We do!" Hank added.

"I'm so scared for her! If I lose my sister, I don't know what I'll do! She's my best friend!"

Emma hugged her other daughter.

"They'll find her," Emma whispered. "I have to believe that they will."

"We were just talking about how she's full of surprises," Hank said. "So we expect her to surprise us and get home. Maybe tomorrow."

"She never stopped surprising us!" Emma said with a sad smile. "Like, remember when she was seven and went missing? And we panicked? But it turned out she was just bringing the cookies we'd just baked down to the senior center home down the road?"

Cassie chuckled. "Oh my god we used to tell that story at like every holiday gathering!"

"Very few people I know have a heart like hers," Hank said.

#

Meanwhile, back on Hellkor, at that moment, Alice was grabbing a large rock off of the ground.

"Die, you piece of shit!" She threw the rock right at the orb.

It barely missed.

#

Back in Oregon, her family traded more surprising Alice stories.

"Remember the time she was sixteen, and they accidentally gave us that Indian movie channel in our satellite TV feed?" Cassie said. "And they were playing that Indian romance movie, and it was like all in Farsi. But Alice actually understood some of what they were saying?" She was looking at both her parents, but she momentarily forgot that her father wasn't there for that one.

"I, uh, would have loved to have seen that," Hank said. He almost got choked up again.

"Oh! Daddy! I'm so sorry!"

"No, no, Cash, it's okay! I…I want to hear all about what I missed! I want all the stories from all of you, about all of you!"

Ever since Hank returned to their lives, they had spent many dinners and nights reminiscing, telling stories about all the years he'd missed. They'd even touched on the time that Alice had attempted suicide, which was a very tough and emotional discussion. But there was still a lot he didn't know, the good and the bad.

Emma kissed her husband. "Hank, when Alice gets back, we'll have another story session, okay?"

"Yes. *When* she gets back."

#

"Well, I think it's those bloody Hellkorians, if you ask me, not the people who got asteroid-smashed!" Julia yelled into her iPad as she had her video conference with Ambassador Harklon and Coordinator Philk. "I mean, if that happened to Earth, that'd definitely nark *me* off! See if *they* have my daughter!"

"Like we said, they're all extinct," Harklon said.

"Well, listen, we have those *Star Trek* shows here on Earth, and I watched some episodes of that one…from back in the eighties… nineties…oh, boy, that bald guy, he was dead sexy he was," Julia said as she sipped her wine. "I mean, whoo! He could get in *my* knickers, lemme tell ya!"

"Uhhh, Mrs. Thompson…"

"Anyway! Listen to me! All right! There was this episode, they were on an alien planet, and all the aliens that were on it were extinct, yeah, like this…Hell Oreos place…and and but the aliens left behind their computers and such. 'Kay? And it was some kind of artificial intelligence, and it kept making trouble after the actual aliens who built it were gone!"

"Wait. So, Mrs. Thompson, if I understand you correctly, you suggest the Hellkorians might all be gone, but maybe they left behind a malevolent A.I.?"

"Well, you said the people who kidnapped them had some sort of super-advanced tech, right? Well, now…" she stopped to take in a gulp of her wine. She quickly swallowed it. She dribbled a little, and she wiped it with her sleeve. "…So, like, if it's *them*, you see, then maybe they *did* do something like that!"

"Actually, that's an intriguing idea, Mrs. Thompson," Ambassador Harklon said.

Julia looked at her wineglass. "And they tell me drinking too much of this is killing my brain cells! Bollocks!"

"Uh, well, we will take your suggestion into consider—"

"Ambassador!" Julia put down her wineglass and brought her face closer to her screen. She suddenly sobbed. "Please find my daughter! She's all I have! You've got to find her!"

"Mrs. Thompson, I assure you, we are doing everything in our power to find her, we promise you!"

"She's literally the best human being I know! She's got so much talent, so much potential! I love her to pieces!" Her sobs got so heavy that they dragged her below her camera.

"Our hearts break for you," Coordinator Philk said softly. "We have faith that we will find her and find all of them. I know this is difficult, but please be patient if you can."

Julia came back up on camera. "Please find her quickly. And thank you."

"We have literally hundreds of people working this problem," Harklon said. "We'll find them. I must go now. Harklon out."

#

Phyllis, Darnell, Marvin, and Min also had a meeting that day with Ambassador Harklon and Coordinator Philk. Min was at Jamar's family home, and Phyllis routed it to their television so that they could all participate easily. Jamar's father, Trent, zoomed in from his office. His wanting to take part surprised Phyllis somewhat, as he had seen none of the boys for several months.

"Are you any closer to finding him?" was one of Phyllis's first questions. It was a sunny spring day out. The sunlight came through the windows so brightly that they had to draw the curtains half-closed so it wasn't hard to see the TV. The cheery weather contrasted with the gloomy emotions of everybody in the room.

"We have some ideas," Harklon began. Then they told them their theories about the losing planets, Fenzzera, the asteroid, and the planet Hellkor.

"So, Fenzerra, if…if that asteroid was as bad as you say it was, wouldn't it have disrupted their technological infrastructure too much to be able to pull this off?" Phyllis asked. "I mean, you said it was only two years ago."

"Yeah, they shouldn't be able to do any of that stuff," Trent said.

"But their amazing development into cloaking technologies is the reason they're a primary candidate," Harklon argued. "And whoever did this was cloaked very well. They even cloaked their vessel's radiation signature, which is very difficult to do."

"I dunno," Marvin said. "My money is on one of those other losers, or maybe that Hell place. The name fits!"

"I agree," Min said. "Yeah, that Hellkor planet. Please look into that one. Please find him!"

"The Mackenzies and Mrs. Thompson also think that planet is a stronger candidate," Philk said. "But like we told them, the Hellko-rians should be extinct."

"But look into it, just in case," Phyllis said. "I mean, you are doing that, right? You cannot leave any stone unturned! Please find my son! I am literally worried sick over this!"

"We are turning over…all the stones," said Harklon, who was unfamiliar with the human expression but figured it out. "We assure you, we are doing everything we can. We have hundreds of people working on this problem. We will find your son. We will find your brother. We will find your boyfriend."

"You'd better find my son!" Trent exclaimed, his bearded, weathered face puckered in anger. "All this shit is all you alien fools' fault!"

"Trent, please chill," Phyllis said. "You've barely talked to him since all this alien stuff began!"

"Not this crap again," Trent said, "you know those fools I supervise at the plant keep me busy as hell, incompetent millennials!"

"Dad, this isn't the time for this!" Marvin exclaimed.

"He just showed up to *show* that he cares!" Darnell said. "But does he *really*?"

"Of course I do!" Trent yelled. "How could you say that?"

"Enough, okay?" Phyllis said, quickly pointing to the screen, then at her sons. "The aliens don't need to see this tired old family argument! They need to find Jamar! Zip it, you three!"

Trent sighed and looked down. "I'm sorry."

"Um, yes, finding Jamar is our primary concern," Harklon said. "Now, if you could please—"

"Please find Jammy!" Min suddenly pleaded. "I'm so worried about him!"

Ambassador Harklon raised their eyebrows. "Jammy?"

"It's her cute nickname for him!" Darnell said. "If he…" he hesitated, cleared his throat, then continued, "*when* he comes back, I plan on makin' fun of him for it."

"WHEN he comes back!" Phyllis said, looking sternly at her son.

"Yeah, *when*!" Trent exclaimed.

"Mama, he's coming back," Marvin said. "We all believe he is."

Phyllis put her hand on his. "Thank you." She hugged him.

"We have two more meetings to get to," Harklon said, "so we

need to get to them—"

"Two?" Phyllis said. "I mean…the Hendersons, and then… *who else*?"

"The Chases."

"*You found them?*" Phyllis replied with a surprised look on her face.

"*They* found *us*," Harklon replied. "When they saw the media coverage of the abduction, they came out of their hiding. Now, please excuse us, we have to go. Remember, we are working hard on finding them. And we will. Harklon out."

"I'm out, too," Trent mumbled. "Break's over anyways." He blipped off the screen.

Phyllis rolled her eyes and sighed.

"Wow," Darnell said. "That Chase dude's been lookin' for his parents for years."

"Well, I'm glad for him, but they better find my son!" Phyllis said. Tears came to her eyes. She pointed at the television, even though it was now off. "It is their fault my son was involved in any of this alien stuff in the first place!"

"But it's helping the Earth, Mama," Marvin said. "They made him into a hero."

"Maybe they made him *dead*, Marvin! Maybe my son is *dead*!"

"Hey," said Min. "I thought we were being optimistic!" Tears came to her eyes. She sniffed.

Phyllis looked down. She sighed. "I'm sorry, Min. You're right. We need to be optimistic."

"He'll be back, Mom," Darnell said, "he will."

#

"Why couldn't you protect my son?!" John yelled at Ambassador Harklon. "I mean, why didn't you have some sort of…I dunno… force field preventing anybody from just being like…beamed up and captured like that?!"

Unlike in Philadelphia, it was thundering and raining in St. Louis. The weather matched the mood of Wyatt's parents.

"Mr. Henderson," Harklon began, "there was a scattering field around the courthouse like we always have around government and judicial buildings, but we do not have one all over the planet. It would take too much energy to maintain. The other teams that were captured were abducted from their home planets. If the humans had been on Earth, they would have been abducted just the same."

"But your prosecution argued in court that the surveillance of Chloe was legal because the humans were under your *protection*!" Christine exclaimed. "So, was my son under your protection or not?!"

"Mrs. Henderson, we assure you, we took all measures that we could think of for their safety like we do for all of our guests. What happened was something that we simply could not have anticipated. We went over most of this in our previous conference. Today, we want to update you on new developments in the search."

"Fine!" John yelled. "What are they?"

Ambassador Harklon told them what he'd told the other families about the suspected losing planets, as well as Hellkor.

"So you guys let an asteroid hit a planet full of people?!" John said. "Yeah, it's probably them! I can tell you that Earth would be furious with you over that! I don't know where you people get off—"

"Honey, please!" Christine said. "They are trying to find Wyatt! Our son! Please, calm down. They're trying to help us." She turned back to their laptop monitor. "Please tell me you're investigating all the leads, even that Hellkor place."

"We are, Mrs. Henderson, we are doing everything we can to find them, including investigating *all* leads."

"I'm sorry, Ambassador, we just don't trust you," John said, still angry. "Wyatt told me that stone quest thing was a sham, that your government lied to them."

"Mr. Henderson, that whole incident was regrettable," Harklon replied. "We plan on making amends for that…"

"Was arresting his girlfriend and threatening her with a long prison time part of those *amends*?"

"She was accused of committing a very serious crime, Mr. Henderson!" Coordinator Philk spoke up. "The enhancement serum—"

"Stop, Philk, enough," Harklon said, holding up a hand. "We do not need to go down that road. What I want to tell you is when we locate and rescue the humans, we plan on offering them compensation for the mistake with the Loovestone quest. Karak was getting something together when they were abducted with the others. It was to be their final act as the *Arkenstar* Ambassador."

"Why was Karak fired?" Christine asked.

"They weren't 'fired' as you humans say. Karak still works for the space station. They will just play a different role now. But this call wasn't to discuss our space station employment. We just wanted to update you on the search, which we have done."

"Do you think you're close?" John asked.

"We believe we are…closer," Harklon said. "I mean, closer than we were a few days ago. We will figure it out soon, I promise you. Now, we must go. We are meeting with one more family."

John thought about that for a second. "Mackenzies, Thompsons, Nelsons, us…well, who's left? Chase doesn't have a family. Does he?"

"He does. We're going to talk to his parents. They tried to contact us yesterday."

"He's been looking for them for a long time!" Christine said.

"And when we find your son and his friends, Mr. Chase will be reunited with them. Now we must go. Harklon out."

#

Lydia and Matthew, Chase's parents, would not be in the same room or even in the same house for the video conference. They had divorced years ago. Lydia was at her house in Mississauga, sitting at her kitchen counter on her iPad, waiting for the call to come. Matthew was on his laptop in his study at his house in Toronto.

Finally, the call came. Both of them answered.

"Mr. and Mrs. Chase, I presume?" Ambassador Harklon said.

"Well, actually, I go by my maiden name now, Finley," Lydia said. "But yes, I am Jacob's mother."

"And I'm his father," Matthew said.

"Oh, I apologize about the name, Ms. Finley. We forget that humans sometimes change their names. I am Ambassador Harklon. This is my associate, Coordinator Philk. We have talked to all the other families today. You were last on the list. To be honest with you, we hadn't anticipated speaking with you today. Mr. Chase has been looking for you two for quite some time."

"What happened with our son? Well, it's kind of a long story," Matthew said. He sighed and looked down.

Lydia sipped a steaming mug of tea that she was drinking that afternoon. "Jacob was…well…*difficult.*"

Matthew rubbed his tired eyes. "To put it mildly."

"I am video conferencing with aliens," Lydia said. "This is not how I ever thought I'd spend a Thursday afternoon."

"It's probably a lot to process," Ambassador Harklon said. "We talk to other alien species daily, so we no longer experience the novelty of it, but I can imagine it must be a lot for you."

"When we saw on the news what happened," Lydia replied, "I just…I mean, I still love my son! And…when the news said that he and his friends were abducted, I just knew it was time, time to stop hiding, to help in any way I could."

"I felt the same way," Matthew said. "I will never stop loving my son. But…it seemed like he had stopped loving us."

"I would think that the fact that he was still searching for you would indicate that he did," Harklon replied, "and likewise, we will not stop searching for him."

"Please find him!" Lydia said. "Do you have any theories as to who took them?"

Harklon told them what they'd told the other families.

"Listen, just find him, please, I don't care which one of them did it," Matthew said.

"I feel the same way," Lydia said.

"We will," Ambassador Harklon said, "we promise you."

Soon, the call ended. And it ended just in time.

"Ambassador!" Philk said as a call was coming in. "The Fenzzera are returning our call!"

"Good, good, maybe we'll finally make some progress in this investigation. Put them on screen."

Their viewscreen came alive again. On it stood a member of an alien species that they hadn't seen in a few years. He was dark-skinned, had a few forehead ridges, and had antennae where most humanoids had ears.

"Hello," Ambassador Harklon said, "we are glad that you called us back. We have some questions—"

"Let me just say that the only reason we are calling you back is morbid curiosity!" the alien man said. "Like, why the hell are you contacting us, expecting us to answer or call back, after what happened?!"

"Look, I am Ambassador Harklon, this is my associate, Coordinator Philk, we have an inquiry for you. Would you please tell us your name?"

"I am Governor Darr," he replied. "I am trying to run what is left of our society! After an asteroid hit us that *you* allowed!"

"Governor Darr, first of all, you have our greatest sympathies for what happened, but we did not send that asteroid to your planet. But we do understand why you're upset with us. Which leads to our inquiry."

"Fine! What is your question, *Deelooveren*?" Darr said their species name as if there was poison in his mouth.

"Recently, last year's Contest-winning team, and many other winning teams from the past, were all abducted. We don't know where they are. Given how bitter your people are toward us—"

"Oh, you have got to be kidding me!" Darr exclaimed. "After letting our entire society almost die, now you insult us by asking if we abducted some aliens we've never even heard of?! Are you serious?!"

"So you had nothing to do with their abductions?"

"Of course not! I guess you don't know because you probably don't care, we've been a bit busy down here! Like trying to rebuild almost our entire society! Dealing with massive climate upheavals! As much as we would actually like to hurt and embarrass you, you're not worth our time! We've got more important things to do than petty revenge plots!"

"So we have just your word on that?"

Darr held out his arms and shook his head. "Well what else do you want from me, from us? Why do you suspect us, with all the other losing teams you've failed to help, whose societies are in shambles now?"

"Your cloaking technology was top tier," Coordinator Philk answered. "Whoever pulled this crime off had excellent cloaking tech. Could there be splinter factions on your planet that your government doesn't—"

"Again, we are too busy, and I mean *all* of us, too busy for that shit! We barely even have any of our technology anymore! You were lucky that we even had the ability to respond to your call. Now leave us alone!" Darr angrily pushed a button, and then he was gone.

"Well," Harklon said, "they were not pleased to hear from us."

"Are we supposed to just take him on his word, the word of an angry government official?"

"No, of course not, we have a ship secretly headed there to run a deep scan of their planet, to look for evidence of what technology they have and search for life signs of any species that's not supposed to be there."

"And Hellkor?"

"Hellkor is over sixty light years away! The president does not want to investigate that lead until we're sure, until we've at least eliminated the Fenzzerans. It'd take a lot of antimatter to go there and back, and we're using a lot right now on the scout ships who are out there finding good candidates for the next Contest."

"But, the next Contest is only five months away. They don't have candidates already?"

"Well, we *do*, but we needed a second run around. We're still investigating the fifth and final planet. Look, this isn't an easy task for me, taking over from Karak this late in the game. I have a lot of catching up to do."

"Well, are there any interesting candidates?"

"Oh yes, a few. There's a species that we've had before in the Contest. The Treylariens. We're giving them another shot. Oh, and also the Skozz. We're giving them another shot, too."

"Why? Why two repeats? We almost never have repeats. But two in one year?"

Harklon glanced around to make sure nobody else was entering the control room. "Look, the truth is, we're running out of planets inhabited by sentient species to choose from. At least in this quadrant of the galaxy. We fear that we're going to start having many repeats. After doing the Contest for so long, this problem was inevitable."

"So, we just…go beyond this quadrant then?"

"We cannot go that far out, not to areas the wormhole network doesn't go to."

"Well, then, what do we do? Do you think that maybe we will just not do the annual Contest anymore?"

Harklon shook their head. "The president and some other higher officials are investigating some intriguing solutions. For years they've been working on a means to travel to other dimensions, other realities. We may be close to opening up such gateways. This could open up almost endless possibilities for planets for the Contest. Maybe even alternative versions of planets we've already had."

Philk opened their eyes wide in wonder. "Intriguing possibilities indeed!"

Ambassador Harklon sighed. They looked at their handlink. "Oh, look. We have more calls to make. The Fargles and the Doo'chen families want to talk. And…the Wistwills? Is that right? They were abducted? I'm surprised that the entire team is still alive."

"They won seventy-five years ago! I'm surprised, too."

"I hope we get this figured out soon and get them home," Harklon said. "If this goes bad, I mean really bad, it would be a huge tragedy. I don't want any of them to die. But if it goes really bad, it could put the whole future of the Contest in jeopardy."

CHAPTER TWELVE: Obstacles

ALICE TRIED to stop the orb from taking Wyatt by throwing rocks at it, but she missed. Other aliens at the campsite tried, but they missed, too.

"Oh god," Wyatt said as the beam of light from the orb enveloped him.

"No!" Chloe screamed.

Seeka also found herself beaming away. The beaming light also surrounded Took'chee, the Doo'chen strategist. Streen, the Norfan strategist, and Johanne, the Wistwill strategist, also began beaming away. Finally, Karak started beaming away.

"We have to stop it!" Captain Flarr yelled.

"How?!" Assistant Meel exclaimed.

"Let's do what the humans are doing!" Coordinator Jeelork yelled as they picked up a rock.

"I hate you!" Chloe screamed at the orb. She also tossed a rock at it. It dodged the rock. As all the strategists—and the Fargle scientist—beamed away, many more rocks flew toward the orb.

Soon, the orb quickly ascended away.

Chloe fell to her knees. She felt broken and helpless. Jamar walked up to her. He put his hand on her shoulder and whispered, "Chloe, he injected himself right as he was about to beam away. He's got the superpowers again. He'll be all right. We're gonna beat this thing now."

"But he can still die," Chloe whimpered. "What are they gonna do to him, Jamar?"

"Nothing," he replied. "I mean, nothing right now. It's got a game it wants us to play. We won't play it if it kills him. Hold onto that, Chloe. He's alright for now."

Chloe got up and hugged Jamar tightly. She sobbed. "I can't do this anymore."

Jamar hugged her tightly. Then he whispered into her ear, "Listen, we have an advantage now. We have the serum. And the thieves are secretly hatching a plan to somehow capture the orb. We're gonna beat this thing, ya hear? We're gonna win this contest, too. Okay?"

Alice approached them and whispered, "Are you sure there's not enough of the plant to make serum for everybody else?"

Jamar shook his head. "*No*. Not that we could find. Another reason to keep a tight lid on this."

Barchell screamed and threw his rock into the fire, causing a plume of sparks to jump out of it. "It's just me! You all still have teams…more or less! But it's up to me now, just me, to save my last teammate!"

"This isn't fair. None of it is," said Farrstead, who was nearby. "And that's the point. Whatever challenge is up ahead, you can do it."

"Farrstead's right, and they're pretty smart," said Alice. "They were our fifth teammate for two rounds of the Contest, so I should know." She smiled at them. Farrstead smiled back.

Chase patted Barchell on the back. "We have your back, Barch. If there's any way we can help you, we will." But then he lowered his voice to a whisper. "And we have that plan, too, don't forget. I think it can work."

Barchell looked at him and slowly nodded.

Chloe and Jamar approached them. "Alice, Chase, we need to have a discussion." Jamar pointed back toward their usual spot at the campfire.

Once they were all there, Jamar whispered to them. "Let's all inject before this new, fresh hell begins. But listen, we can't use the serum in any obvious way. We can't show all our cards. Not yet. So no super speed. Got it?"

Chloe, Alice, and Chase nodded in agreement. Then, they all discreetly got their doses out of their pockets and injected them.

"We're gonna get through this," Jamar said. "We get through this thing, whatever it is, but hopefully, this is the last horrible thing we will let it put us through." He put his fist out. Chloe, Chase, and Alice all fist-bumped him.

"You're right, Jamar, last one," Alice said. "We'll save Wyatt.

We'll get through this. Team Earth: ride or die."

"Ride or die," the others echoed her. But Chloe still looked upset. Her eyes were wet.

Alice reached up and gently put her hands on Chloe's arms. "Hey," she whispered, "Jamar is right. We can do this. Okay? We got this. We need to be strong. Are you ready to be strong?"

Chloe slowly nodded her head. Alice reached up to her eyes and wiped her tears away. Alice then reached up and kissed her on the cheek. "Love you," she whispered.

"Love you, too," Chloe whispered. Then, they both hugged each other tightly.

"Should we hug?" Chase asked Jamar.

Jamar looked at him, a slightly amused look on his face. "Why not, man?"

"Okay," Chase said. Then they both hugged, too. They patted each other's backs. "We got this, big man."

"Yes, whatever it is, we got this."

Chase sighed. "So, umm, have you noticed that all these days with no showers, getting dirty and sweaty, we're all getting pretty ripe?"

"Yup," Jamar said, "and I really wanna stop huggin' now." They both chuckled and separated.

Alice and Chloe separated. Alice waved her hand in front of her nose. "Well, I'm glad that *somebody* finally said it!"

Chloe smiled at her. "Oh, that is coming up your own collar. You smell *way* worse than me." She then pinched her own nose with her fingers. They both laughed.

"No, Chloe, you win the stink contest, trust me!"

Chase sniffed Alice and then Chloe. "Sorry, babe, you're stink-ier," he said to Alice.

"Jacob!" Alice got a mock look of anger on her face.

"Well, only by a *little*!"

"Whatever!" Alice rolled her eyes and then laughed. She made the letter "W" with her hands. As a cloud rolled away from the moon, they got a really good look at each other. They all noticed just how dirty they actually *looked*. And most of them had quite a bit of damage on their uniforms.

"We look like hell," Chase commented.

"Well, we're *in* Hell," Jamar said.

"At least any cuts and bruises we had are gone now," Alice whispered.

Slank lumbered up to them. "You *all* stink!"

Alice stuck her fist out, then with her other hand, pantomimed turning a crank, and she slowly raised her middle finger up at him. Chase chuckled.

The orb descended. But it didn't come as low as it usually did. "If you want to save your friends, follow me!" It drifted away from them, toward the edge of the campsite.

Alice shrugged at her teammates. They all rolled their eyes and shrugged, too. They followed the orb. So did all the others.

They began a trek through the thick forest ahead. The further they headed away from the campfire, the colder the air and the darker the night got.

"Where the bloody hell are we going?" Chloe whispered. The moon above provided little light, as the tree cover above became thick. They could barely see where they were going. But they kept following the orb, which only provided a minuscule amount of additional light.

They had to push past thick brush and tall grass to continue the walk. Many of them, including Alice, tripped and almost fell. Slank's hulking figure had little an issue with the thick foliage. Strange, alien-sounding birds cooed, cawed, and screeched at them. The buzzing and chirping of alien insects increased in volume and thickness as they continued. The thick forest surrounded them with earthy, mossy, and various floral odors.

Soon, the brush got thick enough that they all had to use their knives as small machetes to clear it from out in front of them. Barchell accidentally nicked Alice in her arm once in a clearing attempt. She winced in pain.

"Careful, Barchell!" But then he saw it. He saw the tiny cut disappear. He pointed at it and looked her in the eyes. Alice gave him a stern but pleading look. She subtly and slowly shook her head.

He got the message. Alice breathed a sigh of relief, and they moved on.

#

Soon, the forest thinned out. They came upon an open area that was well lit by the moon. But the relief they all felt was short-lived.

Several meters in front of them was a stream. Mist, or maybe steam, curled upward from it. It was bubbling, but worryingly, it also hissed. A strong acidic odor wafting from it strung their noses. Beyond the stream, there was a straight line of bushes. The humans used their super vision to check them out. There were hives of flying insects in the bushes.

Beyond the bushes, the ground ended. There was a cavern there, with ropes connecting the side they were on to the other side. Then, they saw the worst sight. At the tops of small stone pyramids were their teammates. They were all spread-eagle and tied to the pyramids by their arms and legs. There were gags in their mouths.

Even though the other aliens didn't have the super vision, they apparently could still see that well enough, as everybody gasped in fear when they saw it.

"Do you all like obstacle courses?" the orb asked. "Our research tells me that most of you have them on your planets for various reasons. Well, it's time to have some real fun. First, you must cross the stream. Don't worry, it's not very deep, and the current isn't very strong. It should be super easy...well, it would be if the water in the stream wasn't filled with highly corrosive acid, that is. The first challenge is to get through the stream quickly enough so it doesn't melt your boots and then your feet!"

"Jesus Christ," Chase whispered.

"Brilliant idea for a water park," Slank mumbled.

"Oh, shut up, will you?!" Chloe yelled. She wanted to punch his punk mouth right off.

"Then after you survive that, which you might not, just being honest, you have to go past the bushes. Those bushes are filled with hives of bizzers. If you thought the *sniggles* were mean, wait until you meet those little bastards! They will attack you. And their stings have nasty venom that will cause unbearable pain across your nervous systems. You have to run past the bushes fast enough because if you get too many stings, all your body's vital systems will start to shut down, and you will perish. But don't worry! If you survive that one, the next obstacle is easy! Well, comparatively. Nothing will try to attack you or melt your feet. You have to walk across the cavern on the ropes.

"How good is your balance? Time to find out! But don't fall! The cavern's bottom is a *very* long way down. And then, finally, you can get to the pyramids, climb up the vines, and rescue your friends. But you have to be careful not to let any of the thorns on the vines penetrate your skin. They will cause immense pain. They won't kill you, though. So that's good, right?"

"This is some got damn bullshit," Jamar whispered. "Seriously."

"Tightrope artists take *years* to master that!" Chase exclaimed. "How the hell are any of us supposed to do that?!"

"You're more worried about *that* than the acid stream or the friggin' bizzers?" Alice asked.

"Maybe the orb will let us scoot across it?" Chloe said.

"I sure hope so," Jamar said. "But I have a really bad feeling that it won't."

Farine approached them. "That one will be easy for me," she whispered, "provided that the acid stream doesn't destroy my feet. I wish there was time for me to teach all of you how. All I can do is tell you not to look down. Those ropes are thick enough. One foot in front of the other. Just, whatever you do, do *not* look straight down. Just stare at the rope ahead. Got it?"

Farine went around giving the same advice to everybody.

"I'm gonna die!" Jamar whimpered.

Alice jumped up and grabbed his collar, yanked him down to be eye-level with her, and looked him straight in his eyes. "No, you are *not*, Nelson! You will *not* die! You hear me?! You can *do* this!"

"The cavern isn't very wide," Chase said. "Looks like we only have to traverse about ten meters. Alice is right. We can do it."

"Well!" the orb yelled. "What are you all waiting for? There's a time limit of twenty minutes. Better hurry!"

Everybody approached the stream. Farine looked nervous. "I can dance across this. I think."

"You *can*," Alice said. She grabbed Farine's hand. "You're going to dance across it so gracefully it'll be like you're actually walking on the water."

"It'll be like magic, Farine," Chase said. He grabbed her other hand.

Farine smiled. "We can *all* do it, my cuties."

"Stop calling everybody a cutie!" Slank exclaimed. "God, that's annoying! You greenies are very annoying."

Farine stuck her tongue out at him.

"Let's just do it!" Woo'cha exclaimed. "Let's just get this shit over with!" He headed for the stream and ran across it. When he was almost across, he screamed in pain. He stumbled once he reached the other side. He fell on his backside. One of his feet was steaming. When he held it up, they could see that the bottom of his boot was eaten away.

"He got across quickly," Alice said. "He might be fine. But he splashed a lot."

Faa'lark and Murr started sprinting across. But they splashed too much water. They splashed each other, and they screamed in pain. Murr collapsed onto the ground on the other side, grabbing his face with his hand. Faa'lark grabbed his hairy arm.

Slank couldn't help it. He laughed. "Idiots!"

"Everybody else, listen up!" Coordinator Jeelork yelled. "One at a time! We've got to do this one at a time!" They held up a finger. "Are we clear?"

Alice looked at Murr. When he moved his hand, she could see the spot on his face where his flesh was badly burned. "Oh my god!"

"Well, who's next?" Jamar asked.

Farine raised her hand. "Let me go next!" Nobody objected.

Farine swayed her hips and moved her feet around. Then she took in a deep breath and quickly danced across the stream. She barely splashed. Farine yelped in pain when she got to the other side. She limped a little, but she yelled back to them, "I'm fine, just a little burn on my left foot!"

"Well, that's disappointing," Slank said.

"I'll go next!" Farrstead said, raising their hand. They sprinted across on their tip-toes. They screamed in pain when they were almost across. They fell to the ground, yelling, "Shoovignas! Shoovignas!"

"We better move this along," Jamar exclaimed. "We'll run outta time! Jeelork, we should do two at a time, but far enough away from each other."

"Good idea, Mr. Nelson!" Jeelork agreed. "You heard the man! Two at a time, but plenty of distance between each other!"

"Let's go," Alice said to Chase. "Both of us, together."

"How romantic," Chase said. He held up his hand. Alice did, too. "We're next!"

They spread out until they stood about ten feet apart. They looked at each other with love in their eyes. They ran across the stream.

Nearly across, Alice's feet burned. It was like running across boiling water. She screamed, stumbling. Jacob yelled in pain too.

"Jacob, it hurts!" Alice said, sitting on the ground. She looked at her feet. Most of her boot bottoms were eaten away. Her foot pads were bright red with gnarly blisters.

"Hurts like a bitch!" Chase exclaimed. His boots and feet were in the same condition.

Alice quickly scooted to be closer to him. She whispered into his ear. "Hide your feet…*now*!"

Both of them quickly hid their feet as the blisters started healing.

"Bloody hell!" Chloe screamed as she and Jamar came running across.

"Son of a bitch!" Jamar yelled. They collapsed to their knees near their teammates.

Chloe examined her feet. "I just got this foot!"

Murr looked over at Chloe. "What?"

"Never mind!" Chloe yelled.

Slank poised himself to run across. "My turn now, I guess." He ran across. He did it easily. He chuckled when he reached the other side. Slank noticed surprised onlookers. He smiled and lifted his feet up. "Extra thick boots! Think about buying a pair!"

More of the other aliens, two by two, made it across the stream. Soon, the Wistwills were the only three left. They looked terrified to cross. The one that was in the hover chair was being held up by the other two. His hover chair was nearby, destroyed. The orb must have destroyed it. The smoke from the smoldering, sizzling former transportation machine mixed with the white steam from the acidic stream.

"They're so old they must not move very fast," Alice said. The Wistwills stood on the edge of the steaming stream, their scared faces highlighted and shadowed by the moonlight. Jonnifer nervously gripped one of the small, scraggly trees growing near the edge. In eerie timing, they heard a sad, dove-like call from one of the native birds.

"I am really afraid that they won't make it," Chase said. "And those damned Hellkorians destroyed that one's hover chair. This is pure evil!"

"Let's help them somehow," Alice suggested.

"How?" Chloe asked.

"Carry them," Alice whispered. "We can do it." And then, she added, as quietly as her voice box could talk, "And we'll be fine."

"Will the orb let us?" Chase wondered.

"Let's find out," Jamar said. "We're runnin' outta time."

"Philly is right," said Slank, "this is a waste of time! But whatever. I don't care."

Slank stayed behind, but the four of them walked over to the other side of the stream, near where the Wistwills stood. All three wept.

"We're going to help you!" Alice called to them.

"No!" Jonnifer said. "That's very kind of you, but you won't survive going across twice more. We can't ask that of you! We can't let you!"

"We can!" Chloe said. "Trust us, we can!"

"How old are you?" Jonnifer asked.

"I'm twenty years old."

"You're all around that age, aren't you?"

"We are," Chase replied.

"We are all over ninety years old. We've lived a very long life. You four are still so young. We can't let you do this!"

"The clock is ticking," Jamar said.

"If we don't let our secret out, they're gonna die," Alice whispered.

"Listen," Chase said. "We can help you, and we will be fine. We beg you to trust our word on that. Please. Let us help you."

The Wistwills looked at each other. They looked back at the humans. "All right, let's do it," Jonnifer said. "And...*thank you.*"

The humans, one by one, sprinted across the stream. It burned their feet again, and they all yelled in pain. It took them a few minutes, but they stood back up. Chase and Alice grabbed the one that couldn't walk. Jamar and Chloe each let the other two climb onto their backs.

The orb appeared. Its light started flashing. "Okay, you know what? We will allow this. But they won't survive the bizzers!" It ascended.

It was difficult and badly burned their feet again, but the humans got the three Wistwills across the stream.

Chase looked down. Not much was left of his boots. "We're pretty much barefoot now. Is that going to make the rope thing worse or better?"

"Better, I hope," Alice replied.

All of them approached the bushes.

"This is gonna suck more," Jamar mumbled.

Chase grabbed Alice's hand. "I'm terrified."

"Honey…"

"The Phobia Room could have shown me a nest of wasps. I…I can't do this." A tear came down his cheek.

Alice gripped his hand tighter. "You can do this, baby."

"I can't!" Chase exclaimed. "Flying, stinging insects…oh god, it's one of the few things that terrifies me, Al."

She whispered in his ear. "We'll be okay. We can do this. We will heal. Come on. For Wyatt. He needs us, Jacob. Let's do it. We will cross it together. Don't let go of my hand. Okay?"

"It scares the bejeezus outta me, too," Jamar whispered, "but we must do it. For Wyatt. Ride or die."

They could hear them buzzing. The bizzers seemed angry already. It made their souls shudder in fear.

Chloe trembled. "Ride…or…d-die." She swallowed. "I'm terrified of this, too!"

They looked around. Everybody looked just as scared as they were. Except Slank. He looked bored.

"We gotta do this, people!" Jamar exclaimed. "Doing the rope thing and then the vine thing, that'll take a lot of time! We gotta do this *now*!"

He power-walked to the bushes. Alice looked at Jacob, She tightened her grip on his hand. He swallowed. He nodded at her. "Let's go."

It was more horrible than they'd imagined. When they got to the bushes, the insects swarmed. They buzzed. They stung. It felt like super-heated needles puncturing their skin.

The four humans, and almost everybody else, screamed. They panicked. They desperately ran, swatting away as many of them as they could. They only took several seconds to get well past the bushes, but it seemed like much longer.

When they were totally clear of the bushes, the bizzers stopped attacking.

"Oh god, oh, god oh, god, oh god!" Alice screamed as she continued to swat at the bizzers, but they were gone. She was stung at least a half-dozen times. Chase, Jamar, and Chloe didn't do any better.

"Oh god, that was a nightmare!" Chloe whined.

"This whole thing is a goddamned nightmare!" Chase yelled.

"Ow!" Slank said as he swatted a few last bizzers off of his huge arms. "Those little shits *do* hurt!"

"Oh my god," Alice gasped. She looked over at the Wistwills. One of them was writhing around on the ground in pain. Another lay on the ground, completely still. It was Markonis, their scientist, the one who had been in the chair.

Chase tightened both of his fists. A look of rage trembled his face. "I will kill these assholes…I swear to god I will!"

"And…I will help you do it," Alice sobbed.

"We will get them, Chase," Barchell said, who was nearby. "Trust me, we will."

One of the Doo'chen was also on the ground, completely still. It was Flee-cheer, their musician.

"Oh no!" Jonnifer yelled. "Alannis is dead, too!" Now two Wistwills lay on the ground, deceased.

Alice wept. "There's only two of them now. Only two Fargles. Three Doo'chen. All this death, Jacob…it's tearing my heart to shreds."

"Meel!" Coordinator Jeelork exclaimed. Assistant Meel was also on the ground, totally still. "Oh no, Meel! Come on, Meel! Stay with us!"

"It looks like we're the only team left with all the members," Jamar said in a shaky voice. "Which really scares me."

"That'll be a big, fat target on us," Chase said.

Slank raised his hand. "Can I switch teams?"

"Believe me, I wish you could!" Chase exclaimed.

"Look, we have to move on," Jamar said. "Like I keep sayin', the clock is ticking."

The Norfans approached the chasm. There were five ropes, one for each team. Farine slowly did a subtle dance back and forth. So did her teammate. In a moment, everybody had slowly approached the cavern, except Jonnifer. She still knelt by her dead teammates.

"She can't go on," Alice whispered. "She can't do it."

Warm tears flowed from Chloe's eyes. "If she doesn't, Johanne will die!"

"As much as this tears me up inside, Chloe, we…we have to think about our own team now! We have to focus on saving Wyatt!"

"*Finally*, one of you five says something smart!" Slank exclaimed.

"Remember why we won the Contest, Alice!" Chloe buried her face in her hands.

"Chloe, we…we can't help everybody!" Alice said. "We tried! We can't force Jonnifer across. We are running out of time! Wyatt needs us! Wyatt, the man you love, needs us! He is counting on us! On *you*!"

Chloe gasped. She wiped her eyes. She stifled one last sob. "You're right," she whispered. "Wyatt needs us."

When they were ready to go, they noticed Farine hop onto the rope. She easily and quickly got across the chasm, even while dancing a little bit.

Jamar pointed at her. "Now, *that* is just showin' off!"

Slank blinked several times. That actually impressed him. "Hmm…those people actually are talented!"

The other Norfan got across just as easily.

"It's our turn," Alice whispered. "Remember what Farine said. We can do this."

She stepped out onto the rope. Alice breathed several times, through her nose, out her mouth, through her nose, out her mouth. She swallowed hard. Then she started across. The rope was thick. It was a much thicker rope than tightrope artists traversed back on Earth. It wasn't as hard to do as she'd imagined. She decided that being practically barefoot was better. She could grip the rope better with her bare toes. One foot, in front of the other, in front of the other.

In a moment, she was almost there, to the other side. She was going to make it! But then she slipped a little. "Oh god! Oh god! Oh god!" She flailed her arms around, desperately trying to correct her balance.

Chase, Chloe, and Jamar gasped, their hearts skipping a beat. All the color left Jacob's face.

As the rope shook and bounced, Alice's heart pounded so much it threatened to break through her rib cage. *No, no, no!* she thought. She clenched her fists and gritted her teeth. Alice tried gripping the rope as tightly as she could with her toes. And that worked! She held on. It must have been the super strength! She had almost forgotten about it. That's what kept her from falling. As her heart continued to pound, she finished getting across. She breathed a huge sigh of relief and collapsed onto the ground, the beautiful, wonderful solid ground.

"*I made it!*" Alice yelled.

Farine knelt down to her. "I told you that you could, my cutie." She smiled at Alice. She reached out a hand and helped her up.

Chase decided he was next. "All right, piece of cake," he mumbled to himself. "Nothin' to it…"

Right as he put one foot on the rope, he heard screaming. Somebody had just fallen into the chasm, their scream echoing all the way down. He didn't know who it was.

Chase tried to shove that out of his mind. His heart pounded. He licked his lips, then started across. He figured out what Alice had: that the super strength in his toes could help him grip the rope. When he made it across, he collapsed just as Alice had, thanking all the stars for solid ground.

"I'll go," Slank said with a sigh and a shrug. He approached the edge. He stepped out onto the rope. It bent down a little under his weight. Slowly, he traversed the chasm. He was actually a little nervous that he'd fall. But he made it almost to the other edge. However, with less than a foot to go, he slipped, and the rope broke off the cliff due to his weight. He was able to grab the edge of the cliff with one hand.

"Dammit!" Slank yelled. The dirt and stone of the edge that he was clawing cracked and crumbled. "Help!"

Alice knelt down to the edge.

"Don't help him!" Chloe yelled from the other side.

Slank looked up at Alice pleadingly. "We're on the same team, right?"

Alice knelt down to the edge. "You're a serial killer," she said with a subtle nod of her head to the left as she looked into his eyes, as if contemplating either letting him fall or helping him. Slank couldn't tell which. She almost looked like she enjoyed having his fate in her hands.

Slank's breathing became labored. He was actually frightened. "Please…" He tried to reach up with his other hand, but he couldn't reach the edge with it. "Just think of how useful I could be in the next fresh hell they have planned! I figured out Chase was the imposter! Come on!"

Alice looked into his terrified eyes. He really was afraid to die. The ground he clung to was about to completely break away. She didn't have much longer to decide. She sighed and held her hand down. "Grab my hand!" she said with her jaw tight in reluctance. Slank reached up with his other hand and grabbed hers. Slank was so heavy that she doubted that she'd have been able to help him without super strength. With some struggling, she helped bring him up to safety.

Slank stood up and brushed himself off. He looked at Alice. He looked like he wanted to say something but was having trouble getting the words out. But Alice knew what it was.

"You're welcome," she said, her voice dripping in disdain.

Chloe clenched her fists. She opened her mouth to say something.

"Don't!" Jamar said. "Just…don't! You know Alice. Just let it go. Please."

"She should have let him fall!" Chloe growled under her breath.

Jamar sighed and looked at Chloe. "Just…stop. Who's next?"

"I dunno," she said.

"Rock, paper, scissors?"

"All right."

"One, two, three!"

Jamar did a scissor. Chloe did paper.

"Bloody hell," she mumbled. She shook her head.

"Good luck," Jamar said. "But you don't need it. You got this, you hear?"

"I hear you," she whispered, "loud and clear." She approached the chasm. But Slank had broken their rope. The orb descended and beamed its light at their rope. It then reattached the rope to the other side. The orb ascended again.

Chloe sighed, then started across. She almost slipped, but she dug her toes into the rope. That's when she discovered what Alice and Chase had. She smiled when she thought of Jamar's encouragement. "Thank you, Jamar," she whispered to herself. She made it across.

"And then there was one," Jamar mumbled. He approached the rope. His heart pounded as he stepped onto it. "You can do this, Jamar. You can do this. Just look ahead. Remember what Farine said…" He discovered the same ability the others had. And in a moment, he, too, made it across.

All four of them group-hugged when Jamar made it to the other side. Slank just rolled his eyes. He didn't do hugs.

"We did it!" Alice exclaimed. "We made it! We all made it! Oh my god, we made it!" After their celebration was over, they were curious as to who had fallen. They looked to see that Woo'cha was the only Doo'chen standing on the other side. He looked down at the chasm. Sulking, he slowly turned to face the other direction.

"You had pretty good grips on the rope!" The humans noticed that Coordinator Jeelork was next to them. "Humans must have strong feet."

"Yeah, what of it?" Chloe said.

"Well, it's just a little fun fact about humans that I didn't know, I guess," Jeelork replied. They eyed them suspiciously. Then they frowned and walked back to their team.

"They suspect something," Chloe whispered.

Alice tried to say, "They do," but her voice didn't come out. Then she noticed that her neck, like the rest of her body, was covered in sweat. She used a shred of her uniform to dry her neck off and the voice box. She tried to talk again. Again, no voice came out.

Oh no, she thought.

"Uh oh," Jamar whispered.

"Oh shit," Chase said.

Alice thumped the voice box several times. Then it finally made a noise. "Testing," Alice said. Finally, her voice came out again. But something was wrong with it. It was flat-sounding. There was no bass to it. "Oh crap, that isn't good." She suddenly looked near tears. "I don't want to be mute again!"

"We need to save Wyatt!" Jamar said. "We don't have time for this! We must be almost out of time!"

They approached their pyramid.

"Everybody remember climbing the rope in gym class?" Chase asked.

"No," Chloe said. "But I remember, *completely unnecessarily*, climbing a rope several months ago on a mountain!"

"Come on," Jamar said, "let's climb. Avoid the thorns." There were four vines. Alice looked at the other pyramids. There were four vines to climb on each of them, too. But they were the only team that still needed all four.

The orb descended. "One minute left!"

"One minute!" Jamar yelled. "Climb!"

Alice started climbing. She tried to avoid the thorns, but she was more concerned with speed, so she let many thorns painfully slice into her hands. She had done the rope-climbing activity in gym class in high school and she was not good at it. But with the super strength, she could do it. The ease of it surprised her.

The other three had the same experience.

"The Norfans did it on time!" the orb announced. The humans continued their frantic climb.

"The Doo'chen was on time! And so was the Fargle! Oh, oh, and the Deelooveren saved theirs! The humans and the Wistwill are almost out of time!"

Just as Alice and Jamar reached the top, when they were only about five feet from rescuing Wyatt, the orb yelled, "Time's up!"

"NO!" Chloe screamed.

Wyatt's eyes bulged. Suddenly, a sword stabbed him from his back and out his belly. Some of his blood sprayed on Alice, Chloe, and Jamar. Chase was just getting over the edge when it happened. Then, the sword retracted. Wyatt went limp.

"WYATT!" Chloe screamed. She collapsed onto the stone platform and sobbed uncontrollably. Alice, Jamar, and Chase all looked at Wyatt in shock. Tears came to their eyes.

A weird feeling came over Slank, a feeling he hadn't expected. It angered him that he even had the feeling. He was actually sorry that Wyatt died. He felt sorry for Chloe. "What are these people doing to me?" he mumbled to himself.

The orb descended to where it was right in front of Wyatt. "Awwww. Look. Team Earth finally has a casualty! They had a good run, didn't they?"

As the orb appeared to gloat, Jamar, Alice, and Chase noticed something. Wyatt opened his eyes. The horrible sword wound healed. Wyatt actually smiled. He broke the ropes that had tied him up.

He wanted to run out of time, didn't he? thought Alice.

Wyatt ripped off the torso section of his uniform.

"Poor, poor humans, down to four now!" the orb continued to gloat. "And there is only one Wistwill left! Isn't that—?"

Wyatt jumped and, using his uniform as a bag, captured the orb in it. Then he swung it around and smashed it against the pyramid wall. It sounded like a large glass light bulb shattering.

Chloe finally noticed what was going on. "Oh my god!" She sprinted over to Wyatt. "You're alive!"

"Alive, and…" Wyatt kicked the bag. "…kicking!"

Chloe grabbed him and kissed him passionately.

The other humans opened up the bag and looked at what was left of the orb. Apparently it had been a glass shell with items inside.

"Hey, look, there was a toy surprise inside!" Jamar said. He picked up a handheld phaser or laser weapon. And there appeared to be a Deelooveren handlink device.

"What are they doing with this?" Chase said. He examined the handlink. "This is Deelooveren tech!"

Coordinator Jeelork called up to the top of their pyramid. "Looks like the humans have some explaining to do!"

"And it looks like you have some ass-kissin' to do!" Jamar called back.

Once everybody was down from the pyramids, everybody converged on Team Earth to see what they had.

"We have a weapon now!" Barchell said with a big smile on his face.

"Correction," Jamar, who was holding it, replied, "*I* have a weapon now!"

"Can I have it?" Slank asked, his hand out.

"Hell no!" Jamar exclaimed.

"Good work, Mr. Henderson," Karak said. "You may have saved us all. But, I do ask that you explain how you survived."

"Well," Alice said, sighing. "I guess the super cat is out of the bag."

Chase examined the device. "I can beam us all right back to

the campsite with this! Back to the nice, warm campfire!"

"Then let's do it, my cutie!" Farine said as she danced around.

Chase scanned everybody with the device. He even scanned the bodies of the deceased, including the one at the bottom of the cavern. He entered a few commands into the device and got everybody beamed back to the campsite.

Once there they saw the fire was dying down. Barchell and Woo'cha worked to build it back up. Wyatt and Jamar helped dig graves for the deceased. The campsite was also becoming a cemetery. They held small funerals, mostly just moments of silence and some dancing from the Norfans.

"Do you think there will be another orb?" Chloe asked Wyatt.

"I would bet on it," Wyatt replied, "and if there is, we have yet another surprise for it."

"So, how did you get more of the serum?" Karak asked Wyatt.

Wyatt explained how.

"The plant grows *here*?" Karak said. "That is fascinating! How did they get it to grow here? It needs sunlight. And where did you get the other ingredients?"

"I made it with just the plants and water," Jamar said.

"What?" Coordinator Jeelork said. They slowly shook their head. "You shouldn't have messed with something that you don't understand."

"There's a reason that there are other ingredients in the recipe!" Karak said. "You five may have shortened your lifespans significantly! The other ingredients in the serum are designed to mitigate the acceleration of DNA decay! You should not have done this!"

"If we hadn't done it, how many of us would be dead already?" Chloe asked.

"Maybe it was worth it, then, but you still made a huge mistake," Jeelork said.

Karak pointed at Alice, then Chloe. "You two, you may have great difficulty conceiving children now if and when you ever want them!"

"Oh no," Alice whispered.

Jeelork mumbled to Karak, "What if we can give them a solution with the other ingredients back at the station?"

"Yes, that's possible," Karak said. "But there is a short window of time we can do that."

Chase explored the apps on the device and examined its capabilities. "The Hellkorians must have stolen this tech from you Deelooverens."

Karak held out their hand. "I want to see it!"

"No!" Chase said. "I'll hold onto it if you don't mind, or even if you do!"

Barchell and Woo'cha approached him. "Everything is set up for our plan, yes?" said Barchell.

"Yes," Chase said. "But now it will be me and one of my teammates to throw the knives since we have the super vision. Now we can't miss."

"Fine, whatever works," Woo'cha said.

A familiar glowing light appeared high in the sky. A new orb descended. It flashed rapidly.

"You insolent sniggle rats!" the orb yelled. "I don't exactly know what happened to my previous vessel, but that act of insurrection did not go unnoticed! And you will all pay for it! As such, we are going to cut this little event short! One more trial!"

"Fine!" Wyatt yelled. "What is it?!"

The orb giggled. "A fight to the death! All of you will fight each other…to the *death*! Simple. Elegant. And brutally violent. Whoever is left standing is the winner."

Alice walked closer to where the orb hovered. She looked sternly at it.

"*No.*"

"What do you mean '*no*?'" the orb replied.

"I meant 'no.' Is your translator malfunctioning?"

Wyatt stood right next to her. He grabbed her hand. "I'm with her. No."

Chase grabbed her other hand. Chloe grabbed Wyatt's other hand. "No." they both said in unison.

Jamar grabbed Chloe's other hand. "No!"

Farine grabbed Jamar's other hand. "No."

Everybody at the campsite soon joined in on the hand-holding line. Even Jonnifer, the final Wistwill, did.

"What is this?!" the orb yelled.

"We are done playing your sick games," Alice said. "We refuse to play."

"Fine. Then I'll kill you all."

"Go ahead," Wyatt replied. "Do it."

"Do you think that I am joking, human?"

"It doesn't matter," Chloe said. "If we die anyway, then we choose to die with dignity."

"We are not deranged, violent people like you," Barchell said. "Don't forget the reason that our teams won that Contest and why."

"My associate is right," Seeka said. "No more violence."

"We won't participate any further!" Woo'cha yelled.

"The Doo'chen are done with these twisted games!" Tork'chee added.

"The human Chloe is right," Jonnifer said. "I choose to die with dignity. I will not raise a hand to any of these fine people I stand with here tonight!"

"We dance for you no more!" said Farine, Streen, and Murr, all in unison.

"Your petty revenge on the Deelooveren is at an end," Karak said. "My associates and I also refuse to participate any further." Jeelork, Flarr, and Farrstead nodded in agreement.

"You can go straight to Hell," Chase said. "You can't manipulate us anymore."

Slank did not hold anybody's hand, but he still stood near the line. "As much as I hate everybody here, I hate you the most. I'm with them. You can kiss my ass."

"Fine, have it your way," the orb said. "I guess we're done here."

The orb glowed brighter. Some of the people below closed their eyes, peacefully ready for death.

But then Chase let go of the line, grabbed his knife, and tossed it at a nearby tree. Alice did the same, only she tossed her knife at a tree on the opposite side. A large, weighted net fell onto the orb. The thieves all scrambled to grab the net. Barchell picked up a huge boulder. The orb screamed and glowed even brighter, looking like it was about to explode. Barchell yelled a primal scream, then smashed that orb with the boulder.

Quickly, Barchell picked up the boulder again and tossed it to the side. Inside that orb were another handlink and another weapon.

"I'll keep this one," Farine said as she picked up the weapon. Jamar grabbed the handlink.

"Hey, everybody," Chase said as he studied his handlink. "Are you tired of all this cold and darkness?"

"YES!" everybody yelled.

"Well, I can beam us all to the dusk band of the planet! It will be warmer, and there will be a little bit of sunlight! I will beam us right to the capital city. Maybe if we are near government buildings we can get some answers as to what the hell is going on with this planet!"

"Let's go!" Wyatt exclaimed.

"We gotta hurry before another orb comes back!" Jamar said.

Chase clicked some commands onto the handlink. They all beamed away.

CHAPTER THIRTEEN: The Hellkorians

AFTER THEY finished beaming over, they all happily welcomed the scene that greeted their eyes and the warmth that greeted their bodies.

"It's not cold!" Alice exclaimed. She twirled around. "And there's a little bit of light!"

Indeed, they stood on the sidewalk of a city, with streets and buildings of various heights, not very different from the downtown area of an Earth city. The soft yellow and orange lighting seemed like it was sunset at the end of a pleasant spring day. It cast long shadows from their bodies down the sidewalk and onto each other.

Farine danced around. Everybody smiled. It was wonderful, a beautiful change of scenery and temperature. Some of them laughed. Some of them cried happy tears, including Chloe. There were many warm hugs, too.

Maybe the nightmare part of this adventure was over.

But it did not take long for something disturbing about the scene to itch at the backs of their minds.

"Where *is* everybody?" Chase said.

As far as their eyes could see, the city looked abandoned. There was an eerie stillness to everything. A breeze came through, blowing bits of paper through the streets. Vehicles sat on the streets; a thick layer of dust covered them, which they could smell as well as see.

But it did not look completely apocalyptic, which weirdly made it seem even more disturbing. Some lights of the buildings were on. The streetlights also shined.

Slank didn't want to admit it to anybody, but it actually made his skin crawl. He had seen nothing so deserted before, even after all the alien planets he'd visited.

"It's like we'd thought: they're extinct," Karak said. "There must be no living Hellkorians left."

"What about the orbs?" Farine asked.

"Yeah, like, who was running those evil trials?" Chloe said.

"I don't know," Karak said. "We should investigate, see if we can find some answers."

"Let's try in here," Chase said, pointing toward the nearby building. With the ornate doorway and columns in front, it looked like a government facility. They all headed up the marble stairs toward the entrance.

Some in the group mentioned they were hungry. Wyatt suggested that perhaps food was inside.

When they got to the doors, they found them unlocked. They actually slid open for them. For the ones that still had footwear, their footfalls echoed off of the marble floors. For the others, their bare feet made squishy, sticky noises on the floor.

In the middle of the large lobby room they were in was a fountain, spraying and bubbling its crystal clear water.

"Food!" Barchell yelled. There was a machine in the lobby that looked to the humans like an Earth vending machine. There were columns of snack items inside.

"I hope they kept like Twinkies do," Wyatt muttered.

Woo'cha tried to shake the machine to get the goodies to fall out to the bottom. Slank sighed and lumbered up to the machine. "Step aside, Cousin It," Woo'cha grumbled but did as he was told. Slank smashed the glass front of the machine with his fist. Then he grabbed a large pastry treat of some kind. It was flat and rectangular. He ripped open the package and took a bite.

"Mmmmm!" Slank said. "Oh my god, it's ambrosia! Like a donut!"

That's all everybody else needed to hear. They all gathered around the machine, raiding it. They all grabbed various pastries and candies and bags of salty snacks.

"These are stale," Chase said as he munched on one of the salty snacks, "but I don't care! So much better than those damned berries!"

"I am in heaven!" Alice yelled as she chewed a bite of the

thick candy bar she had grabbed. It was like a Snickers bar. It was filled with some sort of nuts or legumes.

Chase was thirsty. He tried out the water at the fountain. He knelt down to it and stuck a finger in it. Chase carefully licked his finger. It tasted just like normal water. He shrugged, brought his hands to his mouth, and sipped some. It was perfect. He'd never thought that he'd enjoy a simple drink of water like that. "The water is good!" Chase yelled.

Everybody gathered around the fountain and slurped up some of the water.

"Mmmm!" Jamar said as he finished the small pie treat he'd picked. "Damn…did Hostess open up a branch on this planet or something?"

After everybody had their fill of snacks and water, Chase, Wyatt, and Karak decided it was time for some serious work. They walked over to what would have been a receptionist station, if anybody actually sat there. It surprised them to find that the station, like all the lights, was still on and had power flowing into it.

"This is so weird," Chase said. The large monitors were touch-screen. He woke one up by running his finger over it. "Everything is just…like…sitting here…waiting for somebody."

Karak activated another screen with their finger. "It is quite disconcerting, Mr. Chase. I agree."

Wyatt activated a screen as well. "It's like…everybody just left. Not like they slowly died out. But left."

Chase thought of something. He walked away from the station and over to a side window. He looked out. "Hey, have you noticed that there's not only no people here…but nothing else? Like, not even animals? No rodents? No birds? Not even insects? I don't see any signs of any animal life at all."

"Check for ambient radiation or something!" Wyatt quickly said to Jamar. "Hurry!"

Jamar had the other orb's handlink. He slipped it out of his pocket and scanned the area. He breathed a sigh of relief. "No, no lethal radiation levels of any sort. Nothing like that."

Karak read something on the screen in front of them. "Take a look at this." They scrolled through a graphical table. It was data on population levels that was cross-referenced with levels of the virus that had caused the Hellkorians' infertility. "The infertility problem wasn't just an issue with the people here in this part of the planet. It was an issue with *everything in the dusk zone. Every* species of fauna went extinct."

"We can't stay here very long," Chase said, "or whatever caused that might still be lingering around and infecting us."

"That's unlikely," Karak said. "The odds would be extremely low that a virus or some other infectious agent on an alien planet would easily jump to a completely foreign species."

"Well," Wyatt said, "myself, Alice, and Chloe can attest to the fact that that *is* possible!"

"Yeah, he's right. We should still find a way to leave ASAP, just in case," Jamar suggested.

"We need more information," Wyatt said, "like about what happened here."

"No, we don't!" Alice was looking at the monitors, too. "We need to find a ship or something and get the hell out of here!"

"I second that!" Woo'cha said.

"I'm with Alice!" Chloe said, raising her hand.

"We need to figure out what abducted and tortured us," Wyatt argued. "Despite outward appearances, *something* is here. The orb kept talking about 'we.' Well, 'we' who? If we don't find out, we could find ourselves back there. We could *all* die next time."

"Artificial intelligence," Jamar suggested, "or A.I.. That's what it could be. Maybe everybody biological died. But what if they left behind sentient A.I.?"

"Oh, yeah," Chloe said. "Or what if, like…the last people that were here found a way to download their minds into their computers?"

"That's possible," Karak said. "Some species that we have encountered have done so. When we encountered them, there was nothing biological left to greet."

"There are scientists in my world experimenting with doing just that right now," Jonnifer said.

Wyatt noticed something on his monitor. "What's this? Hey Alice, can you maybe translate this?"

"I can give it a shot," Alice said. She looked at what he was trying to read. She studied it, but couldn't understand any of the words on the screen. But there was some text next to a pixelated image of a little Hellkorian girl. She had light brown skin, big gray eyes, tiny ears, and curly, flowing black hair. There was a blinking arrow, like a call-to-action graphic. "I think if we press the arrow, we will get information on something. Just a guess." She pressed it.

"Hello!" said a little girl's voice.

Everybody quickly turned around to see a little Hellkorian girl standing in the middle of the lobby. She was the girl pictured in the graphic. She wore a white dress and a big smile.

Chase and Farine aimed their weapons at her.

The girl giggled. "Oh, there's no need for *those*! I am only a hologram. I could not or would not harm you. My name is Ammee. That is a shortened and cutie-fied version of our word for 'information.' That is my purpose. To provide information. I see that you are not from this world. This is very interesting to me. What is your inquiry?"

"Is she like…a walking, talking Alexa?" Alice asked as she chewed on another candy bar.

Chloe spoke to the girl, "Well, let's start with this, Ammee, where is everybody?"

Ammee frowned, looking sad. "They all died, I'm afraid. The last Hellkorian perished twenty-three years ago. She lived to a *very* old age. She outlived not only all the Hellkorians but all the dusk-region species of any creature. Her name was Sleena. She's the one who programmed me. I look like her as a little girl. It had been a very long time since a Hellkorian child walked the planet."

"So that's why you're depicted as a child," Karak said.

Ammee looked at Karak. An angry face came over her. "You are a Deelooveren! I don't wanna talk to you!" She crossed her arms and stuck out her bottom lip.

Karak sighed. So did Farrstead, Captain Flarr, and Coordinator Jeelork.

"So, what is your purpose?" Wyatt asked. "To…provide information on the Hellkorians in case anybody ever came by asking?"

Ammee smiled again. "Yes, indeed! Sleena wanted all the information on the planet and its people and history to be accessible in case the species went totally extinct. She was still desperately trying to find a way to clone herself and others when she died."

"Is there another artificial intelligence here besides you?"

Chase asked.

"Not here, but yes, there are others," Ammee said. "And I don't like *them*. They're mean."

"How are they mean?" Barchell asked.

"They are angry and bitter about what happened," Ammee answered. "They had vowed vengeance on the Deelooveren for what they did." She glanced at Karak. "I don't like you, either, but I would never do what they'd planned on doing, those meanies."

"I think we just had to deal with one of them," Wyatt said. "Or, maybe several of them. It tortured us, put us through grueling trials."

Ammee scoffed. "I told you they were mean!"

"It talked to us through a glowing orb."

Ammee grimaced and shook her head. "Yes, those meanies use those. They don't like to show their faces. Not that they actually have faces, but they could have a face like I do. They like to be mysterious. And mean."

"Yes, they're mean, we've established that," Alice said. "Do you have any more information? It will probably seek us out and go after us again."

"The orb A.I. was programmed by a Hellkorian group that formed shortly after the Deelooveren's 'help' after the Contest. They vowed revenge on the Deelooveren someday. They wanted to include five groups of aliens in their own version of the Contest. It took them a long time to make preparations. It wasn't until now, the human team's win, that they had four whole teams of winners to use, plus a Deelooveren team. Unfortunately for them, they weren't actually alive to see it happen. But their A.I. programs—that they'd copied their personalities into—got to see it through."

Ammee walked toward a corridor that was behind the lobby desk. "Come, come, follow me if you want to see and hear more."

"Well, let's go," Wyatt said to the others. He followed Ammee, then everybody else followed him.

They came to an administrative room. There were many glass tables with computers on them and chairs nearby. Ammee stopped at a painting of a Hellkorian woman whose skin was slightly darker than Ammee's. "This is President Ellore Kot'shim, the final President of the Dusk Zone of Hellkor. She oversaw our people as the fertility crisis reached critical and the population went into steep decline. When the population reduced down to only about a hundred thousand, all global and local governments fell apart. President Kot'shim lost her authority. Do you want to know how she won the final Hellkorian Presidential election?"

"Ummm…sure," Chase said.

"She vowed revenge on the Deelooveren and a plan to get them back and force them to fix the damage they'd done. She won in a landslide."

"So, why this lesson on Hellkorian politics?" Wyatt asked. "You're answering a question we didn't ask."

"Oh, I *am* answering a question you'd asked, you silly human. Kot'shim worked with the scientists and technicians who were working on the A.I. and the orb programs. It might be her mind and personality that is programmed into the particular orb that has been torturing you. She was a real mean lady. All the peaceable Hellkorians were against her. But all the angry ones, the ones angry over what the Deelooveren did to us, they supported her."

"So this President Kot'shim is who's been putting us through all that Hell," Alice said, "well, sort of."

Ammee approached Alice. "Yes, that's correct. And may I say, I have never seen a lady with that colored hair. It's very pretty." Ammee smiled at her.

"Well, thank you, Ammee," Alice said as she bent down to be more level with the little girl.

Ammee giggled. "Now, come, come, I have more to show you."

She skipped across the admin room and headed for a door on the far side of it. Everybody continued to follow her. Farine and the other two Norfans giggled and skipped, too.

Ammee looked back at Farine. "I like her!" She reached up and pushed a button on a wall panel. The door slid open. There was a large scientific laboratory through the door.

Computer panels, scientific equipment, and containers of various chemicals filled the lab. On one long table sat several glass orbs in round metal mounts. Jamar looked around at all the items. "It almost feels like home," he said.

"This is the laboratory where they studied the infertility problem and worked on programming the different A.I.s. This is where they discovered that the infertility problem…" Ammee looked right at Karak. "…*that the Deelooveren caused*…spread all over to *all* the species of fauna in the Dusk Zone. The original infertility problem did not affect other species, by the way. This meant that the Hellkorians that held on, clinging to life, were not only dying of old age but malnutrition, too. They need plants *and* animals in their meals!"

Ammee walked over to an orb. She tapped it twice. It flickered a few times then it glowed. She giggled, then tapped it twice again. It stopped glowing.

"These were the prototypes," Ammee said. "Come, come, there's lots more to learn."

She jogged back out the door they'd come in. Everybody followed. She led them to another room in the building. It had a desk in it and several computer panels. There were many large, framed photographs of what appeared to be other Hellkorian politicians, with President Kot'shim posing with many of them. But the most alarming thing was a photograph of people wearing all black, with round black masks over their heads.

"This is one of the president's personal rooms. There are pictures of people that she really liked. In this picture, she's standing next to Governor Sherree, a man who later went to jail for hurting some women. And in this picture, she's posing with another bad man, who—"

"Are those Jistari?" Chase asked, pointing to the photo of the people in all black.

Ammee looked at the photo. "Oh yes. Those are Jistari. Those weird people were on this planet recruiting members shortly after President Kot'shim was elected. She *really* liked those weirdos!" Ammee sighed. "If the orb that was torturing you was her, she would probably call them and have them come help her. Those mean guys might even be on their way as we speak! So be careful of *that*!"

"Oh no, that's not good," Alice mumbled.

Jonnifer fidgeted and bit her bottom lip. "You were telling us stories about them around the campfire. They sound frightening."

"They are," Chloe said. She breathed in a deep, shaky breath.

"And by the way, you all are dirty and stinky," Ammee said, wrinkling her face up into a sour look. Then she pointed at Wyatt. "And you don't even have a shirt! There are showers in the restrooms and extra government uniforms hanging nearby. If this were back when actual people were running this place, they would not even let you in. Come, I'll show you where they are."

There were indeed showers in the restrooms. Everybody who needed to use the restrooms did, and all of them got cleaned up. Next to the showers were locker rooms they could use to put on their new outfits. Slank just changed back into the full-leather outfit he had been wearing. They all met back up in the lobby.

"I don't approve," Chloe said as she looked down at the two-piece black and dark gray outfit she now wore, "but it's better than a torn-up, muddy and bloody uniform."

"I'm just enjoying being clean!" Alice said. "Clean, warm, a little sunlight, I mean, you spend a week in a place like we were in, you realize how many typical creature comforts that you take for granted."

"This isn't my color!" Woo'cha exclaimed.

"Woo'cha doesn't like something," Jamar said. "Wow, I am so shocked."

"Jamar, you get used to him after…a long time," Tork'chee said.

Ammee appeared again. "Hello, humans, Doo'chen, Fargles, Norfans, Wistwill, and, well, you others. Do you have any other questions?"

"Is there anything else about the Hellkorian culture that you could tell us that might be useful?" Wyatt asked.

"Well, let's see…they were highly technological and interconnected. They had an advanced worldwide communications system and computer network. Until society broke down, they kept in touch with each other via text, video, and hologram chats. Development of their gadgets and technology was top priority…until the revenge plans started, that is. Medical technology was important, too, especially when the fertility crisis began.

"After the Contest, they focused most of that energy on copying the super serum formula. A scientist secretly stowed away on a ship traveling to Loovian, and he brought back a specimen of the plant that provided the main ingredient plus a sample of the completed serum. He and his team tried to cultivate the plant. When that proved to be really hard in the Dusk Zone, he tried on the night side. And, with some altering of its DNA to take in energy the same way native plants did, he was successful.

"The government started making its own enhancement serum in the hopes of healing and prolonging everybody's lifespans. But as you can see, that plan didn't work. But, the scientist who programmed me, she found another way to prolong her life. There is a pool in the back that has liquid in it that is restorative. She created it using some aspects of the serum plus other chemicals. But after a while, like the serum, it stopped working."

"Wait a minute," Wyatt said, "it sounds like you're talking about a fountain of youth. No, I call bullshit."

Ammee giggled. "Fine. Don't believe it. I don't care."

"Wait, wait, hold on, are there any vials of super serum around that we can have?" Alice asked.

"Oh yes, there sure is," Ammee replied. "Here, I'll show you where they are."

They followed Ammee past the desk, down the corridor, and after a few turns, she brought them to a room with medical supplies and chairs. She knocked on a large metal cabinet. "In here!"

Chase approached the cabinet. He grabbed a small handle and tried to open one side of it. But it wouldn't open. It was locked.

Ammee giggled. "It's locked, silly! You think they'd leave that stuff just lying around, easy to steal?"

Chase smiled and shrugged. "Well, how do we unlock it?"

Ammee giggled again. "Well, you're a thief, right? Several of you are! So…get to thieving!"

"Well, yeah, but we're kind of in a hurry. That orb might find us soon," Chase said. "Can you please help us out?"

Ammee pointed at Chase and struck a mock-angry look on her face. "You're supposed to be a great thief, Mister! You disappoint me!" Then she crossed her arms.

Chase actually laughed. He turned around to face the others. "She's adorable, right?"

Alice smiled at him. "She sure is. Now come on. Get it open, stop disappointing this poor girl."

"Okay, okay, fine!" Ammee said. She rolled her eyes. She reached up and waved her hand at a small touch panel on the wall by the cabinet. It awakened. She entered a code on a keypad. The buttons beeped as she did so. A loud click came from the cabinet doors. "Try it now."

Chase opened it. "Whoah." The hologram girl wasn't kidding. Vials of various sizes, hanging inside clips, filled the cabinet. There was one large one.

Ammee noticed Chase staring at the large one. "That's the mega dose! A super, mega dose! It will give you really, really big super strength! You'll be super duper strong!" She flexed her little arms to demonstrate. "Only use it for a really bad emergency, though! It might mess you up!" Then she looked at Slank. "Like…you could end up being a little like *him*. It will cause you to be super angry for a short time! Aggression and rage!"

Chase started taking as many of the vials as he could hold out of the cabinet. "We need a case or a bag."

"This is a bad idea, Mr. Chase," Karak said. "You've had three large doses already."

"This is for the whole team!" Chase said. "Like, everybody here. To help us fight that A.I.. And the Jistari, if they really are on their way."

Barchell and Woo'cha grabbed some vials, too. Farine searched for a suitable container to keep them all in. She found one. There was a metal case sitting on a nearby table. "Put them in here," she said.

"Listen, this is highly inadvisable!" Coordinator Jeelork said. "The enhancement serum is dangerous. You shouldn't be in possession of—"

"You are no longer telling us what to do!" Chase exclaimed. "We're on equal footing here! You have no authority! Not any more! You're not in charge. You're just part of this beleaguered group now. That goes for Karak and the rest of you Deelooveren." Farrstead got a sad look on their face. Then Chase added, "Sorry, Farrstead."

"We are just concerned about your health!" Karak said. "We're not trying to just tell you what to do. We have more experience with the serum. All right, I mean, fine, we can't tell you want to do. But I beg, I *plead* with you, please take what we're saying under advisement."

"Do you think I'm gonna inject myself with a bunch of these?" Chase said. "We're just stockpiling a supply, for the group, for protection."

"It'll be too tempting to overdo it," Jeelork warned.

"We will control ourselves, don't worry," Chase said.

"I want some now!" Slank said. "I'm starting to feel withdrawals."

Chase and the other thieves walked by him. "Go inject one. I don't care. We didn't grab them all."

Slank grinned and ran to the cabinet. He found a dose and immediately injected it.

"As much as I hate to agree with a Deelooveren," Ammee said, "you should be careful. You could end up hopelessly addicted like him."

Chase bent down to her. "We will, I promise."

"You thumb-swear?" Ammee held out her right thumb.

"We humans on Earth do a pinky-swear," Chase said as he held out his right pinky.

"All right, we'll do it your way," Ammee said. They shook pinkies.

"That's adorable," Alice said. "Now, Ammee, we're also looking for a ship. Or weapons. Or anything else that may assist us."

"I can help you get both!" Ammee said. "Anything to help you with those meanies I don't like!"

"Well, please, take us to weapons next!" Wyatt said.

Ammee giggled. "Follow me!"

Ammee led them to a weapons locker room. She used a wall computer panel to unlock all the lockers. They found numerous rifles and handheld guns inside. Many daggers and knives hung on the backs of the lockers.

"The ones with the red trim are laser weapons," Ammee said, "and the ones with blue trim are phasers. The phasers are more powerful but the lasers don't use up all their power as quickly. There are also some projectile weapons and a cache of ammunition for them."

Chase picked up one of the projectile guns. It was like Earth guns. He cocked it and it made a loud metallic clicking ting sound. "That's a satisfying sound, isn't it?"

"I hate those," Alice said.

"But you're gonna grab a phaser, right, something even more deadly?"

"You make a good point. But…a phaser weapon has never

killed a human."

"Not yet."

"I'll have mine on stun, as usual. Unless you load yours with rubber bullets it can't be set on stun."

"Oh, this won't be my primary weapon," Chase said. He grabbed a belt of holsters, buckled it, put the projectile gun in one of the holsters, then he reached for a phaser rifle. "So…you're gonna… *stun* the orbs?"

Alice sighed as she examined her phaser. "Good point. Stun won't be effective. I'll set them to kill."

"Armed to the teeth!" Wyatt exclaimed. He holstered a phaser pistol, a laser pistol, and a few daggers. Then he chuckled and held a dagger with his teeth. He looked at Chloe.

"Oh, armed *literally* to the teeth," Chloe said. "Hilarious, Wyatt." She rolled her eyes, but she also grinned. He put the dagger away. But, as he stood there with a phaser rifle strapped to himself, and several holsters filled with other weapons, something about that made him look sexy to her. She decided not to admit that out loud.

Everybody armed themselves well. Even Jonnifer grabbed a handheld phaser and laser. That's all she could carry.

"We're going to have quite a dance later," Streen said to Farine as she firmly slid a dagger into one of her knife holsters.

"I certainly hope so," Farine said. She examined her phaser pistol. She hit a few buttons and figured out how to set it to kill.

"I feel like I weigh ten more pounds," said Alice. She had a phaser rifle strapped around her body, two holstered pistols—a phaser and a laser—and two holstered daggers.

Chase tapped on Ammee's shoulder. She turned around to face him. "Do you have anything…I dunno…explosive?"

Ammee grinned at Chase. "You mean bombs or something?"

Chase nodded. "Or grenades?"

"Nothing like that here," she said. "You'd find those at one of our military bases. But, there is one thing you might be interested in…"

She walked toward the back of the locker room. Chase followed her. She entered a code into a panel by a special locker. It opened. There was what appeared to be a huge phaser rifle in it. It was longer than a rocket launcher—but thinner. "This thing here is a plasma cannon. You want to kill a bunch of people in one huge shot? Then this weapon is for you. But, I warn you, it's very dangerous. And it is a one-shot deal—although you can move the cannon around as it shoots to get more out of that one shot. But anyway. You get only one shot, and then it needs to be refueled."

Chase slowly reached out for it. He picked it up. It was heavy. That's when he realized that the dose of serum he'd had back at the campsite was wearing off.

"Okay," Wyatt said, "now we need containers to go grab some of that water, some food, and then we need to get that ship."

"Well, there's more snack machines in the building," Ammee said. "And I think there's some bottles around here to store some water in. But the ship you'd need, it's not nearby. Only land vehicles are parked near here. The problem is, the spaceships are several clicks away. And we have only one spaceship capable of interstellar travel. The rest can only go into orbit and go to our moon. And to get that ship, you will have to fight at least one of the orbs. They've been using it. Like, for instance, to capture all of you."

"Well, I guess it's time to jack a spaceship again," Chase said. He smiled at Woo'cha, Barchell, and Farine.

"Sounds groovy, baby!" Farine said. She did a little dance.

"That does sound fun," Woo'cha said.

"Let's do it!" Barchell said.

After securing supplies of food and water, Ammee led them to a nearby parking lot. It was filled with hover cars and hover bikes.

Chase was giddy as he felt the smooth, sleek surface of one of the blue hover bikes. Except for being covered in some dust, he thought it was beautiful. A helmet and eye shields hung off one of the handlebars, like all the hover bikes.

"I think this one is in love," Ammee said, pointing to him. She glanced at Alice. "You should get jealous!"

Alice laughed. "Wow, maybe I should."

Ammee patted the polymer shell of the rear of the bike. "These things get up to two hundred clicks per hour. They were very popular. Why do you think the president ordered so many of them?"

"Screw the cars," Wyatt said, "I'm with you, Chase. These things are fire!" He eyed a cherry red one.

"I have, but have any of you ever driven such a vehicle?"

Chase asked.

"Oh, don't worry, they're easy to drive," Ammee said. "They balance themselves, they can almost drive themselves. A child could drive one!" Then she giggled. "I could…if I wouldn't disappear if I traveled more than a dozen landmeters from the building."

Barchell had already sat on a yellow one. "Oh yes, I approve," he said as he put his helmet on.

Slank got onto a red one. He tossed the helmet aside.

"Wanna ride on back?" Chase asked Alice as he gripped both handlebars.

"Are you kidding? I'm getting my own!" She walked around a yellow one and eyed it hungrily.

"Maybe it's best if we all have our own vehicle," Wyatt suggested. "If the orb, or *orbs*, attack, then the more targets, the better."

Jonnifer stuttered a nervous sigh out of her mouth and nose. "I'd rather drive one of the hover cars." She eyed a purple one and opened the driver side door. It was on the right side.

Wyatt noticed that the driver side of their cars were on the right. "Hey Chloe, you'd be used to these cars!"

"I don't drive," Chloe said.

"What?" Wyatt said. "Really?"

"Sam drives me everywhere," Chloe said. "I never got a license."

"Well, I am today years old when I discovered that about you," Wyatt said with a chuckle. "I guess you'll be, um, getting on the back?" He nodded behind him.

"As much as I'd love to learn to drive one of these things, I think that would be best." She walked over to the backseat. She was glad to find a small helmet was on the seat.

"Wow, space bikes!" said Jamar as he looked at a red one.

Chase shook his head. "Jamar, these aren't space vehicles. Quit saying everything is a space-something just because you see it while we're on a galactic adventure."

"Is that your space opinion?"

Chase sighed. Then he chuckled. "Never mind, dude."

"I recommend we all inject now," Wyatt said. "Do at least one of the small doses, maybe a medium-sized one. We don't want to wait until we're attacked while we're traveling."

Farine put the case of serum vials on the hood of the car Jonnifer had chosen. She opened it up. "Come and get some super juice, my cuties!"

Karak, Jeelork, Farrstead, and Flarr slowly and reluctantly headed over to the case.

"Well, we probably should," Karak said to their colleagues.

"Just a microdose," Jeelork said. "We've all had near our lifetime limit."

"It'll be okay," Farrstead said, "it's better than the potential alternative. Besides, we will need it to keep up with the others."

Ammee pointed to a microdose, "This will last about six hours." She pointed at a medium-sized one. "This will last you several days." She pointed to a large one. "This one will last two weeks." Then she pointed at a vial larger than that. "This will last about one moon cycle." Then she pointed at the mega dose. "This one, don't let its size fool you, it will only last a few hours. Trust me, you don't want it to last longer than that."

Most of them grabbed a medium-sized dose.

After everybody got their doses, they got into their chosen vehicles. Alice barely felt the usual euphoria. She just felt a bit light-headed as she sat down in her hoverbike's seat. It was like that for all the humans, except for Chase. He felt nothing.

"That's my lifetime limit," he mumbled, "or I'm over it."

"Okay," said Ammee, "there's a little storage tray in the front. Open it up. There's a watch to put on your wrist. Once you have the watch on, try the push-start." She flicked her wrist, then a handlink appeared in her hand. She pushed some commands into it. "They're all unlocked now. The car, too. They should be fully charged. The spaceship field should be on the vehicle's navigation system. I'll put it on the screen." She clicked her device again. "If the orbs come and start shooting at you, hit the red panic button on the bottom of the panel. A force field will deploy over the vehicle."

They put all their supplies, the case of serum vials, and the plasma cannon in the back of Jonnifer's car. Karak, Jeelork, and Flarr decided to get in her car with her. Farrstead opted for their own bike.

One by one, they all started their bikes. A few of them had to hit the button twice, but eventually, they all started. There was a subtle whining noise as they started. The engines, as they idled, sounded like miniature jet engines. Alice detected a hint of the scent of ozone in the air once the vehicles were all started.

"The brakes are a pedal at your feet," Ammee said, "and, once you push the smaller button next to the start button to put the vehicle into gear, grip the handlebars for acceleration. The tighter you grip them, the more you accelerate. There is an autopilot you can use. Find the graphic on the front panel that looks like one of us mounted on the bike." Then she showed Jonnifer how to drive the car.

Once they were all ready to go, Chase looked at Alice as he revved his bike's engine. "Wanna race, Al?"

"You ready to lose?" Alice said. She smiled and winked at him. Then she revved her own engine.

"You're on!"

They all turned on the headlights since the twilight was just dark enough to need them.

Ammee suddenly looked bothered by something. She looked around. "Uh oh!" she exclaimed, "I detect that the meanies are coming! They're nearby and angry!"

"Let's go!" Wyatt yelled. Chloe hugged his midsection. He took off, heading for the street. So did everybody else. Alice and Chase kept up with each other. They looked at each other and grinned.

CHAPTER FOURTEEN: The Chase

T HEY TRAVELED extremely fast. It made a few of them nervous. Jonnifer's car mostly kept up with the bikes. All the vehicles hovered about three feet off the ground.

It was a thrilling drive. With the speed and the fresh air hitting their faces, it was exquisite compared to the Hell they'd experienced the previous week. The total openness of the streets made it even better.

Alice heard a noise above them. She looked in her left mirror. One star in the sky was growing in size. No, it wasn't a star. It was an orb!

"We have company!" she yelled into her communicator.

"I saw it, too!" Wyatt said.

"There's two orbs!" Barchell exclaimed as he looked into his mirror.

A phaser blast from one of the orbs hit the street in front of them. They all steered around the blast. They all hit their panic buttons.

"Did you think you were going to get away from us?!" that orb screamed.

It fired several more blasts. They all tried to dodge, but even the blasts that hit them didn't penetrate their force fields.

Alice looked at Chase. "Would you say that I was crazy for finding this fun?!"

"No," Chase said, "this is the most fun I've had in a long time!" He saw an orb in his mirror powering up its phaser. "Yahoo!" he yelled as he pulled to the left to avoid the blast.

A blast hit Alice. It pushed her bike down to where it briefly scraped the pavement of the street. But she dodged the next blast.

Enough of this, Alice thought. She turned on the autopilot. She unholstered her handheld phaser, turned around, and fired at the orb. It quickly moved to avoid getting hit. She fired several more times. She missed it every time. Chloe grumbled some four-letter words under her breath. "They're quick! Like bats!" she said to her communicator.

Chase tried to fire at one, too. It barely dodged the blast. "I almost got one!"

"Almost ain't good enough, Chase!" Jamar exclaimed. He turned around and fired several blasts in rapid succession. He hit an orb! It yelled in triumph as it exploded.

"Nice job, Jamar!" Chloe yelled. She smiled. She got out her laser and phaser weapon, one in each hand. Chloe fired both at the other orb. It shot a phaser blast at their bike. It hit the force field, but it knocked them around a little. Chloe almost fell off. But she used her super strength in her legs to hold onto the bike. She screamed and fired her weapons again. She finally hit and destroyed the second orb. She pumped her hands in the air and yelled in triumph.

"There's more!" Barchell yelled as he looked in his mirror, seeing two more orbs appear.

Farine gripped her handles tightly and accelerated her bike faster.

Karak and Jeelork fired their phaser rifles at the orbs as they hung out the windows of the car.

Chloe kept firing both of her weapons while holding on with her legs. The orbs both started focusing all their fire on her and Wyatt. The bike's force field took several hits. It almost knocked them off the road.

"Great! Now we're their main target!" Wyatt yelled. "Everybody else fire at the orbs, too! They're both firing at just us!" He then veered dramatically to avoid another hit. He almost hit Barchell's bike.

"Watch it, Wyatt!" he yelled.

Slank made a left turn down an alley, separating from the group.

"Where's he going?" Woo'cha asked.

"Dunno!" Chase replied. "Who cares?!"

Chloe successfully shot down another orb. But it was quickly replaced. "How many of these bloody things are there?!"

Suddenly, Slank appeared. He flew off of a nearby roof. He hit and destroyed the two orbs that were in the sky. Then his bike crashed to the ground. After scraping the street for several feet, he regained control of his bike.

"Wow, he *is* smart!" Chase said as he looked in his mirror. "Slank must have gone up the side of a building somehow."

Three new orbs appeared. They all fired at Wyatt and Chloe.

Wyatt cussed loudly as he tried to dodge as many phaser blasts as he could. He hit the brakes. The orbs zoomed by. Then Wyatt and Chloe both fired at the three orbs. They destroyed two of them.

Wyatt high-fived Chloe. Then they took off again.

"Why do they keep wasting all these orbs?" Chase said. "We keep destroying them."

"You might think I'm crazy," said Wyatt, "but every computer, or video game, or whatever, that I've played tells me there should be a big boss battle coming up. I'd rather have that. This crap is just annoying and anti-climactic."

"I don't want a big boss battle!" Alice said.

"Well, Wyatt," Chloe said, "ask, and ye shall receive." A very large orb appeared in the sky. It was bright enough to light up the surrounding landscape like it was another moon.

"Please, Mr. Henderson, don't request any more big boss battles," Jeelork said in a very annoyed tone.

"Sorry, everybody!" Wyatt exclaimed. The orb fired a sustained line of phaser fire at Wyatt's bike. He dodged it, but when he saw that it was powerful enough to tear up the street, he raised his eyebrows. "Oh shit!"

"Don't let that blast hit you!" Chase yelled. "It might break your force field!"

"Maybe we should have opted for the cars!" Jamar exclaimed. He saw the orb in his mirror increasing in brightness, about to fire another blast. It did, and he barely dodged it.

Chloe grinned. This just gave her a bigger target to shoot at! She fired sustained blasts from her phaser and her laser weapons. They hit the orb but only damaged it. It flinched and sparks shot out of one side of it, but it remained in the sky.

It fired a huge blast right at Chloe. It didn't penetrate the force field but it made her heart skip several beats as it exploded right in front of her face. She shielded her head with her arms and clinched her eyes shut. The blast also caused the bike to tip over. Chloe screamed in pain as her leg scraped the pavement. Wyatt got the bike upright again as quickly as he could.

Chloe looked down at her bloody leg. "Bloody hell!" she exclaimed as burning pain consumed her left leg.

"You all right?!" Wyatt asked.

"Your big boss that you requested has messed up my leg, you git!"

"Sorry!"

Chloe looked down at her leg again. The pain was already subsiding, and it was healing.

Chase looked at his navigation console. "We should arrive at that space base soon!"

Jamar, Seeka, and the Deelooverens all fired at the orb at once. It quickly dodged most of the blasts, but two were direct hits. It still stayed in the sky, though, but it rained sparks everywhere.

It fired a phaser blast at the car. Its force field protected it, but the blast caused the car to veer into Seeka's bike. This caused her to hit Tork'chee's bike. Both crashed off to the side. They quickly got up and re-mounted their bikes but it caused them to be significantly behind the others.

"Tork'chee and Seeka bought it!" Chase exclaimed. "I hope they're okay!"

"Should we slow down?" Alice asked.

Wyatt saw another enormous orb coming into view. "No! There's another mega orb! They'll have to catch up!"

Jamar finished off the damaged orb and turned his fire to the new mega orb. It seemed faster than the previous one. "I think they're adapting or something! I can't even come close to hitting the new one!"

Barchell slowed down. "Sorry, I can't leave my last teammate behind, I'm slowing down."

"Same here," said Woo'cha.

"I would probably do the same thing, but be careful!" Wyatt said. "They'll pick you off easier if you're separated from the rest of us!"

When the new orb fired large phaser blasts, Slank veered off again. He tried zooming up the side of a building again and blasting off of a roof at the orb. It expected it. It had a phaser blast ready for him. It was a direct hit. Slank and his bike, separated from each other, crashed down to the ground.

"Slank is out! Maybe down for the count!" Chase yelled.

"Gee, poor guy," Alice said, rolling her eyes.

"He's got so much serum in him. He'll probably be fine!" Wyatt said. "Not that I actually care or anything."

Slank hit the pavement hard and rolled about twenty meters. It knocked him unconscious and severely damaged his body, but it didn't kill him. But everybody just left him there, even the orbs.

"I really hate to say this…but…Slank *was* helping," Alice said.

"You know he was probably going to kill us once he no longer needed us for anything!" Chase replied.

"He already had that chance back there, and for some reason, he didn't!"

"We can't go back for him anyway!" Wyatt said as he narrowly dodged a big phaser blast that left a giant hole in the pavement behind them.

"Maybe we need to use the plasma cannon!" Chase suggested.

"No, not yet," Coordinator Jeelork said. "We can beat this thing with our phasers."

Chloe aimed her phaser rifle at the orb. She fired a continuous blast at it and nicked it. "I got it! Barely! It's still up!"

Karak, Jeelork, and Flarr tried firing out their windows again at the orb. This time, they used their phaser rifles. It fired back. They barely got back in the windows in time, and Jonnifer barely dodged the blast.

"You're very good at this!" Jeelork said to Jonnifer.

"What? Driving?" Jonnifer narrowed her eyes. "You say that because I'm ninety-two years old? I used to drive in automobile races when I was younger, back on my world! You want to see some driving, Jeelork?! Well, strap in!"

Jonnifer punched the accelerator, and the vehicle zoomed past several of the bikes. She dodged not only phaser blasts but the other vehicles, and she sped ahead of all of them.

"Holy shit!" Alice exclaimed. "Jonnifer can drive!"

Chase laughed but a phaser blast that hit his bike cut him off. It burned his right arm as the force field partially failed. He screamed multiple obscenities as the intense burning pain gripped all the tissues on his arm.

"Jacob! Are you okay?" Alice asked.

He squinted his eyes, gritted his teeth, and grunted in pain. "No, not really!"

Chloe saw what had happened to Chase. She had to stop the orb before it killed anybody. She unleashed a relentless assault on the orb. Chloe screamed as she did so. The orb fired back, and again, a phaser blast exploded right in Chloe's face; she put her arms in front of her head. This time, the force field partially failed. Chloe screamed as it burned her arms, chest, and part of her face.

"Chloe!" Wyatt yelled. He turned around to see her doubled over, in horrible pain, as she screamed and cried. "Should…should we stop?!"

"No!" Chloe said between additional cries of pain. "No, we can't stop! Keep going!"

Her assault had heavily damaged the orb, though. Karak and Jeelork finished it off. That was the last orb in the sky.

"We're almost to the spaceship lot!" Chase said. "I hope we can get there before another orb shows up!"

Chloe, still in intense pain, looked at her arms. She could see the burns healing. She was suddenly starving. She thought of how badly Chase was burned during the battle simulations during the Contest. Chloe could feel the burns on her face healing, too.

Finally, they reached the spaceship lot. They all flew straight for the largest ship, which Ammee had told them was the interstellar ship.

Not everybody arrived. Barchell and his remaining teammate, and Woo'cha and his remaining teammate, didn't arrive. Chase touched his communicator. "Woo'cha! Barchell! Come in!"

"Are they out of communications range?" Jamar asked.

"They shouldn't be!" Chase said.

A moment later, Barchell and Seeka arrived.

"Do you know what happened to the Doo'chen?" Chase asked Barchell.

"No, I didn't. They were right behind us, though," Barchell replied.

"Come on," Farine said, "let's steal this ship." She danced toward it.

Chloe, completely healed, opened the back door of Jonnifer's car. She quickly opened the case of food they'd brought and started almost inhaling several snacks.

"Careful, Chloe, you'll choke!" Wyatt exclaimed.

"Shut up!" Chloe replied, her voice thick with the food she was still chewing.

Chase, Farine, and Barchell approached the ship. It was long, sleek, and silver-colored. It had two large thruster engines in the back.

They approached the main door. Chase tried grabbing the handle. The door was locked. There was a touch panel next to the door. He touched it, and it came alive.

"I guess we need to enter a code," Barchell said.

"Al!" Chase called.

She came over. "Yes, Jake?"

"Can you translate anything that this panel says?"

"Well, I picked up a few things, reading a few documents back at the government building," Alice said. "These buttons are definitely numbers. But that's all I can tell you without hours of study and a codex."

"I have an idea," Chase said. He got out the handlink he had and scanned the panel. He determined which buttons had the most fingerprints. "These four buttons here make up the code to unlock it. But, what order they are…"

"People usually press the last button the hardest when entering a code, yes?" Alice said.

"Yes, good thinking!" Chase scanned again. He determined which button had the most complete fingerprints. "This button here was probably always the last one pushed."

"That narrows the potential combinations down to," Barchell said, "…to nine-hundred ninety-nine or so."

Farine looked nervous. "More orbs will probably come soon!" She was no longer actually dancing. It looked more like fidgeting. Then, a look of excitement came over her face. "If you got this handlink from the orb, maybe it can unlock it. Maybe it knows!"

"Good idea!" Chase swiped and clicked through several apps on the device. "I think I've got it! This might be it!" He found an app for the ship they were standing in front of. He clicked on the door of the 3D illustration of the ship. Four buttons on the panel lit up in a certain sequence. Then the door slid up.

Farine clapped. She started jumping up and down and dancing. Alice chuckled at her. "Wow, you're excited!"

"Everybody, let's get on the ship!" Chase exclaimed.

"Whoo'cha and Tork'chee?" Barchell asked.

Alice tried to tell them to wait, but she again found her voice box not working. She thumped it several times. She tried to talk again. Again, it didn't work.

"Oh no," Jacob said. Again and again, she tried, but the voice box wouldn't work. She shook her head. She banged the side of the ship with her fist.

Karak approached Alice. "Let me see it, Alice." Karak examined the voice box. They hit a tiny button on it. The battery tray slid out. The little battery was corroded. "This is what's been going wrong with it. Somehow, sweat or water got into it at some point. I'm sorry, Alice. I don't think we'll get it working again." They slid the battery back in.

"No!" Alice mouthed. Tears came to her eyes. She thumped it many more times. "Come on!" Those words came out. She looked excited. She tried to talk again. But nothing came out. Alice tried again and again to talk, but she remained silent. She hung her head down. She placed her face in her hands. Jacob gently grabbed her and hugged her. She buried her head into his chest.

I'm mute again, Alice thought.

Alice separated from Jacob, wiped her eyes, and pointed at the door. It was time to go. There wasn't time for this. She wiped another stray tear away and motioned for everybody to board the ship.

Chloe came to the door but stopped. She put her hands on Alice's shoulders. "I'm so sorry, love." She hugged Alice. She smiled and hugged Chloe back. After they parted, Chloe boarded the ship. Before Karak got on, they also stopped to talk to Alice.

"I promise you, we'll replicate a new one once we get back. Look, I know since the quest debacle, you don't trust me as much as you once did or trust any of us very much. But please believe me. I still care very much for you and your friends. It does break my heart to see you in such distress." They gently placed a hand on Alice's cheek. Alice gently put her hand on Karak's. She smiled at them.

Karak smiled back.

When everybody was on the ship, Chase tried contacting the Doo'chen again. He couldn't raise them. He sadly shook his head.

"How long should we wait?" Farrstead asked.

"Not another minute!" Wyatt looked out the window and saw three large flashing orbs rapidly approaching. "We need to take off!"

Alice pushed the button to close the door. She looked longingly out a nearby window.

Jamar knew what was bothering her. "We can't wait any longer, I know you hate leaving anybody behind."

Alice looked at Jamar with wet, crinkled eyes then down at her feet.

Jamar gently placed his warm hand on her shoulder. "I'm sorry. You'll be talkin' again soon. When we get back. But I can understand you. Even when you're not talking."

Alice looked up and smiled at Jamar. He smiled back.

Chase and Farine sat in the pilot chairs. They frantically tried to figure out how to fly the ship. Chase was using the handlink to look up instructions.

"Chase!" Wyatt said. "They're getting closer!"

"I'm trying, Wyatt!" Chase clicked some buttons on the drive panel. This caused a loud whining and rumbling in the back of the ship as the engines started up. The ship shook.

"Taking off soon!" Farine yelled. "Take your seats!"

There were several rows of seats in the middle of the ship. Everybody found one.

As the ship lurched for the planet's stratosphere, the large orbs fired at it. It caused the ship to shake.

"Shields holding!" Farine said.

Soon, they were in space and leaving the planet's orbit.

"I never thought I'd be so happy to say goodbye to such a shit planet!" Chloe exclaimed.

Chase sighed. "I really feel bad for leaving the Doo'chen behind!"

"When we reach communications range with any Deelooveren ships, we'll request a rescue party for them," Karak said.

"That nightmare is finally over!" Wyatt said. "Let's celebrate!" He opened the snack case. "There's not much left!"

Chloe nervously chuckled. "Umm…sorry 'bout that."

Wyatt then got up and emptied the cases they had. He found mental drawers on the port side of the ship. He put all the food in one drawer. And he put all the serum doses in another. Then he put the plasma cannon in the weapons locker.

"We'll get to the wormhole network in about twenty minutes," Chase said. "Let's go to about half-light, Farine."

"Got it."

Alice observed the two of them working together. Despite her efforts to push the feeling out of her mind, she felt some jealousy. A terrible thought crept forth from the back of her mind: that those two actually made more sense together than she and Jacob. She shook her head as if she could shake the thought out of her ears.

Jamar observed Alice looking at them. He gently elbow-bumped her arm. "Hey. He's hella in love with you. I've rarely seen a man love a woman more than he loves you."

Alice looked at Jamar. She smiled. "You're such a good friend," she tried to say, forgetting that she could no longer talk. Then she sighed out of frustration.

"I know what you said, hon," Jamar said, "don't worry."

Farine looked at something on the long-range scanners. "What's this?"

Chase looked at it, too. "It's a large ship."

Jeelork stood up, walked up behind Chase and Farine, and looked at the panel. "Oh no. This is not good."

"Who is it?" Chase asked.

"It's a Jistari Gauntlet, what they call their biggest ship," Jeelork said, "It's massive. It's about the size of a small town."

"And it's rapidly headed our way!" Farine added.

"Go to full sublight now!" Jeelork said. "Our only hope is to outrun it!"

"Maximum speed!" Chase said. "It's not fast enough! They're almost upon us!"

"Why aren't they attacking?" Farine said. "They are within weapons range."

"They don't want to kill us with phasers," Jeelork mumbled.

In a moment, they had a visual of the ship. It was large, mostly black, and it looked almost like a giant egg in space. A large door on the ship was opening.

"Oh no, this can't be good," Chase said.

The ship suddenly shook.

"They've locked on a tractor beam!" Farine exclaimed.

Jeelork slowly shook their head back and forth. "Everybody…
ready your weapons."

CHAPTER FIFTEEN: The Gauntlet

AT JEELORK'S behest, everybody who had weapons snapped them out of their holsters, and, if they were phaser or laser weapons, tapped the buttons to charge them up. The shrill electronic whines of the weapons charging up filled the room's soundscape.

"We need to destroy the source of the tractor beam!" Chase yelled as he sat his phaser next to his drive console.

"With what?" Farine said as she studied her console. "I can't locate weapons…if this ship even has weapons."

Jeelork quickly found the port tactical station and plopped themself in it. They studied the computer panel. "It's got some laser weapons. I'll try firing."

They fired the ship's laser cannon at the Jistari ship. It did nothing.

Jeelork angrily slapped their panel.

Chase punched the accelerator to break them free of the tractor beam. The ship violently shook.

"The tractor beam is holding!" Farine said, her voice trembling. "Stop trying to break free of it, or you'll tear the ship apart!"

"Dammit!" Chase stopped the engines. "So we're just screwed then?"

"Yes, Mr. Chase," Jeelork said, "and we're now being sucked in."

"We're going inside their ship?" Chloe said.

"Like Jonas being swallowed by the whale," Wyatt mumbled.

"Once inside, we'll fire lasers," Chase said. He smiled.

The viewscreen and the windows showed they were indeed being pulled into the opening of the Jistari ship. Soon, all they could see was the inside of that ship, in what looked like a docking bay.

Then, their ship lost power. Everything stopped working except for some dim emergency lights and artificial gravity.

"No, Mr. Chase, we won't be firing lasers," Jeelork said.

Alice looked scared. But then she quickly got up from her seat and readied her weapons. So did everybody else.

"If we're going down, it's not without a fight!" Jamar grabbed all the weapons he could carry.

"I say bring it on!" Chloe checked to make sure that her phaser rifle was still at its highest setting.

"I don't have weapons or combat training," Jonnifer said.

"We'll protect you!" Wyatt said as he set his rifle to the highest setting.

Chase turned his all the way up, too. "Wyatt, please tell me you've got a brilliant plan!"

"Workin' on it!"

"Try to restore power!" Jamar said.

"I'm trying!" Chase said. He tried activating the panel in front of him. "If there's a way, it must be done manually." He tried using the handlink to interface with the ship's systems. He couldn't make the link. But he did notice something he didn't enjoy seeing. "There are multiple heat signatures converging on this location. Here they come."

"Is the bloody door locked?" Chloe ran over to the main door. She tried to open it to make sure it was.

"Everybody stay away from the windows," Barchell suggested.

"Chloe, grab the handle of the door," Chase said, "they'll probably try to open it. Use your super strength to keep it closed if they do."

Alice walked over to the door, too, and readied her phaser rifle.

"If we let them open the door, we can kill them as they come in," Wyatt said, "create like a choke point."

"They're too smart for that," Jeelork said.

"Then how else do they plan on getting to us?" Wyatt asked.

"The Jistari are very patient, which I believe you've already learned," Karak said. "They also like to use psychological attacks. They might circle around the ship for hours to make us anxious, an attempt to drive us crazy."

"We can be patient," Jamar said.

"Until we're out of food and water," Chloe countered.

"Well, shit, that's a good point."

"Let's shoot them through the windows," Seeka suggested.

"No, that's what they want us to do," Jeelork said. "And once the windows are broken, that's how they come in to get us."

"Well, we have time to come up with a plan," Wyatt said. "Let's just sit tight for a while, and let's wait before we do anything."

So they waited. Twenty minutes went by. The Jistari that had surrounded the ship began lightly tapping on its deflector shield, which made a sharp pinging noise. One, two, three. One, two, three. One, two, three. They repeated the pattern with precise accuracy but on different spots on the ship. One of them would tap three times. Then there'd be thirty seconds of silence. Then, another three taps.

"Ah, their infamous tap torture," Karak said. "This is one of the Jistari's techniques for driving people mad, getting them to come out of hiding or a building. Do something to ignore it."

About a half-hour into the tapping, Alice felt uneasy. She tried holding her hands over her ears. But it did not totally drown out the sounds of the tapping.

"Do they ever stop the tapping?!" Seeka exclaimed. She looked really on edge.

"Seeka, just ignore it," Barchell said. "They're trying to mess with our minds. Don't let them." But it was affecting him as well. The tapping felt like they were doing it right on his head. He knew it was only a matter of time before they mentally broke him.

Tap-tap-tap...tap-tap-tap...tap-tap-tap...tap-tap-tap...tap-tap-tap! And on and on the tapping went.

Chloe sat on the floor near the door, curled up and holding her hands over her ears as tightly as she could. She wondered how much longer she could handle it.

Wyatt tried to think of some sort of plan or strategy, but the tapping was too distracting. It made it hard for him to think. He, too, tried holding his hands over his ears.

"This is worse than some of the torture we received on Hellkor," Chase said.

"I wish I had my violin," Chloe said. "Or if I'd kept the cheap one they gave me on the planet. I could play some music."

Jonnifer paced back and forth. She hummed a Wistwill song to herself. But she looked very anxious, the way she was slightly trembling and clenching and unclenching her fists.

Streen had her face buried in her hands. She was crying. Murr tried dancing while clenching his hands to his ears.

Farrstead slowly chewed on a snack. It was one of the crunchy ones, and they had hoped that the loud crunch noises the snack made would drown out the tapping. But it didn't.

Jamar also hummed a song to himself. It didn't help as much as he'd hoped it would.

After another twenty minutes went by, Chloe had almost had all she could take. "Let's just kill them! We have enough weapons, let's just get out there and bloody kill them!"

"We need a plan, Chloe!" Chase yelled. "Or they'll cut all of our heads off! We don't have the body shields this time!"

#

Another hour went by. The intermittent tapping continued the whole time.

Karak, Flarr, Jeelork, and Farrstead stood in a circle, holding hands, humming a Deelooveren song together. It had a soulful tone to it.

"Hey Clo, let's sing Hallelujah again," Jamar said, "have ourselves a little concert in here."

"Okay, we can try it," Chloe said. They stood together and started singing the song together, this time as a duet.

"What is this song?" Streen asked. "I don't like it!"

"Shut up, Streen, it's beautiful!" Farine said.

Between that and the incessant tapping, Chloe and Jamar couldn't get in sync. They weren't singing their best. Chloe kept going off-note.

During the second stanza, she quit. "I can't do it!" She buried her face in her hands.

"We have to try again!" Jamar exclaimed.

Jonnifer wept while Alice consoled her with gentle shoulder rubs.

An idea finally came to Wyatt. "Can you still access a transporter with the handlink, Chase?"

He examined his handlink. "Well, actually…maybe…we might be close enough to Hellkor to be able to use their transporting system…but it's risky…we'd be at risk of signal degradation if we use it."

"Dude, we have got to do *something* before everybody loses their shit!"

"If only the ship had power, we could use it as a power boost to the transporter," Farine said. "I'm going to go to the lower deck to see if I can figure out how to manually get some power back online. See ya, cuties!"

She got out of her seat and headed for the center of the ship, where the stairwell was.

"Chloe, come on," Jamar said. He gently grabbed her shoulder. "We can save us all if we can really get it going."

"Leave me be, Jamar!" Chloe squirmed away from him.

Karak squeezed Jeelork and Farrstead's hands tighter as they tried to hold on to their sanity.

"Ow!" Farrstead said. "Are you okay, Karak?"

"I am near my limit, I'm afraid," Karak said as they shut their eyes tightly, "let's try humming louder, please."

Suddenly, full power came back to the ship. The lights all came back on, and all the ship's systems hummed again.

"She did it!" Chase said. But then, just as suddenly as the power came back on, it shut back off.

Wyatt banged the wall. "The Jistari must have detected we got it back on and shut it right back off! They must have some way to do that with any ship in their hangar."

Chase pressed on his communicator. "Try it again, Farine! I'll randomly adjust the modulations to the shield frequencies. Maybe we can delay the next shutdown."

"Okay!" Farine replied.

In a moment, the power came back on. Chase frantically entered commands into the handlink. "Okay, the ship's computer will now keep randomly modulating the deflector shields."

The power stayed on this time. "It's working," Wyatt said. "Good, good. Now I suggest we beam in and out of the ship, quickly, start picking them off. Maybe one by one."

"That could work," Jeelork said. "It's very dangerous, though. The Jistari are quick, quicker than you can imagine."

"Not quicker than our super speed," Wyatt replied. "Let's sort of act like them. Boom! Beam out, kill, beam back. Let's out-stealth them."

"This is going to be tricky. I have to deactivate the shields for a half-second each time I beam somebody. Okay, well, who wants to go first?" Chase asked.

Alice raised her hand. But Chase wasn't looking at her. So she loudly punched the nearby wall. Chase looked behind him. "You want to go first, Alice?"

Alice nodded vigorously.

"I don't think that's—"

Alice loudly thumped her own chest. She narrowed her eyes at him and pursed her lips.

"Okay, okay," Chase said, "all right, you're first."

She readied her phaser rifle. She wore a stern frown on her face. Chase clicked on his device. Blue sparkles surrounded Alice, and she vanished.

Once outside their ship, Alice aimed at the first Jistari she saw and fired. She hit them. They fell, and Alice beamed back inside the ship.

"I heard your phaser go off. Did you get one?" Chase asked.

Alice smiled and gave him a thumbs-up.

Chase smiled at Alice. "You're stunning, aren't you?"

She grinned and nodded and mouthed, "Yes, I am."

Chase chuckled and sighed. "That's not what I meant. But, yes, Alice, you are stunning." He tapped his phaser. But she knew what he'd meant. She shook her head at him and tapped her own phaser.

"I want to go next!" Barchell said.

"All right," Chase said. He beamed Barchell out. They heard his phaser go off.

He beamed Barchell back in. "I got one!"

Wyatt nodded. "Good, good, this is working so far! I want to be next!"

Chase beamed him out. Then quickly beamed him back in.

"Damn, I missed!" Wyatt yelled.

"Well, maybe on your next turn!" Chase said. "We shouldn't

beam the same person out twice in a row. Keep them guessing! Who's next?"

"Me!" Farine jumped up and down.

Chase beamed her out. He waited a few seconds, then beamed her back in. But when she returned, she was yelling in pain. She doubled over and fell to her knees.

"Farine!" Chase said. He ran to check on her.

She grimaced in extreme pain. "I got a slice to my belly just as I beamed back." She bled profusely. "But…I got one!" She cried in pain again. "Ugh, I think I'm holding my guts in!"

"Ew!" Chloe said.'

"Oh my god!" Chase yelled.

"Don't worry, cutie, I'm healing. Hurry, beam somebody else! We have to continue!"

"Beam me next!" Jamar said. He gripped his rifle tight. He aimed it forward.

Chase beamed him out.

Jamar beamed right in front of a Jistari. He fired immediately. They didn't have time to dodge. "Yes!" Jamar yelled as he beamed back into the ship. Before he was completely gone, a Jistari sliced at his back.

"Ahh!" Jamar yelled when he appeared. He bled from a slice down his back.

"Let me look!" Chloe said. She examined his cut. "This isn't very deep. It's already closing up."

"Hurts like a bitch, though!" Jamar yelled.

Farrstead raised their hand. "I'm next!"

"Okay, Farrstead, but you have less time, given the last two injuries. You have to shoot as soon as you materialize, whether you miss or not."

"Got it!"

Chase beamed them out. Then he beamed them back in.

"Did you get one?"

"I might have," Farrstead said. "You beamed me back so quickly I'm not sure."

"I'm up!" Jeelork said. "And give me a few seconds, Mr. Chase." They grinned. "I'm just really ready to shoot something!"

"Well, all right." Chase beamed them out. He waited a few

seconds. He beamed Jeelork back in.

"I got one!" Jeelork raised their rifle in celebration.

"I wanna go next!" Chloe said. She held her rifle in an attack position.

Chase beamed her out.

As soon as Chloe materialized, she found a Jistari and fired. Just as one flew at her, aiming their sword at her neck, she beamed out.

When she materialized on the ship, she yelled, "Bloody hell!" and put her free hand to her neck. She then examined her hand, glad to see there was no blood on it. "I almost lost my bloody head!"

"This is getting dangerous," Chase said.

"I'm going again!" Wyatt said. "I need to get one!"

Chase beamed him out. Wyatt materialized right in front of two Jistari. He fired and hit one, but the other one sliced at his neck. His super speed and beam-out both saved his life. He reported that to Chase.

"Okay, everybody, I have an idea," Chase said. "There aren't that many left in the hangar. Do you want to get them all at once?"

"Hell, yes!" Jamar replied.

"Well, according to the heat signatures surrounding the ship, they're converging on a spot near the rear of the ship. This could be bad. They might be planning on damaging the engine. But good for us. I can beam us all, or, well, most of us, to a spot right around the corner. I can extend the ship's deflector shield to temporarily cover us at that spot."

"Perfect!" Wyatt said. "Wait. I thought only I was supposed to have the good plans."

Chase laughed. "You can't hog them all!" Then he looked over at Farine. "Hey, are you okay?"

Farine moved her arms away from her abdomen. The cut was almost gone, and all the surrounding blood was dry. "Almost healed."

"So, how many of you want to attend this massacre?" Chase asked the group. Everybody but Seeka and Jonnifer raised their hands.

"Let's do this!" Chase beamed them all to that spot. All the Jistari quickly wheeled around to face them. Everybody in the group fired their phasers. Half of the Jistari quickly dodged the attacks by jumping and flipping out of the way. They attacked the group but could not penetrate the ship's deflector shield. The group continued firing their phaser rifles until all were down but one. Chloe got that one by throwing a dagger into their head.

"Nice shot!" Jeelork said to Chloe.

She smiled at them. "Yeah, I guess I am getting pretty good at that."

Chase pointed to a computer panel on the wall of the hangar. "If we're gonna escape this place, we have to access that panel, deactivate the tractor beam, and open the door."

"I can do it," Farine said.

"No, I got it," Chase said.

Alice grabbed Chase's shoulder. She pointed at the ship.

"Look, I know it's outside the deflector shield, I'll only be a minute," Jacob said. He strode over to the panel. He pushed a button on it. "Anybody know Jistari access codes?"

Suddenly a Jistari appeared from under the shadow of the ship. They fired their blow dart at Chase. The dart hit Chase's neck, but he quickly yanked it out and fired his phaser at the Jistari and killed them.

"Ow," Chase said. He smashed the tiny dart up and tossed it aside.

He ran back to the group.

Alice immediately grabbed him and examined where the dart had hit him. "I'll be fine! The super serum will heal it."

"He's right, don't worry," Jeelork said to Alice. "The serum can handle that stuff, like the sniggle venom."

Chase felt dizzy. He leaned against the side of the ship. Alice looked concerned. She looked at his neck again. "I'm fine! Just a bit of dizziness. That's all." Then he stood straight up. "See? Fine. Now, let's all get back on the ship. I will see if I can access the panel from the ship using my handlink."

Once they were back on the ship, Chase noticed that another ship out in space was calling them. It was a Deelooveren ship. "Hey, maybe the rescue squad is coming!"

"Excellent!" Wyatt said.

"I had a feeling that they would figure out where we were," Karak said, "Although I am a bit surprised it took them this long."

"Several ships are coming," said Chase, "I see them on the sensors." He answered the call.

A Deelooveren in the typical all-black guard uniform appeared on the viewscreen. "Mr. Chase! I didn't expect to see you on that ship! Wow, I see many of the other abductees are with you!"

"Some of us unfortunately didn't make it," Chase said.

"We have a long and weird story to tell you," Chloe said, "but first, can you please rescue us from inside this Jistari ship?"

"We have an entire armada coming!" the Deelooveren captain said. "Deactivate your shields so we can beam you all over to our ship."

Chase deactivated the shields. "Okay, please, get us the hell out of here before more Jistari crash our party!"

Blue beams of light surrounded everybody on the ship.

CHAPTER SIXTEEN: Rescued

WHEN THEY were all on the Deelooveren ship, Chase immediately grabbed Alice and hugged and kissed her. "We made it, babe!" Alice smiled and nodded at him. She looked lovingly into his eyes. Then she kissed him again.

"I, for one, am so glad that stupid hellish experience is over!" Jamar yelled.

"Time to party, cuties!" Farine said. She danced.

"Hello," said the Deelooveren captain. "I'm the captain of this vessel. I'd like to know what happened. What did the Hellkorians do to you all?"

"Before we get into that," Chase said, "you've got to rescue two that we'd left behind on the planet that might still be alive. Two Doo'chen."

Alice held up three fingers. Chase rolled his eyes. "And… Slank was down there with us."

"Slank?" the captain said. "We've been trying to apprehend him for years! We will be very pleased to finally have him incarcerated! Anyway, we will extract him and the two Doo'chen from the surface."

"The Jistari ship is aiming their weapons at us!" a Deelooveren pilot at the drive station exclaimed.

"Aim our weapons at it!" the captain said. "And tell all the other ships to do the same!"

When the Jistari ship had six Deelooveren battleships aiming their weapons at them, it decided that was too much. It lurched forward, then raced away.

"Looks like we were too rich for their blood!" Chase said.

"Damn!" Wyatt said. "We had some great weapons and a

bunch of vials of super serum on that Hellkorian ship!"

"Well, we don't need them now!" Chloe said. "We're saved!" She hugged Wyatt warmly.

"Let's get back to the *Arkenstar* Station as quickly as possible," Karak said. "We have *a lot* of things to sort out."

When the ship entered the wormhole network, Chase took Alice by the hand. He led her to a sleeping quarters near the back to speak to her in private.

Alice shrugged. She got a slightly worried look on her face. But Jacob smiled at her to reassure her that nothing was wrong. "Alice Mackenzie, after months of indecision, I've finally decided. I want to stay on Earth. No more space adventures. Especially after that hellish experience. I want to be with you always and forever. And I want to marry you as soon as we get back to Earth."

Alice immediately teared up and smiled a big, loving, toothy smile. She looked so happy that she didn't need to actually speak what she was feeling. She grabbed Jacob and hugged him tightly…almost too tightly.

"Super strength!" Jacob grunted. Alice quickly let go and mouthed, "I'm sorry." Then Alice kissed him more deeply and more passionately than she ever had. Jacob had never felt so much love from her. He wanted nothing more than to spend the rest of his life with her.

After making out for several more minutes, hand-in-hand, they returned to the front of the ship. Wyatt, Chloe, and Jamar turned to look at them. They all smiled at them like maybe they knew what Chase was about to tell them.

"Jamar, Wyatt, do you two want to be my groomsmen?" Chase asked.

Jamar smiled bigger than Chase had ever seen him smile before. "Hell yeah, man! So you're finally doing it?"

"Me, too!" Wyatt said. "Do you have a date?"

"We want to as soon as we can after we get back to Earth!" Chase replied.

Alice pointed at Chloe. Then pointed back at herself and Chase.

Chloe smiled and chuckled happily. "Oh, darling, I'd love to be your bridesmaid!"

"Your sister will be the other one?" Chase asked her. She nodded vigorously.

"In fact," Chase announced to the group, "you are all invited to the wedding! If you can make it to Earth, that is!"

"Weddings are groovy!" Farine exclaimed. "I'm in!"

Once they made it back to the *Arkenstar*, Karak beamed into the human suite with a gift. Alice beamed when she saw they were holding a new voice box.

"We made sure this one has a better seal to prevent water or sweat damage," Karak said. They helped Alice put it on.

The first thing Alice used it to say was "I love you, baby!" to Jacob.

"I love you more than anything on Earth...or in space!" Jacob replied. They kissed, deeply and lovingly.

Jamar looked at Wyatt. "So, you gonna put a ring on it, too, bro?"

Wyatt shot Jamar a look of annoyance. "Shhh!"

Chloe looked at Wyatt playfully. "Oh no," Wyatt said as he rolled his eyes. They all laughed.

"We rescued the two Doo'chen," Karak announced, "and we apprehended Slank. He was still alive, unfortunately. And we have captured and deactivated all the malevolent artificial intelligences on Hellkor. They will not trouble anybody any further. Now, would you all like to talk to your families?"

After Karak left to give them privacy, they called their families, who were thrilled to hear from them and that they were doing well. The humans couldn't wait to get back to Earth to see them.

But it wasn't time to leave for Earth just yet.

Karak soon returned to the human suite. But they weren't alone. They beamed in with Prime Minister Vale.

"Prime Minister!" Chase exclaimed. "To what do we owe the pleasure of your visit?"

The Prime Minister retrieved an item from their pocket. It was a gray and violet ribbon with a medal attached to it. It reminded Chase of the prize they'd earned at the end of the Contest, but smaller.

"We have a small token of appreciation for you, Mr. Chase," Vale said. "Karak and Jeelork informed me of how brave you were and how instrumental you were in helping them survive down on

Hellkor. On behalf of the *Arkenstar* and the Deelooveren government, we'd like to give you a medal of honor."

"But, it wasn't just me!" Chase said. He gestured to his friends. "They all helped!"

"But you figured out how to beam them all to the Dusk Zone," Vale said. "And you braved a Jistari attack to reach the special computer panel to free you all while in that Gauntlet. Please accept this small token of our appreciation."

Chase smiled at Vale.

"Don't worry, bud, you earned it!" Jamar exclaimed.

"Well, alright, I humbly accept," Chase said. He bowed and let Vale put the medal around his neck.

Alice beamed at him. "It looks great on you, honey!"

"Maybe you should wear it at the wedding!" Chloe said.

Chase grinned as he thought about the upcoming wedding.

Yes, the wedding!

#

When it was time to return to Earth, all of them were in a good mood. The misery of Hellkor was way at the backs of their minds. But of course, one of the pilots just had to mention it.

Captains Flarr and Sloo were more than happy to pilot the ship again that took the five humans back to Earth.

"Just how did I know that it would be you two again?" Chase said when he boarded the ship.

"We just love you five!" Captain Flarr said. "Especially since you helped keep me alive and get me rescued!"

"He told me part of the story," Sloo said, "and wow, sounds absolutely horrible."

"It was," Chase said, "and I am so glad it's over."

"But, hey, we heard about the medal!" Flarr said. "We think you earned it!"

He looked around at his four teammates. He looked down at the medal and smiled. "It was a team effort, though. We *all* contributed!" The other four smiled back at him.

After they got to their seats, Chase realized that, out of all the return trips to Earth, he'd not been as excited to return home as he was this time. He held Alice's hand for almost the entire trip home.

"Oh Jacob," Alice whispered when they were about halfway

home, "I have rarely ever felt this happy."

"Same here, babe," Jacob said. He gripped her hand tighter.

"We have to start planning the wedding as soon as we get back," Alice said. She put her head on his shoulder.

"Al, I want you to know that you get whatever you want, whatever flowers, whatever colors you want…"

"Jacob, what I want is *you*. You, standing with me at the altar, professing your love to me, telling me you're going to be with me forever…" Alice got choked up but tried to continue, "and that…*that's* what's most important."

Jacob reached out and gently stroked her hair. "I am so glad that you're not going to be a *bridezilla*." They chuckled.

"Well, if the cake sucks, then you might see me complain," Alice said, "I *love* cake!"

"I'll keep that in mind!"

"Are we invited?" Captain Sloo asked.

"Sure, Captains!" Chase replied. "Although, I don't know where to send the invitations. Or…how they'd get there."

"How about we just be a couple of wedding crashers?" Captain Flarr said.

"I approve of that!" Alice said with a chuckle.

"Yeah, just fly on down!" Chase said. "Just…do *not* damage the wedding cake!"

Everybody laughed.

"Sounds like you want to have an outdoor wedding," Alice said.

"An outdoor wedding would be lovely!" Chase replied.

Jacob did not let go of the hand of the love of his life the rest of the trip home.

CHAPTER SEVENTEEN: They Do

T HE PLANNING of the wedding went by like a blur. Chase and Alice did it as quickly as possible. Both of them were too impatient for it to take months, or as it does with some people, years, to plan it. They were eager to have it done by the end of April. Alice picked the perfect location: at her parents' house in Oregon, in their huge, lush backyard. Alice said there was simply no other place she'd wanted to have it, and Chase agreed.

"Nervous?" Wyatt asked him on the day of. He, Wyatt, and Jamar were straightening out their tuxedo bow ties and putting on their cuff links in Alice's father's study.

Chase thought about it. He slowly smiled and shook his head. "No, actually, weirdly, I'm not. And I think it's because it feels so right. It's so perfect. Alice was right. The tuxedos, the colors, the seating chart, none of that is important. I just can't wait to say 'I do.'"

"I'm happy for you, man," Jamar said. He held out his arms. Jacob happily embraced him. Then he hugged Wyatt, too.

"You two are the best friends a guy could ever ask for," Chase said, "I mean it, I really do. But…" He looked out the window to the backyard, where all the wedding guests were sitting in white, ornate lawn chairs. "…it's time to marry my very best friend."

"It's kinda hard to believe that we're here, y'know," Jamar said, "I mean, like, it was still less than a year ago that we all met. But after everything we've been through, it seems like longer. We have come a long way since that first night we all woke up in that room. And, I have to tell ya, that first little flirt you had with Alice that night, I saw something. I wondered if something special was beginning."

"Well, gee," Chase said, "would it ruin the warmth and love of this moment if I admitted that the first thing I thought was, 'Wow, this chick is cute, I'd like to bang her?'"

Wyatt chuckled. "No, dude, no, it would not. Don't ever tell Chloe this, I mean, *NEVER* tell her, but that was pretty much my first thought, too."

"Oh really?" Chase said, frowning. "I see, I see!" He got out his phone.

"Wait, what are you doing?" Wyatt said.

"Oh, just texting Chloe something," Chase said.

"Oh no, you don't!" Wyatt said. He tried to grab Chase's phone, but Chase ran to the other side of the room. He laughed at Wyatt. "Just kidding!" They all three laughed.

Wyatt looked at his smartwatch. "Dude, it's almost time."

Chase heard the music start. Chloe began playing *Here Comes the Bride* on her violin. "It is time, indeed."

"We didn't have a bachelor party!" Jamar said. "In all the crazy, last-minute wedding planning, we didn't even think of the bachelor party!"

"Well, maybe it's just as well that we skipped getting blackout drunk and stealing Mike Tyson's tiger!" Chase said.

Jamar clapped and laughed. "Good point, dude! But don't worry. We'll take ya to see some strippers in due time!"

"That would be very thoughtful of you two!" Chase said. "Just…don't tell Alice!"

"Let's go, dude," Wyatt said as he clapped his hand on Chase's shoulder, "this is the one thing you do *not* want to be late for!"

It was a sunny, beautiful day out, the perfect temperature. Chase could not have asked for better weather. Hank marched down the aisle with Alice, the most beautiful bride he'd ever seen. She had the prettiest white dress, her golden hair was falling around her face in shiny, perfect curls. Chase had never seen a more pretty, gorgeous woman in all his life.

And he was about to marry her.

"I'm the luckiest man on Earth," he mumbled to himself as he waited for her to get to the altar. He was smiling so big, and for so many sustained minutes, his face muscles felt sore.

But the way she smiled back at him, though, it was magical.

As the preacher said the usual wedding spiel, he barely listened. He just looked into Alice's beautiful hazel eyes. She looked so lovingly back at him, he wondered if she, too, wasn't listening to the officiator.

Then, it was time to say their own personal vows.

"Alice," Chase began, "I thought I had my whole life figured out before…as a weird fate would have it…I was abducted by aliens last August. I was just going to spend my days pool hustling and thieving, but then I encountered the greatest theft I'd ever experienced… when you stole my heart." Jacob got choked up and had difficulty continuing. "During that second challenge, when you kissed me, you made me feel more alive than I ever had before. And you have continued to do that every day that I've known you. You're the best friend I've ever had. And I love you. And I can't wait to spend the rest of my life with you."

Tears streamed down Alice's face. She looked up into Jacob's eyes. "Jacob Chase…I never knew I could love a man as much as I love you. It was your greatest heist ever when *you* stole *my* heart…"

Jacob noticed something. There was nothing on Alice's neck. She didn't have her voice box on. So how was she talking?

"…and I was never happier to have something stolen from me…"

Jacob looked at the audience. His parents were there. He didn't remember inviting them. He didn't remember *finding* them.

"…and…Jacob…w-what's wrong? You look like something is—"

"How are you talking?" Chase asked. "You don't have your—"

"Just please let me finish my vow," Alice said. "I was getting to the best part."

"You can't be talking without your voice box," Chase whispered, "that's impossible."

Chase looked around. Suddenly, nobody else was there but he and Alice.

"Oh no," Chase said, "oh no, oh no…" He slowly shook his head.

Alice gently grabbed his face. "Jacob, please, please, let's just say 'I do' and kiss me. We've waited for this day our whole lives."

"Oh my god, this isn't real!" Jacob said.

"Yes, it is!" Alice said. "You have to listen to me. Now more than ever. Jacob, you have to stay in this moment with me. Stay in this moment with me. Just focus on me and what I'm saying. Please kiss me."

Jacob started crying, but he kissed her. It felt so loving and sweet.

But it wasn't real.

Chase panicked when he realized what was going on. "Oh no! Oh god. I'm...I'm not ready!"

"Jacob, please!" Alice grabbed his face again. "Just stay in this moment forever! We can do that! Just me and you, and our love! And be at peace!"

"I'm not ready Alice! No! I don't...I don't wanna go!" The sun above had become a giant, white light. "Alice, I don't wanna go!"

"CHASE!" he heard somebody's echoing voice yell from a far-off place.

"Then *don't* go!" Alice said. "Stay with me! Here! Forever! In this moment!"

Jacob sobbed. "I don't want to die! No! Not yet. I want...I want..." He looked around. "I want to do this *for real*! That part of this fantasy was real! I was going to tell you when we got home, what I'd decided! No, no, NO! This can't be happening! I've finally truly found something I want to live for!"

Alice looked at him with sad eyes. "I love you, Jacob Chase."

"I love—" Chase choked. He could no longer talk. The wedding scene began to fade away. The sky above got stormy and dark. He grabbed Alice and hugged her. He clung to her as he clung to life itself as much as he still could.

And then, it was like he was back in the Phobia Room.

All he could see and feel was nothingness.

CHAPTER EIGHTEEN: Gone

"WE'RE LOSIIN' him!" Jamar yelled. He did more chest compressions on his friend Chase. "Come on, man! Come on! Come back to us!".

Rivers of tears flowed down Alice's face as she knelt on the ship's floor, her hands up in a praying position, pleading for Jamar to bring him back, pleading to whatever higher power was watching over them to save Jacob.

"You can do it, Jamar!" Chloe said. "I believe in you! You can save him!" She was crying, too. "Do it, darling, do it for Alice!"

"Ride or die!" Wyatt exclaimed.

"Oh no," Karak whispered, "oh no, no, no…"

"He's not responding," Jamar said, tears freely flowing from his eyes, too. "Oh please, come on, man, please breathe for me…why isn't the goddamn serum helping?!"

Jamar did more breaths. He did more compressions. But he was gone.

Jacob Chase was gone. And Jamar knew it.

Jamar stopped. He sobbed. Alice stood up and started slapping him on the back. Jamar turned to her, his face wet with tears. "I'm… I'm sorry Alice…he's dead."

Alice pushed Jamar aside so hard he hit the opposite wall. She started her own chest compressions.

No! No! Noooooo! You're not dead, Jacob! Please no! She clenched her fists together and she punched his chest several times. But all she did was crack his ribs.

She bulged her eyes out in shock. She just held her shaky hands out in front of her face, not knowing what to do with them. Alice didn't know what to do. How could this be happening?! This can't be happening!

She looked at Chase's eyes. They were half-open, lifeless… the Jistari dart had killed him. The love of her life was dead.

Alice's chest heaved in pure sadness and shock. If she'd had a voice she'd have been screaming in sorrow. But all she could do was shut her eyes tight, wringing out more tears of infinite sadness, and open her mouth in a silent scream of her heartache. Then she buried her face into Jacob's chest, her arms laid over his body.

Chloe hugged Wyatt. She sobbed, too. Wyatt also cried.

"I'm so sorry, Alice," Jamar cried. "I'm so sorry I couldn't save him."

Wyatt gestured for him to come over to him and Chloe. "C'mere, man."

Jamar came to them and they all three hugged each other.

Farine also cried. "Goodbye…my…cutie," she tried to say between sobs.

Alice continued to silently sob and weep.

Even Karak wept. They held hands with Farrstead, who was also crying.

Alice, through her tears, noticed something. The edge of something white was sticking out of the breast pocket of his shirt. She plucked it out. It was the card that had been in his case on Hellkor.

"It's his card," Jamar said. "He never said what it—"

Alice flipped it around and held it up so they could all see it.

"You'll be dead soon," it read. She tossed it aside and resumed weeping for him.

Chloe knelt down to Alice. She put her hand on Alice's back. "I'm so sorry, darling," she whispered. "He was a good man, I loved him, too."

"We all did, Alice," Jamar whispered. He and Wyatt joined Chloe in trying to console Alice. But she was inconsolable.

"He was a good thief," Barchell said, "and a good man." He wiped a few tears from his eyes.

It took some time, but Chloe eventually got Alice to let go of Chase and hug her. Alice continued to sob. "I'm sorry, love," Chloe whispered in her ear. She gently kissed Alice's cheek. "Cry as long as you need to." In a few moments, Alice decided she was done crying.

She parted from Chloe, looked at her lovingly, then wiped her eyes with her hands.

There were important things to do. Her eyes were still red and wet, but she was done with all that. She stood up and left the medical room. The others followed her. She pointed to the main computer panel in the front.

"Right, the Jistari," Wyatt whispered, "We'd better figure this out before more of us die." He approached the computer panel and also looked at Chase's handlink.

Chloe wiped her eyes and looked at the sensor readout. It showed a map of the ship. "Look, most of the Jistari are here, on the main bridge. They must have given up on torturing us."

Jamar looked at Alice. "No, they haven't." Alice looked at Jamar. A new tear rolled down her cheek but she quickly wiped it away.

Wyatt looked at the screen. He traced the corridors and passageways with his finger. "How do we get there? To this bridge? I don't see an obvious door. I just see a wall here. We need to get to that bridge somehow."

"How about we *don't*?" Streen said. "Do we want anybody *else* to die?"

"If we don't escape the Gauntlet, we *all* will," Jamar countered.

"We will think of a good attack and escape tactic," Wyatt said. "We almost had a good one. If Chase had been able to…" He stopped himself. He put his fingers under his glasses and rubbed his eyes.

After Chase had gotten hit with the dart, he had tried to brush it off like he was fine. Then he got dizzy and fell to his knees. He got back up, insisting he was fine. But when they got inside the ship, he suddenly swayed back and forth. Then he fell to the floor. Alice immediately tended to him. She picked him up and brought him to the medical bay and put him on a table.

She had tried so hard to wake him. But he wouldn't wake up. And then, he started dying. And they were mostly helpless to stop it. They all watched in agony as their good friend Jacob Chase passed away.

"I know, man," Jamar mumbled. "If we try that panel again, we'd better be damned sure this whole hanger is clear. I wish we'd checked this map again before…"

He stopped talking as well as he got choked up. "He should have waited. I should have stopped him…"

Wyatt turned to Jamar. "Don't blame yourself, okay? It's not your fault. It's not mine, or anybody's, but that killer that hid in the shadows. He…or she…is to blame. Alright?"

"I know," Jamar whispered, "I know. It's just…I just wish…"

"I know," Wyatt said, "you did everything you could for him."

Chloe wrapped her arms around both of them. They all three hugged for a moment. Then they parted.

Chloe noticed Alice was no longer standing there. "Where'd Alice go?"

Jamar looked around. "Maybe she needs a minute…or sixty… alone."

Wyatt looked around, too. "She was pretty adamant that we find the remaining Jistari. Why would she—?" A thought occurred to him. One of the weapons lockers was open. He pointed at it. "Wasn't that where we'd stored the plasma cannon?"

Jamar and Chloe looked at it, too.

Jamar pushed his communicator. "Alice, come in."

"She can't talk, remember?" Wyatt said.

"Oh no," Jamar said, "Yeah, I think that locker was the one we had the cannon in."

"You don't think she'd—?"

"What if they'd killed Chloe?" Jamar said. Wyatt swallowed nervously.

Chloe slid open the drawer where they'd kept all the serum doses in. "Guys…I have more bad news. The super mega dose is gone."

"What?" Jamar ran over to the drawer to look at it, too. He looked at the floor. He saw and pointed at the empty vial.

"Oh shit," Wyatt said.

"Oh no," Jamar whispered.

"She took the mega dose?" Barchell said. "Oh guys, this is bad. So bad. Remember what Ammee said?"

"What's she going to do?" asked Murr.

"Oh no," Farine mumbled, her eyes open as wide as they could be.

"We have to stop her!" Chloe exclaimed.

"How?" Wyatt said. "Stop her from doing what?! She can't get into the main bridge. There isn't a visible door for it!"

Jamar pointed at the wall outside the bridge on the map. "Naw, dude, she took the super mega dose…she's gonna *make one*."

"Oh my god," Chloe whispered. "She'll destroy herself."

Chloe ran for the door.

"Chloe, wait!" Wyatt yelled. Chloe opened the door and ran out. Wyatt chased her. "Chloe, stop, please!"

"I have to try to stop her!"

"You won't be able to!"

"I have to try!"

#

The Jistari bridge crew were busy preparing to leave and head back to the ship's moon base. Some were checking the engine integrity. Others were checking on the antimatter core. Others were working on figuring out how to disable the shields on the ship the humans were occupying so they could get inside it and kill them all and be done with it. When they needed to speak to each other, they used hand signals. Anybody non-Jistari, should they have found themselves on that bridge, would have found it eerily quiet. The Jistari computer panels were even silent. Any and all button clicks or swiping or scrolling didn't make beeping or any other sounds.

The quietness, however, came to an abrupt end.

Suddenly, something rammed into one of the panels in the metal wall behind them. It shook the whole bridge. The thunder from the assault on the wall rolled around the room. Most of them turned to look at the wall. The whole panel was bent. It was like somebody behind the wall hit it with a giant battering ram. Some of them became alarmed, a state that Jistari rarely found themselves in.

BAM! Whatever was battering the wall smashed into the same panel again. The whole bridge shook. The lights flickered. The wall became even more bent. BAM! With another hit, the wall panel looked like it was about to come loose. Sparks flew from the wiring inside it that connected it to the other panels.

All the Jistari in the bridge readied their weapons for whatever was about to appear.

With one final thunderous crash, the panel flew off the wall and raced across the room, almost smashing into one of the crew members.

In the new doorway stood the small, blonde human. She held a large weapon in her left hand, and her right arm was bloody and mangled. It barely looked like an arm anymore. A look of pure fury and rage was on her sweaty, glistening, grimaced face. Loud cracks came from her arm as it jerked and shuddered back into its original shape. It rapidly healed.

Some of the Jistari quickly threw daggers and knives at her. Her body became a blur as she dodged each weapon with unnatural speed. The knives harmlessly flew out the new doorway or stuck in the remaining wall.

Alice had never felt so angry, so furious, so vengeful than she had in that moment. If she had a voice, she would have been screaming. She did that in her mind instead. Alice grabbed the plasma cannon with her other arm so she held it with both. She hit the charging button. It whined as it built up power.

Then she fired it.

All the Jistari tried to dodge the plasma beam as she swept it across the room. A strong ozone odor came from the hot stream. The heat from it was intense, like somebody had just opened a nearby broiler. The Jistari crouched, they jumped, they flipped, but it was all no use. With that plasma stream, Alice disintegrated all of them, except for one who found a lucky spot under a computer panel near the front.

When that one plasma cannon shot was used-up, Alice dropped the glowing, smoking weapon, letting it hit the floor with a loud clang and thud. The sole surviving Jistari threw a dagger right at Alice's face. She swatted it away as if it had been a housefly and sent it clanging away.

"Alice!" she heard Chloe yell from somewhere behind her.

The Jistari stood up and crouched to a defensive posture. Alice, her chest heaving, her breathing heavy, stomped over to them. Each stomp from her super-powered feet shook the bridge. The Jistari unsheathed their sword. In a few milliseconds Alice was right in their face, grabbing the sword and smashing it to pieces. They grabbed another dagger but Alice grabbed their hand and crushed their hand and their dagger. The snaps and cracks from the hand being crushed sharply echoed off the metal bridge walls. The Jistari tried to punch with their other hand and kick Alice but the assault had no effect. She healed every wound lightning fast.

Alice grabbed the Jistari by their neck. They grabbed her wrist but could do nothing.

"Alice!" Chloe yelled. "What are you doing?! Just…just kill them, or, have mercy, one of the two!"

The Jistari choked. Alice grabbed their mask and ripped it off to see the face of the person she was about to end. She tossed it across the room.

This one was a human. A woman…a young Asian woman. She looked to be of Japanese descent. *She was one of the Earth recruits!*

"Alice, stop! She's a human!" Chloe was now right behind Alice.

The woman struggled as Alice tightened her grip on her neck. She stared blankly at Alice. Alice still wore her look of rage.

The woman repeatedly kicked at Alice's legs and abdomen, but her efforts had little effect. Alice barely felt the pain, and any wound from those slight attacks almost instantly healed.

"Please, love, please let her go," Chloe pleaded. She was now right next to Alice. "We…we'll take her prisoner. She has family back on Earth wondering where she went, why she was taken from them. Alice! She's a kid! She looks like a teenager!"

Chloe found the situation eerie and disturbing, Neither one of them could talk. The Jistari woman couldn't plead for her life. And Alice couldn't explain why she was about to kill her.

The woman used her non-smashed hand to withdraw one more weapon: another dagger. She stabbed it right into Alice's chok-ing hand, which sent droplets of blood into both of their faces. Alice didn't even flinch. She just grabbed the dagger with her other hand and tossed it aside.

"ALICE, STOP THIS!" Chloe screamed. "I BEG YOU!"

Alice drifted her gaze onto Chloe.

"This isn't you," Chloe said. "Please, listen, I can't imagine the pain you're going through. Just…look at her. This isn't what you do. It isn't what *we* do."

Fury still burned in Alice's eyes, and her face was grimaced in pure anger…but she also appeared to listen.

She looked back at the woman she was strangling. She was

now barely moving. Her eyes were rolling up into her head. Her face was now a sickly shade of blue.

Alice let go. The Jistari woman fell to the floor. She wheezed for breath and coughed. The girl looked at Alice, then Chloe. She looked surprised.

Chloe aimed her handheld phaser at the woman. "Just stay right there. Don't try anything and we'll let you live."

Wyatt appeared. "Oh shit. Another human Jistari?" Then he looked around. "Holy shit. It looks like I was late to a massacre." He looked at the plasma cannon. White smoke still curled out of the end of it.

The Jistari woman found a dagger nearby on the floor. She grabbed it. Chloe quickly stunned her.

Alice looked at the woman. Then she looked at Chloe. She was crying again. Her face was tightened up in a look of anguish. Chloe grabbed Alice and hugged her. She kissed the top of her head.

Jamar came onto the bridge, too. He looked around at all the dead Jistari bits. He whistled. "Daaammmmmn."

He walked over to where Wyatt, Chloe, and Alice stood. He looked down at the girl. "Another human Jistari?"

"Yeah," Wyatt said, "I wonder how many there are."

"If we're gonna do something, we'd better do it," Jamar said. "There are more all around the ship. We have a short window of time here." Alice parted from Chloe and then pointed at the device Wyatt held. He held it out. Alice wiped her eyes and grabbed it. She typed a message into it and handed it back to Wyatt.

Wyatt read it. "We need to return to the planet and find that restoration pool that Ammee talked about. I want to put Jacob's body into it and see what happens. It's worth a try. Can we please do that?"

"Alice, it sounds mythical," Wyatt said. "I mean, when she mentioned it, I personally didn't believe it. It sounds like the fountain of youth myth from Earth.'

Alice brought her hands together in a begging motion.

Jamar sighed. "What do we have to lose, man? We can do this. For him. For her."

"First, we have to figure out how to get the hell out of here." Chloe bent down and picked up the Jistari woman. "She's coming back with us. We need to investigate just how many Jistari humans there might be, and how often they come to Earth to recruit. Maybe we can find her family when we get back."

Wyatt approached one of their computer panels. He couldn't read any of the words. But he swiped through a few apps and saw what appeared to be a map of the ship. He pressed on what looked like the hangar. He sighed. "If I knew what the hell I was doing, I could maybe unlock the hangar. I could even set this Gauntlet to self-destruct or something."

Jamar looked at the heat signatures on the map on Wyatt's device. "We gotta hurry."

"Hey, I think I figured something out," Wyatt said. "If I do this…it might unlock the hangar doors." He tapped the graphic of the hangar doors. They turned from red to green. "I wish I could do more. I wish Alice could translate this language."

Alice walked over to the computer panels. She quickly scrolled through some of their text. Her eyes did that crazy fast reading thing she did back when the Loovestone quest began.

"Maybe she's using that super duper serum dose," Jamar suggested.

Alice ran through several interfaces. She did some things. Chloe, Jamar, and Wyatt didn't understand what she was doing. Suddenly, red lights all around the bridge started blinking. She turned, then grabbed Wyatt's device out of his hands. Alice typed into it. She handed it back to him.

"I deactivated the engines and tractor beam. I initiated self-destruct. Let's get the hell out of here."

They quickly left the bridge. Then found their way back to the Hellkorian ship.

"Alice," Karak said when they got back inside the ship, "I got your voice box working again. Sort of." They handed Alice the device. "I cleaned some of the corrosion as best I could."

Alice put the voice box back on. "Hello," she said. It was a little broken up, and the volume was lower than normal, but it was indeed working. Sort of.

"Thank you," Alice said. "We need to get out of here."

"Alice helped us turn off the engines," Wyatt said. "She could translate their language. She also deactivated the tractor beam and initiated a self-destruct sequence. We need to take off as quickly as possible."

He and Chloe sat down at the pilot and co-pilot seats.

"I've been itching to try this again," Chloe said.

The engines of the ship roared to life. They began to take off as dozens of Jistari ran into the hangar. But they left the Gauntlet and sped away at top speed. As they fled back to Hellkor the Jistari ship exploded in a giant yellow and white glow.

#

Back on Hellkor, they went back to the government building. Wyatt, Chloe, Jamar, and Alice—holding Chase's body—entered the building. Ammee appeared.

"Oh no!" Ammee said. "What happened?"

"Jistari killed him," Alice said. "Where's that pool you spoke of?"

"It's in the back," Ammee said. "But I don't think it will—"

"Show me to it!" Alice said.

"Follow me," Ammee whispered. She frowned as she gestured for Alice to follow.

She led them through the building and out the back door. There was a pool of silver liquid in the back. It shimmered in the moonlight, and the partial dusk sunlight.

Alice slowly walked into the pool, still holding Chase's body. The further she walked into the pool, the deeper it got. It stopped descending when she was chest-deep into the cool, thick liquid.

"Come on, baby, come on," Alice whispered. She let Jacob float in it. The silver water seemed to shimmer a little more when it touched him. It also did that when it touched Alice. She decided to completely submerge Jacob into it. She also dipped her head under the water briefly.

Her friends and Ammee stood at the edge of the pool, watching, waiting, curious whether it would work or not.

Alice stayed in the pool for about ten minutes. Jacob's body remained limp. He was still dead. Alice cried again. Her tears dripped into the pool.

"I'm sorry," Ammee said, "it's not supposed to work on somebody who's been dead for more than a few minutes. I truly am sorry, and sad for you."

Alice slowly emerged from the pool. She looked lovingly at

Jacob's face. She looked at the others. "I guess it was a long shot."

Something sounded weird with what she had said, like there was an echo of her voice.

"Did anybody hear a reverb?" Jamar asked.

"It sounded like...she had two voices," Wyatt said.

Alice looked at Wyatt, and then down at her voice box. "It must still be malfunctioning." Again, they heard the same echo.

Wyatt pointed at her neck. "Alice, let me take your voice box off." She bent her head down. Wyatt reached to the back of her neck and unclasped it. "Now...speak."

"Wyatt, I can't talk without—" A look of surprise slowly crept across her face. She looked at each of them, her mouth partially agape.

"The pool does work!" Chloe exclaimed. "Alice, it fixed your voice! You can talk again!"

"I...I can." Alice gulped. She could not only hear it, she could feel it. Her throat, her natural voice box, felt normal again. "I can talk again." She looked down at Jacob. "You hear that, baby? I can talk again." She sniffed. New tears came to her eyes again. "I can talk again...and he's not here to hear it."

"I'm glad you can talk again," Ammee said, "but I wish your friend hadn't died."

"You're a very kind A.I., sweetie," Alice said to her. She couldn't believe that Ammee wasn't a real child. "Thank you."

Ammee approached Alice and hugged her. Alice smiled a sad smile.

"We should leave before the orbs come back," Wyatt suggested.

As they all walked back to the front entrance, Ammee waved goodbye to them. "I'll miss you! Thanks for visiting again!"

Alice turned and looked back at her. "Goodbye!" She turned to the others and whispered, "Do you think she's sad to be all alone all the time?"

"She's just a sophisticated A.I.," Wyatt said, "so probably not."

As Alice stepped onto the ship again, she whispered to Jacob, "I'm sorry I couldn't bring you back." She kissed his forehead.

"Hey!" Right before they closed the door they heard a familiar voice outside. It was Woo'cha. He and Tork'chee were running toward the ship. "You'd better not leave me behind again!"

"Woo'cha, you're okay!" Barchell said.

"No thanks to you guys for leaving us behind!" The Doo'chen both boarded. That's when Woo'cha saw Alice carrying Chase. "Hey, what's wrong with Chase?"

"He's dead," Alice said.

"What?!" Woo'cha jogged up to Alice to examine him. "Oh no, what happened?!"

"Jistari blow dart," Alice replied.

Woo'cha looked sincerely at Alice. "I'm so sorry. This makes me sad. He was one of the best thieves…and one of the best men I've ever known." He put a hand on her shoulder.

Alice smiled at him. "Thank you." She went to the medical bay and placed him back on one of the tables. That's when she saw that the Jistari woman they'd captured was awake and sitting up. They'd chained her to the table so she couldn't escape. The ship didn't have any sort of brig or jail cells. She looked at Alice. She yanked on her chains. Her crushed hand was all bandaged up.

"I'm sorry for almost killing you," Alice said. Alice could see the red marks from her fingers were still on the girl's throat.

The woman just stared at Alice. Then Alice tried to talk to her, "I wish you could tell me which part of Earth you came—"

The woman spat at Alice, hitting her face. Alice sighed. She grabbed a nearby towel and wiped it off. "Okay. Nevermind. Good talk."

On her way back to the front of the ship, Alice encountered Farine.

"Couldn't bring him back?" Farine asked.

"No," Alice whispered. She sadly shook her head.

"Wait…you can talk. I mean really talk!"

"Yeah," Alice said, "that trip to the pool turned out to not be totally useless."

"I'm glad you got your voice back," Farine said, "but…I'm so sorry it didn't bring Jacob back." She reached out and grabbed Alice's hands. "I miss him dearly."

"I will, too," Alice said. Farine sobbed. Alice sighed. "Oh no, you're gonna make me cry again."

Farine sniffed and wiped her eyes. "I'm sorry."

Alice suddenly felt woozy and a little nauseous. She had to

lean against the nearest wall.

"Alice, what's wrong?" Farine asked.

"I…I don't know," she said. Farine helped her to a seat in the front.

"What's wrong with her?" Jamar asked.

"I don't know," Farine said, "she looked like she was going to faint."

Alice grunted in pain. "Oh, what is this?!" Her whole body ached. She suddenly felt weak. "I feel…so…weak."

"Serum withdrawal," Karak said. They frowned at Alice. "You are unfortunately experiencing consequences from taking the mega dose. I was afraid that this would happen."

"Oh, this is bad," Alice said. She writhed in her seat.

"Back at the *Arkenstar,* we have medication that can help," Karak said.

Wyatt struggled with the flight controls. "I don't know how to do this," he said, "I can't find the wormhole network. If we don't then this trip is going to take a lot longer than expected."

"How much longer?" Chloe asked.

"About nine-hundred years longer, give or take," Wyatt replied. "I wish that Chase…" He sighed.

"I know, love," Chloe whispered. She put her hand on his.

Captain Flarr walked up to the controls. "How about an actual spaceship pilot handle this?"

"Sure, go ahead." Wyatt got up. Flarr sat down.

Jamar noticed Alice doubling over again, her eyes clenched shut. She groaned. He gently put his hand on her back.

"You okay, girl?"

"Do…I…look…okay?" Alice responded, between groans. All of her muscles ached and felt weak. Sweat beaded all over her face and dripped down onto her neck. She wasn't sure where she was or what she was doing.

Alice looked at Jamar. "What's going on? What ship are we on?"

"We are on a Hellkorian ship trying to get home. You don't look so good."

"Where's Jacob?!" She looked to see she was sitting next to Chloe, Jamar, and Wyatt. "Where is he?"

Chloe put her hand on Alice's shoulder. "Alice…"

Alice batted her hand away. "Don't touch me!" She doubled over again. "Chloe's coming onto me!" She stroked her face into her hands.

She whimpered. "What is going on? Why do I feel this way?"

"It's the super serum, love, it's withdrawal," Chloe said. "It's from the—"

"If I take more, it'll make this feeling go away!" Alice unbuckled her belt and ran over to the drawer where all the vials were.

"No!" Wyatt said. He got up to go after her. So did Chloe.

Alice got it open and grabbed a microdose vial. "Just a microdose." She was shaking so much she could barely hold on to it.

Wyatt grabbed it from her. "This'll make it *worse!*"

Alice whipped around to face him. "Give it back!" She grabbed for it but Wyatt backed up. Alice drew back a fist, intent on punching him. Chloe grabbed her arm. Alice growled, then turned and punched her elbow into Chloe's face. She yelled in pain and stumbled back against the wall.

Alice went for Wyatt again. "Alice, please try to think! The more you do now, the more addicted you will become, the worse the withdrawal will be!"

Karak tried to stand between them. "Please listen to him! He's right!"

The ship lurched. Everybody standing almost fell.

"Entering the network!" Flarr said. "ETA to the *Arkenstar* is about an hour!"

Alice whipped her knife out. She lunged at Wyatt. He backed away quickly.

"Give it to me!" Alice yelled. "I have to make this feeling stop! I have to make this misery, this sadness, this *pain*, this…this… all this…" She trembled so much she could barely hold the knife. "I NEED TO MAKE ALL THIS STOP! I need to stop this deep, aching hole in my soul!"

She found herself surrounded by Wyatt, Chloe, Jamar, Karak, Farrstead, and Farine. "Just one more microdose! Just one more! Please!"

"The grief she's feeling is making it exponentially worse," Karak whispered.

Chloe tasted the metallic liquid of her blood on her lip. She realized her nose was bleeding from Alice's elbow. She quickly wiped her nose with her sleeve and stood up. "Alice, I wish I could take all your pain away! It breaks my heart to see you this way! Please, I beg you, put the knife down. We can talk about it. And…and…now you *can* talk about it!"

Alice, still brandishing the knife, whipped around to face Chloe, who backed away quickly.

But not quickly enough.

Chloe quickly grabbed her throat with her hand. Her eyes bulged.

"Oh my god!" Alice screamed. She looked down at her hand. There was blood on her knife. She dropped it, letting it clang to the metal floor.

"Chloe!" Wyatt screamed. He ran to her. "Let me see, let me see!" He tried to pull Chloe's hand away from her throat. She let him. It was a slight cut.

"I think…I'll be alright," Chloe managed to say between chokes.

"We still need to apply pressure," Wyatt said. Farine appeared beside them holding a towel. He put it to her throat.

Alice fell to her knees. She looked down at her hands. One of them had Chloe's blood on it.

"Wh-what have I done?!"

"She's gonna be alright," Jamar said. He knelt down to Alice. "You hear? It was just an accident and it's not a bad cut. Okay? Just an accident."

She looked pleadingly at Jamar. "Help me, Jamar. I need help. Please help!"

"Anything, anything you need, except more of that serum, anything else. I'm here for you."

Karak helped Wyatt examine Chloe's cut on her throat. "Thank Molltock this cut isn't deep! We can fix it when we get back to the station."

"I just want to go home," Chloe said in a scratchy voice.

"Maybe don't talk until we get you stitched up," Wyatt suggested. "That's gotta hurt."

"It really does hurt," she whispered. She winced.

Jamar held Alice as they rested in his seat. She was shaking and sweating. "J-J-J-Jamar…t-t-tell them…tell them to turn the…the heat down. It's too hot."

"All right, all right," Jamar whispered. "Hey Captain Flarr, can we turn it down a few degrees?"

"Maybe one or two, Mr. Nelson," they replied. They entered a command into the panel in front of them.

"Th-th-thank you, Jamar." Her trembling increased. Her sweating increased. Jamar wondered how she felt too hot but yet she vigorously shivered.

"No problem, hon," Jamar said. "I got ya. Okay?"

Alice whimpered and groaned. "Why did he have to die, Jamar?" She sobbed, which made her tremble more.

"Oh, hon, I don't know, he was trying to help. He was being the hero…the hero that he was. A very good man. I loved him like he was a brother."

"He was a hero," Alice mumbled. "I love him…so much…"

"I know, hon, I know."

"Oh god, this hurts so much!" Alice yelled. "I feel like I'm on fire! Why does this hurt so much?! Everything sucks so much! Why is everything so bad right now?!"

Jamar held her tighter. "I dunno, Alice. I'm a scientist, not a philosopher. I wish I had all the answers for you. All I can tell you is, this serum has a helluva withdrawal. But I'm here to help you through it. I got ya. Not lettin' go. I love ya."

"I luh luh love you, too, Jamar. Thank you. I…I don't know what…I'd do…without a friend like you."

"Ditto, sweetie. Ditto."

Alice shook violently. "Oh god! Oh god it hurts so bad! Everything hurts!"

Alice felt so hot it felt like she was cooking. All of her muscles felt weak and useless, but the extremely tight pain made it also feel like something was trying to rip them from her bones. All that, added to the curdling nausea and pounding headache, made for the most horrible physical experience of her life. Her vision was now blurry. Every super power that the serum had given her was reversing dramatically.

"Oh god, oh god, oh god, oh god!" Alice exclaimed as her whole body shook. She felt as if she was totally losing control of it.

She cried, she sobbed, mostly from the unbearable pain. Alice looked up at Jamar but his face was just a dark blur. Her vision was now almost completely useless.

"Shhhhh, shhhh," Jamar said as he massaged her arm, "you're gonna get through this. Ya hear? We'll be back to the station soon. You'll get that medicine. And it'll all be better. You hear?"

Alice's eyes rolled up into her head.

"Alice? Alice?!"

Her mouth foamed. She jerked and shook like she was having a seizure.

"Oh no!" Jamar said.

"Jesus!" Wyatt exclaimed.

"Help!" Jamar tightened his grip on her as it became almost impossible to hold her stable.

"My god, I've never seen a withdrawal so bad," Karak said. "Flarr, can we get there faster?"

"I doubt it," Flarr said as they swiped through the drive apps. "These Hellkorians did not know how to make a very efficient antimatter core. These engines are far inferior to ours...or most other antimatter engines that I've seen. But...I might be able to get us a little more speed."

"Please get us there faster!" Jamar exclaimed. Alice continued to seize.

Jamar gently put her on the floor, on her side. She continued to foam at her mouth and violently jerk over and over again.

"What are you doing?" Wyatt asked.

"This is the best thing for her," Jamar said as vomit spewed from her mouth. The sharp, sour odor from it filled the nearby air.

Chloe looked worried and afraid as she observed what was happening to Alice. "Please help her!" she wheezed.

Wyatt turned to Chloe. "Please stop trying to talk, honey, until they get your throat fixed up."

Alice stopped seizing. Jamar examined her.

"Is she okay?" Wyatt asked.

"She's still breathing, and she has a strong pulse," Jamar said as he held one of her wrists. "She's just unconscious now. Her pulse is really fast, though."

"We'll be exiting the network soon," Flarr announced. "This whole nightmare will truly be behind us soon."

"I sure hope so," Jamar said as he brushed some of Alice's hair out of her face and used the towel to wipe her mouth.

CHAPTER NINETEEN: Funeral for a Friend

IN AN hour they made it to the *Arkenstar* Station. As soon as they got there, they took Chloe and Alice to the medical facility. They also took Chase's body to a stasis pod to prevent decomposition.

"I've never seen a serum withdrawal this extensive," said Dr. Wikket as they tended to Alice. They injected her with the medicine to help her with the withdrawal.

"Is she gonna be okay?" Jamar asked.

"This medicine will help her immediate crisis," Dr. Wikket said, "but, my experience tells me that she will deal with this recurrence for a very long time. Maybe the rest of her life. That's why the serum is so dangerous if used improperly." Dr. Wikket glanced at Chloe as another medic closed up her throat wound.

Alice awakened. She opened her eyes. "What's going on?"

"We're back at the *Arkenstar*," Jamar answered. "They're taking care of you."

Dr. Wikket scrunched a confused look onto their face. "Hey, I just remembered something. She shouldn't be able to talk. How is she talking? She's not wearing her voice box."

"It was healed," Jamar said.

"That's impossible!" the doctor said. "The voice-destroyer's damage can't be healed or fixed."

"Y'know, why is that anyway?" Jamar asked. "Nobody has ever explained that to me."

"It damages the larynx and vocal folds and it creates a permanent stasis field so they forever stay in that damaged state. They can't heal and can't be repaired. And the stasis field cannot be removed. How that part of it works is somewhat of a mystery. Whoever invented the device died a long time ago. It's been around a few centuries.

They took the secret of how exactly it works to the grave. All the devices out there now are replicants of the original ones. The only progress we've made is to temporarily disrupt the stasis field with a tiny electromagnetic pulse but the field returns in a few seconds.

"Now that I've answered your question, please answer mine. I must know how this was healed. She'd be the first-ever documented case of damage from the voice destroyer being totally healed."

"Well, on Hellkor, the last surviving Hellkorian was a scientist, and she created some kind of pool with silver water that was restorative," Jamar explained. "Like…it could heal anything. At first, we didn't believe it. She put Chase in it…" Jamar sighed. So did Alice. "…but when she put him in it…well, it didn't save him. But it brought back her voice."

"Well I want to see this stuff!" Dr. Wikket put their device away that they'd used to inject Alice. "I must book a trip to Hellkor! I mean…the entire Galactic Union medical community has to see this stuff. This could revolutionize…well…*everything*."

"It's a finite resource," Alice said, "I mean…once it's used up…"

"We can copy and replicate almost anything, Miss Mackenzie," Dr. Wikket said. "But…this liquid…maybe a medical doctor *and* a physicist needs to look at the stuff. Like maybe it has a temporal property to it."

"Time?" Jamar said.

"Like maybe it restores tissues to a previous state in time, yes. I mean…the scientists who have been trying to think of a way to fix the damage the z'choti does, the only solution they've come to is to try to somehow revert the tissue to a previous state in time."

"Time-traveling medicine?" Chloe said. "Well, the longer I do this space stuff, the weirder and weirder stuff I hear about."

Alice got off the table. "I have work to do."

"What is it?" Chloe said.

"Jacob's funeral," she answered, "he told me when those Hell Trials began that if he died, he wanted his funeral to be a space funeral, like on *Star Trek*. He felt it's where he belonged. He said that a memorial service on Earth afterward would be fine, but he wants his body to go out into space. I need to talk to the station authorities." She looked directly at Dr. Wikket. "If Karak is no longer in charge here, then who is?"

"Ambassador Harklon is," the doctor replied.

Alice was about to touch her communicator but the doctor stopped her. "Don't use those here. The Hellkorians gave you those." They took it out of her ear. Then they went around and took the communicators from each of the other humans. Then they tossed them in the garbage.

"Hold on please," Dr. Wikket said, in Deelooveren, which the humans didn't understand. They went to a replicator. They asked the computer to give them four new communicators for the humans. Four new ones appeared. The doctor grabbed them and handed them out.

"Can you understand me?" Dr. Wikket asked.

"Yes," Alice said. Then she touched it. "Hello, I'm trying to reach Ambassador Harklon?"

"The ambassador is very busy at the moment, it might be a minute. They are busy with preparations for the next Contest."

"Oh wow," Alice said.

"More Contests," Wyatt said. "That's right. They do it every year."

"None of this bloody stuff would have happened if it wasn't for that Contest!" Chloe exclaimed.

Alice looked sad again. "Jacob would still be alive."

"But you would have never met him," Jamar said.

"But he would still be alive!"

Wyatt grabbed Chloe's hand. "But none of us would have ever met each other."

"Look, guys, let's not go down this existential crisis road," Jamar said, "what's happened has happened. What's done is done. It's not like we can go back into time and…" But he trailed off.

"Yes," Alice said, "we can, actually."

Dr. Wikket waved one of their fingers. "No, don't even think it. No, you can't. Not to change anything that you're talking about. It is absolutely against the time travel rules. You'd create paradoxes, chaos in the timelines. You can't."

"Screw the rules!" Alice exclaimed. "Where's the nearest time travel wormhole?!"

"No!" Dr. Wikket said. "That information is restricted. You can't do it, and that's final. I'm sorry. I'm really sorry about what happened to Mr. Chase. But we can't allow mucking up the timelines. I can scarcely imagine all the unintended consequences of such an endeavor."

Wyatt sighed and slowly shook his head. "Dr. Wikket is right, Alice. We can't go messing around with time like that."

Alice closed her eyes tightly. "Dammit," she muttered.

"Hello humans," said a voice in all the humans' communicators, "this is Ambassador Harklon. If you are finished in medical, please head to your suite of the station. I will meet you there."

Wyatt was glad for the communication, as it broke the building tension and changed the subject. Alice sighed heavily and headed for the exit doors. The others followed her.

The shuttle ride to their area was mostly quiet. There were no other aliens riding the shuttles that day.

"Even if we could use a time travel wormhole," Wyatt said, "I mean…what could we even do? We can't undo everything that's happened. We literally saved the world. We wouldn't be friends. And if you somehow save Chase…I mean even that would create a paradox. Because if he hadn't died we wouldn't have been time traveling to begin with."

"We can't do it, because we didn't do it," Jamar said. "I mean, if my thinking on time travel is correct. That's what Karak said when we suggested time travel to fix the Feeijing's world."

"But, some science fiction stuff I've seen suggests that it doesn't create a paradox. It creates a new timeline," Chloe said. "Right?"

"Maybe it'd create a new timeline where we are *all* dead," Wyatt countered. "What Alice did afterward was a bit crazy, but… maybe it saved us all, allowed us to escape."

"Everything happens for a reason, maybe," Jamar said.

"That's not comforting!" Alice said. She rubbed her eyes. She was trying not to cry again.

"It wasn't supposed to be."

#

When they arrived back in their suite, they all sat around the conference table. Ambassador Harklon beamed in. They wore an outfit very similar to the one that Karak wore the first time they met them: a formal outfit that seemed to be a combination of a business suit and a dress.

"Hello, I am Ambassador Harklon. I now occupy the role that Karak used to. First of all, I want to express my deepest condolences for your loss. Mr. Chase was a valuable asset to your team and we appreciated everything he did for us during that quest. He was a valuable friend to the Deelooveren."

"Thank you, Ambassador," Alice said. "And, I have a request."

"What is it, Miss Mackenzie?"

"Jacob wanted a space funeral. He intimated that to me back on Hellkor. Can we please arrange that here?"

"Yes, yes, of course, we do that sometimes, we've had them here on the station before. We have a special airlock facility for that. We will assist in the arrangements in whatever way we can. It is the least we can do."

"And then you can take us home afterward?" Chloe asked.

"Yes, of course," the Ambassador replied. "We can have a meal prepared for you in the dining room. I'm sure it's been a while since you've gotten any proper food."

"It's also been a while since we've gotten proper sleep," Wyatt said. His head was actually down on the table.

Everybody then realized just how tired they were.

"How long has it been since we actually got some sleep?" Jamar asked.

"Too bloody long," Chloe said as she also put her head down.

"You are welcome to use the dormitory rooms to get some rest," Harklon said. They pointed toward the door to the dormitory.

"I'll sleep later," Alice said. "I have things to do."

"Alice, you need some sleep," Wyatt said, "I'm sure it can wait. We probably haven't slept for like two days."

"I was just unconscious for a few hours, I'm fine," Alice said.

"But—"

"Jacob needs me, Wyatt!" Alice said while banging her fist on the table. She looked down and unclenched her fist. She sighed. "I'm…I'm sorry. I…maybe I should get a few hours of sleep."

"It's good timing, too," Harklon said. "The station was just about to enter night mode. And by the way, all your families were very happy to hear that you're all okay. You may call them later if you like, but we told them that you'd all probably want to get some sleep first."

They all thanked Harklon and agreed that they needed sleep.

#

Alice tried to sleep that night. But it was a very restless sleep. She couldn't stop thinking about things like returning to Earth, seeing her family again, and planning Jacob's funeral. She cried some when she thought about how she and Jacob used to sleep together in that room. Her bed felt empty without him.

#

In the morning, she got up first. She could barely sleep anyway. She cleaned up. As expected, the clothing that was available to dress herself in was the old red Team Earth uniform. She actually enjoyed putting it on. It was familiar. It reminded her of better times and it felt good to rid herself of anything connected to Hellkor.

Even though it was useless for communication of any kind on the station, Alice opened up the nightstand drawer and got her cell phone out. They'd made sure it was charged up for her. She face-logged into it and immediately scrolled through her photos to find that perfect, beautiful photo of her and Jacob, taken right before they left the *Arkenstar* Station after the Contest. She reached out with her finger and touched the photo. She put her phone to her face and gave the picture a tiny kiss.

It was still night mode when she entered the dining area. Karak sitting at the table surprised her.

"Oh, good morning," Alice said, "what are you doing here?"

"I figured you'd be up early," Karak said. "I wanted to be here to talk to you. I know about the funeral plans. And I want to help in any way that I can. But that's not all I want to help with."

"Thank you, but what else?" Alice poured herself a cup of coffee. She was glad to see that some coffee was already brewed.

"I know grief is always different for different people and situations, but when I lost Zeeler, I was devastated. So I thought maybe I could help you through that grief since I recently went through it myself."

"That's very kind of you," Alice said. She sat down next to Karak, cradling her warm cup of coffee in her hands.

"First of all—and this was a hard lesson for myself—you are still here. And you are still loved by others. You still have to take care of yourself. Mr. Chase was very important, very important to you, obviously. But don't forget just how important *you* are. To others and to yourself. When I first lost Zeeler, I didn't properly grieve at first. I threw myself into my work. I didn't sleep or eat properly for a while. I…I started making bad decisions. Maybe some of the bad decisions I made regarding the quest were part of that. I made terrible mistakes. I lost your team's trust. I'm still sorry and ashamed about that."

Alice put down her coffee. She put her hand on Karak's hand. "Thank you. And…yes. You're right. I need to take care of myself, which is why I tried to get to sleep last night. But unfortunately, I didn't sleep much. And as far as trusting you…I think that I do trust you. But I don't trust the Deelooveren in general. I'm sorry."

"That's fair," Karak said, "and I understand."

Alice sipped her coffee. She noticed that her muscles ached again. She winced in pain.

Karak sighed. "It looks like you're in pain again. I can get you more withdrawal medicine. Do you need more?"

"No…I'm…I'm fine, I think. It's not that bad. After I have a little food, I need to start with the funeral preparations."

"The other thieves heard about the funeral. Deelan, Farine, Barchell, and Woo'cha want to help. They think that some of the people that they'd helped after the quest want to pay their respects. Like the parents of the children that they had saved. They are communicating with them."

Alice thought of something…actually *somebody*…that she'd forgotten about. "Hey, that Jistari woman, where is she? When we return to Earth, are we taking her? Maybe we can find her family."

"She's currently in one of the containment cells. We aren't sure taking her back to Earth is a good idea. She's very dangerous. She's a highly-trained killer and a brainwashed member of a cult. She probably no longer has any semblance of her previous identity. We have begun an investigation to determine how extensive the Jistari recruitment on Earth has been. We will cooperate with your planet's detectives and law enforcement, too. But we warn you, if you take her back, she could escape. And she will kill anybody who tries to stop her from getting back to the Jistari."

"But…she's just a kid."

"An extremely deadly kid."

Alice sighed.

"You have a very loving heart, Alice. It's commendable. But it may not be possible to save her. But…with extreme caution…maybe we can try."

"Thank you," Alice whispered.

A few minutes later, the lights brightened, and day mode began. Karak tapped something on her handlink. A breakfast spread appeared on the table. Alice grabbed an apple. She crunched into it.

Shortly thereafter, her four…no…three teammates entered the room. They also wore the familiar red uniforms with black trim. It was difficult to see them all without Jacob among them. It briefly choked her up. It was a reminder that he was truly gone. They were now a team of four.

"Real food," Jamar whispered. He almost sprinted over to the table.

Karak grew a subtle smile on their face.

"Oh my god," Chloe said as she shoved some purple grapes into her mouth, "Oh…my…god…so much better than those bloody berries!"

"Indeed, Miss Thompson," Karak said with a chuckle.

Somewhat of a show of gluttony occurred during the meal, but nobody blamed them. It was the first meal of good food since they'd left Earth to go to Chloe's trial. Even Alice indulged more than just that apple she'd started with. She had a plate of pancakes, raspberries, and blueberries.

After breakfast, they all had video calls with their families. They were all filled with joy to see them again. They had been worried that the worst had happened.

"We can't wait to see you again, sweetie!" Hank said to his daughter at the end of their call. But he didn't smile much. "And, again, I'm sorry about Chase. I know that you'll make sure he has a proper send-off."

"Thanks, Dad," Alice said, "goodbye."

After the call was over, Ambassador Harklon informed her that she had another call. Alice looked confused. "But…who?"

"Mr. Chase's parents," Harklon replied.

Alice's eyes almost popped out in surprise. She leaned toward Harklon. "What?! *You found them?*"

"Yes. Well, they sort of found us. I'm sorry, I'm kind of springing this on you. They already know that he's dead. But they wanted to talk to one of you today, and I figured that you were the best person for that. You got to know him the best this past year."

"I...I don't know if I can!"

"Please try. His poor parents...they were looking forward to speaking with their son again for the first time in so long. Then, their hopes were dashed. After that, they longed to at least speak with somebody who'd had an intimate connection with him."

Alice sighed. She put herself into their shoes, and their hearts, and she knew Harklon was right. She had to do it.

"Patch them through," Alice said.

Lydia and Matthew appeared on the screen. Unlike before, this time, they were in the same room. When they'd learned that their son had died, they had decided to put their animosity aside and console each other.

"Mr. and Mrs. Chase?" Alice said. A look of sadness had already crept into her eyes.

"Actually," Lydia said, "um...never mind. Yes. And you are... Alice?"

"Yes, that's me."

"You...you were with our son?" Matthew asked.

"Yes, we were...a couple. I love...I, um, loved him very much. I need to tell you that your son is...was...a good man."

"Jacob was a good man, Matt," Lydia said, "you hear that?"

Matthew visibly got choked up.

"He really was," Alice said. "I know that...he had a questionable occupation, but, his heart, it was beautiful. I saw it. I know that you were disappointed in him, but you should be proud of what he did out here. He was a valuable friend, a valuable member of this team, and last month he helped rescue a bunch of children. He was a wonderful person."

"He loved you?" Lydia asked.

"Yes, he did, and I loved him. And he always showed me how much he loved me. He made me feel loved. But not just *me*. He showed us all out here how much he cared. He became such good friends with Wyatt, Chloe, and Jamar, too. They loved him, too. He told me that it was the first time in his life that he ever had such good friends, that he felt like he was part of a team, a part of something important."

"Did he, um, ever talk about us?" Matthew asked.

"Yes, he did. He missed you. Jacob was trying to find you. He generally spoke positively about you two, and he felt bad that he had left like he did. He felt bad about that might have affected you two. He'd wanted to apologize for it if he ever found you."

"His apology is accepted," Lydia said, "and...we forgive him."

"Yes, we do," Matthew added. "To be frank with you, before today, I'd never thought I'd be proud of him for something. But, what you've told us...it's very heartening. I'm very glad that my son has left a legacy behind to be proud of."

The conversation continued for about another half hour. Alice told them all about her experiences with Jacob, their adventures together, and all the good he'd done on those adventures.

When it was over, Alice felt good. She was glad that she did it. She made a connection with Jacob's parents that helped her feel like part of him was still there. It was comforting. It partially healed her heart.

#

Karak helped Alice plan the funeral. She found that there wasn't as much to do as she'd thought. But the part of the planning that made her feel sad, despite the wonderful relationship she'd had with him, was guessing his preferences. It painfully helped her realize just how much she hadn't yet learned about him. Like Karak was going to program the replicator with his favorite kind of flower, but Alice didn't know what it was. But then, when she sent a message to his parents asking, they didn't know, either.

Alice wanted Chloe to play his favorite song, but she sadly did not know that, either. This one his parents *did* know. It was "Black Parade" by My Chemical Romance. Alice didn't even know he was a fan of that specific genre of music.

Chloe said she could play the song and that she'd love to do it. Alice thanked her.

The hardest part was choosing which space coffin to send him off in. The Deelooveren had a selection of them to choose from, but they also told her they could replicate a new one if none of those would do. But Alice, glad that she knew what his favorite color was, chose a dark blue one. Their large size surprised her. They were the size of a tiny ship to better survive the ravages of space than a small coffin would. And the ship, with its own antimatter power core, would

maintain the stasis field forever, or at least as long as the ship remained intact.

The next day, the ceremony commenced. The humans all wore
formal black outfits. And Chloe, similar to her preference at the winner's ceremony, had opted for a suit and tie.

When Alice, Wyatt, Chloe, and Jamar arrived, they were glad
to see some familiar faces.

"Great sadness in our hearts," Soojen said as he greeted them.
The entire Feeijing team was there. Along with Soojen, Fijaa, Deelan, Mootak, and Foojar were present. The humans were happy to see
them.

"Much shock in my mind when this news of sadness entered
my ears," Deelan said. "And…there's something I want to put in your
ears that maybe was not in your mind."

"What is it?" Alice said.

"The choice in his mind was Earth and *you*. He put that in my
ears before fitting in the trip to Loovian."

Alice's eyes grew wet. "I wonder why didn't he tell me when
he'd had the chance?"

"He desired to wait until he lived in the right moment," Deelan
replied.

Alice hugged him. "Thank you for telling me, Deelan."

"Problem not," he replied.

She was more surprised to see Marner there, the Venure thief
that they'd played against in the Contest.

"I never thought I'd see one of you again," Alice said to him.

"When I heard, I had to be here," Marner said with a hint of
sadness in his eye. "He was a great thief, and I have a lot of respect for
him. So I wanted to pay those respects."

"Thank you," Alice said.

When the coffin ship was in place near the airlock's force field
and everybody was seated, the ceremony began. Chloe began it by
playing *Amazing Grace,* and Jamar accompanied her by singing the
lyrics. Alice wept as they did so. So did Jamar, Wyatt, and Chloe.
Tears dripped from her eyes as she played the song with the beautiful,
mellifluous notes that she could produce with her Stradivarius violin.
And Jamar also cried as he sang his heart out.

A profound gesture uplifted Alice's heart. Eight of the alien children that Chase had helped rescue and their parents were at the ceremony. Each child held a single flower picked from their home planets. Each of them, dressed in either their little dresses or little suits, walked up and carefully placed their flowers near the front of the coffin. One particular little girl, who was very pale with violet hair and antennae, wearing a large, pretty bow on the back of her dress, hesitated. She looked at Alice and smiled at her before putting her flower down. Alice, with tears streaming down her eyes, smiled back at her.

When it was time for Alice to stand at the podium before the audience and in front of Jacob's coffin to give the speech that she'd prepared, she could barely do it. She had a handlink in front of her that she'd written the speech on, but she just set it aside. She sniffed, then began.

"I wrote a speech, but…and this rarely happens with me… written language is failing me. I need to say this purely from my heart. And, standing before you all, here, today, in front of all this love you all have shown, my heart tells me that this man, Jacob Chase, was, and still is, worthy of all of it." She stopped for several seconds to try to compose herself. "I can think of few people who are as worthy of it as he is. Let's just address the elephant in the room, as we humans like to say, and, yes, he has a questionable past, like all the thieves here today. But he sought redemption, and he sought to use his skills for good. And he loved all that he loved with *all* of his heart."

She couldn't stop it anymore. She broke down and sobbed. Chloe stood up from her seat and walked to the podium, the heels of her shoes clicking onto the thinly carpeted metal floor. She reached out and took one of Alice's hands into hers. She held it firmly and lovingly.

Alice sniffed, and, with her wet eyes, she looked into hers. "Thank you, Chloe," she whispered.

But Alice continued to sob. She couldn't stop. Chloe cleared her throat and finished for her. "Jacob Chase was a wonderful man! One of the finest men, and humans, I've ever had the pleasure to meet. I say this with no doubt in my heart!" But then, she added, with a slight smile, "Even though when I first met him, I didn't like him. But here's the thing about Chase, as he'd liked to be called, the more you get to know him, the more you cannot help but like him…and, later, love him, as I do." Tears came to her eyes, too, but she continued. "He ended up being one of the dearest friends I've ever had, and I will cherish the memories of that friendship forever! From here, to the end of the galaxy, and back. I will truly miss him. And I will *never* forget him."

Not a single eye in the funeral room stayed dry as Chloe said those words.

Jamar and Wyatt joined them at the podium.

Jamar, quite choked up himself, tried several times to also give his own little speech. But he couldn't. "Aw, hell," he managed to say between sniffs, "ditto what they said!" He nodded to Chloe and Alice.

"Jamar is right," Wyatt said as he wiped his eyes, "they said it perfectly." Then all four joined hands.

"Jacob," Alice said as she looked out to the room at nobody in particular, "I don't know if…if somehow you can hear all this, but I want you to know that I love you and that you are worthy! Because you had doubted that you were, you saddled yourself with too much self-doubt! But you *are* worthy! I mean that with *all* of my heart… and soul!"

All four of them, still joined hand-in-hand, raised their hands to the air.

"For Chase!" Wyatt said.

"For Chase!" Chloe echoed him. Jamar said it, too.

Then, with all eyes on Alice, she said it, too. "For Chase!" She looked backward at the coffin. "I'll miss you, my love," she whispered.

Moments later, Chloe played his favorite song, solo, with no singing. It was beautiful.

Then it was time. Karak stood at the podium.

"As is Deelooveren tradition, with interstellar funerals, we now commit the remains of Jacob Chase to the deep expanse, to continue his journey. He was a fine human, one I am glad to have known. I will never forget him. We, my people and I, honor him. We wish him luck on the rest of his adventures in the universe." They turned and looked at the coffin. They brought their hands up and clasped their hands together, a traditional Deelooveren gesture of love and honor. From their seats, Coordinator Jeelork and Engineer Farrstead did the same.

The ship coffin hummed. It hovered off of the floor.

Alice collapsed to her knees, sobbing uncontrollably. Wyatt, Jamar, and Chloe knelt down, too, consoling her as best they could. The ship slowly passed through the force field, then traveled out into space. Through soaked eyes, Alice watched it get smaller and smaller as it traveled out into the galaxy.

CHAPTER TWENTY: The Slithertown Rescue

FOLLOWING THE funeral, there was a banquet in the ballroom with food and drinks to celebrate the life of Jacob Chase. The humans and the thieves sat at the same large table.

"It was a beautiful ceremony, wasn't it?" Chloe said to Alice.

"It was," Alice replied. Her eyes were still red and sore from all the crying. "And thank you so much for the beautiful words you said."

"It was my pleasure, love," Chloe whispered.

Alice sipped her drink, but as she swallowed, she wondered something. She looked at Deelan, Farine, Barchell, and Woo'cha, who were all seated next to each other. "I just realized that Jacob, nor any of you, had ever told me the full story of when you all rescued the children at Slithertown. I would like to hear it."

"So would I," Wyatt said. "I mean, I was very glad to hear that you all pulled it off. It broke our hearts to have to leave those kids behind to continue the quest."

"Sure," Barchell said. "But before I begin, I have to give credit to Farine. She was the one who'd advocated that we do it. She brought us all together for it."

"We had to rescue those little cuties!" Farine said. "I was insistent. I'm glad you all listened."

Barchell snickered. "We had to, ummm, *borrow* a Deelooveren ship to do it."

"Oh, '*borrow*,' I see," Alice said. "Yes, you guys *borrow* a lot of things don't you?" Chloe was glad to see a slight smile on her face.

"I was on Loovian for a scheduled visit," Farine said as she held her drink aloft casually, "and it was in a shipyard being repaired. They, well, didn't exactly lock the doors adequately enough."

Alice sighed and slightly shook her head. "At least you used it for a good purpose."

"Don't tell her about the Kastonian jewels," Barchell whispered.

"The what?" Chloe said.

"Let's just move on, okay!" Farine said quickly. She took a big gulp of her drink.

"Yes, get to better story, let's do now," Deelan said with a sly smile.

Alice looked at them with mock disapproval. "You thieves, I swear…"

"I just want to say, before we really deep-dive into the story," said Farine, "and I don't say this just because we're here right now to celebrate his life, but even though the rescue was my idea, Chase was the true hero of this story."

"Absolutely!" Barchell said. "We could not have pulled it off without him."

"Well, please explain," Alice said, "I'd really love to hear this story."

#

"Chase!" Ambassador Karak yelled. "Are you piloting that ship that's gone missing?!"

They were on the communications screen, looking quite angry.

"What, Ambassador?" Chase said. "Gee, you're breaking up, so much static, what was that about a ship?"

"I know you can hear me clearly! I'm not stupid!"

Chase made fake static noises with his mouth. "Hold on…not sure I'm hearing you correctly…did you just say that you're stupid?!"

Kara's face trembled in anger. "Really? I mean…*really*?!"

"I think they said they can't hear you clearly!" said Farine, Chase's copilot.

"Farine, you know I didn't—" Karak sighed and shook their head. They also rolled their eyes. "This is what we get for having thieves in the Contest."

"After we are finished rescuing these children," Chase said, "which, by the way, is a *very noble cause*, we can circle back around to this missing ship business that you're talking about!"

"If you had just asked—"

"Oh no, Ambassador, we're entering a black hole! We're losing you!"

"Oh, come on! You are *not* entering a—"

Chase hung up on them. "Dang it, what is wrong with these communications systems?"

"We should run a full diagnostic!" Barchell said, trying to hold back laughter.

Farine giggled. "Well, let's do that later, my cuties! We are currently dancing into Slithertown!"

"Turning on the cloak!" Chase said. "I'm sure they won't be happy to see a Deelooveren ship again!"

The ship shimmered into an invisible state as they approached the moon's upper atmosphere.

"I'll tell you who won't like seeing the two of us again!" Farine said. "Tark and Lady Pain!"

"Yeah, let's hope we don't have to, um, have a conversation with them."

"Didn't you say that your girlfriend killed Scort?" Barchell asked.

Chase smiled. "Yes she did! And now, we're here to rescue all those children he'd had abducted and finish the job that she'd started."

They landed the ship near the club in a large, secluded alleyway near the outskirts of the main downtown area.

After arming themselves, they got off the ship. Chase looked at the deep orange shades in the sky as the sun was setting. "I'm glad it's not raining this time."

"We have to be very careful," Barchell said as he examined his phaser rifle. "No serum this time."

"We can do it," Chase said, "no fights unless absolutely necessary. This has to be as surgical as possible. Get in, get the kids, get out." He got out his handlink. They all gathered around. He had a floor plan of the club on the screen. He pointed to the back room. "The kids should be here."

"Are you sure?" Barchell asked.

"This is where they were last time." Then he pointed to other spots on the floor plan. "There will be guards here, and here. We need to make as little noise as possible. We need to sneak up on them and stab them in the back with our knives. Only use phasers as a last resort. Got it?"

"Won't they be expecting us to come back?!" Woo'cha said. "This is an insane plan."

"Then why the hell did you come, anyway?" Barchell asked him. "To be the team's complainer?"

Woo'cha sighed and looked at him. "I just…okay, good point. Let's do this."

Chase rolled his eyes. "Glad you're on board, Zendeck!"

They had to walk about a kilometer to get to the club. When they got there, Woo'cha and Barchell headed toward the main entrance.

"Stop, cuties!" Farine said. "We're not going in the main entrance."

"Oh yeah, good idea," Barchell said. "Let's find a back entrance."

Chase pointed to it on his device. "I believe the back entrance is here. It's where they take in deliveries of food and such."

They headed for a retaining wall on the side of the club. Chase scanned the wall with his device. Then he transformed everybody's uniform to match the wall.

"I love this Deelooveren tech," Barchell said as he looked at his arms.

"It was Wyatt's idea to use it this way," Chase said, "mad props to him."

#

"Well, I'm glad he gave me credit!" Wyatt held up his drink.

"Shhh!" Chloe said, "Don't interrupt! We're about to get to the rescue part!"

#

The thieves crept around to the back of the club. So far nobody had detected their presence. When they arrived near the back entrance, there was a delivery taking place. A small cargo ship was unloading several boxes of something. A swarthy alien wearing a filthy tee shirt and baggy, dirty pants was carrying the boxes into the doorway.

"Good," Farine whispered, "we won't have to break into it. Let's sneak in next time he goes inside with a box."

Chase changed their uniforms again to resemble the back of the building. They successfully snuck into the entrance. Chase changed their appearance again to resemble the pale orange paint of the walls of that area of the club.

"Their choice of paint color might be the most criminal thing about this place," Farine whispered.

"Hey," Barchell said, "we're a pale orange color like that when we're born."

"Sorry, Barch," Farine replied.

"Very nice color, in my eyes," Deelan lied.

"Whatever," Barchell replied.

"This way," Chase whispered, He gestured for them to follow him as he turned a corner. "Now's a good time to get out your knives."

He and Farine slipped theirs out of their pockets. Barchell and Woo'cha did the same. Before long they came to the room with the children. Like before, they observed kids of many different races chained up to each other and the walls. Chase was glad that he recognized a few of them so he saw it as a second chance for them. There were guards there, the same race as Tark. They busily discussed something with each other. They tried to overhear them. All they could make out was something about a potential buyer arriving soon. They had little time.

"Gimme more!" yelled a female somebody from the nearby corridor. It was some junkie pleading with a dealer most likely. "I need more fixion!"

"This place is terrible," Barchell whispered.

Chase put his finger out his mouth. "Shhh," he quietly shushed him.

Farine gasped when she noticed one of the children was her own race. A little Norfan girl was chained to the wall, and to a male child of some other race. Her eyes were wet like she had recently cried.

"She will be free soon," Chase whispered in her ear. He was so close to her hair that he could smell its floral scent.

Chase and Barchell slowly approached the backs of the guards. Chase pointed at their heads. Barchell nodded. Stabbing them there would ensure an instant kill.

Farine, Woo'cha, and Deelan crept near the children. They had their knives and lock picks out.

Chase and Barchell each killed a guard by stabbing them

through the backs of their necks to their throats to make sure they couldn't scream. The guards fell to the floor. Chase hated having to kill somebody that way…or murder anybody in *any* way…but his primary concern was freeing the children. He justified it in his mind as anybody who helps the trafficking of children deserved it.

Some of the kids noticed the guards falling down. They frantically looked around. Then the thieves showed themselves to the children.

"We're here to rescue you," Chase whispered. But he noticed that none of them had translating communicators. So he just tried to shush them, hoping they'd understand that meant to be quiet. Fortunately, they got the message. Farine could convey the message to the Norfan girl.

The thieves were all able to pick the locks of the wrist and ankle bracelets on all the children. When the children realized maybe this meant they were being rescued, some of them got excited. One of them—a pale little girl with antennae—grabbed Chase and hugged him. She sobbed a joyful cry. This moved Chase so much that he teared up. He warmly hugged her back.

"Hugs later!" Barchell said in a loud whisper. "We gotta go!"

Chase parted with the girl, then he pointed toward the direction of the rear of the club. She smiled and nodded at him. But before they moved, she grabbed his hand. She reached her face up and kissed his cheek. Chase, moved again by the affection, briefly touched the spot where she'd kissed him. He smiled and slowly nodded at her.

Soon they all sneaked toward the rear corridor of the building. Unfortunately, it would not be this easy.

"What the hell?!"

Chase spun his head around. Lady Pain and Tark suddenly stood there. It was Lady Pain who had yelled.

Chase got both of his handheld phasers out. "Everybody, go! I'll take care of them!"

"Chase!" Farine yelled.

"Go! The children are more important! If I survive I'll catch up to you!"

"*You!*" Lady Pain yelled. "You must have titanium balls to come back here!"

"Well, they're made of *something* hard!" Chase replied.

"As much as I agreed that Scort was a sick bastard, I can't let millions of bunds of gold walk out that door!"

"Well, you either do that, or die!" Chase aimed his phasers.

"*You're* the one who's going to die, human!" Tark yelled.

Chase dropped to his knees as they fired their phasers at his head. He shot back. He hit Tark, killing him, but he missed Lady Pain. She deftly dodged his shots. She fired back but Chase rolled away, barely avoiding getting shot. Chase fired several more shots in rapid succession and missed. It temporarily overheated his phaser. Lady Pain did the same to her weapon.

But she whipped out a dagger. She lunged at him. He jumped away from her, but not quickly enough. She sliced his cheek with her sharp blade. Chase fired his phaser again. Lady Pain dodged it. She aimed her own phaser.

Chase got behind a metal box to use it as cover as she fired. He grabbed at his cheek as the cut sharply hurt. His bloody fingers showed the cut was bad. He shook his hand, then popped back up and fired, missing her. She shot back at him and missed, too.

"If you truly believe Scort was evil for the child trafficking business, then let them go!"

"I can't!"

"Your heart can't be that dark!" Chase replied. "They're children, for crying out loud! You know it's wrong and evil! If you really are human, then show some humanity!"

"I...I can't! It's too much money!"

"Please let us go. We can make it look good. Like you really tried to stop us and failed! Please!"

Lady Pain sighed heavily.

"Please, Lady! You know it's the right thing to do!"

"Um...okay." Lady Pain lowered her weapon. "Just...go. I hope you find their families. Get the hell out quickly before I change my mind!"

"Thank you!" Chase said. He stood up. "I really appreciate—"

"GO!"

Chase needed no more prompting. He ran out of the room. Lady Pain fired several times at him as he ran off, missing on purpose.

Chase caught up with the others by sprinting out the door and away from the club.

"I'm so glad you made it out!" Farine yelled. "Oh no, you're cut!"

"It's fine!" Chase said. "Just a scratch!"

Farine grabbed him and hugged him. Then she quickly kissed him. (Barchell and the others left that part of the story out.)

"We're not safe yet!" Chase said. "Come on, back to the ship, quickly!"

But they couldn't run as fast as they could. They were herding about a dozen children who were escaping with them.

When they heard yelling behind them, Barchell yelled, "Grab some kids! We gotta run faster!"

"Why don't we beam out?!" Woo'cha yelled.

"The ship's broken transporter was the reason it was in the repair bay!" Chase yelled.

Each of them grabbed a few kids. They could indeed grab all of them. This helped them increase their speed.

"I really…wish…we had…the serum…now," Chase panted. It had been a while since he'd run this fast or this long. His lungs and legs burned.

When they got to the ship Chase remotely opened the door. They all quickly scrambled inside. Just then phaser blasts started to hit the ship. They barely missed them.

"We gotta go!" Barchell yelled as he closed the door.

Farine and Chase returned to the pilot's chairs. Chase initiated the take-off sequence.

#

"…and we successfully escaped," Barchell said, concluding the story.

"And, we used the Deelooveren database of alien races to identify which planets all the children belonged to, and we brought them back to their families," Farine added.

Alice held her hand to her mouth. She looked near tears. "Oh my god," she gasped, "he was even more brave than I already knew he was."

Jamar gently put his hand on her other one.

"And that pale little girl that hugged him was that same one that looked at you during the funeral," Barchell said. "Her name is Lorine. Her family had been looking for her for over a year. Chase helped end her parents' anguish.'"

Alice smiled. She tried not to get choked up. She swallowed hard. "He did good," she whispered. "He did so much good. I wish…I wish I could tell him."

"I think you just did," Jamar said. "Maybe he's listening. I believe he is."

Alice turned to look at him. "Thank you, Jamar," she said.

Wyatt held up his drink. "To Chase," he said. "Let's toast to one of the best men, one of the biggest hearts, one of the most loving men I've ever known. He was a damned fine thief…not because he could swipe all of our wallets without us knowing, because he could swipe all of our hearts…without us knowing."

"Hear, hear!" Jamar said. "To Chase!" They all raised their drinks, and the rest of them yelled "To Chase!" as they clinked their drinks together.

#

Later, when it was late, when the banquet was winding down, Alice saw Farine standing by one of the windows that looked out into space. Farine stood there, quiet, maybe contemplating something. She approached Farine. She heard her coming, and turned to greet her. "Hey," she whispered.

"There's a lovely view of that nebula tonight," Alice said.

Farine nodded. "How far do you think he's traveled?"

Alice shrugged. "He'll never travel far from us."

Farine smiled. "You have such a way with words. I guess that's why you were the linguist of your team."

Alice smiled, too. But then her smile faded. "I want to ask you something."

"What?"

Alice paused for a few seconds. She had to build up a little courage. "Did you love him?"

Farine also hesitated. She turned back around to where she faced the window again. "Yes, almost everybody at that funeral today did."

"No, I mean…did you *really* love him?"

A moment of silence followed where all they could hear was the hum of the station's systems and far-off chatter from the people still in the ballroom. Alice looked at Farine's face in her reflection in the window. She could tell that Farine struggled with something in her mind.

Farine hung her head low. "Yes." She sighed. "I'm sorry."

Alice put her hand on Farine's shoulder. "There's no need to apologize, it's okay," she whispered. "I think he loved you, too. And…that's also okay."

Farine turned to look into Alice's eyes. "How…are you possible? I mean…how does a person as wonderful and as pure as you exist? You're one of the most beautiful souls I've ever known."

Alice frowned. "I'm not that pure. You know what happened back on that Jistari ship."

Farine looked sincerely into Alice's eyes. "You were angry."

"I don't think it's a good excuse for murdering so many people in one blast of a plasma cannon. I wonder how many more of them were human." Alice now hung her head low.

"The serum caused that rage. You heard what Ammee said."

Alice looked back up at Farine. "But I chose to inject it."

Farine sighed. "I guess none of us are perfect."

"None of us are, Farine."

Farine hesitated. She needed to build up a little courage to ask her next question. "Do you…do you think he knew?"

"That you loved him?"

"Yes."

"I think he did," Alice whispered, "because, you know him, one of the most observant people I've ever known. Not much gets past him. Trust me. He knew."

Farine's eyes teared up. "I miss him terribly. It tears me up inside."

Alice had hardly ever seen Farine so sad, so not chill—only a few times back on Hellkor.

"Come here," Alice said. She embraced Farine.

"Alice, why doesn't this upset you more?"

Alice parted from the hug so she could look her in the eyes. "Trust me, if you'd tried to take him from me, I would have kicked your ass." Farine's mouth stuttered into a smile. Both of them had a slight, sad chuckle.

"You would have *tried*." Both of them chuckled some more. But they both still had tears in their eyes that they had to wipe away.

Alice grinned. "No, I would have succeeded…*my cutie*." Then they both full-on laughed.

After the laughter died down, Farine had another question. "How do you do that?"

"Do what?"

"Help people feel better like that?"

"I'm not sure. It's just…always something I've been able to do. I can't explain it."

"I can." Farine pointed at Alice's chest.

Alice looked down. "My breasts?"

Farine burst into laughter. She actually bent down a little and stood straight back up. "No, silly! Your heart!"

Alice laughed, too. "I know what you meant. And…yeah… that's what they tell me. I just do the best I can, like most people. I empathize. It's just who I am.

"But…Farine…I have to tell you…you do the same thing. Like with your sweet words and your little dance…it puts a smile on anybody's face. It always has the same effect on me."

Farine chuckled. "Not Queeza Tash."

Alice chuckled, too. "Okay, that's *one* exception."

"Hey, Alice, you wanna know something?"

"Yeah?"

"I haven't known you that long, but I love you, too. I want to always have you as a friend. Can you always be my friend?"

"Yes, of course! And I love you, too!" Alice hugged her.

Then they both looked out the window together, wondering how far out there the man they both loved was.

CHAPTER TWENTY-ONE: The Recruit

T HE NEXT day, the humans were scheduled to go home: all five of them.

Alice went down to the containment cell to try, once again, to communicate with the Jistari woman. She approached the cell. The young Asian woman just stood there, looking out with a blank expression on her face. Alice wondered if she'd heard her approaching. Or if she'd been standing like that for hours.

Alice decided to also stand there, on the other side of the force field, and stare right back at her for a few moments. Her stomach felt queasy for a moment when she looked at the black, blue, and yellow marks on her neck where she had nearly strangled her to death.

Alice continued to stare at her. The woman barely blinked. She was utterly unreadable. It was almost as if she wasn't even human.

"Who *are* you?" Alice wondered out loud.

She didn't respond.

"Who *were* you?" Alice said, deciding that was the more pertinent question.

Again, the woman didn't respond.

"What did they do to you?"

This time, and it was barely detectable, she flinched. She ever-so-slightly flinched. She swallowed.

"You had a name once. A family. One who loved you. They probably miss you now. Do you ever think about them? They're probably thinking about you right now."

The woman's face softened slightly. Like the flinch, it was nearly imperceptible. Perhaps she was human after all.

Alice got something out of her pocket. It was a huge risk, but she had to do it. She approached the force field. She pressed the button next to the cell, quickly threw the device into the cell, and pushed the button to reactivate the force field.

It was Alice's voice box. "Put it on."

The woman flinched again. She slowly looked down at the voice box. Then she looked back up at Alice.

"Please. Put it on. It's important."

The woman looked back down at the voice box. Then back at Alice.

"Please."

The Jistari woman bent down and picked the voice box up. She examined it.

"Put it around your neck. It will allow you to talk. Don't be alarmed when the voice sounds like mine. This used to be mine."

The woman looked at Alice. Then she slowly put it on, which actually surprised her.

"Thank you for putting it on. Now, please answer my question. Who are you?"

"Jistari," she answered. It was eerie that it was Alice's own voice talking to her.

"Who were you before?"

"Jistari." She talked flat and devoid of emotion.

"No, no, you weren't."

"Jistari. Always."

Alice slowly shook her head. "You were a beautiful, vibrant girl once. Before they took you. That is what I believe."

A moment of silence followed. The woman continued to stare at Alice. It was unnerving. Alice wondered what was going on inside that head of hers. She had never found somebody so hard to read.

Alice needed to think of a new strategy. She felt like it was her mission to reach the woman before they returned to Earth. Maybe it was a fool's errand. But she felt like it was something she had to do. Or at least try. She just knew she had to, down to her very soul. Something told her that she needed to do this, that it was important. She sighed and paced back and forth.

But then, the woman surprised her. It was so unexpected that it almost made her jump.

"Why didn't you kill me?"

Alice stopped pacing. She walked closer to the force field. "I almost did."

The girl looked to the left, then the right, like she briefly thought something over. "Why didn't you?"

Alice inched even closer to the force field. "My friend begged me not to. She got me to see that it was something I shouldn't do."

"Why?"

Alice gave it some thought. "Because…because you're human."

"I am Jistari."

Alice shook her head. "Be that as it may, you are from Earth. My world. You were born human. And up until a certain point, you were raised human."

"You should have killed me," the woman said as she inched slightly closer to the force field.

This puzzled Alice. "Why?"

"Because if I can, I will not hesitate to kill you."

Alice cocked her head slightly to the left. She felt a twinge of annoyance. "Even after I showed you mercy?"

"Mercy is weakness."

Alice drew even closer to the force field. She could come no closer to it. "No. It's *strength*. Mercy is risky. It requires courage. Weakness is giving in! I was weak when I almost killed you! I was a mess of anger and grief. I lost all control. I was showing weakness, *not* strength, when I was about to snap your neck in two."

The woman slightly craned her neck. She seemed to think about what Alice had said.

"Hate is what made me attack you. But love stayed my hand. Love for my friend. And my love for humanity."

The woman looked slightly confused, like she didn't understand something Alice had said. "What is that?" she asked.

"What's…what?"

"That word you said."

"Which word?"

"Love. What is that?"

Hearing the woman ask that question tore Alice up inside. It blew her mind. How could somebody not know what love was? How was it possible that she didn't remember what the word was? She grunted as she tried to maintain her composure. It made her feel sick that this woman was so far gone that she didn't know, or remember, what love was.

"What is wrong?" the woman asked.

Alice used all the willpower she had to keep herself from sobbing. "It makes me profoundly sad that you don't know what love is."

The woman blinked at Alice. "Sadness is weakness."

"No, it isn't," Alice said.

Something was happening with the woman. Her cool demeanor showed cracks. "What is love?! I mean...I actually do remember the word but...what is it, exactly?!" This time she asked with a slight impatience in her tone.

"I don't...I don't know how to explain it."

"*Try.*"

"The man that the Jistari killed, I loved him. And when the Jistari killed him, I felt such sadness and loss that I went into that rage."

"Love causes rage?"

"No!" Alice stopped and thought about it. This was testing her command of language. She now wished she'd been a poet. "Love... can cause many other emotions. It's...complicated. It's...caring, affection, connection. It's an emotion. Some people say it's a verb. To love somebody is an action. It's also a feeling...a deep caring. Sometimes it's like a fire...that consumes you. Like when it's passion. Does that make sense?"

The Jistari woman moved her eyes around, like she was thinking. "I..." Finally Alice could read something in her. Something, a thought, or maybe a memory, was occurring to her. "I...was loved... once."

"Yes, I don't doubt that."

"Do...do the Jistari love me?"

Alice slowly shook her head. "I don't think they do. I'm sorry. It seems that they just regard you as...like, just another member, a killer. You provide a utility."

"Love is not usefulness?"

"No. It's much more than that."

The woman grew silent again.

"Do you remember who you were?" Alice asked. "Like... when you were loved?"

"I am Jis—" The woman stopped. Alice could see her swallowing. She blinked several times in rapid succession. Her eyes suddenly looked a little more reflective. Was she about to finally show emotion?

"*Who are you*?" Alice whispered.

"I am *nobody*!"

Her outburst shocked Alice. It caused her to step backward. The woman had finally shown emotion.

"I am Jistari!" she yelled.

"Who were you *before that*?!"

"I was—" She trembled. Her lips quivered.

"Yes? You were…?"

"What are you doing to me?" she whispered.

"Showing you that you are a human person with an identity. That you were somebody before the Jistari took you from Earth."

"Why?"

"Because we're taking you back to Earth. I want to reunite you with your family."

"My family is Jistari."

"Yes. And then before Jistari, they were…?"

"They—" Again, she trembled. Her breathing became slightly labored. "They were…I was…I was loved."

"Yes, you were," Alice said. She came as close to the force field that she could. "Who loved you?"

"My mo—" She closed her eyes tightly. She shook her head. She put her hands on the sides of her face. She shook her head again. "Stop it!"

"Do you remember your mother?"

The woman shut her eyes tighter. "I…remember…" Then Alice saw it. A single tear formed at the corner of one of her eyes.

"What was your name?" Alice asked. "Do you remember?"

"Shut up!"

"What was it?"

The woman ripped off the voice box, threw it onto the floor, and stomped on it, smashing it to pieces. She threw a punch at the force field right at Alice's face. It knocked her back against the opposite wall. It stung her nose a little, but it didn't do any damage. She rubbed her nose and checked for blood. But there wasn't any.

Chloe entered the corridor and walked down to the cell. She

saw Alice checking her nose. "I came to see if you'd made any progress. What happened?"

"I got too close to the force field, I'm fine."

Chloe looked at the Jistari woman and the smashed bits of the
voice box. "What's that rubbish on the floor of her cell?"

"My voice box," Alice replied.

"Well…I'm, um, glad you don't need it anymore."

"Yeah, I used it to talk to her. It didn't go so well. Come on,
I'll tell you more." Alice led Chloe away from the woman's cell and
toward the entrance of the brig.

Alice recapped for Chloe the progress she'd made and the conversation she'd had with the woman.

Chloe looked upset and shook her head when Alice was done.
"I'm sorry…she didn't remember what love is?"

"Yeah," Alice said.

"Oh my god," Chloe said. "That's so bloody sad."

"Oh, that almost broke me, Chloe, seriously. Hearing that tore
up my soul. It ripped me to pieces."

Chloe sighed. "You know, Alice, honestly, you're a bit dramat-
ic sometimes."

Alice narrowed her eyes at Chloe. But then she slowly rolled
her eyes. "OK… that's fair."

Chloe smiled and snickered at her. "I'm sorry, love."

Alice sighed and chuckled a little, too. "It's true, it's true. But,
really, though, it *is* super sad, not remembering love."

"I agree. It sucks that you didn't get her name. Without that,
how are we going to figure out who she belongs to?"'

Alice thought about it for a few seconds. Then she shook her
head. "You know what? Why does that have to be my job, or ours, to
figure that out? There are people, you know, *detectives*, on Earth that
figure that shit out? Let's just let them figure it out, so we can freakin'
get back to our normal lives! We have been burdened with too much!"

"Yeah!" Chloe said. "You're right! God, yeah, you are so right!
Enough of all of this bollocks!" She waved her hand around. "Let's
just go the hell home and, finally, leave all this rubbish behind! Like,
go back to when our lives *weren't constantly in danger*!"

As much as Alice wanted that possibility to be true, she knew
it wasn't. She felt a little sad again as that reality struck her. "Chloe,

that may not be entirely possible, though. The Hellkorian A.I. would have abducted us from Earth if we hadn't been on Loovian. They abducted the others from their home planets. We're famous now on Earth. We made intergalactic enemies. One of those space gangsters or the Jistari might come after us. Hell, we have *human* assassins after us! We opened Pandora's space box and can't close it again. Who knows what's next? Our lives may be in constant danger now, no matter what we do."

"Well…that's a very disturbing thought."

"Maybe…maybe we really do need to be under the Deelooveren's protection. Maybe they weren't being bad or wrong to watch us. Maybe they're right, and that…we *should* trust them. Or maybe…"

"Maybe…what?"

"Maybe…we shouldn't even go back to Earth."

"What?"

"No, I mean…so like, we go back, as scheduled. Have a good visit. But then come back here. Maybe Jacob had a good thought… after all we've been through, maybe out here is where we belong now. Or at least me."

"That thought got him killed!"

A pinch of anger entered Alice's mind. "Aren't you listening? Going back home and staying *there* could get us killed. At least here, I mean, on this station, not out seeking space gangsters or whatever, but right here on this station, which has armed guards and deflector shields, we'd be safer!"

Chloe sighed. "You are…not without a point."

"I mean…I'm like…thinking about all this right now as I'm saying it…it actually sounds interesting. Like, staying here, working for the station, if they'll have me. I could help with translations, with the language barriers…all the new aliens coming in to participate in the Contests every year. And *you*…you could train them to learn combat techniques for the trials. Think about it. I'm actually getting kind of excited thinking about it."

"Yeah?" Chloe frowned. She thought about it, too. "What about Wyatt and Jamar?"

"Let's talk to them about it. Let's see what they think. Like, discuss it during the trip back to Earth."

"Wyatt and I could be…with each other every day. No more

flying back and forth between London and St. Louis. Alice…your idea is *intriguing*."

Alice smiled at Chloe. "We could *all* be together all the time."

Chloe smiled, too. She grabbed Alice's hands and held them on her own. "That sounds…*lovely*."

#

When it was time to leave, the four humans met at the airlock. Alice, Jamar, Chloe, and Wyatt, with bags of their belongings, were ready to go. Chloe also had her violin case. Alice was in pain. The withdrawals were back. Her breathing was labored and she had trouble standing there.

"Are you okay?" Wyatt asked her.

"Not really," Alice said. "But…I'm dealing. I got another dose of the medicine earlier. And Karak gave me a few more doses to take back with me. But they warned me not to take it until the withdrawals got unbearably bad. If I use the medicine too much it will become ineffective."

Two Deelooveren guards appeared, escorting the Jistari woman. She was in the large, titanium restraints, similar to the ones that Leeka had used. The woman had a blank expression on her face.

"I hope they can figure out who she belongs to," Wyatt said.

"That's not our problem," Alice said.

"Why not?"

"Because it doesn't have to be, Wyatt!" Alice sighed and rubbed her face with her hand. "I'm sorry. I'm irritable right now. I just think that maybe we're overburdening ourselves. We don't have to solve everybody's problems." Alice looked at the woman again. She no longer had a blank expression. She looked right at Alice. She thought she detected a very subtle pleading expression on her face.

Did she want Alice to help her?

"Alice, it's what we do," Jamar said. "I want to help her. I feel like it's something we gotta do."

"We are making sure she gets back to Earth," Chloe said. "We *are* helping her. But what else can we do? Detectives will figure it out. They'll use her DNA or picture or something."

Right after the airlock doors opened, Karak came around the corner. "Wait," they said. They held a new voice box in their hands.

Alice looked at them. "I don't think I'll ever need another one of those."

"No," Karak said, "I heard that you used your old voice box on the Jistari woman. I had a new one made, programmed with the voice this woman likely had, based on the DNA scans we did of her. You can use it if you try to speak with her again."

"She'll probably smash it again."

"They're not difficult to replicate."

Karak gave it to Alice. "Well, thank you. When we get back to Earth, investigators can use it to talk to her, too, maybe help her figure out who her family is."

Alice held onto the device. It was time to get to the ship. They all said goodbye to Karak.

"Wait!" Farine came running around the corner. "I couldn't let you all leave without saying goodbye!"

"Awww, I'm glad you didn't miss us!" Chloe said.

Alice held out her arms. "Me, too!" She hugged Farine warmly. Each of them took turns hugging her goodbye.

"We'll miss you," Wyatt said, "too bad we didn't get to get dance lessons from you."

"You never know," Alice said with a mischievous smile, "maybe we'll get them sometime later."

"You know what?" Jamar said. "Maybe we will."

"Well, then, maybe I'll see you later, my cuties!" Farine did a particular dance where she clasped her hands together, moved her arms as if they were an ocean wave, and shuffled her feet around. "This is my peoples' goodbye dance."

Alice smiled as she tried to emulate her. Then Chloe, Wyatt, and Jamar tried to copy the dance, too. They didn't do so well, but it still made Farine happy.

She giggled. "Not bad, not bad!"

The four humans chuckled as they looked at each other, amused by how they were all mostly failing at copying her. "Not that good, either!" Alice exclaimed.

"When we meet again, I'll try to teach you the Hello dance," Farine said as she giggled.

"I look forward to it, love!" Chloe said.

They all said goodbye again.

#

"I had a feeling it'd be you two," Wyatt said when they boarded the slip. Captains Flarr and Sloo were at the drive controls.

"Well, we requested it this time," Captain Flarr said.

Sloo counted. "Hey, there's only four of them."

Captain Flarr quickly tried to shush them.

"What?" Sloo whispered. Flarr whispered in their ear about what happened to Chase.

Sloo looked at the humans as they finished boarding. "I'm so sorry for your loss. I didn't know…"

"It's okay," Alice replied, "and thank you."

Later, Alice went down to the lower level to communicate with the Jistari woman again. One of the guards turned off the force field, and Alice handed the woman the voice box. The guard quickly turned the force field back on.

Round three, Alice thought.

The woman surprised Alice by putting the voice box on without hesitation.

"Do you wanna talk more, then?" Alice asked.

"Yes," she said. Alice was glad she wasn't listening to her in her own voice again.

"Good. Do you remember what your name was?"

"I…I think it was…Akiko. I think that was my first name."

"Okay, good. I have a name to call you. Akiko, my name is—"

"Alice," Akiko said. When she saw Alice was a little surprised, she said, "I am mute, not deaf."

"Oh, right. I'm sorry."

"You should have killed me."

"We've already been over that, Akiko."

"If I get free, I will kill you."

Alice scoffed. "I am trying to help you, you know!"

"You should not help me."

"Well, I don't believe that you're beyond help. And I believe what happened to you was not your fault."

"You believe the Jistari kidnap people. You believe wrong. They recruit, they do not abduct."

"What age were you when they took—" Alice stopped herself, hesitated, shook her head slightly, then continued. "When they…met you? And what age are you now?"

"I do not know my age," Akiko replied. "But…I believe I am…somewhere between seventeen and nineteen."

"What age were you when they… 'recruited' you?"

"I believe I was…nine? Ten?"

"You were a child, Akiko! It wasn't fair what they did to you. I don't care how willing you think you were."

"They showed me a better path."

"They showed you a path away from love! You forgot what love was! There is no way in hell that that's a better path."

"Love is weakness."

"No!" Alice yelled. She banged the nearby phaser locker. "Dammit, no! See what they've done to you? Last time we talked you said that you remembered being loved. Now, tell me that's a bad memory."

Akiko didn't answer. But she looked like she was becoming slightly emotional again.

"Is it a bad memory, Akiko? Is it, or is it not?"

Akiko remained silent. But she swallowed, and her bottom lip quivered.

"Answer me!" Akiko didn't answer. Alice sighed. "Akiko, if you didn't want to listen to me, answer all my questions, then why did you want to talk? Why did you put it on?"

"I…I don't know."

"Okay, let's circle back to the love thing. Where are you from?"

"I am from Jistari Moon 876, in the Florian system."

"No. Where on *Earth* are you from? America? Japan? I can't tell if you're using the translator or not."

"I was born in New York, in the US. My parents…" Akiko hesitated. She looked like she was suddenly getting choked up. "My parents are from Japan."

"Okay, so, the Jistari are coming to Earth recruiting. They've been to New York. This is good to know."

"What are you going to do with that information?!" Akiko exclaimed.

Alice approached the force field. "Stop them from breaking up any more families," she whispered, almost in an angry hiss.

Akiko's face trembled. "My family was weak!" She said it in an angry tone, but despite that she was near sobbing.

"No, they weren't! And you know it!" Alice backed away from the force field. "I got the information I need. I have other things to do."

Alice headed for the stairs.

"Wait!" Akiko yelled.

Alice stopped. She turned around. "What?"

Akiko just stood there, unmoving. A few tears trickled down her cheeks.

Alice approached the force field again. "*What?*"

"I…I don't understand…these feelings that I'm having."

"It's simple, Akiko. You're starting to remember that you're human."

"Help me understand them!" Akiko exclaimed.

"You say you want to kill me, yet you plea for my help?"

"I…I…I think I'm changing my mind…like you did."

Alice scrunched her mouth to the left. "Well, that's a start. But…Akiko, you need therapy. *Years* of it. I'm not a therapist. It's not my expertise. Language is. But not psychology or psychotherapy. I'm sorry."

Alice walked away again.

"Wait, please!"

Alice turned back to her. "We can talk again when you are certain you've changed your mind about killing me! Are you certain?"

Akiko didn't answer.

"That's what I thought!" Alice ascended to the upper level.

"Alice!" Akiko yelled. But Alice shut the door.

CHAPTER TWENTY-TWO: Home

W HEN THE trip home was well underway, after Alice got back to her seat, the others wanted to know how the conversation with the Jistari woman went.

The body aches from the serum withdrawal suddenly hit Alice again. She grunted and doubled over. "It…went…fine." She took in a deep breath and sat straight up again. She slowly blew the breath out. "I got some more information."

"Like what?" Chloe asked.

"Her first name…Akiko. She lived in New York. So that's at least one place on Earth the Jistari are invading to recruit."

"New York City? State?" Jamar said.

"She wasn't more specific, sorry. But she did mention that they took her away as a child, like nine or ten years old."

"Well, that's sad, but, having more information, this is good," Wyatt said. "We have more information to give the authorities. Maybe they, with the help of the Deelooveren, can put a stop to this."

"Why do they need the Deelooveren?" Chloe asked.

"Wyatt's right, we've seen what the Jistari can do," Alice replied. "Human authorities aren't ready to deal with them without help from people who've dealt with them before."

#

Halfway through the trip, Alice pitched her idea to the rest of the team to go back to the *Arkenstar* and become staff. Unbeknownst to them, she had already pitched the idea before they'd left to Ambassador Harklon, and they were amenable to it.

"So, my idea, and of course you are all free to do what you want, is that we become *Arkenstar* staff, help them with the Contests, in training, in planning, and all of us could use our particular talents.

I know the idea of, again, spending so much time away from Earth would be unpalatable, but we all have to admit, we're not safe there, even being under the Deelooveren's protection."

"I agree," Chloe said. "And I've already decided that I am on board. She's right. On Earth we are in more danger, and we put our families in danger. I think it really gives me a sense of purpose."

"I'm gonna need to think about this," Jamar said. "I mean...I was in the middle of doing research for a big paper."

"I'm going to think on it, too," Wyatt said, "but, I think it's a very interesting idea. But, spending so much time away from Earth, we'd have to have plenty of sunny holosuite time."

"I'm sure we could do that," Alice said.

"We would of course come back and visit Earth often," Chloe said.

"Harklon said when I talked to them that that wouldn't be a problem," Alice added.

"Yeah, sure, we trust that," Jamar said. "It's not like the Deelooveren never lie to us!"

Alice sighed. "I get it, I get the doubt. It's fair. We do have to make somewhat of a leap of faith that might be unearned. So yeah, this plan is not without its risk."

"You know what?" Wyatt said. "Screw it, I'm in! If I get to see Chloe a lot more often, I'm for it!" He looked at Chloe. She looked back at him with a huge smile. She grabbed him and she kissed him.

"Damn PDA again," Jamar said, "if I do it, you all are gonna—" But he looked at Alice and he stopped. "Oh...Alice...I'm sorry, I..."

Alice placed a hand on his leg. "Jamar, it's okay. It hasn't been that long. We're not all used to it yet."

"What are we doing with that Jistari woman?" Sloo asked Flarr.

"We're dropping her and the guards off at the offices of some investigators in this place called New York. Like...they call them the Federal Bureau of Investigations."

"We just say FBI," Alice said. "They should help find her family."

"Well, I, for one, hope they do," Flarr said, "since you said they kidnapped her as a child."

When they entered the Terran system, the trip was almost over.

Alice was first on the list to drop off. When the ship arrived at Earth they headed for Oregon. When the ship hovered over her family's home, they observed a fiasco below. Reporters and media vans were everywhere. It was around 8:00 PM, but the ground was still bathed in plenty of light.

"They must know about Jacob," Alice whispered as she looked out the window. "I'm not ready for this."

"We're about to drop her off in the hornet's nest," Jamar said.

"Change of plan!" Chloe exclaimed. "Drop me off here! With Alice! I'll go back home to London later."

Captain Flarr pointed to an informational panel in front of them. "But my orders—"

"To hell with your orders!" Chloe said. "Drop me off *here!*"

Wyatt raised his hand. "Drop me off here, too, please."

"Me, too," Jamar said.

Alice's cell phone rang. At first she didn't recognize what the noise was, it had been so long since she'd used it. But then she did, and she answered it. It was her father.

"Hey, Dad."

"Is that you, up in that spaceship?"

"Yes, we were about to beam down."

"What the hell is going on?! They got here an hour ago."

"They must have heard about Jacob."

"Well, I promise you, it wasn't *me* who leaked that news. And…when you said 'we…?'"

"We're *all* coming down, Dad, please get the extra chairs from the basement. Love you, bye." She hung up.

She stood up and turned to her friends so she could address them all. "Thank you all so much for coming down with me. I really appreciate it…not letting me face all that alone. You're three of the best friends that…" She paused as she got choked up. "…that any girl…or anybody…could ask for."

"No problem, hon," Jamar replied, "we got you."

"Ride or die," Chloe said.

"Well, are you all ready for an impromptu press conference?" Wyatt said.

"After the hell we've been through lately," Chloe said, "I'm ready for almost *anything*."

#

It turned out that the media circus was not only about Chase's death, but the fact that they were found and returning home. They were hungry for the story about what had happened to them, and where they'd been.

They beamed down, and shortly afterward, they indeed gave an impromptu press conference near Alice's driveway. She barely got to hug her mother, father, and sister before all of that began.

The reporters asked them about who had abducted them, where they were taken, how Chase died, and just about every detail about the whole ordeal. Thousands of photos were taken of them. It was the first time that human media ever got images of them wearing their red team uniforms. They immediately became the number-one subject trending on all social media. #TeamEarthReturns became one of the most popular hashtag of the day.

So did #RIPChase.

#

After the press conference was over, Jamar, Wyatt, and Chloe had brief phone conversations with their families to explain their delay in coming home. The Mackenzies invited everybody into their home. They had made dinner but didn't have enough food for three extra people.

"That's okay," Chloe said as she got her phone out, "I'll order us all a feast. Just tell me what you're all in the mood for, and I'll have it delivered."

"Being rich must be awesome," Jamar said.

She grinned at him. "It *is!*"

"Honey, look!" Hank said. He pointed at the television. Alice looked at it. What she saw brought her to tears. It was a CNN report about an unplanned memorial service for Chase out in the street in front of the apartment complex he'd been living in. Hundreds of fans of his, from all over Ontario, gathered there, holding candles, and hanging flowers and pictures of him on the chain link fence.

"Oh my god, Daddy!"

"They now know what you always knew," Hank whispered, "what a hero he truly was."

"He was a good man, sweetie," Emma said. She put her arm around her daughter. "I'm so sorry that you lost him. The world did truly lose a hero."

"Thanks, Mom!" Alice whispered. She hugged her.

The report mentioned the huge story that broke during their press conference, about how he had helped save the alien children. The headline "Jacob Chase: Space Hero" flashed onto the screen as the memorial footage continued.

"Wow," Cassie said, "just look at that." She turned to look at Chloe, Jamar, and Wyatt. "Do you three have fans like that?"

All three smiled and laughed a little. "Well," said Chloe, "I get a fair amount of social media mentions and DMs…sadly, a lot of them are wildly inappropriate…but I think Chase's rugged good looks got him quite a horde of young lady stans."

"Hey, what about *my* rugged good looks?" Wyatt asked.

Chloe laughed. She put her arm around Wyatt. "Oh, babe, you are *very* handsome…and sexy…but in a sweet kind of nerdy way… which I adore…but…just *look* at Chase's photo on the screen right now. I mean, that chiseled jawline, his eyes, his hair…I mean…just look at him!"

"Plus the mystery of him!" Cassie added. "I mean, he was missing for a while…then he was missing again…and then again… and the mystery of his past…that certainly added something! I mean… my friends, they just lapped that all up! They would *not* stop asking me about him since he was dating my sister!"

Wyatt sighed. He rolled his eyes. "Yeah…you two have a point."

"If I was a teenage girl…" Jamar mumbled as he stared at the screen. Everybody looked at him.

"If you were what?" Chloe asked.

Jamar nervously looked back at her. "Oh. Did I say that out loud?"

Chloe beamed at him. "Yeah, ya did."

Alice laughed. "You guys…" She sighed. "I love you!" And she looked back at the screen. "And…I love you!" she added in a whisper. She blew him a kiss before his image vanished and the news report moved on.

#

Later, the dinner that Chloe had generously paid for, arrived. It was a full spread of Japanese fare from a nearby sushi restaurant. They all ate around the dinner table, trading stories of their adventures, with a poignant focus on Chase. At first, they mostly avoided the stories of the misery on Hellkor, as everybody tried to steer the conversation to more uplifting subjects.

"So, wait, wait," Hank said, "after Chase saved those children…very noble thing…he and his thief friends just had to go steal some jewels from some other planet?"

"Well, Barchell *claimed* that they needed to sell them to buy more antimatter fuel," Alice said. "I mean, they had a bunch of planets to travel to to get those kids home!"

"Well, I guess fuel prices are also bad all over the galaxy, huh?!" Hank said. Everybody laughed.

But the sad moments did come up and Alice's parents were shocked at what she and her friends had to go through.

When Alice briefly spoke about the Phobia Room, her mother could barely listen to it. "Oh my god," she whispered, "it just breaks my brain to hear about you going through that. If those aliens weren't all already dead, I'd go kill them."

"Mom, I'm okay now," Alice said. She grabbed her hand. "Really, I am."

But later, Alice wasn't exactly okay. She felt the withdrawal pain again. She tried to hide it but her anguish was noticeable.

"Take the medicine that Karak gave you, honey!" Emma insisted.

"No, Mom, they only gave me a few doses of that. It's not bad enough. I just need some ibuprofen."

"Okay, I'll get you some," Emma said as she got up.

The conversation lingered well into the night. Alice got a sick feeling in the pit of her stomach. But this time, it wasn't because of the serum withdrawal. It was because of the news she'd needed to deliver to her family.

While they were continuing the conversation in the living room while enjoying some drinks, Alice decided to broach the subject at a lull in the conversation.

"Mom, Dad, Cassie, I have something to say, an announcement of sorts, and it's not going to be easy to say," Alice said.

"Oh my god, you're pregnant!" Emma blurted.

Alice shook her head. "What? No! Why did you jump so fast

to *that* conclusion?"

"Ummm," Emma said, "well I…I mean, since…I mean, that would have been something difficult to announce because…okay. I'll shut up. Go on."

Alice sighed. "Okay, so here it goes. I'm going back to that space station…semi-permanently…to be on their staff."

Emma slapped the coffee table. "No!" She almost spilled her drink.

"Honey, why?!" Hank said. "We just got you back! We were worried sick!"

"Guys, I don't mean like tomorrow or even next week, okay? But…soon."

"You can't!" Emma stood up. "No, no!"

"Mom, please, let me explain!"

"No!" Emma yelled again.

Hank grabbed her hand. "Honey, please, let Alice explain. I want to hear this. You know how smart our daughter is. She must have a good reason. Please, sit and listen to her."

Still trembling, Emma slowly sat back down on the couch.

"Mom, the biggest reason is we're not safe here," she said. "And Chloe and Wyatt want to do it, too, and Jamar is thinking about it, mostly for this reason. If the Hellkorians hadn't abducted us on Loovian, they would have done it here. I recently realized that going back to the normal life I had before all of this is just not possible. We've made dangerous enemies. The Deelooveren said they'd protect us, but we're not going to be completely safe here on Earth ever again. And this makes our families—you two and Cassie—not safe, either. Not as long as we're here. And Jacob…" She swallowed hard. "Jacob…he's proof of this." She sighed loudly to keep herself from crying again. "If you really think about it, you know that I'm right. I mean, just look!" She pointed to the window. "Some of them are still here! And we were done talking to them hours ago! *Nothing* will be normal with any of the four of us ever again."

"We tried to go back to our dorms, to our classes, to get our degrees," Wyatt said, "but Mr. and Mrs. Mackenzie, look what happened."

Emma took a sip of her drink and swallowed it. "So that's it? You just don't feel safe here?"

"No, it's more than that, Mom. Just think about what I do. Just think about what my career goal was. To be a translator for, like, the UN or something, to learn so many languages, to be a language and translation expert. Now I will learn and help translate the languages of aliens from other planets! I will get to the point where I don't even need the ear communicator to speak to the Deelooveren. I'm going to start learning their language right away. This is exciting! My brain is hungry for this! I actually don't think I've ever been more excited about something! I am going to help them with the languages of all the new alien teams coming in for the Contests. And I will help those aliens."

"I'm going to help them train, like with fighting skills," Chloe said. "I could work with Coordinator Jeelork. Their main assistant sadly died on Hellkor."

"And I can probably help them program or invent new games for the trials," Wyatt added. They all looked at Jamar.

"Listen, I was right in the middle of research for this huge paper I was gonna be co-author on," he said, "I still have some things to work out. I'm still not sure what I'm gonna do."

"Why do you think you'll be safer there?" Cassie asked.

"Big phaser cannons, deflector shields, Deelooveren guards everywhere," Alice said.

"But you said those space ninjas attacked after that quest and infiltrated the station and killed a bunch of people!"

"Cassie, they investigated what happened, and they have plugged security holes since. But, see, this is exactly my point! We'd be even *more* vulnerable to them here! And they know Earth. They've been here!"

"What?!" Hank said. "You never mentioned that before! When were they here?!"

"I didn't want to worry you, Dad, that's why I didn't say something sooner. We're not exactly sure when they were here. The Deelooveren authorities and the FBI, and maybe the UN, working together, are gonna try to figure that out. Maybe even the CIA, who knows? I dunno. But…after Jacob died…I…I killed a bunch of them. And…there was one that I let live. She turned out to be human. They've recruited on Earth."

Emma, Hank, and Cassie all had a difficult time processing

the fact that Alice had killed somebody—much less a bunch of somebodies. They were stunned by that revelation.

"You…you've killed people?" Hank said. "A…bunch of people? Those…space ninjas?"

"Dozens of them," Alice said. She quickly gulped her drink. She looked down in shame.

Emma couldn't believe what she'd just heard. "I'm not judging…they were bad guys…they killed your boyfriend…but…I just…I can't wrap my head around you killing anybody. As much as you hate spiders, you don't even like to kill *them*. But my little girl killing *people*? Even bad people. I just…I need time to process this."

"And you almost killed a human one?" Hank said.

"A Japanese-American girl who is in her late teens," Alice said. "She was taken by them when she was around nine or ten. I was shocked when I tore her mask off and realized she was human."

"I killed a human man during that attack on the space station," Chloe said. "That's when we first got evidence that the Jistari were recruiting on Earth. That makes two humans recruited that we know of. Who knows how many more?"

"Jesus, Alice, what did you use to kill them?" Cassie asked. "A machine gun or something?"

"A plasma cannon. And I was hopped up on that super serum dose, the one I told you about. I was kind of like a Terminator. And…I don't say that to sound cool. I lost a little bit of my humanity when I did that. I wish I could take it back. I was angry and vengeful. I was very far from being myself."

Alice flashed back to the memory of the event. She saw them again, the Jistari, trying desperately to avoid getting obliterated by the plasma blast. She wished she could erase that memory.

"Wow," Emma whispered. With a big, long gulp, she finished her drink.

"See what I mean?" Alice said. "*Everything* is different now. *I'm* different now. Nothing can go back to how it was before all this. Not for us, at least."

#

The conversation continued until late in the night. They worked out some logistics, like how often she was going to contact them while she was away, how often she would come back for visits, things like that.

They eventually all went to bed, with Chloe, Jamar, and Wyatt sleeping on couches. The next day Chloe bought herself and Jamar and Wyatt flights home. And they all went home to tell their own families about the plan.

#

Julia took the news of Chloe going back to the station about as well as Alice's mother had.

"You can't do this!" Julia yelled to her daughter as they discussed it in their breakfast nook. Chloe had decided to tell her mother as they drank some morning tea.

"I can, Mum, and I *am*," Chloe replied.

"You've lost your bloody mind!"

"If you just let me explain, you will see that it would make less sense *not* to."

Chloe then explained to her mother most of what Alice had said to her family, mostly about the safety issue.

Julia sipped her tea as she thought about it. "But…what about the leukemia? What if it comes back? And you're way out there in space?"

"Mum, the Deelooveren has much more advanced medical treatments than we do on Earth. It would probably be even better for me there! They might even be able to cure it! Wouldn't that be wonderful?"

"It would be…" She still looked unconvinced. But tears came to her eyes. "I can't lose you, darling!"

"Mum, you won't! Did you not hear everything I *just* said? If I do this, I will be even more safe than I would be *here*!"

"But, I will hardly ever see you!"

"Mum, did you think I was going to live here forever? I only had two more years of University until getting my undergrad. I was going to leave the nest soon anyway. Can't you understand how exciting this opportunity is? I might even be able to somehow finish the degree. Ever since COVID they do remote classes anyway!"

"I don't think they had intended for you to Zoom in from halfway across the galaxy, dear!"

Chloe snickered. "Oh, Mum, perhaps not."

Julia thought about it some more. She sipped her tea

thoughtfully. "What's your father gonna say?"

"I don't think he'll give a shit! I've barely seen him at all in the past three months! He keeps going to Paris for these business trips, and honestly, side note, you should *really* start getting suspicious about that!"

"I already am! But drop this subject, please, I don't wanna bloody talk about it!"

"Okay, okay, subject dropped." Chloe sighed. But she looked back at her mother.

"Well, um, we can probably have the Deelooveren spy on him…" After she said it, a sly smile spread across Chloe's face. She brought her steaming cup of tea to her mouth to get a drink, but she still looked slyly at her mother through the steam.

Julia thought about it. "You don't say…?"

Chloe sipped her tea. Then, so did her mother.

#

When Jamar told his family about possibly going back to the station, they had a somewhat different reaction.

"But, sweetie, what would you do on the station full-time?" Phyllis asked Jamar. "And what about your paper?"

"Well, there's still some stuff I gotta work out."

"Awww, Jam, that sounds dope!" Darnell said. "You get to be the space hero all the time?! I'm jelly!"

"Ditto what he said, man!" Marvin exclaimed. "That's gonna be fire! Meeting all these new aliens all the time! *Hey, can we visit you there?*"

"Maybe you can visit. I dunno. But, well, won't you guys miss me?"

"Aw, you know we love ya, bro!" Marvin said. "But just think about all the science shit you'll get to do…in friggin' *space*! Stuff you can't do *here*, I bet!"

Jamar hadn't even thought about that. A smile slowly spread across his face. "You know what, you're right! Man. My mind is reeling right now about that! Just imagine the papers I can get published on alien tech, alien chemistry! Alien *bio*-chemistry!"

"But, honey, what about Min?!" Phyllis asked. "She is on her way over here now. What are you gonna tell *her*?"

"Well, I was thinking…*if I did this*…and I still haven't decided that I will…that I'd see if she wanted to come back there with me."

"Dude, you're gonna have a hell of a time convincing her of *that*," Darnell said, "I mean, shit, you know her family barely even approves of you dating her to begin with."

"Well, she's an adult. It's not their decision, now is it?" Jamar pointed out.

"It ain't that simple, and you *know* it ain't!" Darnell pointed at Jamar as he said it.

"I am with Darnell," Marvin said, "it isn't happening! So if you decide to do this, you better let her off easy and quick, like ripping off a band-aid, 'cause man, she doesn't deserve to have her feelings messed around with. I care about her like she's a sister now."

Jamar looked surprised at his brother. "Marv…I didn't know you felt that way!"

"I do, too!" Darnell said. "You're pretty oblivious sometimes, aren't ya, Jam?"

"Look, I am *not* dumping Min! Okay? That is not—"

"Dumping me?" Everybody looked in the direction of the foyer. Min had let herself in. "Jammy…why would you dump me? What…what's going on?" A very worried expression was on her face.

Jamar ran over to her. "I wouldn't. I love you!" He grabbed her hands. "You came in the middle of a conversation here. The TLDR version: I might, I stress, *might* go back to the *Arkenstar* Station and work there. Like, full time or something."

Min's eyes narrowed in anger at him. "And if you did that, then yes, you *would* need to dump me! Or I could dump *you*."

Jamar shook his head. "No, girl, no! No! Just…let me explain something…"

"This had better be good," Min said.

Jamar went over Alice's idea. He also went over the points she'd made about their safety, although he tried to summarize it more quickly than she had. But then, at the end, he added, "And if I did it, I want you to come with me."

"Come with you?" Min screwed up her face in confusion. "Like…*to space*?"

"Yeah! It'd be awesome, right?!"

"And meet aliens?" Min added. She didn't look mad anymore.

"Yes!" Jamar said. He looked hopefully at her.

A big smile spread across her face. "*Hell yeah,* I wanna go to space! Are you freakin' kidding me? Where the hell do I sign up?!" She loudly clapped her hands together.

Jamar slowly turned his head to look at his brothers with the most smug facial expression he could muster.

"Now, um, what was that you two were saying?"

#

After Wyatt had a long conversation with his parents about his most recent adventure, he added, at the tail end of it, "Oh yeah. And I want to go back to space and live and work on the *Arkenstar* Station and see Chloe almost every day!" Then he got up from the kitchen table and ran for the stairs. "I'm gonna pack now!"

Christine looked at John. He looked at her. Christine stood up from the table. "Wait…*what*?!"

CHAPTER TWENTY-THREE: The Next Contestants

Three Months Later...

IT WAS a busy time at the *Arkenstar* Station. Excitement was at every turn, every door, every bulkhead, in every room. Everybody on the station was busy with preparations for the 671st Planetorial Quest Trials.

The five alien races and teams had been selected: the Treylariens, the Skozz, the Hoo, the Mmm'chons, and the Fitzgarls.

The Treylariens, who had been in the Contest before, were tall, scaly, gray aliens.

The Skozz, who had also been in the Contest before, were short, blue aliens with housefly-like wings on their backs, but they couldn't really use them to fly, just mostly hover.

The Hoo were a three-eyed, pale-skinned species with short tails.

The Mmm'chons were a race with skin so dark it was essentially black, but their strikingly bright blue eyes made for an interesting contrast.

And the Fitzgarls were another reptilian race, similar in looks to the Sarrnacks from the previous year, but they had a peaceful demeanor.

Alice hurried down the corridor to the control room. She was going over a translation she had done of the Mmm'chons' language as she entered. Unlike the last Contest, she wore an official Deelooveren staff uniform, which was gray with violet trim. But, at her request, and the rest of her teammates, a small diamond-shaped patch of red with a black border was added to the right shoulder as a means of continuity with their race's team colors. But her outfit wasn't the only thing that changed recently. Her hair was much shorter than it used to be.

"Ambassador Harklon, I have something for you!" Alice said, in the Deelooveren's language, which she no longer had to use the translator for.

"The Mmm'chon translation matrix?" Harklon asked.

"Yes, it's ready for upload." She handed Harklon the tablet she'd been carrying.

"Excellent work, Miss Mackenzie!" They grabbed the tablet from her and went over it, swiping through the information. "Very, very good! Almost not in time, though! Cutting it close!"

"Come on, Ambassador, I told you it'd take time! Their race speaks partially in hand gestures. That added this whole different dynamic to their language. I had to work out how our translator would handle it. I had to work with Engineer Farrstead on making the communicators project holographic hand gestures to everybody they talk to! And they also helped me get cameras on all of them so it will record their hand gestures and translate them into words!"

"Oh yes, yes, and Farrstead said that that's been installed on all the communicators! Excellent work! You know, I had a feeling that you'd be a great addition to our staff!"

"Now, if you'll excuse me, I have lunch with Wyatt, Chloe, Jamar, and Farine to finalize exercises for the orientation training sessions and go over changes to the trials."

"Well, don't let me keep you!"

Alice quickly left. As she reached the door, a withdrawal pain hit her. She had to stop for a second to process it, but then she continued on.

Alice headed for the shuttles, but she looked at the time on her handlink. She would be late. "Computer, transport me to holosuite C!" A blue light surrounded her, and she vanished.

Alice smiled and breathed in the fresh, meadow air when she finished beaming into the holosuite. They waited for her at a picnic table in the middle of a park setting. There was a small pond nearby with a bubbling fountain in the middle of it. A nice, pleasant, breezy, sunny day was programmed into the simulation. It was wonderful that they got to experience pleasant, planetary weather on a station out in space.

"Hi, guys!" Alice said as she approached the table. Her fellow humans wore the same uniform she did.

"Hey, girl!" Jamar said. Min sat next to him. She looked around the scenery with wonder in her eyes. She stood out from the rest, wearing a bright sundress.

"This is like the third time now I've been in a holosuite," Min said, "but I still can't get over how real this all seems. I mean, they even got all the scents correct!"

"It truly is amazing," Jamar said, "and I've been doing these for a year now!"

"Hey, my cutie!" Farine said. "Did you get that translation done?"

Alice rolled her eyes. "Oh, I did, but man, that one was a bitch!"

"Oh," Chloe said as she moved her arms around, "that bloody hand gesture thing?"

"Curious," Wyatt said, "how did you resolve that problem?"

"Engineer Farrstead helped me get the translator working with a holo-emitter to make it look as if everybody talking to them is doing the hand gestures."

"Wow, what a creative solution!" Wyatt said. "Maybe you could help me with mine, then. That Wargames sim upgrade I've been working on, I can't quite get the—"

"No," Alice pointed her finger at Wyatt. "Don't you dare rope me into anything else! I've got another translation matrix to finish, and a problem to fix with the Fitzgarl's translation. I have coffee with Coordinator Karak later to discuss last minute changes to the history videos, a video call with my family…"

"We get it, we get it, you're busy!" Chloe said. She took a bite of her sandwich. "But you weren't too busy to get that haircut yesterday."

Alice ran her finger through her hair. "I needed a change. And all this running around makes my head sweat too much, I needed less hair."

"Well I love it!" Jamar said. "It's kinda like a blonde version of Trinity's hair in *The Matrix*."

"Thanks, Jamar!" Alice looked at the pond. Ducks were splashing in it. "Look! They added ducks!"

"They were there yesterday," Jamar said. "You didn't notice 'em!"

"Oh my god, maybe I *should* slow it down a little," Alice said. She got her cheese sandwich out of her bag and chomped into it.

"You may have taken on a little too much," Wyatt said.

"I have to make sure the Contest goes perfectly! They're counting on me!"

"Harklon shouldn't have asked you to do more than just the translation stuff," Jamar said. "I'm a little worried about ya."

"So many things are related and tied to the language stuff, Jamar," Alice replied, with food still in her mouth, "that's what you don't understand!" She swallowed her bite. "Okay, everybody, please report your progress to me."

"Okay, *Manager Alice*," Jamar said.

Alice rolled her eyes and laughed. "Oh, come on, you don't have to say it like *that*! You'll probably all get official titles soon, too!"

"So, what are the names, again, of all the races?" Wyatt asked.

"The Treylariens, the Skozz, the Mmm'chons, the Fitzgarls and the Hoo," Alice answered.

"The who?" Jamar said.

"The Hoo—" Alice sighed. "Okay, Jamar, *that* joke is going to get old *real fast*!"

"So," said Wyatt, "they're a rock band, I take it?"

"And that one!"

"*Whoooooo are you…hoo hoo,*" Jamar sang.

"*And* that one!"

Everybody laughed.

"So, I heard that the Treylariens and the Skozz are repeats?" Wyatt said. "Two repeats in one year. I mean, that's unheard of, right?"

"As I understand it, after six hundred seventy-one Contests, they're running out of planets with sentient races to pick from," Alice replied. "In fact, at a senior staff meeting yesterday, somebody suggested that next year's Contest might have to be all repeats."

"Hmm, that's over three thousand planets," Jamar said. "But the Drake Equation estimated there could be up to millions with sentient life in the Milky Way."

"Yeah, but, we're talking about just this quadrant of the galaxy that the wormhole network can get to," Alice pointed out. "And millions was the very high end of the estimate anyway. Listen, we do not have time to get into these weeds, okay? I came here to get your status reports. Let's please get that done."

"Well, I finished coming up with the new, fun editions to the Zerrdon item warehouse!" Farine announced. "The thieves will love it!" She also wore the same uniform but her team color badge was green.

Alice looked at her suspiciously. "What did you do, Farine?"

Farine giggled. "What? You don't trust me?"

"Farine…"

"I added a few Zerrdonian monkey rats to scurry about to make it more realistic!"

"How so?"

"Well, I read that they are often in warehouses on Zerrdonan! Come on! It'll make it more challenging!"

Alice smiled at her. "Okay, okay, let's see how it goes. But if nobody passes the challenge, they won't be there next year, got it?"

"Got it!"

"Yeah," Alice said, "the thieves will…" Jacob popped into her head. She quickly cleared her throat. She sighed. "The thieves will find it more challenging, you're right. But, okay, you were also working on making the orientation test for the thieves different?"

"We're adding how they have to steal from a thief! Like… me!" Farine giggled. "I mean, I can't think of a more challenging pick-pocket test than stealing from another thief."

"Sounds good! I can't wait to see how that plays out!"

"In some ways, this is more fun than actually doing the Contest!' Jamar said. "I mean, now we get to decide what their tormen—I mean, what their *challenges* will be!"

That elicited a few chuckles around the table.

"What do you have…*Jammy*?" Alice said.

He forcefully put his sandwich down. "Now, see, I, see, I done…I told you…I…" He looked at Min. "See what you did?!"

Min giggled and slurped her juice box while looking up into the clear blue sky, trying to look as innocent as possible. In Jamar's eyes, that was not difficult at all for her to do.

Jamar shook his head. "Well, I am done totally redesigning that lame-ass science skills test at the orientation. Now, I gotta do a test run this afternoon with Coordinator Jeelork. I already emailed you the deets."

"Excellent!" Manager Alice said. "Now, Chloe, go!"

"Well, I thought, since we are now adding fighting training to orientation, that we needed to program the Zerrdon, in the music and martial arts round, to be harder to beat and to be more menacing."

"Chloe, I like it! But can that be completed by the time we get to that round?"

"Oh, it will be! The programmer this morning said that they're almost done."

"Just make sure nobody gets actually stabbed!" Jamar said.

Alice smiled. "Don't worry, Jamar, the Deelooveren made sure there's extra security in all the sims, more firewalls or whatever they call it. I also told them to add an extra 'Are You Sure?' prompt if anybody turns off the safety filters."

"Have them add a 'Are You REALLY Sure?' prompt," Wyatt suggested.

Alice laughed. "I'll run it by them, Wyatt!"

"Now," Wyatt said, "on my war games changes, I really think the translations on some of the on-screen instructions need some tweaking…"

Alice loudly sighed and rolled her eyes. "All right, all right, I'll look at it! But not before the Contest begins. But I'll look at it before we get to that round, I promise."

"Thank you," Wyatt replied. "But as far as any other changes, Farrstead and I made sure all the maps are updated with the new team colors, but besides that, I think it's ready to go."

"Good!" Alice said. "Okay, now it's *my* turn. Now, I have decided to make the language round *dramatically* different!"

"Hold up!" Jamar said. "Weren't you just talking about how busy you are? So why be so extra for your thing?"

"It is so worth it! Listen to this: I decided to recreate Queeza Tash's riddle maze for the translation trial! They not only have to translate the riddles, but they have to *solve the riddles*!" Alice smiled and gleefully rubbed her hands together. When they didn't begin applauding, she added, "Well, what do you all think?"

Jamar chuckled. "As long as there aren't any sniggles, I'm down for it!"

"No, Jamar, no sniggles," Alice said as she pointed at him. "But, please, don't tempt me to add them…because I might do it!"

Jamar laughed. Then, he quietly started chanting, "Add the sniggles! Add the sniggles!" He gently thumped the table with the beat of his chanting. Then Farine, Chloe, and Wyatt followed his lead and started chanting it, too.

Alice chuckled. "Oh, stop it, you guys, I swear!"

"Umm…what's a *sniggle*?" Min asked.

A few snickers traveled around the table. Alice grinned and clicked something on her device. A sniggle appeared on the ground by Min.

"Oh, this is a sniggle? Oh, look at it, it's so cute!" She bent down closer to it and waved to it. "Hi there!"

Suddenly, the sniggle hissed at her and bared all its razor-sharp teeth.

"Dyaaahhh!" Min quickly backed away. "*What the hell*?!"

Alice made it disappear, and everybody at the table, except Min, burst out into hearty laughter.

"Seriously!" Min said. "What…what is up with those things?!"

"They're deadly!" Jamar said. "I'll fill you in more later! But if you ever see one, you better *run*! Run like hell!"

"Wait a minute," Wyatt said, "hold on, did Ambassador Harklon approve that huge change?"

Alice looked up at the sky. "Ummm…well…"

"They didn't, did they?"

"Well, they did say, 'Make it different.' So…I did."

"Alice! If it's one major thing I know from my game design jobs is that a major change like that has to go through proper approvals."

Alice gave him a playfully stern look. "Look, Wyatt, Ambassador Harklon likes me. I'm kicking so much ass at this job. I'm not worried about it. I can get them to approve almost *anything*. Okay?"

"Okay, if you say so!"

The table got quiet as they all ate their food. But it wasn't long before Chloe was curious about something.

"Hey, Alice, how is Akiko? Have you heard any updates lately?"

"Last I heard, she's still in intense therapy and that she's still dangerous. But there's been some progress, little by little. Her parents are still hopeful they'll have their daughter back someday. It's basically a long deprogramming process. There's been tiny breakthroughs here and there."

"I can imagine if she were my kid, I'd remain hopeful," Wyatt said. "But they'll never get their daughter back, not like how she was before."

Alice sighed. "But maybe they'll get somebody resembling their daughter…eventually. I want that for them."

"Me, too," Jamar said.

After discussing a few more items of station business, the lunch meeting concluded.

Everybody else headed for the main door of the holosuite, which to them, at that moment, looked like the entrance to a quaint little wooden cottage. But Alice stayed standing near the pond.

Wyatt stopped. He looked back at Alice.

"I thought you were super busy," Wyatt said as a nearby holographic bird sang a song.

Chloe also stopped. She looked back at him. "Wyatt, just don't."

Alice looked back at both of them. "I won't be long." She walked toward the shore.

"She'll never truly heal from it," Wyatt whispered to Chloe. "I don't think it's healthy."

"I know you care a lot for her, as we all do, and it's sweet, but this is her choice. It's not our business." She gently grabbed Wyatt's arm. "Come on. Let's go. The Contest starts in two days. They arrive tomorrow. We have last-minute preparations."

Wyatt sighed. "Okay. You're right."

They both headed out of the holosuite.

Breezing through the mildly warm air, Alice approached the man who was skipping flat rocks across the pond. His back was still to her. She traversed the soft grass meadow until she got to the shoreline.

"That last one was a good one," Alice said. "It almost made it to the other side."

The man turned around. He smiled at her. "Hey, Al. I thought that lunch would never end."

There he was again, Jacob Chase, looking just how he'd

looked right before leaving Earth to go save the alien children. As a duck splashed by in the nearby pond, Alice reached up and stroked his stubbly chin and cheek. She looked into his eyes.

"You're so real," she whispered.

"Of course I am. That's how he wanted me. As real as I could be."

"You even smell like him."

Chase laughed. The bright sunlight reflected off of his shiny, dark hair. His mischievous eyes sparkled almost as much as the simulated sun overhead. "Well, I hope that's a good thing!"

Alice let out a slight laugh. "Yes, it is."

"I like your hair like that," he said.

"Thanks. The others…well, mostly Wyatt…tell me that this is unhealthy, that it's keeping me from moving on."

"Well, what do *you* think?"

Alice noticed more ducks floating by, splashing and floating. Everything was so peaceful at that moment, including Alice's heart.

"I'm not sure. They may have a point."

"Because I'm not real?"

"You seem so real." Alice reached up and softly kissed him. "That felt really real."

"I exist solely for you, like the real Chase intended. He wanted this for you."

"I've never asked this before…because I didn't want to spoil the illusion…but…why did he have you programmed? You have all of his memories up until right after the mission to save the children, yes?"

"That's correct. And the reason why? Well, I had a really strong feeling that I would soon have a mission that I wasn't going to come back from. Especially with me no longer able to have any super serum."

"I love you."

"I love you, too."'

"But do you, *really*?"

"Do *you*, really? I mean, you know I'm not real."

"Do you really have feelings? Like…are you sentient?"

Chase frowned. He sighed and reached out and touched Alice's hair. "I like to think I am. It seems like I do, I don't know."

"But…you just stand here, waiting for me, skipping rocks."

"Sure, when this program is running. If we were, say, at an orchard, I'd be picking apples. If we were in downtown Toronto, I'd be hustling some chumps." He smiled.

"But you can't leave the holosuite."

"So that makes me not real, then, I guess. But it's okay. The feelings that matter are yours. He…I…the thing we wanted most in the universe was for you to be happy."

"But why'd you leave, then? Again?"

"Look, I haven't told you this before, but before the upload, he had made a decision. And that decision was you. To be with you always and forever. To have the wedding. Live wherever you wanted to. I was all in. After the Slithertown mission, that was it."

Alice smiled and started crying. A nearby bird chirped a merry song, sharply contrasting with her feelings at the moment. "Deelan already told me."

"He's a good friend." Jacob reached up and wiped some of her tears away with his thumb. "You're not like anybody he'd ever met before. I don't think this program could ever truly express to you just how much he loved you. How much…*I* love you."

Alice wrapped her arms around Jacob and hugged him. "I loved you so much."

"I know. *He* knew. He had no doubt." He hugged her back with a warm, loving embrace.

Alice sighed. "I could just…stay here with you forever."

"You had things to get to, didn't you?"

Alice parted from him. She wiped her eyes. "Yes."

"See you tomorrow?"

Alice looked at him, a very sad expression on her face. "No… not tomorrow."

"Then when?"

Alice shook her head. "I don't know. I…I realized something a few moments ago."

"What's that?"

"That maybe they're right."

A tear fell down Chase's face. "That you…need to move on."

"You even cry!" Alice gasped. She reached out and wiped his tear away.

"Do what is best for *you*, my love. Don't worry about me."

"I will…but I do. So…goodbye."

"Bye."

"Computer…" Alice hesitated a gut-wrenching hesitation. "…end program."

Jacob, the park, and the pond all vanished. She was now just in a dull, gray room. It reflected her emotions at the moment.

As Alice left the holosuite, she cried like she'd lost him all over again.

#

That night, Wyatt, Chloe, Jamar, Min, and Farine waited for Alice in the human's dining room. They eventually had to start eating without her, as she was running late.

They were going over the different alien races that were about to arrive.

"So," Wyatt said as he activated a three-dimensional holographic image of the Skozz. It showed a male and a female. "These are the Skozz."

"Oh, right, these guys are blue, too," Chloe said, "and…didn't they tell us that those wings don't actually allow them to fly?"

"Nope, they just hover," Wyatt said. He clicked something. The 3D Skozz buzzed their wings. All they did was hover off the ground a few feet.

"I wonder if it helps them dance," Farine said as she danced a little in her chair.

Min giggled. "Your people really do love dancing!"

"It is literally in our DNA!"

"You know, what a crazy life we now have," Wyatt said. "And we have an even crazier one ahead. When you really think about it, take stock of it all. It truly is amazing. The fi—four…" He looked at Farine. "No, the five of us, we have done things and been places that no other human has ever done." He pointed to the door at the end of the dining room. "And it all started in there, one fateful night, about a year ago."

"Who would have ever guessed that being abducted against your will would lead to such good times!" Chloe said as she gestured toward the door.

Wyatt looked at the door. "Do…do you wanna go in there? I

mean…we haven't been in there since that night. I mean, we could just like…take a look."

"I understand nostalgia, Wyatt," Jamar said, "but there is literally nothing in there. What's to look at?"

Wyatt got up. "Well, I'm feeling nostalgic." He went over to the door. He clicked the button on the wall panel to open it. At first, they could see nothing but blackness. Wyatt located the lights button on the panel and turned them on.

"There it is," whispered Chloe. She had walked up behind Wyatt and put her arm around his shoulders.

Memories came back to Wyatt of that night. "I woke up around…there." He pointed to the spot. "And, Alice, she woke up second, she was about…here. And you, Chloe, I think you woke up in that spot. Jamar was here, I think." And then he pointed toward the back. "And…Chase was there."

When Chloe noticed Wyatt get emotional, she gently kissed his cheek. "I think you're right, darling," she whispered, "you have a sharp memory."

Farine and Jamar appeared behind them.

"You all woke up in *there*?" Farine asked. "How weird. My team all woke up in our dining area."

"What?!" Chloe said.

"You gotta be shittin' me!" Jamar exclaimed.

"Well, keep in mind, my Contest was like thirty years ago. Maybe they did things differently then."

"Thirty years ago?" Chloe said. "I forgot it was that long ago. Can I say that you do not look like you're that old?"

Farine giggled. She looked coyly at Chloe. "Thanks, my cutie! Well, my race lives on average to around a hundred and fifty, so we age slower than yours does."

Finally, Alice beamed in. She saw them all looking in the room. "What are you guys doing?"

"Strolling down memory lane," Jamar answered.

"There's literally nothing in there!" Alice said.

Jamar pointed at her. "That's exactly what *I* said!"

"Oh, but on that subject, I am making damned sure that none of the new aliens experience what we did. That shit is just unacceptable."

"Farine just told us that her team woke up in their dining room!" Wyatt said.

"What?!" Alice yelled.

"That's what *I* said!" Chloe exclaimed.

Farine giggled. "No offense, but you four are entertaining." She then did a little dance.

Wyatt chuckled. "Well, I, for one, am glad we amuse you." He clicked the button to shut the door.

"Let's eat!" Jamar said. "You were a half hour late, Alice, and my tummy is growling!"

Alice slowly shook her head at Jamar and smiled at him. "Why am I not surprised that you're the hungriest one?" She clicked something on her handlink, and a feast beamed onto the table.

"I will never get used to this!" Jamar exclaimed as he sat in his chair.

"Since we're feeling nostalgic, I had the same exact feast beamed onto the table that was here our first, confusing night."

Chloe was already tearing into a steak. "I thought this all looked familiar."

"All right, kooshkas!" Farine happily grabbed a stick of some kind of white meat that was wrapped in little green vines. "Yummy! The station's replicators always make great kooshkas!"

"Of course I also made sure there were some Norfan dishes!"

Jamar gnawed on a barbecue rib. "Makes these perfect, too!"

Alice smiled when she noticed some poutine on the table. It had been there for Chase. She grabbed a fork and took a bite. It was good.

#

The next afternoon was one of the busiest ones the humans had ever seen. The ships would arrive soon with the five teams of five aliens. They were scrambling with last-minute preparations.

Manager Alice ran down a corridor with Engineer Farrstead, who was trying to keep up with her. "These Fitzgarl clicks are wrong!" She played a series of them.

"They sound right to me!" Farrstead said.

"They're not going to have *any* idea as to what *anybody* is saying!" Alice rolled her eyes. She played a recording of the correct clicks. "This is what they're supposed to sound like!"

Farrstead listened carefully. "I, um, don't hear a difference."

"Trust me, *they* will!"

They strode into the control room. "We've got to hurry and fix these clicks. They arrive in twenty minutes!" Farrstead hurried and sat at their usual station.

"Manager Alice!" Somebody else was calling to her. She ran over to Programmer Shellob's station.

"Yes, what is it?"

"The Hoo are starting to wake up already, and they're still on their ship!"

"Well, why is this *my* problem? Where's Dr. Wikket?!"

"They're, umm, in the bathroom."

"Oh, great, grandest time for a nature call!" Alice threw up her hands and rolled her eyes. She hit her communicator. "Jamar, come in!"

"Yes, ma'am?"

"The Hoo's ship, we need to pump its air with something that'll knock them out again."

"Who's ship?"

"JAMAR!" Alice yelled.

Jamar quickly laughed. "I'm sorry, I'm sorry, uhh…let's see. If what I've studied about their anatomy is correct, diffuse about five percent more carbon monoxide into their air mixture. That should do the trick."

"Thanks, Jamar!" Then she turned to Shellob. "Five percent more carbon monoxide in their air supply!"

"Got it!"

She glanced at the schedule on her handlink to make sure everything else was on track.

"No, no, no! Somebody please tell me why the Skozz are arriving ten minutes early!"

"It doesn't matter!" Farrstead said. "They've been here before, they knew about all this, they're not unconscious. I think they requested their ship fly faster. They were anxious to get here, is all."

Alice put a firm hand on Farrstead's shoulder. "But their *rooms* aren't ready yet!" She scoffed. "Okay, fine, whatever! Not everything has to be perfect. But those clicks do! How are we doing on fixing those clicks?"

Farrstead clicked some commands into their console. It played a clip of Fitzgarl translation.

"Good, good, yes, the clicks are correct now!"

Alice's communicator beeped. "Manager Alice?" It was Farine's voice.

"Yes, Farine?"

"The Treylarien thief stole a handheld phaser from their ship's weapons locker!"

"What?! Oh, for the love of—What the hell are any weapons even *doing* on the transport ships?!"

"It was an inventory mistake. Don't worry. I'm working on the problem. I just wanted to let you know what was going on."

"These repeats, I swear, I say they still should have been unconscious! Farine, control your thieves, please!"

Farine giggled. "Oh, my cutest cutie! Surely, you've been around us galactic thieves long enough to know that's almost impossible!"

"Oh, Farine! Just...just take care of the problem!"

"I already have. I just remotely deactivated the weapon...and all the others on that ship."

"*Others*?!" Alice groaned. "Okay, whatever. Mackenzie out!"

Her communicator beeped again. "Alice, it's Chloe!"

"Yes, Chloe, what is it?!"

"Wow, are you in a bad mood?"

"Kind of! Putting out multiple fires over here! Please tell me that you don't have a fire."

"Well, kind of."

Alice rolled her eyes. "Oh, great! What is it?"

"The fight training for orientation tomorrow morning...I discovered a teeny tiny snag in the plan..."

"Okay, *WHAT*?!"

"Even with the super serum, I just discovered that the Skozz have bones more brittle than the others, which could be a problem. It was a problem last time they were in the Contest fifty years ago."

"How the hell did they evolve to have brittle bones? How would their species even survive?"

"Well, gravity on their planet is weaker than most humanoids' planets."

"Well, figure something out! You have until tomorrow morning! Alice out!"

Ambassador Harklon entered the control room accompanied by Coordinator Karak. Alice was glad to see them both, especially Karak.

"Where have you two been?!" She held out her arms in frustration. But she did smile a little. "Seriously, how did you get all this done before *I* worked here?!"

They both laughed. "I'm wondering that myself!" Ambassador Harklon said.

"Well," Karak said, "if you recall, it, well, didn't go all that smoothly!"

"Oh, yeah, right, we were stuck in that room for an hour before you came and got us! Good point!"

Karak laughed.

Alice laughed, too. "Oh, I get it, you think that's funny?"

"Well, it's funny *now*! A year later! Right?!"

Alice shook her head at Coordinator Karak. "Okay, fine, it's a *little* funny!"

"Well, thanks to you, Miss Mackenzie, we're not going to have that problem this year. I am very impressed with your work. I have to admit it, when you first pitched your idea to me, I was very skeptical. For hundreds of years, only the Deelooveren have handled the Contest. No *Arkenstar* Station staff have ever been any species but mine. But I must say, you and your friends have brought fresh ideas to the table and come up with very interesting solutions! This will be a most interesting Contest indeed!"

"Well, thank you, and you're welcome! I agree. It's going to be very interesting. But now that you and Harklon are here, I'm gonna go take a break! I skipped lunch, and I am running on fumes!"

"Go, go take that break, Miss Mackenzie!" Harklon said. "You've earned it!"

After she was gone, Harklon mumbled to Karak, "How's that work on the gateway coming along?"

"It's almost ready for test travelers," they replied.

"Excellent!" Harklon replied.

#

Alice ate a slice of cheese pizza as she emerged from the cafeteria. She headed to the ballroom. She was finished with it by the time she walked into it. There, around the center of the room, stood her friends.

"Are we all ready?" Alice asked as she still had a bit of cheese in her mouth. She wiped some sauce off her mouth with a napkin.

"As ready as I'll *ever* be," Wyatt said.

"Anybody nervous?"

"I am!" Chloe said. "Just a bit of the butterflies."

"Oh, I just feel like I wanna vomit is all," Jamar said, "no big deal."

"Let's dance into this, my cuties!" Farine said.

Alice looked at her device. "It's almost time."

"Okay, so like…what's the best first thing to say to them?" Wyatt asked.

Alice playfully scoffed at him. "Well, *you're* the one with all the best strategies, Wyatt! You tell *me*!"

Chloe looked at him. "Yeah. I mean, come on. It seems like everybody wants to depend on Alice for everything now since she's been so good at managing all this! Give her a bloody break!"

"Well, we're just making her earn that title!" Wyatt said. "You know, that thing that they haven't given to any of the rest of us."

Alice smiled at him. "Wyatt, you'll get them soon enough. I submitted an official request today to grant titles to all of you. You all deserve it!"

"Thanks, love!" Chloe said.

Alice looked at the time again. "Okay. We have to all beam into our assigned team suites now…well, in about a minute."

Jamar held out his fist. "One last fist bump?"

"One last fist bump!" Wyatt exclaimed. They all bumped fists.

"Okay, ready?!" Alice said.

"Ready!" the others all yelled at once.

"Let's do this, people!" Alice exclaimed.

Blue beams of light surrounded all of them. Then they vanished.

#

Millions of kilometers from the *Arkenstar* Station, out in deep space, Jacob Chase's coffin ship drifted further and further out. It was silent. Alone. But peaceful.

But that changed.

A large Jistari ship, another one of their Gauntlets, slowly approached the coffin. Its docking bay opened like it was the ship's mouth, and it was about to swallow a tiny treat.

Once it was inside the ship, the docking bay doors closed. For several moments, the coffin just sat in the bay. Silent. And alone.

But a Jistari crew person in a control room several decks above the docking bay deactivated the stasis field in the coffin ship.

That's when Jacob Chase, for the first time in six months, opened his eyes.

EPILOGUE

ALICE WAS up later than the others, as per usual, well past the start of night mode. She sat at the dining table drinking a steaming cup of nighttime herbal tea. She scrolled through a report on her handlink of the progress of the Contestants. Orientation Day was over, and it was time to begin the trials.

Alice clicked on a video to watch some of the aliens racing each other around the track. She chuckled slightly when a few of them inevitably wiped out while zooming round the first turn. She sipped more of her tea and then scrolled past it to look at the science test results again. The Hoo scientist had won. She seemed to have a lot of potential. Alice wondered how she'd do leading their team in the first trial.

A little window popped up on the top right of her device. It was Ambassador Harklon video-calling her. Alice clicked on it. "Yes, Ambassador?"

"There's a distress call coming into the station from a ship one light year away. It sounds urgent," they said.

"Well, why are you telling me? That stuff would be above my pay grade."

"The reason I'm calling is, well, the audio, the person begging for help, she sounds like she's you! So I wanted to call and make sure you're okay, that you're still at the station."

"She sounds like me?"

"*Exactly* like you! And also…she claims her name is Alice. And…the signal is coming from a Deelooveren ship, but the transponder signal identity is unknown, not a registered ID anywhere in our fleet."

Alice paused for a moment to think. "Can you please patch

the distress call to the monitor in here, our dining room? And if there's video, please patch that in, too."

"Okay, sure," Harklon said.

In a few seconds the viewscreen at the back of the dining room flickered on. Video appeared, but it was distorted with lots of interference. At first, she couldn't really make anything out. And very choppy audio accompanied it.

Alice walked over to the viewscreen. She went to a communications app on her handlink and did what she could to clean up the signal. It worked.

Then, on the screen was a young blonde woman. Her hair was different—it was tied back in a ponytail—but it was *her*. It was almost like looking into a mirror. She bled from a wound on the side of her head. A fountain of sparks rained from a computer panel behind her. Alice could see four other humans at ship stations around her. Three of them she didn't recognize. But one of them looked like Chloe but with much shorter hair and a red patch over one of her eyes.

The woman yelled at the screen, some of her audio being scrambled with interference. "This is Captain Alice Mackenzie of— oovern ship *Moondown*—under attack by Jistar—shields at five per-cent…" But she stopped. She stared at Alice. Her eyes opened wider. "Who…who the hell are *you*?!"

Alice tossed her device onto the table. She stepped closer to the screen.

"Who the hell am *I*?! Um…who the hell are *you*?!"

The two women named Alice Mackenzie continued to stare at each other during a moment of confusion for both of them.

Then, the signal cut out in a fizzle of static.

If you liked this book, please give it a review on Amazon:

COMING SOON:

THE OTHER FIVE

Fall 2024

In the fourth installment of the gripping "FIVE" series, tensions flare as Team Earth finds themselves facing their toughest challenge yet: an alternate version of their team from another universe, with alternatve versions of Alice and Chloe. When The Other Five arrive from a darker universe with dangerous cargo, chaos errupts abord the *Arkenstar* space station. As the two teams clash, Manager Alice must confront haunting visions of her lost lover, Chase, while the fate of the station hangs in the balance. Can the power of love ovdercome the darkness within, or will The Other Five's sinister plans tear them apart forever? Join the adventure as alliances are tested, friendships are forged, and the true meaning of redemption is revealed in *The Other Five*!

www.ingramcontent.com/pod-product-compliance
Lightning Source LLC
Chambersburg PA
CBHW061943170626
46813CB00006B/2509